The House of the Dawn.

When Sancha Dared the Trail Alone.

[Page 214]

The House of the Dawn

by

MARAH ELLIS RYAN

Author of
"Indian Love Letters"
"For the Soul of Rafael"
"The Woman of the Twilight", etc.

Illustrated and Decorated
by
HANSON BOOTH

CHICAGO
A. C. McCLURG & CO.
1914

W. F. Hall Printing Co., Chicago

To my
Friends, Red, and White,
of the
Indian Desert

CONTENTS

ILLUSTRATIONS

The House of the Dawn

CHAPTER I

DON JUAN TELLS IT

I, too, Perdida, would venture my soul
If your heart true should love me!
If your lips red should touch me!
I, too, Querida, would venture a soul
If your white hand should lead me!

UNDER my balcony in the Mexican night a singer sweeps the strings of his guitar until they thrill and plead to the maid behind the bars in the house opposite. So much is she of the shadow there that I only see her when a white bodice presses forward against the grating — or a little hand lets fall a yellow rose in the starlight.

His eyes and his thoughts are for her, and hers go to him with the rose. Their own little romance looms so big with import that to neither comes special thought of the song itself, or the " Doña Perdida " of whom the song was made.

Yet it is not so long ago — a mere yesterday. Either of the lovers opposite might have gazed up at her grandeur as she looked with young, eager, seeking eyes

I

from the balcony of the viceroy's palace — that palace from which her trail was planned to the northland of the Indians.

No, it is not so long ago. I am still here waiting word of her, yet those two children of the yellow rose and the guitar have their own way of making a man feel old; and that song of " Perdida " —

It is not to be thought that our Sancha was christened " Perdida " — or the " Lost One " — far from it. Her cousin, the Archbishop and Viceroy, could have told them how nearly royal was her blood and how weighty her name. But he, good man, had closed on himself the doors of a monastery in Spain ere the Brotherhood blotted out her name from the lists of Christian folk here in Mexico.

" Perdida," heretic, without the faith, they said when her name was publicly burned at the *auto-da-fé*. Yet the saints knew she had strong faith — a faith so large that it bridged ocean and desert. By faith alone her vision of love grew into a living thing so great that all the needs of smaller souls fell from her as a garment cast aside. Not once, I know, did she ever look backward with a sigh to that garment of gilded magnificence. I cross myself as I write it, lest the devil, who is always busy, think that I approve her mad sacrifice, and the angels know my will was good to put a stop to it in the very beginning, had it been in the power of a lad, half sick with his own love, of which he was too young to tell.

But the years change one, and while I wait, or while I seek, I shall make record of the days in the land of the barbarians, for not again in one life may a man come close to so great a love, whether in outlaw or true son of the church; and beside me there is none left alive who knew how the bond grew between those two, and how it strengthened with each hard stroke of fortune until the courts and palaces of men seemed but trifling things in exchange for sanctuary in the "House of the Dawn."

Bernal Diaz, after his campaigns, made written record of the things he saw and did in the pagan cities and the wilderness, and it is good and true reading, though at times terrible, as one must expect a soldier's tale of conquest to be. For myself, I must set down plainly that I got not even a smell of conquest such as his, though I crossed the water with all the faith of Sancho Panza in winning, at the very least, a governor's staff; and like him had more routings than any lad of adventure ever sees in his most dismal dreams. Gold there was, and silver in plenty — but the brown people took their toll.

Added to all this was the fact that I followed a mistress instead of a master — and a mistress whose beauty was an unbelievable wonder of earth. All boys, and even men, feel like that concerning the charm some one maid has given out to the world, but the charm of our Sancha is a living charm today, here in this city of Mexico; and the singing of that song — "Perdida" — brings it back to me like a sweep of music in a night of roses.

It was but yesterday I heard a padre chiding a singer of the song; also he discoursed on the devilish impiety of it. I stood aside, silent, and listened while he said plainly that the nameless "Doña Perdida" was bewitched and enchanted by one of the workers on earth for the prince of darkness, and that the singer must do penance by ten Ave Marias before the miracle picture of Our Lady in the Chapel.

Muttering and admonishing the singer, he shuffled into the cool dusk of the sanctuary and bent where the wonderful face smiles from the frame like a living maid gazing down from a golden window of paradise into the world. As if on the top of the world she stands there, with the drifting clouds of white back of her, the silver white doves above, and the sun's rays touching the white drapery over her head like a glory crown. White — all white but the rose-leaf flesh, the wide, gray, seeking eyes, and the dark braids of hair down either shoulder and near touching the fawn on which her hand rests.

I had thoughts of my own as to the horror of the padre if I should tell him that the lost soul of the forbidden song and the Virgin of the Fawn were one and the same, and that the radiant glory crown was inspired by a full white skirt drawn upward over the head of the maid as a shield from the sun on a far-away hill of Andalucia. Even the home forest of that fawn I could have told, and solved a knotty problem; for the graceful animal of soft shy eyes had caused much discourse among the ecclesiastics, by the reason that no record of the Holy Evangelists held any word of such a companion of the forest for Our Lady of Light. A lamb might have been understood — but a wild, care-free creature of the wilderness! I know Padre Felipe gave advice that it be painted over, and that lilies be painted, instead. His reason was that pagan false gods of old

Rome were such wild things of forest or sylvan places;
among them a piper of devilish music, with the horns
and haunches of a goat. I never dare inquire too
closely as to the relationship between a kid and a fawn,
or betray special interest in the controversy — content
that it has quieted down, and that the symbol of the
wilderness is left beside her in her high place against
the sky.

So I kept to myself what I knew of the miracle of
that picture, having no desire to follow the convicted
of sin in line to the next roastings at the *quemadora* —
and if I had but hinted that my own hands had made
the sandals for the slender feet of the virgin on the canvas, well — at the very mildest — I would have been
possessed of a devil, and sheltered the rest of my days
in a monastery, and my worldly goods divided between
the King and the Holy Brotherhood.

They have already made some blessed and fanciful
tales about the picture, intended to affect anyone prone
to heretical doubts; for even a Jew must believe when
it is shown that the artist painted it in prison with no
woman to look at, and that Our Lady herself came to
him and showed herself, that his soul might be saved
by faith and the church be made a place of pilgrimage
in her honor, which it is today. Sermons have been
preached on that picture, and I have been sorely puzzled at some of them, since it would seem that Our
Lady's discernment was at fault in that she elected to
show herself only to a heretic possessed of the devil,
who still continued, in spite of her graciousness, to be
possessed by devils.

But, as I wish to live in comfort if I am to live at

all, I keep a long face and my tongue between my teeth when these mystical tales are told, and in time I gain almost the name of being a *religioso* because of the many times I kneel at that altar, and dream away the hours there.

I go to look at the dear little bare feet in the sandals I made, and it gives me comfort to see the serene joy of life in her eyes, and know that if she continues to live the joy is still hers — for if it ever left she would die, and that of course would be best. There are women, and men too, who live on with a life all patches and scraps of what they meant it to be, but I know our Sancha, whose name is forbidden, would go into death as to a royal audience, gracious and unbroken.

CHAPTER II

THE BETROTHAL

A LITTLE queen, Sancha seemed to me, that far-away day of her betrothal! She was twelve, and Marco nineteen, and he was to sail in a week with his uncle, Rodrigo de Ordoño, to one of the provinces of Mexico. I was fourteen and was jealous of him because he was going out into a world of mysteries, and it was easy to see from the petting of the women that life was arranged for him in pleasant places! His suit of velvet was darkest blue, with silver buckles on shoes, and silver buttons wherever there was space for them, and the emerald ring of his father on his hand, while cousin Sancha was laced into a brocade of rose, with the wedding veil of our grandmother, the Marquesa de Llorente, falling to her little slippers, even though caught in many loops through the ancient girdle of golden wires and jeweled butterflies. I always have had suspicions that the girdle was come by through that infidel Moresco grandee, who, it is said, came into the family some generations ago. However, with conveniences to Christian souls — and it may be by some expense to treasure chests — no mention above a whisper had been made of him for a lifetime or two. If a family urges itself not into forgetfulness of heretic blood, the Holy Brotherhood have a

7

way of smelling the trail to it, if there is a *maravedi* to confiscate or a monastery in need of more lands.

Pearls were also about her neck — the first time Sancha had been given the joy of wearing jewels. They at least did not blazon their early pagan possessors, but lay lustrous as moonlight on the flushed marble of her shoulders.

So gorgeous a butterfly she was, and she knew it — - the child coquette — glancing sideways at Marco, and giving look for look at the older men who praised her; kissing Don Rodrigo, her guardian, but with her eyes on Miguel Alrada, the page of Señor Cura. You never would have thought she had lived always among the blessed nuns of St. Dominic, and that when the days of the betrothal fiesta were over she would go again up into the gray walls on the gray hills for five years, until Marco de Ordoño, with happiness well arranged for him, came back from Mexico to claim her.

It is not easy for a shy lad of fourteen to love a tall gallant of nineteen summers when there is a maid between them, not even though he be, in a way, a cousin; but this lack of love was aggravated that day until in my jealousy, and with my murderous thoughts of what I should do to him when I had doubled my height, I was obliged to make confession to Padre Juan of my homicidal intentions.

It was not that he had married her — to me all that betrothal formality in the presence of the family was as a bona fide wedding fiesta — but I was furious because he could have eyes and ears for other maids there. I — I could only sit like an owl in my holiday finery, and blink and wonder at the beauty of her, while he not

only had smiles and honey words for others but danced
with them after the supper!

It never entered my loyal mind to question why she
also was gay as a bird of springtime, and in no way
chary of her hands, or her glances, or her soft laughter,
as she chose to dance with every eager youth. I was
not jealous of them. I have grown to know I was jealous for her — in truth I was a little fanatic who resented
that there should be other idols in the world than
my own.

Even now, when I think over those child hours, I
cannot see why, in her brocade, and the pearls, and the
wonderful lace, she was not more inspiring to an artist
than on the hill with bare feet in sandals, and her white
skirt over her head; but poets and artists are curious.
I, perhaps, keep the only picture of her in the betrothal
dress, and that is in my mind, stamped there by the
information that in future she was to belong to Marco
de Ordoño.

It is a mistake to think children do not suffer deeply;
within their hearts are the seeds of all tragedies. A
strange painter was there from Valencia, and the
portrait he had painted of Marco was framed and in
the sala, for all to see. Don Rodrigo, who had arranged
the betrothal, as I thought later, to get the Llorente y
Rivera treasures in his own family chests lest they come
to me, well, Don Rodrigo was all smiling, and everybody's friend that day. He had great good nature in
the arrangement of the money of other people — most
of his own had been lost in various venturings. So he
had made decision that before they set sail for Mexico
he would have the portrait made to comfort admiring

aunts and a grandmother who mourned the departure of Marco's handsome self.

And it was a picture! All of velvet suit and satin linings, and the sword of his father, the general, in his ringed hand. People came in and looked at it, and praised. Marco took all the prettiest girls and asked each one to gaze on it sometimes and think of him when he was risking his life among the red barbarians. I know, for I heard three of them offer to pray for him. I think I waited near it to hear if cousin Sancha would also offer to pray for him, but Sancha was occupied with that lank Miguel, and coquetted till I was sorely tempted to remind her that Sister Teresa would give her short space for the wearing of brocades, and back in the convent she would be but a little student again, of as little importance as myself.

It was there, while looking at the picture, that I noticed Tristan Rueda, the foster brother of Marco. I had never known him to come much where the gay crowds were, and I had heard he was a poor relation, but whose relation I did not know. He did not look poor, and was taller than Marco. I knew they had the same nurse, Luiza, who once lived in the mountains, and had married a soldier, Mateo Gomez, and gone with him to Mexico; and it was thought a convenient thing that Don Rodrigo and Marco would go where a good housewife would be, as it were, waiting for them, and glad to be once more under the old family rule.

All those matters were talked over in the preparation for their journey, and I was wild with impatience at my lack of years, so eager was I to take ship and cross seas, and conquer worlds!

I did not know that height or years could not always win the thing desired. While I sat, glowering at the fine picture and eating my heart out with a boy's longings, Rodrigo stopped to talk to Tristan where he stood looking at the painting in the gorgeous gilded frame.

"You write a pretty letter, Tristan," he said, "and I have thought of it much while you were at the school, but it suits not my arrangements that you should go with us now. For one more year I need you here; then come and welcome. In a year my cousin Carlos will be back from Austria. In his hands all the properties will have good care. But until then I must leave some one in trust, and who knows so well as you all the lands, and the herds, and the accounts? For five years you have saved me every coin that was saved in the timber or the herds — Marco has no head that way!"

"True, Marco has not," agreed Tristan. He looked sulky, and not a traveling companion to wish for.

"No — and softly, Tristan, lad — I fancy there are even moments when he is more than a little jealous that you are as my right hand. So, for a year, it seems to me as well that you have a different way of life. One year will do much with a spoiled boy; he will be so sick for home that he will welcome you with a warm heart, and it will be better for both of you to wait until that time."

"Jealous — of me — when he has all this!" Tristan looked ugly as he said it, but in a moment bowed before Don Rodrigo as if in apologizing for a rebellious thought.

"I do not forget, señor, that to you and to the General de Ordoño I owe a debt of which we never speak. I cannot pay it to the general except it be by devotion to Marco, his son. I made my vow when I was very little, señor, but each year I repeat it: so long as I live I owe my life to your house; and somewhere, somewhere in the world, another man, perhaps, still lives under the shelter of a monk's robe, and it may be that for his life, also, I owe your house allegiance. I will stay, señor, until Don Pedro comes back from Austria, though my heart will go ahead of your ship into New Spain."

Don Rodrigo stared at him, and then sat down. His face had gone pale and red again as he looked at Tristan Rueda, who spoke so quietly.

"Holy saints!" he whispered. "Then you do remember?"

Tristan said nothing, and Don Rodrigo wiped his face, and looked as sick as a fat man sitting upright could look, and I made myself small in the corner behind a black carved chair taller than myself. I did not understand at all, but Don Rodrigo was the good-natured, gambling soldier, yet strong in all family councils, and a thing to frighten him was surely a thing of much import. I had no desire to listen, yet dared not move for fear of drawing their attention.

"You are a man," said Don Rodrigo after a silence in which I wondered my heart thumps did not give warning that I was so few paces from them. "Years do not always make the man, but you have held the secret of men since you were the height of my knee, and asked never a question! Santa Maria, lad, how could you remember?"

"I remember because I was carried all a long night ride from the mountains under a man's cloak; the man kissed me, and we wept together. I did not know why. It was to this room he brought me, and from the window I saw the river and the ships; that was the first time I had looked on ships, and I could not forget that. General de Ordoño put his hands on my head, and said I was not to be afraid; also that Marco would be as my brother. I do not recall the days after that for a long time — only that one day and that ride in the dark."

"Yet you speak of — another life — another," Don Rodrigo almost said the words in a whisper, and caught the sleeve of Tristan, looking up into his face, for the lad was still standing as at first, looking at the gorgeous picture of Marco.

"Yes, señor, but that was afterwards, long afterwards. General de Ordoño was dying, and priests came. One who came was the man of that night ride. After the funeral there were ships sailing to Mexico, and you took Marco and other children and me down to the shore to see the people. Among them was my man of the ride. He went away in the boat, and until now I have been waiting to follow to Mexico. I do not ask his name. I heard you call him Fernandito, and you said the robe of a monk was a better garment for him than a *sanbenito*. I do not know what he had done to earn the *sanbenito*."

"He did no wrong to any one, unless it be the holy saints, and they are good to forgive," said Don Rodrigo, crossing himself, and I was well frightened then, for while the monk's robe is for the service of the saints, the *sanbenito* is the yellow, glaring, hideous thing worn by heretics on the way to the *auto-da-fé* when there is a burning of sinners for the purifying of the world.

That was a big day in my boyhood. I had wished for height and years because I was jealous of Marco de Ordoño, but hidden there in the corner. I was willing to give up even the inches I had, so eager was I to shrink and be safe from discovery, for as in a bad dream I was afraid of the things I was hearing, yet scarcely knew why.

"You are a man, comrade," said Don Rodrigo, "but, Santa Maria, you have given me a fright! To think that the head of a child could hold all that danger for years, and never speak!"

Then the fine painter of the picture came in, and other friends, and Padre Juan, and in the crowd I could slip from my corner and stand among them unnoticed, and hear the words of praise, until Padre Juan put his hand on the shoulder of Tristan Rueda, and said before them all:

"Here, also, we may have a Velasquez or a Murillo some fine day! For his own joy he painted on our chapel of Santa Cecelia for a year, and did more of the angels in the frieze than the foreigner who got the pay for it."

This caused much surprise to me, for I had only heard of Tristan Rueda as the assistant of Don Rodrigo, and he looked red and sulky, with all eyes turned to him.

"So," said the painter in a sweet and honeyed way, as if to a child, "so you have ambitions? That is to be commended; but the labor is great, and only the few succeed."

"My ambitions, señor, will seem to you but slender. I have only made drawings to pass time while herding sheep," said Tristan, and his shrug and glance at the canvas in the gold frame were very nearly insulting. He would not be patronized by any one, and it was easy to see he did not relish the kind padre's good intent.

"Ah, only pastime for a shepherd!" and the painter stroked his beard, and measured the lad with his eyes. "Then as a shepherd, will you give us your free opinion of this portrait of Señor Don Marco de Ordoño?"

"Since you request it, señor, I would say that Marco is handsome enough without all that gold; you have made him grander than the pope. Also, to my eyes, the sword of his father has no fit place in the lily hand you have given to Marco. It is not the great general's son you have painted, señor, but a pretty page; only petticoats are needed to make him a fine lady in waiting."

And with a really beautiful bow to the painter, and the padre, and Don Rodrigo, he walked out and left them staring, and I think I was the only one of them all to see that Marco himself was at that moment about to enter from the patio with another maid to view the picture. They had halted, heard every word, and the girl, with her head held high in anger, drew Marco away along the corridor — and this time the girl was cousin Sancha herself! He seemed to be trying as best he might to loosen her fingers from about his arm, but gave it up; that child was strong as a young tigress, and she was tense with the dread of duels and death, and all the other tragic dreams so much a part of a girl's romance.

I did not wait to hear how Padre Juan and Don Rodrigo smoothed the ruffled humor of the painter. No doubt they told him that the lad had in truth lived his summers with the herdsmen and the timber cutters, and had gained a certain rustic disdain of the luxurious. But however they patched it up, I ran after cousin Sancha and found her half in tears with rage.

"Who is he — this Tristan Rueda?" she demanded. "No, I have never seen him. How should I see sheep-men in the convent? No, I saw only the back of his head, but that was enough! Rueda! *I* shall call him 'El Negrido,' because he has black hair curled at the ends like a Moor! I know he is hideous! I do not see how it is, Marco, that you ever were friends with him — he is not worthy since he mocks at your beautiful picture — him — El Negrido!"

In her fine rage and her attack on Tristan, Marco felt himself much comforted, and when I left them he was giving fond promise to spare Tristan's life, but also promised to ignore him from that time forth; which, by the way, he could not so easily do, as that "lady in waiting" got abroad and caused some laughter, and the following day a threat was made by Marco to chastise Tristan, whereupon Tristan hurt his pride some more, also his body, and made Marco go and confess to Don Rodrigo why it was done.

I thought of course Tristan would go back to the hills at once, that day of the betrothal, or to the house of Padre Juan; but long after the moon was up, and the music of the dancing had caused me to fall asleep on a seat outside the window of the sala, I was lifted in strong arms and carried to the room across the patio where the boy guests were to sleep; and as my fine holiday shoes were slipped off, and my clothes were unfastened with care, my curiosity conquered my sleepy head for a little, and I was made sorry to see it was Tristan Rueda who cared for me — for if cousin Sancha could find no good in him, how could I, her devoted slave, accept his favors? I comforted myself with the thought that she had not actually bound me with a promise to refuse his friendship, well though I knew she would have done so had she thought of it!

"Oh, Don Tristan! I thought you had gone back to your sheep, or to pray to your angels in the chapel," I whispered, "for she is very, very angry, and she will not let cousin Marco be friends with you, ever."

"That may be," he said as he slipped off the sleeves of my jacket.

"She does not know you, of course, or she would not call you El Negrido instead of Rueda," I continued. "It is because your hair is so black. She only saw your head, and heard your voice; and you — you did not get to see her at all, and she is so fine!"

"So very fine," he agreed. So he must have seen her while I slept. "But you also have black hair, little comrade, yet she is kind to you."

"You do not know how terrible Sancha can be when she is in a rage," I persisted. "I have seen her break things when she is in anger. It is better, I think, if you make more angels, and — pray to them. She hates you very, very much."

"I know," he whispered, and if he said anything more, I did not hear it. He laid me on the pillow, covered me over, and blew out the candle, and I knew nothing more until the other boys were throwing their shoes at me in the morning, and daring me to come with them and run naked down to the river for a swim before anyone but Santiago, the old watchman, was awake.

And that was the end of the betrothal day of cousin Sancha. Looking backward, it seems that while it was a great and full day to me, of which I was conscious, it was a day of fate for others more important than I, and their after years were framed by it.

CHAPTER III

THE THINGS FORBIDDEN

IT IS strange how quickly a slip of a girl makes a boy feel that she is a woman, while the boy is still a boy.

So quickly did cousin Sancha shoot up tall and slender, like a young palm by a living spring, that I flushed hot and cold as I kissed her six months later, and she patted my cheek and called me "Juanito Chiquito," and thanked me for a pet fawn I had sent, and asked me if I wanted to see the Indian dolls sent her by Marco from Mexico!

I cared as little as most boys for dolls, but I lied graciously, and with Padre Juan I spent a wonder day at the convent and looked at dolls, and spelled out the letters sent with them, and was too surprised to make comment when I saw the letters were not from, but about, Marco. He was at the De Ordoño mines in the interior, not convenient to the seacoast, or in the way of letters; thus a monk who was a friend of Don Rodrigo wrote for them all family letters, and they were sent to the good abbess, Mother Maria Cecilia, so that, as far as I could see, the letters were for the relations, and Sancha was regarded as a babe for whom only dolls were fitting pastime.

But the pages glowed with the beauty and the fine

success of Marco as communicated by the writer, Fray Fernando Alcatraz. The Ordoño mines at San Luis Potosí were in a fair way to make all their fortunes; the only difficulty was to secure a steady supply of native slaves for the work; there had been some rebellious in various ways, but in the end all would come right; Marco was attached to Fray Payo, the venerable Archbishop and Viceroy, and was in a fair way to climb high in the viceregal court; and so on, and so on.

All the letters were of the same things, and each carried the love and the blessings of Don Rodrigo and Marco and the priest who wrote it — and a doll or a string of beads.

"From Fray Payo and Don Rodrigo and Marco and the learned priest, I get dolls and strings of beads," said Sancha with disdain, "beads of turquoise, and of wood, of berries, and stone, and shell. I shall weave them all into a robe for the wedding dress, there will soon be enough to cover me!"

We laughed over how she would look in the wedding dress of beads, and then we fell to choosing which of the dresses of the Indian dolls would be most becoming. They were of even greater variety of material than the beads, and ranged from husks of maize to carvings of stone. I know now that those things which the white people named dolls were really effigies and figurines of their false gods and goddesses, and I wonder much that they escaped the sharp eyes of the officers of the Inquisition.

One doll wore woven sandals of grasses, and on these Sancha set her heart — she so dearly loved to run shoeless, and sandals like these would be so nearly nothing

on her feet. I had watched the village girls braid their
hats from the straw of the wild oats until I had the trick
of it, and with the footgear of the little Indian field god
for a pattern, I took strips of palm and braided them
and formed the fabric to her foot, and added to the
band across the ankle the silver buckles from my own
shoes, so that I had the joy of seeing her dance in them
with delight and spread her petticoats in a profound
mocking bow to me. And at that very moment the
Abbess and Padre Juan came into the garden, and tried
to look severe, and ended by laughing. Then they took
us in to the refectory, where we had bread and honey
and milk before we went back to the town below.

Sancha, with Sister Teresa, walked with us along the
path, and the fawn was led by Sancha, for already it had
learned the hand from which its food came. I looked
back at them as they stood at the edge of the olive wood,
and noted that Sancha was taller than little Sister Teresa,
and that over her head, in a way she had, she cast the
soft white skirt from the back as a shield against the
sun. The straight long folds of it either side her face,
and down to her feet, added to her height. It was not
as if a long white scarf had been flung over her head,
but rather as if close folded wings of white were either
side the slender figure, meeting overhead. It made her
look very curious with the flare of the sun back of her.
I thought of an angel I had once seen in a picture with
Joseph the carpenter. Yet Sancha herself was not like
an angel at all.

As we went down the steep way of the hill, Padre
Juan remarked that he must ask Tristan Rueda to send
some competent man to repair the chapel of the convent

where a storm had done damage; there were some capable lay brothers at the monastery who could do the work and repair the frescoes, but Tristan always knew the one who would be best, and it might be that he would himself give an eye to it, despite the fact that his days were very full with preparations for the voyage through the sea of the north to the New World.

Don Carlos had made the journey back from Austria sooner than hoped for. Within a week the *San Clemente* would spread her wings for the western shores and, if the saints willed, Tristan would be aboard of her, free at last to live his own life. Through all his boyhood, he had seemed, in some strange way, a willing, yet dominating vassal of De Ordoño's.

Padre Juan grumbled about this vassalage more than a little that day, for he had a great belief that Tristan came perilously near to being a genius — a lad who could manage herds, and cure the murrain in sheep with the skill of the devil-possessed Moors, and who could copy in fairest beauty the ancient writings of the Fathers. An entire volume had he done for Padre Juan on the life and works of the well beloved San Juan Bautista, his patron saint, and each page had its own illuminated letters of blue and of gold, as was custom with all holy books of an older day — I should see it! Not another like it anywhere! Padre Juan thought he painted no more saints or angels; Tristan had never talked of such work since a day when the Bishop had warned him it would mean much gold and a lifetime. Also there had been some ill feeling among the De Ordoño cousins against him because of that ugly estimate of the portrait of Marco for which much good money had been paid.

Tristan had so much of almost heretical independence about so many of the things of life that Padre Juan could never understand why he made himself do the will of the De Ordoño family, even to smothering his own talents that their sheep be rightly tended, and their olive and orange orchards rightly cared for.

So the padre grumbled and discoursed over his favorite pupil all down the road to the town, and thus I learned that Tristan Rueda did not tell all of his life and thoughts at confession, which unsafe habit helps to make a path for the devil to walk over and whisper heretical things, especially in the ears of a genius. Did not that word mean to be possessed by genii? And were there not malicious spirits together with saintly ones in that list? If not, why did the church and the priests have to work so endlessly to exorcise them?

I had these thoughts, but I dared not offend Padre Juan by speech of them. Orphan as I was, with only Sancha, Marquesa de Llorente y Rivera as a near relative, it was kind Padre Juan who made the world seem like a home place to me, just as the good abbess of the convent was mother to Sancha. Two nestless birds were we, despite the countless branches of the family tree on which we might roost and welcome.

For myself, I confess that the only branch holding dreams of mine was that one most powerful, across the seas in New Spain. To have a great-uncle who was both archbishop and viceroy of Mexico made me count the days until I, too, might fare forth to adventure, and I was ever measuring my height, and walking with head high held, to make myself grow tall more quickly.

Also, I was like the shadow of Tristan Rueda from

the time I learned he was to sail in the *San Clemente.*
I had a holiday of two weeks from school, and all of it
was spent to fetch or carry for him, or seek out the
things he needed for the far journey. He was always
gentle with me; took me into shops and among boat-
men; bought himself a strong chest from a home-coming
merchant, and together we packed it in joy. At my wish,
he wrote a letter for me to Fray Payo de Rivera, the
Viceroy, asking that some place be made for me, if it
were but to lace his shoes — a boy would need no great
height for that! I also asked his gracious notice for my
friend, Tristan, and signed the letter with the name of
my mother, who had been with the angels before I
could even recall her, and also my own name in full,
Juan Estevan Maria Llorente y Rivera, that he might
not fail to see I was of his own family. I think now
that my determination to go was made when I read
those letters with report of the high estate of Marco de
Ordoño under the patronage of a viceroy of our family.

Between jealousy of Marco and emulation of Tristan,
I was well nigh sleepless during those last days before
the sailing. We slept together in the De Ordoño home,
for Tristan was commissioned to take charge of much
wealth in goods for Don Rodrigo. There were bales of
fine cloths, casks of Greek and Spanish wine, priests'
vestments with wonderful embroideries done by the
blessed nuns in the convent, and silks of richness,
worked over and bordered with threads of gold. Also
there were statues of four saints for the church of San
Carlos, carved of wood, with eyes of glass, and a wonderful enamel of wax, painted to the life as to face and
hands. A bit of the gold on the carven lace draperies

had been rubbed off by some accident, and at the last Tristan spent precious time in regilding them, that no little curve or edge should be less than perfect.

This pleased Padre Juan very much. I heard his commendation at the same time that he was giving priestly warning concerning all books to be taken, for strict though the Holy Brotherhood might be in loyal Spain, it was but mild ruling to that of Mexico, where, perhaps because of the native converts, religion must not even be discussed, and those who went to the New World for greater freedom found themselves there under the iron heel of the Inquisition.

"Yet I have heard there are lands of the north coast where the Dutch and English and some French live who have cast free from Rome," said Tristan.

"Keep you far from such shores, lest the seas rise up to engulf the lands! Whence comes your knowledge?"

"I hear the sailors talk, and the merchants; there is always talk of the new lands. We all listen."

"Then take not Juan with you to the warehouses, no good can be learned from the discourse of heretical travelers."

"Yet," ventured Tristan, "if Christoval Colon had not listened to the heresies of a round world, we would not be sending these saints to the western heathen this day."

Padre Juan looked at him strangely.

"Tristan, you are only a youth, yet I must warn you not to say words like that, the *San Clemente* might sail without you if such words reached the Brotherhood. It savors of careless speaking of forbidden things. And

that name ' Colon,' and ' Christoval,' why give the Spanish name to a man of Italy? "

" We hear it sometimes."

" Then you should also hear that it has been forbidden."

" I was reading the letters in his book at the monastery
to learn things of New Spain, and all the letters are in
Spanish and were so signed; none in Italian, so I
thought — "

" Think no more, and speak no more on that matter,"
said Padre Juan in a tone that set me quaking. " The
reasons why are not to be spoken of; it is forbidden."

" Yes, father," said Tristan obediently, and went on
with his careful work on the statute, though I slipped
out of the strong room as soon as might be, and was
relieved to see Padre Juan follow soon. I sat on the
veranda to watch if by any chance he turned towards
the office of the tribunal, but to my relief, he went on
the way to the chapel. I never before had heard Padre
Juan speak with severity to Tristan Rueda — it was as
if my world were turning topsy-turvy.

And the night was the equal of that day in surprises.
It may have been the excitement by which I was kept
wakeful, or the very dread of that shadowy Holy Brotherhood whose eyes were everywhere. Be that as it
may, I wakened suddenly with a fright at the silence,
for there was not even the sound of the breath of Tristan
in the room, and in the sickly light of the old moon, I
crept to his bed and found his pillow empty. Also the
bed was cold. Scarcely within an hour had he lain
there.

The wonder is that I did not call aloud. It was the

thing I wanted first to do. But that warning of **Padre**
Juan's still ringing in my ears brought me a terror, and
also a desire to find Tristan in silence, if I alone could
find him at all.

The cocks were crowing, though there was no dawn.
Could it be that he had risen while it was yet night to
work on his tasks?

Quiet as might be, I slipped into clothing, and, without shoes, went through the halls and down the stone
steps to the door of the strong room where the things
of merchandise were kept. Beyond were the foreign
wines and other importations. In the anteroom his
work on the carven saints had seemed finished.

But through the keyhole a light came, and I heard
strange noises as of an auger and then of muffled ham-
merings. Try as I would, I could not see farther than
the little circle gained by one eye at the keyhole, but
the ancient musty treasure chest of General de Ordoño
was in the corner. I saw Tristan open it with a key
and then I scarcely dared breathe — so eager was I to
see the treasure there.

I might as well have taken my comfort in bed for all
the treasure, not a thing could I see but rolls of parchment and some brown books; then with a sharp knife,
Tristan cut the leather cover from every book and tossed
the covers back into the open chest! That was a thing
so at variance with his every previous act that I was
given a fright by it. There was no sacrifice Tristan
Rueda would not make if, by any privation, he might
earn or borrow books. He had the knack of languages,
and would chaffer with a Greek sailor for even a book
of prayers in a foreign tongue. His love of books was

so pronounced that Padre Juan was wise in giving him warning as to the laws of Mexico.

When one is startled or badly frightened, he does not think, he only feels; and I was filled with an unreasoning fear that Tristan had gone mad, all alone there in the night. In a shrill whisper I tried to reassure him of my presence, though I was strongly put to it not to turn and run blindly, screaming for everybody.

Tristan opened the door, perhaps fearing the thing I was tempted to, and his face was death white in the light of the candle, as he dragged me in, his hand over my mouth.

"You have risked your life, your freedom, and more than that," he said; "but now that you are here, stay you must to the end. You may have it in your power for the rest of your life to send me to hell, when the thought comes to you, Juanito. Tend your thoughts that way? or may I trust the man your boyhood will make?"

My teeth were like castanets in their chatter, for I could only shake and stare at that which I saw. San Pedro, with the keys of heaven in his hand, lay flat on his back on the floor, and was made hollow from his feet up and in that cavity were packed rolls of parchment. Santa Cecilia was treated likewise, but a block, cunningly contrived, fitted over the work and was fresh painted with blue and gilding. I saw then why Tristan had much care of the saints donated to Mexican chapels. Also there was a cask of Greek wine emptied into a great jar, and the cask was packed with books to the right weight, and around them fresh straw.

"Speak you, Juanito, but speak in whispers."

" What — what would chance to you if " —

" There would be a fine burning at the next *auto-da-fé*, but first there would be one here, for the brandy in that corner would take fire and all within these walls would go up in smoke before you would be let go to give warning. Even then it might be thought that you only dreamed all you think you see here! It would be a loss to learning if the books were destroyed, and men are hungry for learning. Speak now, Juanito, but think if you have faith in yourself to be silent always."

I tried to think, but all that came in my head was the voice of Don Rodrigo when he had said to Tristan in the sala, " You are a man, comrade ; years do not always make a man, but you have held the secret of men since you were the height of my knee."

I had been thrilled by that praise, for it had been wrung from a frightened old soldier, and now I was to be put to the test as to whether I also could ever compel such approval. That, I am sure, was the thing which urged me to whisper, " I can be silent, Tristan."

With a bit of old canvas he covered again the keyhole from which a draft had made it fall, and then in silence he bound my eyes, and led me to a seat.

" It is only that you see no more than you already have," he said, " for that will be trouble enough for you to keep ever out of your confessions. I can waste no time taking you back to bed, and what is to be done must be finished before dawn."

So I sat there and shook with fear, and smelled the paint, and heard him use the muffled hammer, and move heavy casks, and at last gather up in a canvas all the broken wood bored from the central blocks of the wooden saints, and when my eyes were uncovered, we bore it to the river and cast it in.

The gray of day was coming when we climbed the stairs and were back in our beds.

" For the comfort of your own soul, Juanito, I will tell you that there is no word of evil in all the books you saw hidden there. The man who turned the key on them was General de Ordoño. He was a stanch son of the church, but also a loyal friend. The books belonged to a friend who is dead to the world — a letter I found tells me this — and the knowledge in the books is now for me, if God, the Father, sends good wind to our sails."

It was a comfort that he assured me there was no evil, for Tristan was ever truthful to boldness.

No other word passed between us concerning that night of work in the strong room, but he put his hands on my shoulders and looked very hard into my eyes before the last boat left shore for the *San Clemente,* and then he took my hands close in his.

" Juanito, you have a friend waiting in the New World if ever you should set sail there," he promised, and then he said no more, but bent his head to the blessing of Padre Juan, and I went back, sad enough, to the chapel, with the hope that my viceregal uncle would send for me soon as might be.

The secret of that night gave me vast importance in my own thoughts. I had asked no question of the books and parchments, sure that if the General de Ordoño had hidden them away, it must have been for a good purpose. It never occurred to my childish mind that the general was not as much scholar as soldier, or that the contents of the books were not known to him. Like Don Rodrigo, his brother, he had been the ranging adventurer rather than the student.

As the years passed after Tristan's going, strange tales came eastward over the seas in every ship, until all the youth and half the priesthood were stung by the gadfly of unrest to garner gold or heathen souls in the New World. Padre Juan, traveling to Cordoba, brought me a wonder feast of intelligence from the letters of Tristan — the De Ordoño mines were even more rich than Don Rodrigo had hoped; Marco was in such favor that it was said a high official would not be averse to giving his daughter to a husband of such riches, though Don Rodrigo would see to it that this should not come about, for his heart was set on uniting the families of De Ordoño and De Llorente y Rivera.

Of Tristan there were no great riches told, but adventures even more dear to the heart of a boy. He had gone north into the heathen land with a godly friar whose mission work was as a miracle, so many of the pagans had he won for salvation. Into the far wilderness they had gone, and the walls of chapels and convents were rising toward heaven as quickly as the poor heathen could shape the timber and make the bricks.

Not so much news did he send of the cities of the new land, except that they were unduly housing too many of the idle adventurers who lounged in sun or shadow, waiting newly arrived riches from the mines, and all the gay carouse of the gamblers' heaven. He, Tristan, escaped all such danger by lack of gold, and by the garb of the convent. He went as a lay brother with Fray Fernando, as the dress of the order was a help in herding the flocks of heathen lambs. Already he was learning the language, and noting down many of their strange thoughts of the false gods to which they had in ignorance given worship.

Padre Juan was very happy over this word. It was as if his pupil were already on the golden ladder to a Bishop's mitre, at least. If he was not to be a painter of saints, he might do even better and become a saint himself in his zeal for converts!

Our good Padre Juan read into that account more, I think, than he got out of it. I had not seen so much of saintliness in the spirit of Tristan Rueda; and that he wore on his journeys the robe of a monk, was as if he had protected his legs with a new sort of boot or armor to fit the desert he was to cross.

Of cousin Sancha, Padre Juan had little to say, except that she had grown more tall. There is not much else a priest may tell a lad concerning a maid.

But I was soon to need no messenger to tell me anything. From the archbishop came the word for which I had prayed rather than hoped. I was to see a bit of the world, and fit myself in good time for even a place at court, if need be. I was chosen as one of the pages in his train, and this ended my school days and took me to Seville for the requisite preparation.

CHAPTER IV

IN MEXICO

SO AGAIN I saw Sancha, and felt myself more dumb and stupid than ever in the light of her beauty, for which there were no words.

"But — you are a woman!" I found myself saying as I stared at her, and she laughed — the dear, lighthearted, reckless laugh the good nuns could never tone down to a discreet smile or simper.

" A woman, Juanito mine, and either a married woman or a nun before I am grown much more in height," she said, nodding her pretty head, and her gray eyes darkling. "I am sick of gray walls, and priest letters, and there is no one to tell it to but you. I sang with joy when I heard you were coming. We will go into the orchard where I will bring my love gifts to show you, and there we can talk."

It was like paradise to be with her, and I choked back a sigh as she spoke of her love gifts. Though I should bring down the moon out of the sky for her, she would regard it only as a kinsman's gift.

She came back to me in a little while, with her skirt gathered up and loaded full, as a peasant woman would carry cabbages or onions, and then with a laugh in which there was derision of herself, she let fall her load at my feet — and I stared, and laughed, and then grew sober enough as I saw her eyes.

33

These were her love gifts from over the sea for all the years, and not one thing but the Indian dolls and beads and toys such as had been sent in the very first ship!

"Every homeward vessel shows me I am not forgotten," she said with a little crooked smile. "Yet who is it remembers me? Some one to whom I am still a little child! Here are the letters; they are the same. They come to the Mother Abbess. When that monk, Fray Fernando, was north among the heathen there were no letters. But the end has come. There are lovers in Spain if not over the water — and I have written and told that to Don Rodrigo.

"You have sent a letter, one you wrote?" Our women were not bookish. To read the lives of the saints it was good enough to know how, but the writing of letters was not so well for maids. And in the end you will see that was where the plain trail for trouble began for Sancha.

When I told her that I myself was to sail in the next vessel, and that I would carry the message to Don Rodrigo or to Marco, she was wild with protests that we all could journey to see the world, while for her, a maid, there was nothing to do but stay close at home, and make endless prayers.

"But not to Marco shall you carry word for me," she declared with pride. "It is to Don Rodrigo, Padre Juan is writing the word, for it is only poor old Don Rodrigo who sends the letters — and selects these," and she touched the heap of dolls with her foot. "Poor Don Rodrigo! He made the betrothal, and now he sends all the love gifts! No, if Marco de Ordoño thinks he has taken a step upward in the favor of our family, it may be as well he is given a lesson. I will write him a reminder. I thought I was married to him that day he sailed away, but my mind is changed. If ever I marry him it will be after he has wooed me — and gifts of Indian dolls will not serve."

Here was a new sort of trouble, for I was boy enough to fear that a bearer of fiery messages would lack the welcome I longed for in New Spain. Yet what was there but to do her will, and do it with the best grace I could muster?

She wept at our parting, and kissed me, and after that I knew little of how I tumbled into the small boat at the shore, or how I went up over the side of the ship and landed on the deck, striving as might be to remember that as grandnephew to the viceroy of Mexico I was a personage of importance aboard ship, and that to shed the tears I felt would not be in keeping with my dignities.

From the Azores I sent back a letter to Sancha, telling her all that had happened, and then we set sail out over the untracked waters to the west, and with every dawning and every nightfall the wonder grew in my mind as to the bigness of the man who first ventured there, for we had calms and hurricanes and our own share of sea troubles; added to which was the ever restless watch for English pirates and French corsairs. But at last our stubborn vessel proved her worth by bearing us all safe to Hispaniola where we rested a week for the mending of ship, the taking on of fresh water and other provisions; and I, who, during the hurricanes, had strong conviction that food of earth could never more attract me, was astonished at my own appetite, for surely never

had fruit or meat such wonderful delicacy as that of
the tropic land. This was the effect of the many weeks
of salted pork, and, at the last, none too much of that.

From there, in due time, the *Santa Maria* sailed west-
ward through sea gardens, for the days were few when
we saw neither palm isles, nor canoes of the natives or
traders with fruits, nuts, or fowl for sale.

At Havana ill word was waiting. A ship from Mexico
was in harbor, and there was much of surmise over
changes to be made because of an illness of the viceroy.
His physician had made the statement that his years of
work for church and crown had left their mark, and that
a new archbishop and a new viceroy would be named,
for the good Fray Payo was making arrangements to
resign and end his days in a monastery in the old home-
land of Spain.

Here was a new turn to my wheel of life. Were all
my dreams of viceregal grandeur to melt beneath the
tropic suns? In my excitement I had ill thoughts of a
man who could remain viceroy and archbishop, yet
choose a monk's cowl instead. Why, it was to be a
king so far as power was concerned, and even the
unknown grandnephew might hope to fare well under
such patronage.

Whatever else I heard of concern passed me unheeded.
Even my boy's joy of new sights and new lands was
dampened, and my greatest fear was that I might be
called upon to face about and journey back with him
through the hurricanes to Seville. Yet, would a monk
in a monastery need a page? Could I not hope to live
in New Spain if Marco could live there? I assured
myself yes, and remembered with gladness the words

of Tristan Rueda. There, at least, I would have a friend though all the people of our own family should fail me.

Thus I argued myself across the seas from Havana, and questioned with eagerness the first man aboard at Vera Cruz. The viceroy was able to walk again, but he had gone through two months' siege of fever, and was peacefully preparing for retirement. The man spoken of as his successor was Don Tomas Antonio, Marquis de la Laguna, Conde de Parades, and it was said that the ruling of the new day would have diversions of its own and have little likeness to the six years of the rule of the good priest, Don Payo de Rivera.

By this I gathered that the new ruler would at least be of the world, worldly, and that a page of his would see gayer life than with an archbishop. In fact and in truth, I see myself now as a selfish little animal, measuring the greatest only by their ability to confer favors. I was at the same time homesick, if I may call it so, at losing the only relation I knew of in Mexico. He had seemed to me as a bond with Sancha, though he had never seen either of us!

Each new thing I saw on the great journey I wished for the able pen of a Diaz that I might make clear the picture of it for her, but when the great enchantment of white Orizaba met my eyes above the palms, I knew no pen was equal to the writing of its beauties. The natives call it Mountain of the Star, and Tristan told me, long after, that it was used by the ancient priests as a range finder for the stars forming the heart of heaven — our Polaris and his circling companions of the Serpent and the Eagle.

Of all that paganism I knew nothing then or of the mythology of the red tribes, but it is easy to believe when looking on Orizaba that its meaning was linked with the sky and its sacred things.

A slender, pale priest with a curious Indian rosary of crude turquoise and shell was with the cavalcade going up from the seashore, and he told us much of the strange land and places, and at Pueblo de los Angels he was greeted with glad looks. Little brown, naked babes were held out to him for his smile, and doors were open to his friends. I was told that in an epidemic he had remained to care for the stricken, after all other help had fled, and the Indians came near to worship of him. His help had been great to Fray Payo, and he knew the tribes from Yucatan to the pueblos of the Rio Brava del Norte. He could speak in the tongué of many, and was called "El Sabio." I heard that term so often that I took it to be his title. And then an old soldier whom we met on the trail doffed his hat and saluted him as Don Fernando, and I knew that the slender man with the face like old ivory was the friend of the De Ordoños and the writer of the letters to the abbess; also he was the miracle worker with whom Tristan had made the journey to the far north!

It was the first time, I think, that my mind was consciously impressed by force of character apart from all the trappings of circumstance and state. Don Fernando wore a habit that was old and somewhat frayed as to sleeves and hem, and we had some richly dressed merchants, together with men of family, in that group of travelers; yet among them all the quiet Don Fernando won central place without striving, and the most pre-

tentious listened when he spoke. I learned that the
turquoise and shell beads were gifts of Indio tribes.

He bade me ride beside him, and showed me such
kindness as a traveler might, but of the many questions
concerning Marco and his magnificence he could tell
me little; only, Fray Payo had opened the door for him,
and his handsome face had won its own way to prefer-
ment.

As to Tristan, he had made great headway with the
strange picture-writing records of the heathen, and
already he had ranged afar on every quest the church
could send him, thus adding greatly to this knowledge.
Also, he had painted in a chapel a frieze of angels, and
the native chiefs had been duly impressed by those spirit
faces gazing down from the clouds. The result had
been curious. Tristan, though not in holy orders, or
like to be, had been given high place in the minds of the
brown people; his fame had traveled because it was
thought by them that he could see the spirit people
whom the heathens were convinced were everywhere.
While the brown priests could see them only after long
fasting and prayers, this white youth with the brushes
could see them at all times! When a revolt threatened
at the mines, he had saved the lives of Marco and Don
Rodrigo by learning of the secret leader, and painting
his portrait with a fiery devil peering over his shoulder.
The sight of it frightened every native to his knees.
The leader was shunned and would have been killed by
his comrades but for Tristan, who saved him and sent
him north to his own forests. Thus he both bettered
conditions and saved lives, and despite his short stay in
Mexico, his fame had traveled in strange ways into far

deserts and jungles. Don Payo would gladly have held him in the town, but Tristan had the blood of rangers in his veins, and was restless for the free wild places.

Thus I learned more in riding beside Don Fernando than ever went over the seas to Spain. The name of Tristan was as a key to his heart, and while love and loyalty were as a blanket to cover the acts of a De Ordoño, I could easily perceive that Marco, with all his pride, stood not so high as Tristan, the ranger, might stand if he chose.

Lad though I was, I could see why the walls of palace and monastery were left behind him, despite all exalted patronage. It was the first time he had ever ranged free, and of patronage, in a way, he had been given more than made for his happiness, since it chained him to a certain allegiance to the house of De Ordoño.

The air was like wine to me where we rode hour by hour above the palms and into the oaks and pines, with ever the snow peaks white in the sun, or rosy long after the sun was gone. I wondered not at the witchery by which Marco was held from Spain, though it was true he could not even think how fair Sancha had grown!

Don Fernando knew also Luiza, who had married the soldier Gomez, and to her home he took me that I might make myself fit for the presence of the viceroy after all the journey, and when I saw pretty Anita there, the daughter of Luiza's first husband, I wondered that no mention of her was in all the letters home; for Anita Gomez was sparkling as the water of a fountain in the sun, a slender flitting wisp of a girl, with big eyes of brown.

Luiza wept at the messages sent from home, and

showed all deference to Don Fernando, and many kindnesses to me, and made plans to house me in her own
home, if by chance the illness of the viceroy should make
delay as to my comfort in the palace.

So I found a good nest, and a welcome comforting to
a strange lad in a strange land. Through the little court,
Anita took me to the cell-like room of Tristan's choice,
and showed me his Indian mats, and rugs, and strange
arms and paintings.

"But those we never touch, for the records are
pagan," she said with a little shrinking. "He studies
out the meanings, and puts them in good Spanish for
the archbishop. But these days he is out somewhere
with the tribes, and you can have his room if need. Tristan is rich in beds, for there is ever one for him at the
monastery of San Carlos. They are glad when he goes
there, for he is helping Fray Bernardino with the
paintings.

"And what of Marco, señorita?" I asked, and thought
how much prettier she was when the red flushed her
cheek at the question.

"I — I am not so exalted that your excellency should
give me 'señorita'," she said slowly, and when the color
went again from her face it left her pale. I did not know
then what I learned later, that pretty Anita was a child
of love, and that Luiza did a Christian thing when she
married the father, and took the little orphan to her own
heart.

"But what of Marco? does he also abide with you
when here from the mines?" I asked.

"Not — now," she said. "Since Don Tristan is here,
Don Marco is more with his palace friends, and it is

very gay there. This is very plain, as you see, señor."

Anita had the pretty, friendly ways of a servant who has pride in service, and quickly made clear the remembrance that I was not only a tired lad off a journey, but that I was a Llorente y Rivera and the grandnephew of the viceroy. But as I put on my finest apparel, I was more than a little oppressed, and longed for a voice of other shores that would call me " Juanito."

My luck would have it that my regal and priestly relative was sleeping when I made my visit, and a very learned gentleman, Don Martin de Silva, the vicar general, saw to it that I was provided with a companion of my own age, Gilberto Lanchitas, whose uncle was prior of the *consulado*. Together we climbed stairs and looked from towers out over the wondrous valley of the Mexicos ; and the perfection of it all was enough to astonish even the most loyal Sevillan, for it was no new city, as a Spaniard might expect, but everywhere there were traces of ancientness and mysteries. An old temple was being torn down in a garden back of Chapultepec, where we went on horseback, and the brown people stood by and watched the carven stone being carted on wooden wheels for the building of a stable ; and I thought, and crossed myself at the same time, of the chapel of Charles the Fifth, set in the midst of the Moorish marbles of Cordoba. Even as a boy it seemed to me sacrilege of beauty.

But Gilberto took little heed, and could tell me little enough of Mexico. All his thought was centered on learning the latest news of Spain, and what was said of the death of Don Juan of Austria, and what of the queen mother and the court intrigues, and so on. All I heard from him was gossip of the viceregal succession and the probable archbishop. There were aspirants for both posts of honor — and also questionings as to whether new dignitaries would be sent out from Spain. Gilberto had an eye to his own advancement, and plied his arts to make his virtues known to me, as a relative of the viceroy; as if he had not spent years himself in shadow of the palace, whilst I was the stranger.

Such discourse was of small profit to me, for he was of the milk-and-water sort, ever intent on his own apparel and questions of the latest fashions and favorites at court. So, soon as might be in courtesy, I slipped away to range alone and, though I knew it not then, I crossed with an adventure my first day in the garden of the palace.

I had no intent to listen, but the voice inside the barred window of the patio was the sweetest one could wish to hear; it had the deep seductive notes and again the lightness of love music. Truly, to this day, I have not heard more wondrous tones in a speaking voice than those of Doña Perfecta de Dasmarinas.

She was laughing gently as if teasing some one, and then she said, "But truly, Don Marco, if you in truth seek to serve me, how is it that your friend, Don Tristan, never again comes as I request? If he paints angels for a chapel, why should he not paint another face — it may be — for a palace?"

There were some hesitant murmurings in a voice I knew after all the years, and those two names — Marco and Tristan — made me hold my breath.

"It is not for myself I care," continued the lady, "but when one has been married to a man, the padre ever tells a woman to seek to pleasure her husband, and this is a thing upon which his mind is set. Who knows what honors there will be to divide when Don Payo goes? Is your friend blind, that he ranges with the brown people for empty learning, when his talents should hold him here?"

Marco assured her that he had only returned from San Luis Potosi that hour, and that he had faithfully borne her message to Tristan of the honor she had suggested, also that Tristan had been booted and spurred for a sally to the north, and made comment that the painting of beauty was a joy not allowed to a *maestro de campo.*

Perhaps the lady knew Marco was framing his words as best he could to please her, for she was silent a bit as if in thought, and then said, "Remember that I have trusted you in this. Don Eduardo wants the portrait of me, yet will he value it the more if I surprise him with it, and " — she laughed softly — " when the new viceroy comes in, I may have friends to ask favors for."

Then a youthful lady quickly crossed the corridor and entered the room. I heard her called Doña Mercedes by Marco.

"Perfecta," she said with coldness, "your husband is waiting. He thinks you in the chapel at confession."

"I am this little minute returned through the garden and stop to greet Don Marco. He is as a stranger from those rich mines of his. Shall we ask him to the ball with us tonight?"

Then their voices went away, and I hurried through the garden and around to the entrance of the palace that I might see them come out.

Doña Perfecta fitted her seductive voice. Her hair was of red gold and her eyes brown, and her every movement had the slow grace by which you were made to wonder that each turn of her head, or her eyes, was more lovely than the last. And to think that Tristan turned away to barbarians when he could paint such beauty!

Doña Mercedes was not beautiful, but looked very capable — also she looked not well pleased, and she stepped into the waiting carriage without the helping hand of Marco de Ordoño. He assisted Doña Perfecta, saluted the gentleman who entered the carriage with them, and then stood uncovered, a very courtly, handsome figure, as they drove away. No wonder Sancha had held him so long as an ideal in her heart. I thought, and still think, Marco de Ordoño the very handsomest man I ever had sight of.

That he had joy in seeing me again he gave every sign of in courtesy, though he looked me over, made comment on my growth, and wondered at my coming. Why had I journeyed from my comfort to far uncertainties?

I told him that Sancha decided those far uncertainties must have great and strange charms that he did not return from them to claim his betrothed. He laughed at that, and stared at me, and looked after the carriage.

"Is that her wording, or your own?" he asked, "and are there messages for me? Come within."

I was presented to people of distinction, and noted how, even in their courtesy, they were curious. Thus at the very gate of the new life I saw the uneasiness of the office-holding, office-seeking men, for whom life might be changed by the threatened new rule. The very courtiers, and some of them men of talents, had the natural curiosity as to a new seeker of even a small office, especially one of the blood of the viceroy.

Through these several signs and the banter of Marco de Ordoño, my heart was low enough in my boots ere the time came that I should be brought to his eminent excellency, the priestly viceroy. Strange enough it is that the little, frittering minds take the courage out of one, while the big, simple souls provide with a glance all that you lack. Thus it was with Fray Payo Enriqez de Rivera, the archbishop and viceroy of Mexico. His hand met mine, and his other hand was on my shoulder as he gave me welcome, and at once he spoke significantly: I was not to lose courage in the new land for want of a patron; he would make that his own charge, whether he stayed or sailed for Spain.

Fray Fernando was by his side, and, I gave a guess, had divined my boyish uncertainties. Thus life, at a moment, took on a different color to me, and I could enter into the gaieties of the youths, and take less to heart the raillery of Marco over a stray lad seeking adventure.

Also I was housed in the palace, and to give me acquaintance and ease of mind, was made page, and Gilberto's was the task of guide and friend in the new and care-free office to which I was assigned.

CHAPTER V

THE LESSON OF LISPANOS TO HERETICAL SOULS

THE frail health of Don Payo made clear that his viceregal office was a burden he would gladly lay aside, and in the following days I had many opportunities of seeing how, little by little, he was making all plans to shift safely the weight of both church and state from his own shoulders.

To Marco I said little as might be of Sancha — all the more so that she had sent him no direct message by me. All that came was safe within the scroll to Don Rodrigo. From the gossip of Gilberto I divined that Marco had no need to languish for maids across the water, when the best doors of Mexico were opened wide for him. I fancied it gave him a swaggering arrogance when her name was mentioned, knowing well that I dared not express in words my own dumb rage at his carelessness. Between women and the desire of Fray Payo to show preference to the son of General de Ordoño, Marco was at a point where, without surprise, the hand of a king or the glove of a princess might be offered him without his special wonder. Thus his handsome face had spoiled him, and, as was apparent, secret meetings were given him by lovely ladies who should have been at confession.

And back in Seville Sancha must make herself content with Indian dolls and prayers and strings of beads.

So, to all Marco's questions as to word from Sancha, I gave him nothing, since the word was to Don Rodrigo, and was well sealed.

My great desire was to make the journey to the mines, but Don Fernando advised against it, as the Indian clans had been making trouble in that region, or in one I should have to cross, and Don Rodrigo would be in the city as soon as all grew quiet again.

It was while I was waiting his return, and learning the ways of the town and people, that I gained knowledge that Padre Juan, back in Seville, was well informed as to the strictures placed on all of Mexico by the Holy Brotherhood. The rule of Fray Payo was questionably mild in their eyes, and as I saw long lines of the penitents doing the stations in the garb of shame, I heard much of grumbling that the Judaizing apostates, or the pestilent Lutherans, were shown prolonged mercy under Fray Payo — and the penance of weekly processions and edifying sermons was little short of encouragement to iniquity. There had been no burnings out of sinful souls for many weeks. More than one of the devout openly prophesied either epidemics or earthquakings, if holy church grew lax in its prosecutions of heretics.

So a company, including Marco, was sent riding bravely north to Texcuco where, report said, a new Christian family had refused to eat good pork, and added to this the further damning evidence that neither father nor son worked the fields on a Saturday. Therefore the case against them was heavy with dire import. Many maintained that so flagrant an affair must be beyond even the mercy or lenient word of the viceroy. And thus did I learn, little by little, of the warring of factions, and the reasons why a man, old in service as was Don Payo, would be glad to put aside the honors, and the endless fight for lives.

Marco rode back looking like a hero, with his arm in a sling from some accident, and the suspected men and women were led with their hands tied and ropes about their necks, staggering at the heels of the horses. They were pelted through the streets to the prison, and there was more excitement than over a fight with Indians, for it was said that heretical books, and even a Bible, had been found hidden under their shelled maize in the bins.

A great scandal was made over the matter, for the Lispano family were not insignificant. Their holdings in land were important, as was even the tax to the crown on their mines at Zacatecas. I found the good Luiza weeping over their downfall, for their province in Spain was her own. But Anita, exclaiming with youth's impetuosity against the trailing of ladies of delicacy through the dust at the heels of troopers, was given a word of caution and hard query by her confessor. What sympathy could a true daughter of holy church hold for those who made plain choice of the devil and his instruments? To either read of religion or discuss it was forbidden, as she well knew — and there was the damning evidence of a pious *mestizo* major-domo that pork was not eaten at the Lispano table! Of a certainty the evil would be burnt out of their souls and their bodies at the next *auto-da-fé*.

For myself, I cared not much for the meat of a pig, where fish and good chicken were in plenty, despite which, for many a day after that, I refused every dish, no matter how tempting, unless pork was somehow used in it.

Thus was my mind impressed by the sight of the white-haired man and his drooping daughters staggering in weariness through the dust. Sons and a nephew were also there, but they were more able. I saw Doña Perfecta look down from a balcony and heard her comment on the white skin of the shoulder of one prisoner; it had not occurred to her that a Jewess was so fair.

It was my first sight of the work of the Brotherhood in the New World, and has never left me. It is not that it was more severe than in Spain. Yet in the older land affairs were conducted with a difference. A man might be caged, or he might wear chains through the street to prison, but a certain decorum was observed; there were no white-faced girls with half-naked backs, drawn with ropes at the heels of prancing horses. Marco rode well, and lifted his feathered hat to Doña Perfecta, and to his saddlebow was tied the rope of the youngest maid. And back of this triumphant procession for the faith stood groups of the dark-skinned natives, staring at the pious work of civilization in their land.

The prison was full, due, said the grumblers, to the inactivity of Fray Payo to order executions. But Fray Payo was again ill in health and could not have the care of even so important a matter, so it was left for the *audiencia* to assist the Brotherhood as well as may be, and in the end the Lispano family were prisoned in a warehouse double guarded for lack of dungeon room.

I tell of this unfortunate family whose names I had not even known, because out of their trial, and their end, came illuminating things to me. They were judged and condemned, as all knew, before any open audience was given to the evidence. But in the end a public sentence was the usual form, whereby all might be warned against apostasy. I do not recall that a word was uttered by the prisoners, though the recorder read aloud their words and admissions under the torture. There was no recanting except by the nephew, so all knew he would be conducted as a trophy of glory in the next procession. The others were sullen and dumb as they heard the sentence that they be burnt together, and their lands and mines revert to the crown, except for the gift to the *mestizo* of a certain competence in proof that the Brotherhood ever favored its faithful sons.

Yet all this was a thing of custom; and I listened beside Don Fernando and felt the tremble of his slender hand on my arm. Always he was white, yet at their sentence his face grew whiter, or his eyes burned more darkly, for I could but note it, and ask if he were ill in health.

I had no answer, for he was staring at the recorder, who, with the help of another monk, was fishing from a rawhide bag the pestilent books found hidden in the maize bins. The Prosecutor for the Faith assured all who listened that in the pages of those volumes, without covers, was contained iniquity enough to either raise devils from hell, or sink all the land under their feet to the regions of the fiends themselves! He admonished one and all to attend a special mass for the reason that their eyes had even rested on the forbidden and outlawed volumes. Among them were translations from the disgraced Luther, books in Hebrew, and more than half of a Bible — all contentious and pernicious, and prone to establish insurrection and heresy wherever introduced.

Many at the trial got away quickly, or turned their glances otherwise than on that stack of condemned iniquity. But my own feet seemed stuck fast to the tiles of the floor, my eyes bulging at the stack of books in front of the stubborn, silent, prisoners. Not one of the books had a cover, and, as in a dream, I thought I saw again the open chest in the storeroom of the De Ordoños, and beautiful covers of books flung, one after the other, into its shadows and the lid clamped shut.

But it was not the lid which fell; it was I, and after my head struck the hard tile, I knew nothing until I found myself in a bed in the palace, with Don Fernando beside me, and heard voices saying that even a sight of those volumes of craft cast a spell over me — and some woman also had fainted on hearing they could raise the devil!

I was yet dazed and shaking, and Don Fernando sent the others, Marco and Gilberto among them, reluctant, from the room.

And when I did speak it was whisperingly, and with a dazed mind, for I asked if Tristan were safe.

Don Fernando bent his head, and there were tears in his eyes.

"Safe," he said, "thank God, he is safe somewhere in the wilderness among savages and wild beasts."

Then he sat beside me in silence, until I, feeling better, would have risen, but he took my hand. "It is growing dark," he said, "lie you still and think — and some day tell Tristan. He is eager for books because it is in his blood. He is the son of scholars, yet today you and I have seen souls under a curse because of that hunger. Tell him of that — all of it! In Catholic lands today scholarship must rest. Under the robe alone will he dare study religions, and then only in the books of faith of the one religion. I say this because even the study of the pagan gods may bear ill fruit, and with Fray Payo gone from Mexico, and with me gone, it might at some time of life go hard with him. Even the gods of the sun and those of the stars are held in disrepute by the Brotherhood. Thus you must tell him, for no new archbishop will protect him in his searchings, or ask translations for scholars of the future."

"But you, Don Fernando, he would set more store by word from you on such a serious matter."

"I may not give it, boy. Who can tell the things to come? But if aught should chance me, give to him my blessing and tell him of my pride in him. The pride is great, as my faith in him is great; to Don Rodrigo say I leave to him the thing most precious on earth, and that I take the seal from his lips."

Then he gave me a cup of some bitter tea to quaff, and made the sign over me, and went away. I must have gone to sleep at once for I knew no more until the next day's sun was in my eyes, and Gilberto had me by the shoulder shaking me awake, and babbling of a guard killed, and another one wounded — it was Mateo Gomez, the husband of Luiza — and it was the opinion of Gilberto that now, indeed, the town must have some sanctified burnings to make room in the prison, for it was proved to all that the warehouse would never do.

That sleep of mine was so curious that it was hard to shake out of either my head or my legs, and I wrestled

myself stupidly into my garb, grunting my comment
on his discourse, and was put to it to unravel head or
tail of it.

But a sniff of fresh air and a cup of cocoa took the
numbness out of me, and I had sense to sit in silence
while Gilberto talked. There were tales abroad of
enchantings of the devil, for no locks had been broken,
and no eyes had seen the going. Yet the Lispano family
had certainly been borne away — every he and she of
them — by their Master of Evil!

Questioned as to special points, all that was known
was that a pious monk had obtained order from the
Brotherhood to use his utmost strivings to bring the
victims of Satan to open confession as to the accursed
volumes found in the maize bin. Armed with the order
of the Holy Office, the doors had opened to him, but no
one had ever seen him come again from behind the heavy
locked doors of the warehouse. Yet was the warehouse
empty! One guard was found who looked as if the devil
himself had had the strangling of him, for iron fingers
had most certainly sunk into his throat until the life was
gone. Also Mateo Gomez, the husband of Luiza, was
found without senses, and with a cut on his head. This
discovery had been at the change of guard at sunrise,
and the captain of the guard was up for reprimand, and
was a deposed man at the very mildest. Gilberto wondered who would be named as the new captain, and
mentioned the name of Marco, for Marco had helped
bring in the heretics.

And from that, in another minute, Gilberto was back
at his old subject of preferments and intrigues, and
thought it in the power of Don Eduardo Vidal de

Dasmarinas to see that Marco had first chance, and his word would go far.

I heard it all with little thought of Marco or his chances, for my head was in a whirl as to the enchantments sent by the devil to free the old man and his daughters. It had all been done in a haste scarcely human, for there were men of degree — and women too — held safe behind the prison bars for suspected heresy these many years. We saw them in the lurid *sanbenitos* — the very color of flames — each week in the procession of the penitents. Yet this family, convicted of apostasy, heresy, and traffic with the Prince of Darkness, had rested in prison but one setting of the sun after their sentence had been thundered at them by the Prosecutor for the Faith. All the evidence was most certainly in favor of infernal agencies — a fact dwelt upon by the Holy Office as the only method by which their own efforts for the faith could have been made void. For myself, the question I most wanted to ask stuck in my throat, and I made my way to the house of Luiza to ask after Mateo, for whose health I cared little. He was the scheming, truculent member of a household otherwise pleasant. His subservience to me as the relative of the viceroy was embarrassingly pronounced. I had the custom of visiting the good Luiza when the husband was on duty elsewhere.

But that morning I was as one driven there to hear the thing I dared not ask, and I found the two women all but frantic between the crippled man and the curious crowd, from which came every variety of tale as to demoniac assaults and their consequences. Poor Luiza knew not whether to pray for his physical recovery, lest the devil should still withhold his wits, and Anita was weeping in sympathy and lamenting the absence of Don Tristan — for with him at home he would surely find Don Fernando, and that was the only intelligent name Mateo had muttered.

"Was Fray Fernando his confessor?" I asked, with my eyes on the floor and my heart thumping.

"Surely not — it is Fray Felipe, and already he has been here, and was of comfort. But know you not that it was Fray Fernando himself who was spirited away with those heretic Lispanos who chose to follow the dead law of Moses rather than the way of the cross?"

"No one has told me," I said.

"Well, it is so. I shed tears to see those ladies dragged by soldiers through the dust of the streets — in shame before even their own brown slaves. But I might have saved my pity, as Fray Felipe told us both; for the fiend himself was certainly master of the beauty of those Lispano girls, and it has proved itself. How else could all within those walls have been thus suddenly spirited away?"

"Ay," ventured Anita, "even Don Fernando, whom all knew as a holy person, who else than he, so worshiped by the Indios? For his sake they would make themselves as a carpet for his feet."

I looked at the ugly cut on the head of Mateo. He had been struck down, and fallen on a sharp stone. The fall had been heavy, and there was a fracture of the skull, but there were no other marks. Evidently only one stroke had been needed.

"If Don Tristan were only here!" moaned Luiza, over and over. "What can a woman do with a wounded

man on her hands, and a guard outside her door? My
wits are all but gone."

"I am here at your service," I said with kind intent;
"and there is Marco de Ordoño, your nursling as well
as Don Tristan. It is even said that his name is mentioned as captain of the guard. You will have an official
friend in high places."

I spoke lightly to reassure her, but was little prepared
for the frightened look she gave towards pretty Anita,
who was at the moment outside the door, listening to the
condolings of a woman neighbor.

"Send Don Marco not here, lest there be troubles for
a priest to mend!" she mumbled apart to me as she
changed the wet bandages and filled a basin with water
fresh from an olla. "Know you not that Don Tristan
has laid a threat against him?"

This was news to me, as I had learned nothing to
indicate there was ill will between them, and I said so.

"Not on other matters," agreed Luiza, "but the girl
is as a little sister to Don Tristan, and — as you may
know — Don Marco whispers at many windows, and
wins his way through many doors. The saints alone
know how hard it is to guard a girl, but Don Tristan
knows somewhat, and Don Marco had his warning to
walk in other streets. It makes it hard for me, for Mateo
favored him, as it was one ladder to a step up at the
palace."

"What do you mean by all that? What girl?"

She nodded her head towards Anita.

"God alone knows how it will end," she said, "for the
child no longer opens her heart to me. She trusts and
reverences Don Tristan for his brother spirit, but what

she dreams of the other, no soul can tell. I never trust
her out of my sight but for confession or mass, and then
a neighbor walks beside, for how could I live if a boy
and girl love should end in a murder? Don Tristan
made the threat to trail him to hell if he did her wrong,
and the threat of Tristan was a thing to fear."

Here was a new turn in fortune's wheel in the new
land where I had thought life would be free and simple.
I recalled the blush of Anita when I had asked of Marco
that first day. At one time he had housed there; no
doubt he still would have had that pleasure but for the
most unchristian threat of Tristan.

I went back to the palace, and listened to words of
sympathy over my faint of the day before. Two women
had also fallen unconscious through the devilish enchantments abroad, and one of them had become a mother in
the night. So, in one way and another, there were waves
of gossip surging about me, and I could easily sit silent,
and listen to good purpose. Fray Payo was ill from the
excitement, and would see no one, and to Don Martin
de Silva was given the task of dealing with the Holy
Office, and getting to the bottom of the affair.

But all I could learn was that it was Don Fernando
himself who had put in the reasonable request that the
" reconciled " nephew of Lispano be separated from the
convicted apostates before an attempt be made to reach
their sinful souls. And it stood to reason, also, that a
priest who had won savage idolaters from their false
gods would be the one man most like to win these
heretics from their pernicious ways. But for all the
wisdom, and reasonableness of it, the officials had nothing left but a dead man, an empty prison, and no trace

of two maids and four men who had gone under the earth or into the air.

The guards were questioned at every side of the city, but except for an Indian fiesta out by Tlacopan, and some of their brood going and coming, the streets had been still of all traffic; neither man nor woman had been abroad more than was the custom until the hour of early mass at the cathedral. I heard Marco tell Doña Perfecta and her cousin Mercedes all this, as he rode in after making a circle of highways north and south to establish the fact that no such group of refugees could have passed the guards on the way to either coast. And how could they have carried with them a man so noticeable as Don Fernando?

It was the opinion of Marco that Don Fernando had been killed by the heretics, and would be found in due time, under the tiles, or in some other secret place.

Thus was all conjecture seething and bubbling to no purpose, when Don Rodrigo rode into the city. In Spain I had not loved Don Rodrigo beyond reason, but at sight of him in Mexico I could have kissed his dusty boots. Don Payo was by far too eminent for a confidant, but Don Rodrigo was nearer the earth — and, it was reasonable to suppose, would know the other half of most I had to tell him.

As soon as might be, I followed him from the house of Luiza to his lodgings near the monastery, and gave myself credit for even that patience. I had stood by, silent as a fish, while he had been overwhelmed by all the news, and all the surmises of the many others, but when I tagged at his heels, he bade me come along as a good-natured man may throw a kind word to a stray puppy.

Not that a companion as mute as I was a thing to wish for, but after all, I had messages from home, and must be accepted as the bearer.

Had I been less near to bursting, I might have had a certain pride in changing his mind, or in the mere astonishing of him, but I was far beyond all that in my suppressed terror.

I gave him the folded and sealed packet from the abbess, which he accepted with the sigh of a martyr. Well he knew it would involve a letter of duty — the aftermath of his long-ago matchmaking. His manner plainly betrayed that the reading of that might wait until supper had been eaten.

So long as others were in hearing I told him the latest news of his friends and family and the captain I sailed with, and all such topics of common question.

Then, while I poured for him a cup of Greek wine sent by Padre Juan, I gave him the message of Don Fernando.

He let fall the cup, and the wine soaked into his sleeve and dripped to the floor while he stared at me. I poured him another cup, for he looked as if he needed it.

" Say that again," he whispered, yet put out his hand to stop me when I would have spoken aloud.

" Lower," he said, and I repeated:

" ' To Don Rodrigo I leave the thing most precious on earth, and I take the seal from his lips.' "

" God! " he said, and quaffed the wine, and sat staring at nothing for what seemed a long time. I knew he was thinking of the trial and the mystery.

" Holy God! " he whispered again, " then he knew it was the end of him! "

I had thought as much myself, yet it spelled out none of the riddle of his disappearance.

"Indians," he said in the same tone, "Indians! For him or for Tristan they will do the impossible things. Yet what could the Lispanos mean to him? Fernando was not heretic."

"But he had love of study. He — he gave me a warning against seeking knowledge except in churchly books," I ventured. "The holy prior said there was enough of evil in the Lispano books to enchant an army. It may have been that they began in all innocence — with the books — and then the evil grew in them. I only know he left a warning with me, and — went away."

I did not tell him the warning was not for me, for I could see that of the books he knew nothing. Books might be housed under his very nose for a lifetime, yet he would not have thought to turn a leaf.

"Indians!" he said again, "and it will go hard in the mines without him. The Indians rebel at another confessor — there his strength lay."

"And what of Tristan's strength?"

"The less said of that the better. The lad gets under their skin as though he had suckled the same breast. A new day will come to us all when Fray Payo goes — and the less said of Tristan and his Indian strength the better. It came some way by the help of Fernando, but the pupil out-distanced the master. And if you are a friend, you will caution him that pagan records had best be forgotten: no new viceroy or archbishop will serve as patron in that — and there is the Holy Office with its thousand eyes!"

CHAPTER VI

TRISTAN THE RANGER

THE letter from Spain was forgotten by Don Rodrigo in the excitement of the Lispano matter, and the mystery of Don Fernando. He was careful not to betray all he felt concerning the latter, not sure of the wisdom of open avowal. The clergy grew cautious about expressing themselves, and were alert for every word of interest that was dropped by anyone. The common people might have their own fancies regarding diabolical agencies in the matter, but the Holy Office had ears open for temporal evidence. I myself was never so devoted to the interests of Don Payo. I scarce moved away from the antechamber of his excellency, and came near to losing the use of my tongue, lest I should say the wrong thing.

Then, one day of beauty, when the winter rain made the world sparkle anew, Tristan Rueda rode from the north; and when he was hailed, I stared and choked, and tried in vain to say the civil thing, but could not, for my own amazement at the new Tristan, who now had the look of a sad and bitter man stamped on the features of youth.

I was not alone in the wonder. There were many questions asked of his health, and I heard comments of various sorts. He had ridden away ruddy and careless,

62

and came back pale and hard, as from a campaign where he had fared ill.

Yet he took both my hands in the old friendly way, and looked in my eyes, and when he went in to Fray Payo, I was the only one who went with him. To the message of Don Fernando he had listened with sudden tears, and he did not let go my hand. My venerable relative smiled on us both, and the others in the room were sent away.

Then Tristan took from under his cloak a girdle of cord and a rosary of brown wood and turquoise and shell beads with a silver crucifix, and laid them on the knee of Don Payo.

Don Payo knew that crucifix, and his hands trembled pitifully as he touched it.

" Where? " he said, and that was all.

" In the waters north of the Panuco."

" Dead? "

" Dead many days, and alone. There was a boat and a storm. If others were there they escaped north or went to the bottom, but the Indios found no boat."

Fray Payo asked for a map, and traced with his finger the long line of coast past Florida to the Virginias. Then he traced the great river from the north, and sat in thought.

" That way the countries of the French could be reached," he said, "but the wide lands of the pagans would have to be crossed — and with women! It took Alvarado and his men ninety days to reach Panuco, and they had no women. It is seven years since the French Jesuit and the merchant came down the mighty river whose source is said to be somewhere in Kathay. It

may be that people of a colony have followed their trail
by ship or land, and that beyond the Texas, these refugees will be hidden and guarded. But the way is
through such a wilderness as to appall the bravest. Such,
Tristan, is the only refuge for the benighted souls fleeing
from the true God."

Tristan was white and silent while that wonderful
old mind thought out the chances against escape of the
scholarly, refined Lispanos, who had been accustomed
only to the luxuries of life.

"Leave these with me," he said at last, "and to both
you lads—silence! Careful thought must be given ere
a brother monk is held forth to blame or shame, and
such a brother! Every turquoise bead and every silver
one here is some pledge of prayer from some brown
convert. This is a matter as of our own family."

Then Tristan went out, and I beside him. He had to
listen to all the rumors and conjectures I had learned
by heart, and I wondered that he kept his face steady,
knowing what he knew.

"These are the ends to which a fool's hunger for
knowledge may bring his friends if they try to help
him!" he said to me. "Be you content, Juanito, with
the little learning of a harmless man."

And beyond this he uttered no word, either then or
later, of the books, or of the people who had hidden
them; but I saw him often poring over the maps of
that north shore, and knew that he thought much of the
trails to be taken for safety, for away beyond there to
the east was the country of the French, and the heretical
Lutherans, and in no other place in the lands of the
New World was there refuge from the Holy Office —

unless, indeed, a sinner might risk himself with the brown pagans, and few souls could brave that choice.

Yet, in after days, I took note that from every trader or traveler Tristan added to his knowledge of these foreign coasts and the tribes or rulers, and though he said little, his ears were ever open to the older men concerning the missions of the north. These men held much converse over the strange loss of Fray Fernando, whose zeal among the heathen had been great.

Mateo, when he got his wits and his tongue, could tell nothing of that strange going. Don Fernando had gone in to the heretics, and the door had closed. In peace he had done guard service and seen no one; then a blow had made him senseless. He could tell nothing.

But the Lispanos were all burnt in effigy at the next *auto-da-fé* and their names execrated as enchanters and evil heretics.

For myself, I had the feeling that one of the huge volcanos might be fuming and groaning under the very city, so fearful was I that some sort of explosion was due from all the thoughts suppressed. But as the days went by, and nothing further happened, I began to breathe freely, and be a boy again, instead of a scared child.

Don Rodrigo had a touch of the fever, and was bled until some of the color left his ruddy face, and there were days when I was more his page than Don Payo's, for always there was some seasonable thing sent from the kitchen of the viceroy to the old soldier in the inn by the monastery. From there was but the flight of a chicken to the house of Luiza, and thus I saw most of our friends daily.

Tristan had quietly fitted himself into the niche of the cloister life because of some saintly figures with which he was helping Fray Bernardino for the chapel there. Why he did not go — as he so easily could — on some of the adventurous expeditions north or west, would have been a puzzle to me, had it not been for the memories of the Lispano family and the books. He plainly meant to stay in the center of things; yet by taking up the painting he was leaving himself free from all offices by which his feet might be chained, did he again feel the hunger of far quests, and to all Marco's urging he would take but little share in the affairs of state at the palace. Only when Fray Payo sent a call, did he go and go willingly, and his service was great in many matters dealing with the tribes.

To me it was as if he had put aside that search for adventure and strange lore, and was striving to take up, in body and spirit, all the work for the brown pagans which Don Fernando had laid down.

To Don Rodrigo he was doubly devoted in the illness caught in the night mists, or from the evil waters of a bad camp, and Don Rodrigo had much of sympathy for himself over many things those days, when he sat, shaded from the sun, by the great rose tree at the edge of the monastery wall. A ship was to sail for Spain, and by trick or craft a letter must go in exchange for those I had borne to him under seal. Of the contents he had never spoken in my hearing, so I had only my guess as to the messages of Sancha. All I did know was that he had urged Marco to sail for Spain in the train of Don Payo, and had been given good excuses instead of consent.

So I found him one day, grumbling and blinking sleepily across the plaza, where the Indian carriers, with bent backs, passed in line under the pepper trees. They bore loads so great that all but their feet were hidden as they walked patiently on in the sunshine. I have not to this day ceased to wonder at the grave repose of those people who pass on fatefully with our burdens, while we lounge, fretful, in the shadow of walls built from stones of their temples. Whence the endurance?

But Don Rodrigo, fingering the letters from Spain, frowned and looked at them, yet saw only his own troubles.

" They have no cares but for a bowl of meal or a cup of their native brandy," he insisted. " And I — look at the loads I carry! To avoid marriage until my age, yet have the matches to make or hold steady, for every young gallant of the family! What use to pray to the saints if they never keep a man out of trouble? "

" Yet without doubt you will go on paying for good candles the rest of your life," I said, eager to hear his discourse of the letters.

He stared at me.

" A man must be a Christian soul in spite of the devil," he affirmed solemnly, as if recollecting the duty of instructing youth, " and the light of altar candles does give a glow of righteous satisfaction over all." Then, after another stare, " Did you know the jade had learned to write? "

He regarded me as if he thought I was somehow to blame for this objectionable acquirement, but I could only confess I had heard somewhat of her mind on the matter, though I had seen no written evidence.

" Well, it is here," he acknowledged morosely, " a dic-
tated letter to me by the hand of Padre Juan, and a
threat of worse to follow! A prayerful letter from the
abbess, because with neither guardian nor husband to
control her, the little Arab is like to do some wild thing.
Then to Marco a writing of her own — and nothing less
than a return by his own hand will content her! "

I had a glimmer of light on a puzzling matter.

" Is it for that reason the hand of Marco has still the
wrappings of a lameness? " I asked. " I was so silly as
to think it more excuse for the sympathy of ladies; they
ever love a man to need their ministrations."

" The cowl of a monk to you, you learn fast! " he
growled. " Yet under a cowl there is peace, and I half
regret I turned from it at your age. Fine work for me
to have this marriage business on my hands with the
two of them half a world apart. If Fernando — rest his
soul — had lived —"

The whistle of an old Moorish air came along the
corridor. Don Rodrigo listened and then nodded his
head as one who had found a solution of his problem.

" Tristan always knows," he observed; " every man-
jack down-at-the-heels scholar in the city is more or
less in his knowledge. He will find me someone to do
the letters instead of a priest, and as no letter by Marco's
own hand has ever gone to her, how is she, with all her
temper, to know the difference? It will be a discipline
she sorely needs, and it is a kindness, too — for Marco
writes a vile, unreadable scrawl. We will get her an
escribiente of elegance."

Tristan swung along the corridor, humming the air
he had ceased to whistle. His step, in the soft leather

boots, had the virile spring of life in it, eager, yet not impetuous. He looked a strong animal held in check, almost an idler for want of a task he fitted — and dangerous fuel for the fates. I did not reason it out thus, I was too much of a boy, but I was set athrill by the force within him.

He was momentarily elated over some completed work in the chapel. Fray Payo had sent some painters of note to view it, and their praise was high. Fray Bernardino gave him credit, and they had protested against a youth of such talent wasting time on Indian chronicles.

"That marches with my own thought," decided Don Rodrigo; "why rope an Indian in the lake and drag him to shore for baptizing? If they have souls, they have also a saint to drive them in for confession when the time comes."

"Many would wait long for that."

"And better so than that good men should be wasted on them. Think of the army of priests now in the north."

"Mines of turquoise are there, and it is said gold," commented Tristan; "that should be good cause to you, if not the souls."

"Yet the true mines of Mexican gold have never yet been found, with all the aid of converts," grumbled the old man. "A little here and a little there — yes, and much of silver — but the real mines, the great treasure houses, where are they? With all your journeyings have you traced them, or with all your converts?"

"The gold is sacred to the sun god, and to their houses of dawn," said Tristan. "I have never sought by words to find trails to their sacred things. If they want you to know they will tell you with an open heart. If they are made to answer, they will only lie."

" All hopeless sinners given over to the devil! But it was not of their red souls I would talk. It was to ask how far you would go to favor a friend."

" If you are the friend, Don Rodrigo, you know these many years I am bound to your house."

" Hark now! That is it, lad; it is for the house of De Ordoño itself I need loyalty, else how is the house to continue if there are not marriages? and how are marriages to be if there is not love-making of some sort or pretense? "

Tristan smiled, and it was the first smile of his I had seen in Mexico.

" If it is love-making, why not do it yourself? " he asked. " You are substantial, and comely to the eye, even after all your bloodletting."

" But this is a serious matter! " protested the old man. " The ship sails in less than a week, and Marco is useless, and — "

" Tell me," said Tristan.

" It is this. Don Fernando — God rest his soul — has written all the letters for us since we came from Spain. He is gone, yet the letters must be written, more than ever they must be written, for the girl has the devil in her, and demands things. You remember the child, Sancha? "

" I remember."

" Good! Gifts have gone to her from Marco all these years — I myself sent them. Letters have gone for her to Padre Juan or to the abbess — I had them written."

" All this I know," said Tristan, " for all of the letters

from there were among papers of Don Fernando, and Fray Payo gave me the task of sorting them."

" Praise to the saints if you have not destroyed them! This is a day of good fortune. You are yourself so good a scribe and scholar that you will know every worthy scribe in the city who hires his pen and his time."

" That is true, señor. Many of them, failing to find the El Dorado of dreams, are glad to keep accounts, or act as scribe, or turn monk at the last!"

" Softly and with care! Your careless speech may earn for you a trial of the faith some dark day if you guard it not. Monks are vowed to God's service."

" And a fat living here," grinned Tristan.

" Had you and Fray Fernando so fat a living when you were on that desert trail to the north?"

" Let me not remember that time of the lost way in a land of plenty. We dug roots and ate snakes. But Don Fernando was never a monastery man. To me he was ever the soldier who had somehow broken into a cloister."

" That is true, that is how it was," said Don Rodrigo, and sat in silence a space; I started as if to leave them, for it was always a pain for me to hear of Don Fernando in the presence of Tristan. He was guarded even while he seemed careless, and our eyes ever avoided each other.

Don Rodrigo put out his hand to detain me.

" Stay you here, Juanito, unless you are needed elsewhere. You may serve as help, you saw the little spitfire later than I."

" Your pardon, señor, but she is no longer so small," I said.

"Her height has kept pace with her temper, then?"

"About that, señor," I conceded.

"You see, Tristan, that is what I have to deal with —
a temper of pepper, and the height of a woman! I have
asked little help of any but Don Fernando, and he — "

"Señor, many of the tasks he did have been given to
me by Fray Payo. That I work here at the painting for
pure love of it, does not mean that I take no other
duties."

"I could wish Marco as willing. He ever has some
errand of state if I need to talk sense to him — and that
ship must carry a letter to Spain. When I did remind
him of it, he gave me leave to write it; schoolmaids, he
said, were not to his fancy. She could wait there safe
in the convent until he went back; so stands it with
Marco. But Marco should recall that the girl is a little
Arab of temper; truly there was the blood of Moresco in
that family. This letter is not at all 'an you will, your
excellency;' it is a shoulder stroke, direct! 'An you do
not, there are other men, also there are cloisters!' She
is wearied of letters from priest to abbess, and with her
own hand has she learned to write — that she may say
this."

"Life of my soul! this grows amusing. And does
your rebel lady demand of you a letter of love from
Marco?"

"Ay, she does — and if it does not in the first ship,
there are others — comely gallants nearer home — and
there are cloisters."

"That ever Marco should drive a maid to a cloister
for lack of love-making!" said Tristan. "If she were
this side the water he would not let her go begging. I

had a bad hour with him ere he ceased tossing roses or sweetmeats over the wall to the child, Anita. He took it ill at that time, but seems again a friend. And now, señor, to serve you, how can I? "

" Read the letters, and have reply made that is courtly, and what it should be. Save the child's name if you can. And have replies sent to Marco in your care. Thus the maid will be content in the thought that he writes them, and no harm will be done. If you will do this and get the letters to ship, it will be all heavenly harmony instead of cat scratches. It will not be for long; our intent is to go back another springtime."

" Marco knows? "

" Marco knows, and laughs, and says I started it and must finish it. I, who have worked with heart and care to join a marquesa of Llorente y Rivera and De Ordoño! He is an ungrateful donkey, and knows not his own good fortune. Also, he says she should have faith as has he, and no letters would be needed. For myself, I do deplore even the thought of letters, and it goes hard to chide the lad for the same natural feeling. We De Ordoños have never been much with a quill."

" Faith, as he has! " repeated Tristan. " The maid locked tight in a convent, and he ranging the world for pleasure! Which recalls to me a small matter: Is it not by the friendship of Señor Don de Dasmariñas that Marco has lately been shown some special preferences? "

" It may be so; he has said nothing."

" Then you say something, Don Rodrigo, and save troubles to come. Tell him to range elsewhere for sweethearts than so close to forbidden ground. I interfered in one direction, and he would think me turned spy if I should speak of another. At the very mildest, he would take it ill."

"That is true. What is wrong? Are you rivals?"

"Not at all, my heart is at the feet of Mercedes, the cousin of Doña Perfecta. She is safely betrothed to my friend Ernesto Galvez and is not for me; but she is wise — that girl — and sees things. Doña Perfecta will also be wise to hasten the wedding, lest Mercedes see too much. That beauteous Perfecta is a woman ambitious for special place at the palace, and uses all tools to her hand. Also she is a pretty cat, no, rather is she a tigress, and likes pretty boys instead of kittens to play with!"

"Marco would say then that you were safe," said Don Rodrigo, rolling a cigarro, and watching the face of Tristan to see if he flushed, or paled, or lied.

But Tristan only smiled.

"It is true," he said, "my beauty will not make troubles for me. If I told Marco all I could tell, we would end by fighting, and that would win pleasure for none of us. Where is the letter?"

"It is here — all three of them — from the abbess, the priest, and the girl, and the last deserves better treatment than it is getting."

"Also, here is Marco de Ordoño," I warned them as I sighted him across the little plaza. "It will be a joke on Marco that you help save a wife for him from the cloister."

"If there is a joke, it will be on me, that I plan letters of love for a girl over seas when I am thinking only of Mercedes Herrara here in Mexico!"

Later I knew how bravely he lied about that little

matter, though at the time I had a boy's sorrow for him. I knew how it was to adore a divinity at a distance.

Marco shrugged and smiled when he saw the creased and crumpled letters. Don Rodrigo had evidently taken his worries to bed.

"So you have Tristan in it now," he jeered; "but I have a better task for him. Whether with good or ill will, your presence is entreated soon as may be at the house of Señor Don de Dasmarinas. The fame of your churchly paintings is abroad; you are asked again to paint the portrait of the loveliest lady of the land."

Tristan looked at him and smiled.

"One woman at a time," he said; "and if her time ever comes, it must come second."

"Let him alone, Marco," said Don Rodrigo. "He will be our salvation if you give him a free hand. A letter must go on that ship if you want ever to join the De Ordoño with the illustrious family of Llorente y Rivera."

"Does she fancy we carry secretaries to the mines?" growled Marco.

"What she fancies is not spelled out here, though the letter of Padre Juan makes much plain. Here she says, ' It is five years, and I have grown tall. I pray you convey to Don Marco that the Indian dolls he sends have made much merriment for the nuns here at Santa Maria, also that I lately hung each one of them by the neck to a pomegranate tree, and if Padre Juan has a mind to tell you what I said of them he is free to write it in this letter, for I am making *sanbenitos* for each one, and the little pagans will all go into the fire on some fine day!' "

"The little Arab devil!" said Marco. "She was ten when we came from Spain, was she not?"

"Twelve," said Don Rodrigo, "and should she ever hear you call her 'Arab' there would be troubles enough. That Moresco blood was proud as any in Castile; it was used to ruling in other days. And this word of hers is more than the whim of a child. Look to it, Marco, that you lose not a pearl you would gladly wear!"

"In a year we will go back, weighted with treasure — is that not good reason enough for delay? How can a man make love to a girl in far Spain when there are as pretty, here to one's hand?"

"There needs no love-making; the child has never had it, and cannot miss it. But letters of your own writing she does demand."

"I will marry, as I will die, when my time comes," said Marco sulkily, "but to wear out my brain with letters to a little vixen like that — I can't and won't! Also my hand is lame, even if I would — also you can get another priest to write, for after all she has never seen writing of mine. Who is to tell her the difference?"

He looked at me as though I might not be trusted, but Don Rodrigo spoke for me.

"We can trust Juanito. He is too fond of Sancha not to want her happy and safe wedded."

"If it makes her happy," I said, and had doubts.

"How else will it be if only she is quiet and tame for a little longer?"

"A clerkly wife is the last thing I should have asked the saints for," growled Marco, looking at the letters, and throwing them back on the table. "Why could she not be content with trinkets, as would any other maid?"

"Because there is not like her any other maid anywhere in all the rest of the world!" I declared. "She has a brain to think with, and your trinkets have been a jest to her since ever you came away; also your ladies of Mexico are tinsel beside her gold, and no maid of the house of Llorente y Rivera need go pleading for a husband, Señor de Ordoño. She is loyal, but she has no love for you, she only thinks she loves the memory of you."

How I said it — to thrust my tongue into their man's discourse — I could not tell. Never before had I presumed before my elders, but my blood was hot with anger at his easy confidence.

Tristan put his hand on my own as if he feared my effrontery might make trouble, but Marco was so amazed he had no time to be angry. And Don Rodrigo watched me with a curious look.

" It is the same blood, Marco, safe and loyal, yet prone to wild doings in the older days. You had best take that little warning, for wild blood may lead your maid to strange decisions — there is always a cloister — and she mentions that there are also men in Spain! "

" I have thought over the accursed matter until I am past thinking," said Marco, suddenly truculent. "But you and Tristan are not the ones to desert a comrade in trouble. I would as soon hope to preach a sermon as write a letter, while this *escribiente* can write easily as he can eat. Come, Tristan, refresh yourself with a cup to give you heart, and help a comrade. Get a letter written for me before the ship sails."

" I'll write for myself," threatened Tristan, " and steal your maid and her fortune, and the latter, as I see it, would be your greater loss! "

"Lads, lads, this thing is no jest, but a serious matter. The fractious jade says plainly there are gallants in Seville who are not too busy to woo, also that she has misgivings that the convent life may be her true vocation. If no letter goes to her by next ship, I wash my hands of you both, dolts that you are."

There was laughter among us at Don Rodrigo fuming over a letter of love, and Tristan, noting that his heart was in it, spoke up.

"The letter shall go, señor, if it will give you content. Marco must write it, else you and I will do it, and shame him!"

"Done!" said Don Rodrigo, eager as a boy. "We will toss dice to decide which does the task, though if chance be that Marco writes the letter he will drive the maid to a nunnery rather than wed anyone of his name or family. Even the reckonings at the mine he could not keep in a way to be deciphered."

So, with a new jug of wine to give them courage, the dice were thrown, first by Don Rodrigo, who threw seven, then by Marco, who sang in glee and did a caper when he threw but six. And Tristan sat silent when the fates, or the saints, sent double six to his hand that he write letters to the wilful maid across the sea.

There was much rejoicing on the part of Don Rodrigo over this, for he, in all honesty, feared that a letter from Marco would hurt his suit more than help it, and Tristan, once his word was pledged, would carry it through bravely.

Thus it began — the jest in the shade of the monastery wall in Mexico. For myself, I think the guardian angels of all three were taking a siesta that day.

Once it was settled, Marco was gay as a lark, willing to discuss the letter and advise regarding it, but Tristan had the better of him there.

"You will play your hand, or you will keep out of the game," he directed. "Also the letters must come to my hand."

"That is as it should be," and Don Rodrigo passed over the letters. "This donkey — this burro — has sent her only strings of beads until she is all but lost to us. Now, the saints willing, all will go merrily and smooth till we sail home for the wedding, with treasure chests well filled."

"And you, Tristan, shall be my second, and salute the bride," offered Marco in high good spirits.

"Take him away ere I do him harm," said Tristan to Don Rodrigo, "and if he has not made his daily call on the family of De Dasmarinas, this is the hour."

"Family? but there is no family but Doña Perfecta, and — "

"She is quite enough in herself," commented Tristan unfolding the letters, and not even looking up to see the red flush in the face of Marco. "Get you gone and find a messenger to bear the letter to the ship captain. If I am to attend to your affairs of love, give me, at least, privacy."

So they left him, Marco going without further words for a messenger, and Don Rodrigo hobbling in to his couch. When I returned from waiting upon him, Tristan still sat by the table with the unfolded letter in his hand.

"Strange it is that the pearls of life sink often to low usage," he said, when I sat myself quiet beside him;

"and strange that his heart is not touched by that which is good in this."

"Is it truly done by herself?" I asked, for while she had boasted of her new accomplishment, I had seen none of it.

"It truly is — and it is a shame to deceive so fair a soul even though I made promise. His name, at least, I will not sign. I will find some lie to cover that. Who could trick a child heart such as shows itself here? God! how strangely the pearls are portioned!"

This was a new turn, after the jests, and the wine, and the dice, and I knew not whether to take myself away, or how to speak.

"You were right, Juanito," he said at last, "the child but tries to be loyal to a dream of childhood. Hear to this."

Then he read me the letter Marco had laughed at.

To Don Marcos de Ordoño of Mexico,
                    Excellency:
This will be the first of letters writ by my hand. You did not know I write. I have learned for the reason I am weary of priest letters. If you are to be my husband, it is right you should have my first letter. I look at the stars and wonder if the same ones shine where you are now, and I have sent messages some days with the white butterflies, and wished the messages had wings, that they go to you. My own saint is the beautiful one of the white bees who is called the Saint of the Impossible; not yet is she made a saint by the church, but in our hearts she is one. I am not a saint or I could go through the sea to where you are, as did she through walls of stone for holiness. But the mother abbess says a maid must abide at home and wait and make prayers, thinking not of sea journeys. Yet when the stars go over to you in the west I do think of it; and also I make prayers for you in your far travels.

It is not gay to have a life always in a convent, though that thought may not have come to you. This I have told Padre Juan to write for me; but no more priest letters will I send — nor will I read. The letters are most fine, but the only letters I want are from him I am to marry. I cannot marry the priest, also he would not want me. Padre Juan tells me I am rebellious, but I think it is not that. I but ask to know the true thought of the man I may wed.

Therefore my own hand writes, and I am,

Your friend in graciousness,

Encarnacian Maria Emanuella de Llorente y Rivera.

"Proud little lady — lonely, though exalted!" said Tristan. "Think you she would pen this if she knew the course he runs in Mexico?"

"You will not tell her?" I asked, recalling how Don Rodrigo had said that ranging youths often made the best of husbands after the settling down had come.

"No, that I could not do, but the child shall no longer be lonely. It is as a work sent because my own thoughts are not good company. In this I may forget, for a little while."

I did not ask what his own sorrows were; I had grown fearful of knowing too much.

"You will keep this secret?" he asked.

"Yes, if it is the only way for her happiness," I said; for, of course, I believed that when she saw Marco she would be in love as most maids were, and the letters would be forgotten — no matter who did the writing of them.

"You promise?" he insisted. "For I know she is dear to you as a sister."

"That is true. But I give my word. When you, yourself, tell her, I may; but not before."

"When I tell her — ha!" and he had a bitter smile.
"It is so likely that I, of the name of sorrow, should tell
a Marquesa de Llorente y Rivera that I had dared to
write to her letters from a lover! Yet that is my task —
take yourself away while I prepare my soul."

I did so, looking back at him as he sat, chin on hand,
with the jug, and the wine cups, and the open letters on
the table.

It did not seem to me so fitting an altar for the preparation of a soul, and I had my own doubt of a letter to
our Sancha if sent from such a place, yet the very place
may have brought its own help, for the letter was sent,
and in after days my own eyes saw it, and this is it:

To the Lady of the White Butterflies:
It did not come to my mind that you, exalted on the convent
hill, could wish for letters from one far below. But when I
have the word of your hand, my thoughts go over seas to you
more swift than any letter made by man.

I do see the white butterflies here, great ones with wide wings
and velvet soft bodies, but it was the reading of your letter by
which I was able to know the message they strive to give me.
They will never be far from me now, and if I were a knight of
old bearing shield, the butterfly of white should be marked
on it. If I were indeed the knight of an older day I might plead
also for a worn glove. Know you a fair and gracious maid of
the convent hill who would be kind in that?

The land here seems in some things like a country of enchantment — it is so very, very old, and had been sleeping so many
ages when the conquerors came in with rude awakenings. This
is not what is often told, but it is truth, and much evidence of
the truth was swept away or burned by Cortez, and by others
after Cortez.

If you were here you would learn new things of the stars, for
they come close to earth in this high air. Also the pagans had
their own love and worship of them. They call the moon

"mother," and greet her with gifts of grain meal and flowers of the night, tossed upwards. Their sanctuaries were many on the high places, and their shrines in the "houses of the dawn" were dear as are your altars in old Spain. The white butterfly is to them the symbol of the spirit of life, and their other symbols are many.

Do you ever look at the still star of the north, around which others circle? That star is as a god to them for the reason that it is enthroned steadily. Do you ever see that Cassiopeia has the wings of a great eagle, and the curve of the Dipper is like a serpent half twisted in coil? Ever these two change places in the sky. When the eagle is high in the sky the serpent is under the throne of Polaris, and again the eagle circles low, and the serpent curves above. Thus in their pictures these pagans show this endless battle of sky things and earth things, good and evil, light and darkness, and the enthroned star, Polaris, holds the balance. Their standards bore the symbols of this meaning. In desert nights these thoughts, held sacred by them, are told at times, little by little, to a friend, and they make one see how God prepared man by all these wonders for the revelation of the greater Wonder!

I write of the stars because you ask of them, and I see your own constellation in the sky as I write. I saw you once on the convent hill above the olive trees, standing clear against the sky, with the white doves about you. You were Virgo to me, white and serene, I have looked at Virgo many times since then from the wild corners of Mexico, and my thoughts have gone to you — little maid on the hill!

Be lonely no more, but look at the stars at night. Under the feet of Virgo stretches the great Hydra, with the Solitary One, Alphard, beating there its steady warmth as the heart of it. I am thus at your feet, White Virgo! At your feet I will be all the days I have to live, and here I write, that you may know it, the name of

Alphard.

CHAPTER VII

THE AMUSEMENTS OF DONA PERFECTA

AFTER the ship sailed away with that letter, decided by the dice, Tristan kept me closer to him than before, and the barrier was down regarding Sancha. Never before had he spoken of her, but it was, I think, as he said — to talk of places or people over seas took his thoughts from matters troubling him, and they were many.

The plans of Fray Payo were made, and we were both given choice of service in his train. But I looked at Tristan, and his decision was to stay. Don Rodrigo, despite his good days, was not well enough for a journey, and fretted his soul over the mining matters until twice Tristan rode across the wilderness to set things right for him, and I — an adventurer of the wilds at last — rode with him.

But I cared not much for the living at the camps where meat was scarce, and little else plenty but the rich silver in the ore. My own money had gone into shares there, and slaves to work with, but the camp life was tame, and I was glad to ride back.

With the ship of Fray Payo went another letter to Sancha, and then Tristan settled down to make a finish of the painting, and complete some tasks of records left by the departing viceroy.

There was great change of ceremony and state when the new viceroy went in, but it did not lessen the importance of the De Dasmarinas. The office of secretary bestowed upon her husband by the new viceroy, Don Tomas, Conde de Paredes, gave Doña Perfecta opportunities to show favor to whom she chose, and this time it was not Marco who was sent with the message; she came herself to visit the chapel, and Tristan, in a tattered old monk's gown smeared with paint, could do no less than bow when the Fray Bernardino brought her in to see the holy saints all in a row, on either side the altar.

"Is it true, Don Tristan, you have grown so devout that you paint only heavenly things these days?" she asked, and watched him approvingly with those brown slumberous eyes of hers. No one would call Tristan handsome, as was Marco, yet heads did turn to look after him, and his strong dark face made him remembered.

"I dare not say they are of heaven," he answered; "no poor worker of earth may hope for that."

"You might hope for more than you know," she said softly, as Fray Bernardino shuffled away to send someone with wine and sweets to the visitor. "The message that I sent with Don Marco should have told you that."

"Marco is scarce a safe messenger, especially for exalted ladies, Excellencia," and when Tristan said it he looked at her very hard, and with no more of courtesy than he would bestow on a dealer who offered wares he disdained.

"Send that boy away," she said. "How is it you are never alone, whether in the palace, or monk's cell?"

"It is, perhaps, that I have found a comrade."

"Send him away," she said again, and this time she was close beside him, looking up to his face.

"Juanito, the Doña Perfecta would have you see that her carriage is waiting at the portal," said Tristan, and I saw him step back as she caught at his arm.

"You shall not!" she said. "Listen — it is a year since you said ——"

"I was a boy a year ago, señora; also I was proud that you desired the portrait. But in a year one learns ——"

"What did you learn that sent you away — what?"

"Only that my art is not fine enough for your face, Excellencia," he said, and I was so eaten up with curiosity that I peered back and saw the ugly smile on his face.

"It is not that — I know it!" she insisted, and again she caught his arm. "What did that girl tell you — Mercedes? It will be well the day she is safe married, and no time left to play spy!"

"I have no memory of anything told me," he said coldly. "Is his excellency, your husband, Don Eduardo, visiting the monastery today?"

"You know he is not. Listen — things are changed, Tristan. I have power now — and ——"

"So it is said, Excellencia," and his words were like ice, and again the ugly smile was there.

"Who dares say it? I can make them pay if I choose. We have not now a viceroy who is a saint."

"So it is said, Excellencia," and again he smiled.

"Ah! I could — could break my fan in your face!"

"And then, Excellencia?"

"Then weep because I had done it," she whispered,

and again went close to him. "Tristan, why did you steal away to the Indian deserts, and why —— "

"The Indian Desert is a good safe place for weak mortals afraid of temptations, señora."

"Afraid! You?" and she laughed. "You are no more afraid than you are weak. You are only devil-possessed not to grant me that which I desire."

"There are better painters of portraits than I, señora."

"But if I think not? If I have both the viceroy and Don Eduardo eager to please me and give you a good price? Can you not see it is favor from the palace I bring to you? What more can I do?"

"Señora, you do more than I may find thanks for."

"It is not thanks for which I am here — it is that I shall not go out the portal till you promise. The portrait I must have. I will see that the viceroy himself asks for it if I fail."

Tristan looked at her in thought — though many a man would lose every sane thought at sight of her. Perhaps he saw the contest would be endless, and I coulc plainly discern that the favor shown Tristan by her was not a new thing. He could have first place, even while he jeered at Marco for coveting it.

"I will not put his Excellency to the trouble of a request," he said. "If my poor talent is of service, I will, of course, endeavor to make of you a portrait."

"Ah!" and she was a sparkle of gladness in her delight. "And you will come to the palace to paint, and doff that monk's robe, and be human once more?"

"I shall be human enough for the task."

"Task! You speak as if I set you a penance for sins. Yet look you, Tristan, you have promised, and I shall give you else to think of than your pale saints on the wall. You will forget them all."

" All but one — perhaps."

" Which one? " she demanded, and turned to look at those of the chancel.

" The one I have not dared to paint," he said.

" Where is she? "

He smiled, and reached up, catching at a sunbeam making clear its bar of light against a shadow.

" It is that, señora, the unattainable."

" Tah! " and she laughed in derision, " only that! But for these drawings — did you get their faces from sunbeams alone? "

" Not all. I have a little foster sister who is a pretty maid, and she has sat still as a mouse, many times, that I might make drawings of her head or eyes."

" It would please me to see this maid. I bid you bring her to me at the palace."

" The mother must say as to that; and I think she will say no."

" What? Do places go begging in the palace of the viceroy? " she said smilingly. " We will make her future if she is fair. Did I not tell you I would have favors to confer? "

" Favors of the palace are dangerous sometimes to us common people of the cots."

But at that she laughed again, and looked at him.

" *You* of the people of the cots! You look royal enough for a throne, though your name tells me nothing. Tristan, who are you? "

" An adventurer whose name is Tristan — which means sorrow. Find a gayer painter, Doña Perfecta."

" I will have only you. There will be long hours of the work, and you will tell me the things of the far deserts you love more than women."

Then Fray Bernardino came in with the prior and refreshments, and Tristan got away with what civility he could. Doña Perfecta talked with the prior a long time while her horses fretted beyond the portal. If there were any questions she failed to ask concerning Tristan and the family of his foster mother, Luiza Gomez, they were few indeed, and at last she swept away, leaving the impression that she meant to give patronage to all of them, also to send some special gifts to the monastery of San Carlos for the pleasure of her visit. The prior accompanied her to the carriage, well satisfied that he had gained the favor of the new rule in Mexico.

It was not a matter of great surprise to me to learn later that Doña Perfecta had sent for Luiza, who was vastly flattered at preference shown Mateo, who was given place as guard at the palace, while Anita was offered chance to learn embroideries and other fine handicraft, and have training beyond the hope of a pretty *paisana*, which she, in truth, was.

The rage of Mateo and the dismay of Luiza were great when Tristan broke in on the pretty plan with some oaths a Christian could not approve.

" Have I fought and made threats to keep her out of dangerous influences, only to have you toss her into hell to hold patronage for Mateo? " he asked.

" But her excellency, the Doña Perfecta — "

" Ay — yes, I know all of that! " he assented, but he could not say that her excellency had but a whim to learn if Anita were the reason her own enchantments had failed! He knew it, and I knew it, but the good Luiza would have thought me mad had I spoke it. Tristan with his somber eyes and monkish learning was not thought of as a gallant, though it is true that when he rode down the street, heads turned to look at him, and questions were asked by strangers.

Like Doña Perfecta, I had often in my heart the query — " Tristan, who are you? "

Mateo was more than a little surly, and poor Luiza was in despair between the two of them, and out of the despair came an idea.

" Listen, Don Tristan," she begged. " We all know you are right in your thoughts, and always wise, and with gracious care for Anita, but remember your warning against the advances of Don Marco. You told her he had more sweethearts than fingers to his hands and that his thoughts are all for the people exalted and important. Tristan, she is a good child, and she loves you as a sister, but in her heart she does not believe one thing you said, from the smallest to the greatest. The heart of the child is so full of the thought of him that he is to her like an angel of God on the throne. It will always be like that unless we make her see. How can I, when she goes not away from our door but to confession or mass? But at the palace she will see with her own eyes. So I think the saints have sent us this chance to make her sensible, for she is a pious child, but overmuch in love for her own good."

Luiza talked it all over with me many times afterwards, and told how, little by little, Tristan gave way, though he said at the last, " Then you leave me nothing but to keep my word."

"Tristan, your word was to deal him death if he did wrong to her, but that he would not do, and that you could not do."

"Then tell Anita, that I may not be called to," he said. "In all things I am loyal to the De Ordoño except where two maids are in question."

"Two, Don Tristan!"

"Two, and Anita is one of them. Give her warning. She may guard him by guarding herself in the midst of all that tinsel."

So, very quietly, as if there were no gallants ready to war for her, pretty Anita went with Mateo to the palace one morning, and there was passed from guard to lackey until the breakfast room was reached, and Mercedes Herrara looked her over, and took her in charge.

"Though you are too fine of grain to easily find tasks for," she observed, "and I wonder much why the señora has called you here."

But when Tristan came for the first drawing, a light task had been found for her, and she wore a dress of white, and drew the threads for an altar cloth to be embroidered by Doña Perfecta.

"It will be given to the good prior in memory of the visit to the saints," she said, looking at Tristan with a little crooked smile. "Now that I have one of your angels before my eyes in life, I see how good the likeness was made."

"Yes, Anita sits very still, and was good to copy from," said Tristan.

He confessed later that he felt ashamed of his fears over Anita when he found her thus among the women, petted, and talked to, yet not unduly. No men were present, and Doña Mercedes had a kindly notice of the girl.

Doña Perfecta watched carefully the first meeting of Tristan and Anita there, and then turned radiant, and was graciousness itself to everyone, even to me, whom she had sent out of the chancel that she might vent her humor on him!

And having seen that Anita was nothing to Tristan but a kindly charge, it did not enter the thoughts of Doña Perfecta that the quiet maid could ever aspire to the very handsomest gallant in her own following!

The beginning of the picture making, with all the group about her, gave me distrust of Tristan's judgment. Why hold out so stubbornly against the favor other painters envied him? I found myself deciding that he had read monkish books and lived with old thoughts until his views of life were curious.

When I was there Marco never but once entered the room, and then with a brief message from Señor de Dasmarinas. He gave Tristan a playful thrust or two because at last he had been chained and dragged from monastery walls, and then, with a gay salute to Doña Perfecta and a teasing word to Doña Mercedes, he took himself away. If he even glanced at Anita it was as if he had noted a pretty bit of furniture, and the ladies certainly gave no note to her flushed cheek and shy eyes. His familiarity with palace ways and people certainly appeared like a high barrier between them, and though she might admire him more than ever at a distance, she must plainly see that her world of life must ever be far below the ladies who smiled on him there. To me it seemed that the reasoning of Luiza had sense.

After the second day, Doña Perfecta found useful task for her in teaching Indio maids the linen work, and under Doña Mercedes there was a gay group of the young girls in the *ramada* intent on spacing and stitches. I passed them, and spoke. Later I learned that Don Eduardo had made a week's journey to Michoacán, and that Doña Perfecta had sent for Tristan that the painting of the picture might be continued without delay in the sala.

It is not a gracious task to write the record of an exalted lady who makes opportunities for gallants,' and I will only set down here that no one is ever like to know what did chance in the sala that morning. But with the unthinking folly of youth, I did not note the closed door until I had tried to open it, and found the bolt held fast.

With what haste I could, I was making retreat when I heard a chair crash to the floor, and a wicked word or two from Tristan.

He shot back the bolt, and I heard the silks of the lady rustle across the floor.

"Tristan, Tristan!" she said, and he halted in the half-open door lest she echo the call where there was more danger. "Tristan, you will not go like that? And the portrait ——"

He stood very straight and looked at her.

"As I told you, señora, the deserts or the monastery walls are safest! I find I cannot work in this light. I grieve at being a trouble to you, but if Señor de Dasmarinas wishes the portrait, he may be able to arrange to bring you to the monastery — the workroom of Fray Bernardino is a better place."

"I will not go there — I will not! Tristan —— "

"Then I regret I cannot —— "

"You do not mean it — you are mad! I can win you favor, or — I can work you ill."

"Surely, yes," he said, and bowed low. "*Adios,* señora."

"*No!* Tristan, I will go to you, I will do as you say for the portrait. But you are mad, Tristan, quite mad!"

She laughed a little, nervously, as though to pass the scene by as a jest, but he only bowed again, and walked out without seeing me where I stood in the shadow of a pillar. The door of the sala was slammed shut, and I heard the bolt click again.

Tristan lied complacently, and growled that the light came from three sides in the sala, and was a devil of a place to paint anyway; he liked a good tile floor where a bit of trodden charcoal or a drop of paint would make no difference.

And the next day the carriage of the de Dasmarinas was again at the monastery with the lovely Doña Perfecta. And there the painting went on, the Doña Mercedes seated demurely by, with her little embroideries and her velvety black eyes.

Tristan worked, silent and square jawed, while that lovely glowing creature made a blaze of color in an amber silk the color of her eyes. He would stand off and stare at her as if the gracious and exalted lady had been one of the least important of the lay brothers in an old cowl.

Once her husband came to cast an eye on the very safe appearing group, and once the carriage of the viceroy halted there by chance, and the prior was made to feel that Tristan was, indeed, bringing special patronage through the using of Fray Bernardino's workshop. But with it all, Tristan was irritable, and not so good a companion. Always he was courteous to all women; and Doña Mercedes he smiled at as at a comrade, but I could see him hold himself tense if Doña Perfecta came close or touched him. He hated the woman beyond reason, and his very coldness attracted her by its novelty. She sent him letters which he burned, and even to me she made affairs pleasant that he might see all his friends were shown favor. Sometimes she sent a message to him by me, for Marco was getting sulky on her hands, and was not in good humor if Tristan was praised over much.

I tried, as I might — flattered by her sweet voice — to show Tristan what he was throwing away with his sad lack of tact, but he shook me and laughed, and bade me keep clear of her net.

"She is a fair devil, but there is a loathsome feeling here in my heart for her — so what use to reason? Others are glad of her favors, and, as you see, her husband has been made of necessity to the viceroy because of her beauty. If she keeps all those lads dangling — Marco and his sort — His Excellency may well think it is as a careless cloak to cover other sociabilities. But for me she is a sweet poison thing, and if this keeps up —— "

He broke off and laughed, and burned the letter I had taken, and then sought among some old Indian relics until he found an ugly little carving of a woman's figure with the robes and fan of the ruling class.

He looked at it, and laughed again.

"Yesterday she wanted a flower to hold, or some other thing to give her hands occupation," he said, "and it is this I will give her. Thus will I write thoughts into her portrait which every Indio may read as he runs. She hates the Indios — also I think she would need to fear them if chance should take her their way. They often measure rightly the people who would look down on them."

"But the little statue? What is its meaning?"

"She was a queen once here in Mexico, and was a very powerful lady," he said. "Her name would mean nothing to you, but this is the thing for the hands of Doña Perfecta to hold. It will make her own beauty more glowing by contrast."

This he told her when she came, and again when she demurred at the queer little statue and its queer smile.

"But it might be a pagan god, and have evil power!" she protested.

"It is not a god, but a princess so charming that many men died for love of her," said Tristan, carefully mixing his colors, yet watching her with amusement as she held the little gilded figure so curiously made. "There, señora, that is just right for you to hold, and, as I said, the lucky figure shows your white hands more white."

It was the nearest to a compliment she had wrung from him during the painting, and her face flushed with the triumph.

"And men did die for her — truly?" she asked.

"Truly they did. So famous was the love felt for her that images were made also of many of the lovers after they were dead — all this that the land should not forget one who charmed so well."

I could see a laughing devil in the eyes of Tristan while the wife of De Dasmarinas, the friend of a viceroy, held the image, quite content at his words and tone. He even hummed an air as he worked, and then broke off to regard her with pleasure.

Thus went on the portrait he had made protest against doing. All was in harmony except, perhaps, Marco, who fretted at sight of the carriage of Doña Perfecta so often out by the monastery, and once at the palace I saw her slip her hand on his as she chided him for it.

With all this, I think most of us forgot that the girl Anita, with her pretty tasks, was left without company of the ladies for at least an hour or two each day. But Luiza was much pleased that she was seeing the world a little, and acquiring a dignity from the palace air. As for Mateo, he was so proud that two of the family were under patronage of Doña Perfecta that he was slavish as a dog for her, and would have either done murder at her word or made himself a rug for her feet.

CHAPTER VIII

SANCHA TO ALPHARD

IT WAS the day of the last sitting for the picture that word came from Vera Cruz — a ship from Spain was in, and it was my pleasure to ride south, meeting the carriers. Besides a letter for me, there was a thick, soft packet addressed to " Don Marco de Ordoño by the hand of Rueda at Convent of San Carlos in Mexico."

By going to meet the train of packers, I headed the bearer straight to the monastery with no risk of the letter arriving at the hands of Marco. Her own letter to me, full of joy and excitement, showed me that happiness was hers, and I was of a mind that it should not be made subject to the jeers of Marco.

There was a flutter among the women when I entered, waving my letter in triumph, and gave the packet to Tristan.

He held it, staring at the writing on it, and his face flushed warm. His first movement was to put it aside, but the mockery of Doña Mercedes and the half closed eyes of Señora de Dasmarinas warned him that secrecy was not in high favor. An open face would make the matter forgotten more quickly.

So, careless as might be, he lifted a knife from a bench of brushes and tools, cut the cord, and lifted the seal. With the first unfolding of the paper there was a scream

98

of laughter from Doña Mercedes, and the little carved figure slipped from the hand of Doña Perfecta as she stared.

For, from the folded paper there fell a soft glove of kid, fringed with silver, and lay, a white spot on the red tile at the feet of Tristan.

"Ai, ai!" laughed the Doña Mercedes. "The man has made my Ernesto jealous that I am so often in this place of paint and brushes. Now I can tell him he can rest his soul! Don Tristan is guarded by a mistress who sends the glove as promise of the hand. Ai, ai!"

Her merriment gave Tristan a chance to smile with her, and he lifted the glove and thrust it, with the letter, in his belt under the old robe.

"You will note, lovely lady, that I turned nowhere for glove or letter till the day of your betrothal," he said, and she laughed again, and teased him. Those two were ever care-free comrades, and I had been told it was Tristan who had helped Ernesto Galvez to his wooing. Galvez was in the north, and Doña Mercedes made embroideries for her wedding, and jested happily while waiting his return.

Then Tristan lifted the little carven figure and placed it in the hands of Doña Perfecta, and went on with the picture.

"It is the last day I shall tire you, señora," he said, "but there are the last little touches a worker must linger over."

Doña Perfecta said no word, and sat there as steady and cold as the carving of the dead princess of many lovers. Doña Mercedes had eyes for all, and smiled over her pretty silken webs. Her life had not been one of joy in the house of De Dasmarinas, where, beyond doubt, she saw enough to make her dread domestic up-heavals any morning she opened her eyes. It was easy to perceive that her heart was glad of that glove and letter of mystery; it gave a new color to her day, and she ceased not to make merry over it, even singing softly a love song for Tristan of a loved one far away.

But in the midst of it, Doña Perfecta arose, and rustled her silks over the tiles, and stood close to Tristan to look at the picture.

He bent to write with a brush like a needle a strange name on the base of the little carving, then stepped back a pace.

"It is done, Excellencia," he said. "Were it not a portrait it should be called 'Two Queens of Mexico.'"

"That would be treason," said Doña Mercedes, "since there can be only one vicereine in Mexico."

"I doubt if Don Tomas would punish a loyal subject for naming a lady queen of loves," said Tristan.

He was so little given to compliment, and so beyond reason cold to the lady the viceroy certainly delighted to honor, that I was puzzled to understand his words or his mocking smile, for the picture itself was not a thing to smile at. Once at work he had forgotten that she was the sweet poison he had once said, and the painting seemed to me a quite glorious thing, her face like a flower, a string of topaz girding her golden hair, and the amber silk in soft folds about her. One red flower lay in her lap, and her jeweled hand held the ugly Mexican statue while she looked at it as if she would read its riddle of colors and symbols.

"It is then done!" she said, and looked at Tristan.

"Go you out, Mercedes, and see that the carriage is ready for it."

"There would be wisdom in letting it rest here until the drying is complete," he observed.

"And my visits would not be needed for that! Go you out, Mercedes, while I speak with Señor Rueda."

Of course, at that, there was nothing for me but to go out also, which I did, and Doña Mercedes laughed and made a mocking bow to Señora de Dasmarinas when once the corridor hid us.

"Go you out, Mercedes!" she mimicked with slight respect. "Small care she has of me, to send me out with a gallant and no duenna!"

We laughed at and made merry over this in the corridor.

But for all that, we were given a long wait, and I was made to see that Doña Perfecta's selection of a companion had been thought out with care. An older woman could not be dismissed with such briefness, nor keep so silent.

"For the first time in her life Perfecta is made mad by a man unlike all the others," she whispered. "I do not know that she would look at him twice if he were at her call as is Marco de Ordoño — perhaps not. On my soul, I think if he but satisfied her pride to seek her, she would delight in seeing the viceroy send him on missions so far he could never get back! It is her pride he offends at every turn; but it is over a year now, and I never knew her to show favor so long."

"What becomes of those forgotten?" I asked, not because I cared, but the wait was long, and one must not be dull.

Mercedes looked at me, suddenly grave.

"God knows! now that she has power," she said. "When Don Eduardo was but governor of a southern province, there were always troubles with the natives. Young soldiers were needed, and many never came back. It is a nice sign of favor, you know, to be made a lieutenant of guard over the heads of older men! Most youths think it a feather in their cap."

"What of Marco?" I asked.

"Oh, he is safe! Betrothed to a very exalted lady and due to return to Spain any day. She has use for Don Marco and they are well matched. He may be of use to her in Spain if ever she goes back, and she has been of special use to him here. They understand each other — those two! But who understands Don Tristan?"

When Doña Perfecta joined us at the portal, it was without the picture, and only the prior was with her. At that moment the viceroy drove by with Don Eduardo beside him in the carriage, and there were lifted hats and smiles, and all looked so harmless one would never guess the adventures under the thin surface of things.

I made excuse to Doña Perfecta, who was so gracious as to ask me to drive with them, and once they had rolled away, I rushed back to Tristan to read him my letter — my first letter from Sancha! That matter of the glove was a mystery for me as well as for the ladies, and it was many days before it was made clear.

He was alone, the yellow glow of the picture was already turned to the wall, and the letter was open before him.

"Come out into the garden," he said. "There is still

the odor of palace perfumes lingering here. Come out
under the sky."

"See what you have done!" I protested angrily. "You
have made her in love with Marco, so in love that she
has even kind thoughts of you because you have done
him service. I learn new things of him each day, and
love for him is the last thing she should know. Read
the letter!"

So he read aloud:

My dear Cousin Juanito:
I send my blessings and my love to you. I feel today love
for all the world! No more dolls have come, but a letter from
his own hand. His wisdom is beyond that of all the padres.
How sweet it is that you can see him, walk by him, and hear
his voice! Why must maids be left behind? I am wild to follow you! Nothing happens here but what happened to our
grandmothers, and where you are there are new things, and
wonderful things.
Sister Teresa tells me that when the next ship sails, nuns go
to Mexico to establish a convent for Indian maids. I would
wish myself a nun if it were not that he could not wed a nun —
and some day he is to wed with me! I was very wicked to say I
was not his wife; that was childish of me, for I know now in my
heart that the betrothal was as a marriage. Why cannot I also
go over sea when all I love is there with you? I am not now
a child. What use of gold if it takes me not to my dreams?
The world here is empty. Write me by every ship and tell
me how he fares. By the address I see he is friends always
with that Tristan Rueda of whom the padre wrote when he
saved the life of Marco in the wilderness. I think it was he
who put me in a rage once when Marco's picture was new. I
thought of him as a cruel black bear after that, but perhaps he
is not so bad now. I love all who are near to Marco, so give
Tristan Rueda my blessing. Also to Don Rodrigo my saluta-
tion. What word would he have for me if I became a nun that

I might go to Mexico? Frighten them with that so they come home, and quickly!

A good safe ship to take this to you — and the love of your cousin, Sancha.

"You see!" I said, shaking my head with the wisdom of nineteen years. "You all sat here, and threw dice, and made jests, and thought she was a child — but you have made her love him, and raised the devil!"

He looked at me, laughed at my fuming, and then sighed.

"So it seems," said he.

"And the glove — that too was for him," I blundered, "what to do but give it to him, and save trouble in the future for all of us?"

"And have him flaunt it in the sala of Doña Perfecta to make others jealous?"

That silenced me on the matter of the glove, though I thought the least he could do was to give it to me, her kinsman.

"And God only knows what she wrote in the letter," I grumbled.

"God only," he said, "and I."

I saw by that how little use there was to question, though I did sulk over it a little. I had run to him with a free heart and let him read her writing with his own eyes, even her good words of him. And he buckled close his own message, and did not even let me touch the glove.

Yet the letter was to come to me as he least expected, and thus I learned the new Sancha. I give it here as it was written:

To Alphard in the Sky:

I send the glove because I may not send the hand to you. Think in your heart that I only whisper what I say here — for how else might Virgo send message to Alphard but by whisper on the wind? So wise you grow that I write in fear of my simple words, but I think you do know I look at the circling stars to find the wonders you read there — it makes you closer to me. Did you know that long ago there was a legend of a Moor of Granada in our family? He was a prince, and also most wise in star knowledge. That seems true to me now, for your letter wakes things sleeping in my mind, though I have no memory of when they went to sleep. It may sound childish to your wisdom but that is what you make me feel. I have a wish that the sea were not so wide, that I might go where you are and see with you the wonders you write. You write of serpent things which have been things of fear, but as I read, I remember the tale in the "Pentameron" of the serpent who was a prince under enchantment. Then a maid gave him tenderness so that his true spirit awoke, and they lived in happiness in a palace. I do not ask a palace, but your deserts and "houses of dawn" speak their mysteries and beauty to me. This night there is a new moon. I kissed a rose and tossed it up in my gladness to be alive and in your thoughts, then I knelt in the grass and looked and looked as the crescent sunk far in the sky going the path to you. I was trying to know what the red pagans feel when they make the moon prayer, and tears came into my eyes at the beauty of the night, and the wish that you might kneel beside me. Will that night come? I think of the wilderness shrines under the sky, and wish much to know of the "houses of the dawn." It is a marvel that you learn these prayer thoughts and places. Juanito will tell you I have had wild hours of desire to go where you are — but even Juanito does not know how wild! Could Virgo step down and go a-journeying? Why may I not travel when all the others do? I am making prayers to my Saint of the Impossible that this may come to pass. I said a prayer to her when I wrote you my first letter. She made the reply to come on the first ship — is that not a true miracle? For I knew not then there was

anyone in the world to think of me as you think — yet she
brought it to be! Shall we build a shrine to her some fair
day in some secret place where white butterflies are? That is
a dear wish of mine. Is it yours?

Virgo trembles at thought of the great glowing heart of
Hydra under her feet; she would lift him high as her heart
and journey together in the skies where souls grow big and
full of beauty. Thus you will read that Virgo is only a lonely
maid who awaits the day of enchantment when a dream comes
true. This from the hand of   Sancha.

In my letter by the next ship I gave what wise warning I was able against roving maids, and added a cautious word against dreaming that Mexico was another
heaven on earth, for, despite the work of the church, it
yet had its own hells. The men were not yet saints,
nor the women angels. In my own opinion, it would be
better that Marco be called to Spain with Don Rodrigo,
who was ill in health.

I did not add, as was my desire, that no land would
be the richer of him, however far he might journey, for
in every country alike can be found pretty youths who
grow to pretty men and sport a cock's feather, and a
strut, and know how to wear a cloak or hide a woman
under it! So far as I could see, the travels of Marco had
given him no vision broader than that.

But of what use my advice and labored wisdom, when
another of those letters of the dice went forward in the
same ship? I do not think Tristan had a mind contrary
to my own, but of a certainty he had a way of writing
his thoughts in a different manner and the effect was
beyond our knowing. I still think my own the wiser
way, thought it might not so quickly enchant a maid as
this of his.

White Butterfly Lady:

That heart in the sky is at once lifted high at your words, and I wish it were wise to leave go all earthly things on this shore and cross over to your world, or say to you " come! " and count the hours until I dared look on your face.

But even your Saint of the Impossible could scarce bring that to be. Believe me when I say it were an easier task she had when she brought roses from under winter snows. Wondrous with strange beauty though this land may be, all hearts are not joyous here. I could not sadden you with troubles of the earth, and for that reason bade you look to the things of the sky.

The Houses of the Dawn are many from Peru to New Granada. They are the sanctuaries of sun worship, where a priest stands with lifted hands of adoration when his visible symbol of God comes to him out of the darkness. Some of these houses were things of beauty, but many have been destroyed for the gold of their vessels, and for the salvation of souls. In secret places of the deserts and forests they still stand to catch the light on certain high places, and are thought holy. They mean more than a house; they have a sky spirit to lift earth spirits out of darkness. For this reason are they both sanctuaries and places of refuge to the pagan mind — so sure are they that the god of the sun has a care of them.

Records have been made of such matters for Don Payo, but many good Christians do not approve, and there is feeling against speech or writing of these pagan things, and I must write not so much lest your confessor give you warning.

The glove is with me. It is truly to me as the rose of your Santa Rita from under the snow — a blossom I never dared hope would cross the seas to touch my hand! If I could write that which is within me, I could cover much paper to you, but words are weak and even strength must often choose silence. I write here a little song of that silence:

> If Love were mine —
> The love of maid divine to me!
> I'd build a shrine
> Within my heart where none could see.

And there my litany
Of heart beats, endlessly
Would whisper all the vows
I dare not say!

Once when I dreamed of you in a wonderful desert place to the north, I woke with that song singing in my heart. It was long ago, little maid. At that time I did not know white Virgo would ever whisper a warm word to Alphard, who has ever been, in all the night skies, the solitary one. The song is simple, for the reason that the writer is many other things, but not a poet. Yet he does think poet thoughts when Virgo comes into the Mexican sky out of the east. He cannot ever be the prince of the legend of enchantment for you, and his hand can never lead you to a king's palace, but it would be joy to build with you a shrine to the saint of your prayers. I dare not pray at any shrine for that which you make me wish. I am neither wise, nor great, little maid of the white butterflies. I am only a man who wished to make you less lonely. Surely of all the stars of the sky, the Solitary One knows best the hurt of lonely lives. For that I have written you, and for that I bid you know that far below your feet is stretched the guardian one, whose heart is   Alphard.

CHAPTER IX

THE TRIAL OF THE FAITH

A NEW expedition of colonists was fitting out for New Granada of the Rio Grande del Norte, and I was of half a mind to go, for the sheer adventure of new lands, but Don Rodrigo remained stubbornly ill. Thus there were some weeks of nursing, and Tristan was so closely held that I could hope for neither help nor encouragement from him. He was full of regret that he had not urged the old soldier to take ship with Don Payo, and be among his own home kindred if serious sickness should come.

For while there were neither words nor grieving from him, there was little doubt that the loss of Don Fernando was as a support wrested from him, and this, so quickly followed by the departure of Don Payo, left the old man bewildered between illness and the new régime into which it was not so easy to fit himself.

Tristan was the only confidential support left him, and the cares of Tristan made a very full seven days in the week; thus he was ever provided with fair excuses when the messages from Doña Perfecta or Don Eduardo would entreat him to the palace where the portrait was a source of praise. Marco was half inclined to go north because of some gorgeous tales of turquoise found there. Ernesto Galvez had returned, and brought much fine stone, and some encouraging washings of gold. There was a fever in the air over it, and it seemed plain that Doña Perfecta encouraged it so far as Marco de Ordoño was concerned. She stood ready to be his advocate for position and honor, since there should always be men of the ruling class to keep up the dignity of a cavalcade.

Doña Mercedes, happy over her approaching wedding, smiled at me when Marco told us, with a bit of swagger, of the proffered honors.

"Is it that Doña Perfecta would change courtiers?" I asked her.

"It may be, yet he is useful to Perfecta, and I would rather hazard a guess that there is jealousy somewhere."

"Her husband?" I asked, scenting a fine scandal if he should make troubles so late in the day.

"No — Don Eduardo thinks only of holding political powers, or adding to them — he sees little else."

"Then — "

"There is a higher official, you know, than Don Eduardo," she said with a little shrug. "Also there is an old friendship between him and Perfecta. It may be he grows tired of seeing the same pets in the palace. Thank God I shall be safely married and out of it ere long! It is not so easy, Don Juanito, to be an undowered maid in a house of political intrigues. I have learned so much I will scarcely be able to trust my own husband when I get him!"

"Yet there are those who envy you the chance to live at a palace."

"Foolish they! But a soldier's orphan must take what offers. Perfecta has no love for my presence; it

is the safe, placid Don Eduardo who deemed it wise to
remember a far relationship. It left Perfecta not alone
among strangers if he was absent, and odious gossips
would have less to whisper. He is a good soul in intent.
I would have sorrow if she should forget it utterly. She
was but a child widow when she married him — yet not
a child! She picked, not the richest suitor, but the
safest, and one of family. You see already what she
has made him. Yet she encourages him to think he did
it himself, and that she is his greatest admirer! Men
are curious."

To myself I thought women were.

"Tristan knows all these things — think you?" I
asked.

"Why not? He knows old soldiers of her father's
troop. Now that she has won apartments in the palace,
their memories may not prove keen — for she has power,
and God knows what ambition. Vanity alone stands
chance to win her; for she has ever seen lads fight for
her — and needs for her content to ever see it!"

Scarce a week went by after that until she saw more
of it than the greatest coquette could wish, for Marco,
after carrying and showing his commission as *maestro de
campo* for a week, grew suddenly jealous and let the colonists go north without him.

Some way Doña Perfecta got grace for him on the
ground of illness, and another man took charge, for the
whims of Marco had already made too many delays for
his own comfort.

Thus affairs stood, with Marco stalking about sullenly,
when Tristan was called to the palace to help make
straight some records left over from Don Payo's day,

a simple enough thing to everyone else, but a thing of import to the jealous, watchful eyes of Marco.

Doña Mercedes, who told me of it, knew only that Tristan, in leaving the work completed in the hands of Don Eduardo, chanced to halt on the gallery to speak with Anita, who was screened from the garden by the blossoming vines. Tristan had no thought, perhaps, that he was standing outside the private apartment of Doña Perfecta, and after a few words with Anita, passed on and out, to be met by Marco boiling with fury. He saw in Tristan the sole reason of his commission to the provinces, and what he said was heard by all who cared to listen. He accused Tristan of scheming to put him out of favor with the viceroy, and whatever he could recall of patronage accepted by Tristan, he flung in his face under the eyes and ears of all who thronged the court. He fumed that Tristan was trying to climb by clinging to the skirts of a woman, and then he spoke of him as ingrate and baseborn — a peasant who strove to climb palace steps!

Then it was that Tristan, having no weapon, struck him down with his hand, and left him there, stretched on the tiles, with the blood from his nose not adding to his beauty. A cry went up to halt the man who had struck down a gentleman within the palace grounds, but the call came too late, for those nearest had already shrunk back to give Tristan room, and he walked out without a word from first to last.

Straight to the house of Luiza he went, for it was there Don Rodrigo was being nursed. The good woman made many a prayer there, as in spite of all good nursing, the color came not back to the old man, and the flesh was shrinking until his face held deep wrinkles instead of its former plump glow.

Tristan walked past her as he had walked past the people at the palace, and for the first time in his life he had neither courtesy for woman, nor mercy on age. To the comfort of Luiza, Don Rodrigo was having a fairly good sleep, but the hand of Tristan fell on his shoulder as if he might have been a sentry sleeping on post.

"Awake and talk to me," he said. "Who was my father?"

Don Rodrigo opened his eyes, and looked in fear at the hard face.

"Tell me now," said Tristan. "I have had patience. I have had courtesy, I have waited long. But whatever it may do to me, I want the truth if you know it. You must know it if he does!"

"He?" and Don Rodrigo was trembling, "*he?*"

"Marco — he said I was some peasant's bastard whom his family protected."

"Holy God! What did you do?"

"I struck him down in the palace. I want the truth."

Don Rodrigo signed Luiza to leave, and she did, and knelt praying in her kitchen, feeling as if her world were rocking. As boys, Tristan had been master, and now as man he had struck down his foster brother.

"The truth," said Tristan when she had gone. "Who was my father?"

"Tristan, have you never guessed?"

"Yes, many times. You, General de Ordoño, and even —"

Don Rodrigo drew from under his pillow a rosary of brown beads with turquoise and shell interposed.

"It came to me from Don Payo. It is now yours, Tristan, for he was the man:—Fernando."

And Tristan knelt to receive the rosary, and laid his head on the bed, and hid his face because of the tears.

"I dreamed that, and hoped it," he said, "yet it is a bitter word for all that. He gave his life trying to make amends for a folly of mine — and I gave him love as I gave no other."

"So long as he lived you were not to know — but he took the seal from my lips. He saved the life of Pedro, Marco's father — more than his life, for they were prisoners of the Moors — held for ransom. All he ever asked of the De Ordoño in recompense was shelter and secrecy for you."

"If there was secrecy — then Marco told the truth you have all hidden," said Tristan, but Don Rodrigo shook his head.

"See that the door is closed tightly," he said, "for I give you the secret of souls gone to God, and it might be better if I never told; I do not know."

"If I am not of shameful blood, give me the truth of it," said Tristan.

"It were hard to do, if it were not that you have ever read books, and know some things of history which I lack," and the old man was plainly averse to the task. "And so you know there were very wealthy, and very learned Jews of Spain who were banished, and took with them the magic, and it was said accursed knowledge that was theirs."

"I know these things, for even Cristoval Colon would never have got the blessing of the pope or consent of the crown, if a whisper had been let fall of his Jew ancestry."

" You have heard that, too? " whispered Don Rodrigo.
" It is still unsafe to speak of it — the Holy Brotherhood
smothered that knowledge when they found it, for Colon
himself was a good Christian."

" Though his relations were burnt as Jews in Pont-
evedra," said Tristan. " I have seen the records."

" Then forget them ere another sun comes up,"
warned the old man — " that, and your own family
might ——"

" Ah! " and as if a revelation had come to him Tristan
said, " Then *that* is the secret; I am a Jew! "

" You are not a Jew! Your mother was so good a
Christian she was as a saint. My brother loved her, too,
but Fernando won her. You have read, perhaps, the
name of Abarbanel."

" The very learned Jew who was banished? "

" Yes, your mother was of that blood, exiled from
Spain. In Morocco they made marriages with the
priestly Kahn class, but her father married a Christian.
The father saved Fernan and my brother, Pedro, and,
dying, asked one favor — that his daughter Dolores be
brought away from the land of the Moors. They brought
her — smuggled somehow, with her ropes of jewels
worn under the dress of a serving maid. It was the great
adventure. Up in the hills of Antequera Fernan found
a priest, and Pedro was their marriage witness. Up
there Fernan hid her, but the jewels made trouble. A
few were sold — and one was a famous gorget, a royal
gem. The crown and the Brotherhood went on the trail,
for the family holding those trinkets had been sentenced
to perpetual exile; also the officers had stripped those
exiles of gold and lands and jewel casket, and then woke

up to find the casket held only imitations. So it was a serious matter; the jewels had been claimed for the crown and the crown had been cheated. It may be your mother did not even know of this until the search for her was taken up. She was hidden with you, in many places — even in hill caves — and hunted out. Then Pedro took you, and Fernan strove to go north with her and take ship. Well, there was another child, and she went to God on the Galician shore, and her babe went with her. Yes, she was Christian, but she had the blood of Jewish priests, and her family was so strong that no member was to ever set foot on ground of Catholic Spain. She was only a child in those days, and Fernan was only a boy; they thought the Brotherhood would take no note of one little child woman — but they did not know!"

"Does Luiza know?"

"Nothing but what she may think — and that is that you were no doubt of our family. Her first husband gave credit to me, as I was the one bachelor among us. He was planning to make some money by holding my secret, when the devil took him."

"Then I am a Jew," said Tristan again.

"Don't say it!" begged Don Rodrigo. "Fernan and your mother were good Christians ever."

"But my blood is Jewish — my brain is Jewish. It is like a curtain lifted! It gave me the hunger for the study of the gods of the pagans; I wonder, Don Rodrigo, if I searched for the unknown god because I was searching the way back to the god of the ancient Kahns — for that was a royal house, and its symbol was the serpent of wisdom, also there is the same name in the sky gods of these people, and the symbol is the same. It is a priestly caste."

"God forbid you should go deeper into such abominations for the reason that I tell you of your Jewish blood!" groaned Don Rodrigo. "Yes, it was blood of power, too much power to please the kings of Spain. Also, jewels to outshine an ambitious queen are dangerous possessions."

"Then why should Marco shout 'baseborn' at me?" demanded Tristan, but the old man reached out his hand in pleading.

"He does not know; he is an angry child with a lost toy, and blames you, perhaps. But Tristan, your two fathers loved, and starved, and shared prison together. He can never be told that. Are you big enough, Tristan, to know it all and hide it, and not be hurt by his words?"

"I would rather tell the truth in the plaza for all to hear," said Tristan. "Am I to show shame of my blood when kings of old were proud of it?"

But Don Rodrigo caught his hands, and begged him to unsay the words.

"Your friends will be caught in the toils as well as you if ever the Holy Brotherhood should add you to the suspected heretics," he reminded. "You are safe as was your father under the wing of the church, but only the monk's robe saved him at the last. Remember these things, Tristan. No drop of Jewish blood was in him, and no heresy; yet he had to live in shadow and silence because he had fathered the son of the house of exiles. We guarded you as a child, Tristan. He left you to me. You would not undo the work of his life for your safety?"

"No — I will not do that. But silence is bitter; I am proud of the truth, yet must act shame."

"For my sake, Tristan, the sake of an old man. And what of your quarrel with Marco?"

"I would do him no ill except as he earns it. He is much to you, I know, but give him a word that will warn him if ever I need lift hand to him again."

"And you are not cast down at the word I have given you?" asked the old man.

"I? You have opened a window for a dark soul! Don Rodrigo, I have entered this day into a royal heritage, and I have learned why my mother called me the name of sadness."

Then Don Rodrigo told him there were some family records among Don Fernando's papers; they would show him the ancestry of his Christian family. And with some kindly words, the old man wearily turned his head on the pillow, and fell asleep, worn out by the doing of the task he had long promised to do when the time came.

The resentment against Marco seemed to slip out of Tristan's mind, when he learned how very ignorant he had been of all the truth — also how senselessly jealous.

I had been told of the scandal at the palace, so I was waiting outside at a word from Luiza, and when the door opened, and Tristan came into the street, his face held all the radiance of a new day. He walked beside me, scarce heeding my blundering attempts to explain Marco and his jealous furies.

"That will look after itself," he said; "she has him frantic that she seeks importance for him elsewhere than at the palace. It was easy for him to believe I had her ear; he could not see it was Anita with whom I spoke."

"But the insult?"

"It was an ignorant one — for which I may yet give him the sound thrashing he well earned. Yet, for the sake of Don Rodrigo, I might find myself doing him a favor after the thrashing! The old man has been my friend this day. I would do much to make his days content, there may not be so many of them."

There was not in his face a sign of the anger from which the group at the palace had shrunk away, and I had my own wonder as to how a man could, for anyone, show favor after such an insult. But I was soon to learn this, and other things. Marco de Ordoño was only a spoiled and petted child, yet out of his jealous whims came tragic things to all of us, and that encounter in the court was but the beginning.

Doña Perfecta had her own tasks to explain why two men quarreled under her window. Even Don Eduardo was aroused to an interest in this, and there would have been an arrest of Tristan, but for the desire to let the matter go quietly to sleep.

But again did Marco and his jealousy prevent. Notes were exchanged, and Doña Perfecta, with intent to prevail upon him that he follow quickly after the colonists, gave him secret audience of which only Anita was witness. That poor child was desperate with her own secret, as was learned later, and eager to go where Tristan might not follow.

However they planned it, there was some lack of cleverness, and some hand to write a note of warning to Don Tomas; the viceregal palace was used for rendezvous which might make scandals for the future. That writer was never known, but I suspected the man who would have liked to hold the office of secretary, instead of Don Eduardo.

The first I knew of it was a note to Tristan without signature.

If you have power such as is thought at the palace, the nephew of Don Rodrigo is in danger there, in the room of a lady, and the order has come to post extra guard tonight.

Tristan read it, and looked at the time.

" The guard is changed in a few minutes, that will be the time," he said. " In the rooms of a lady — that means she either wants him caught, or urges him to leave the city. In either case — "

He girded the old robe about him, the cowl over his face, and was out into the darkness before the thought was voiced.

In either case, it was the viceroy who was alert instead of the husband. That posting of the guard had its own significance. Ernesto Galvez was of the guard, and was a friend of Don Rodrigo. Evidently he did not want Doña Mercedes in any way concerned with a message.

It was not until later I had time to think this out, for at that time I could only tag at the heels of Tristan, and see him enter by the gate of the garden. Then I strolled to the back to take note of guards and saw none, only three horses held by a young fellow who gave but ungracious greeting as I passed him in the darkness.

I had but reached the corner when a figure in robe and cowl came flying out of the gate.

"Up!" he said to the youth holding the horses. "Up and away ere he finds you! I have the pass."

Whereupon they both tumbled into saddles, and went into darkness, and while I thought the voice was that of Marco, it is not easy to tell of a voice by a whisper, and I was frozen with dread lest I had seen the escape of Doña Perfecta, and her most troublesome favorite, and the scandal would be great.

The echo of the horse hoofs had scarce ended when a troop of men filed along the wall. From the other side of the narrow street I could hear one laugh, "What sort of night bird, think you, we spread the net for?" he asked.

There was no answer, for at that moment a door opened in the wall at the back, and a light from the garden came through, and in the light stood Tristan as he stepped quickly out to the darkness.

But not quick enough, for from each side a guard moved. I was standing square in the light; it was dim, yet enough to show him my face, and with a hurtling run he staggered back the guard and leaped across the space to me. I could only stare, for it was as if he meant to assault me that he plunged forward; and, stepping back, I did trip and fall, and he dropped beside me.

It surely looked to the others as if he had stumbled over me, but his knee touched the ground only enough for the ruse, and his hand was on my breast, and under my cloak was thrust a flat small packet, filling me with fear.

Then he arose, and the guards were upon him, and he laughed as he turned to walk with them.

"You are wrong, my friends," he said. "I am not a brigand that you need arms to take me, now I know who you are. I deemed you highwaymen when I sought to leap clear of you."

They led him away for all that, and I followed, at a distance, past the palace, where naught was to be learned. A word with Doña Mercedes showed me she was panic stricken, Doña Perfecta knew nothing, or would tell nothing.

And I, failing to see Tristan or learn aught at the prison, made my way back to bed and tossed, sleepless, until morning, with the little packet under my pillow. He had uttered no word to me, but I knew that the glove I had coveted was at last in my keeping — yet no pleasure came with it.

The viceroy had not caught the man he hoped, and someone had to pay for that. I do not think in the beginning he would have given special thought to the affair of Tristan, had Doña Perfecta not lost her head. But she was more than a little amazed to learn that while Marco had escaped, it had not been alone. Anita Gomez was also gone, and Luiza in the first fright, had asked concerning Marco, whereupon others about the palace remembered many things! Doña Perfecta was quite happy over this matter of Anita. It made clear all the jealousy of Marco — it was Anita with whom Tristan talked back of the lattice, and was the plain cause of the quarrel, and so on, and so on!

All was fish to her net, and the going of Anita was to her a blessing sent by the angels.

And then the real thunderbolt fell, and her little power dwindled until she was frantic. Just as she had planned how to appear as a guardian angel to Tristan, and thus make him her debtor forever, a stronger hand than hers was laid upon him, and beyond that was terror and sickness of heart for all of us.

For Mateo Gomez went to confession.

That sounds as slight a thing as that Marco had shown jealous temper.

Yet all these lives were entwined until I began to think no look or word was without weight, and the confession of Mateo was a weighty matter indeed. It placed a guard at the door of Don Rodrigo, and gave a definite charge against Tristan, who had failed to accuse himself of the evil of Jewish blood!

And poor Luiza, who retired to pray during that confession of Don Rodrigo, had given no thought that Mateo was in bed in the adjoining room, and was, in one hour, more important in the eyes of the Inquisition than ever before in his entire life.

Don Rodrigo was questioned by the officers, and came near to dying at the first shock, then braced himself like an old soldier facing a charge and told all, as Mateo had heard. The people were all dead — his brother Pedro, his friend, Fernando Alcatraz, and the Christian girl, Dolores Maria Kahn. Yes, many jewels had been in her hands, so he had been told, and because of that hidden wealth, she had been searched for until she died, so he had heard, and his brother who would have wedded her but that Fernando had her love, was their friend while he lived, and hid the child for them. Jewels and books also he hid, for the father of Dolores was very learned, and a great collector of knowledge, and the books were for the son of his daughter if there should be one, for he believed that the God of Moses would in time lead his people into peace, and they must know the records of their race and their clans.

No, Don Rodrigo knew not what had been the end of the books. Pedro had them in charge in Spain, but Pedro died. It might be Fernando could have told, but Fernando also was dead, and as for the boy — how could he be blamed for all this of which he knew nothing? He had not even known the name of either father or mother.

So all at once everybody knew at least that Marco was wrong — for a Kahn and an Abarbanel could not be base in caste, however evil their souls might be through following the dead laws of Moses and ignoring the sanctified path to the new dispensation.

With all the help of Doña Perfecta, who was most willing to help, I could get no glimpse or speech with Tristan other than to look on, as all the town did, at the procession of the penitents for the mass at San Francisco, and even there the guard encouraged no discourse. But I could see him — walking strong and with head high held. All the moody dark was gone from his face. At last the mystery was over; he knew now the reasons he had been hidden under a strange name, and there was a most unchristian pride in his glance.

Doña Mercedes whispered a prayer as she gazed.

"It is as though he welcomed martyrdom," she whispered. "What is in his heart that he walks like that?"

"It is the thought of his people, and his pride to know of them," I said, and I read him truly in that.

"But he is Christian — he wears a rosary," persisted Doña Perfecta.

"Yet he has uttered heretical words according to

report," said Don Eduardo. "His statement that the tribes of the deserts have no devil and get along very well without one has been discussed with much feeling, and you perhaps have not heard of his statement that our blessed Lord lived a Jew and died a Jew."

"Does he dare to argue in words like that in the very shadow of death?" gasped his wife. "If he were a saint from heaven he could not hope for help."

So thought we all, and wondered much that there was no word of torture; for they were suddenly connecting this with the Lispano matter, through Fray Fernando, but for reasons of their own did not press this. And that Tristan wore the rosary of Don Fernando was made clear, with no attempt at secrecy. It had been found on the drowned body and entrusted to Don Payo; this could be verified when a ship sailed.

But under the tiles in the cell of Fray Fernando there were found some curious things, very puzzling. There were books, and there were records of note: the two century old list of the outfitting of the first expedition to the Indies, and the names of the various Jews who furnished the money — Santangel and Sanchez at the head — both *marranos*, though high in affairs of state. Diego de Deza, the learned theologian of Jewish blood, who had Columbus received at Salamanca. There was also the account of the second expedition, financed with Jewish money — this time, however, it was taken in tribute from exiles. The list was very long and complete in its devilish intent, and proved that Jewish gold opened up a new world, and that there had been no royal gifts from the crown; all given by them was the permit to sail, and honors if the navigator earned them.

These were things long whispered of but never before seen in writing by the Inquisition in Mexico. All such records were thought to have been burned by the faithful. Yet here it was, beside a copy in Latin of "The Hope of Israel," by Menasseh ben Israel. This contained a devilish record of native Jews among the Indians of South America, and part of the contents was the copy of an address to a man named Cromwell, in an attempt to gain freedom for Jews to abide in England.

All this was a firebrand, indeed! But Tristan told gladly all the officers of the Inquisition had to ask. He had read this record as he read every record telling him aught of the origin of the tribes of America. If they came from ancient Jews, then it should be an easier task to learn their histories. He confessed that he did not himself believe the tribes were, or ever had been, Jews — it was even easier to think that these Indians were the older people.

"What meaning had your impious words of the dead tribes of Israel and the false gods of these red Indios?" demanded the prosecutor, and all who heard were sure at last that Tristan could have no chance, for his interest in the pagan creed was known to be great.

"I do not recall what I said, holy father, but I knew the Kahns were a priestly caste — that even kings had been known to change records that they might claim descent from them, the highest. Also that word, 'kan,' means the sky and the things of the sky to certain of these tribes, and their priest-kings use it also in their names. It seems the pagan mind goes ever to the sky, and the sun, and the stars, for their god-thoughts. To me it was strange they should thus use the word by

which the family of Aaron, the high priest, was called;
these have also their high priests, who, after death, they
pray to as gods, and know by that sky name!"

And Tristan was so suddenly interested in tracing
these strange links of human thought, that he was eager
as a boy to follow a game, and forgot he was on trial
for his faith and his life until the prosecutor frowned,
and pointed to the dangerous volume of Menasseh ben.
Israel.

"Did you not know you committed the deadly sin
by application to the works of a heretic?" he demanded.

"Holy father, much of my work for three years has
been making records of the pagan beliefs here for the
archbishop. Thus was I ever delving in heretical material and constantly adding all I might to my knowledge. Some saintly priests have done the same and
were not questioned."

This of course was a fact, for under Fray Payo freedom of a sort had flourished.

"Do you not know," thundered the prosecutor, "that
your inheritance of blood has given you a pernicious
tendency to read evil into the records where a Christian
would read good?"

"I have not been conscious of the evil."

"Do you deny the Jew blood animating you?"

"No, holy father, they tell me I have it, and it is a
new matter to me. My parents were Christian."

"You deny the Jewish blood?"

"How can I? You have there my family records.
You can prove me the same amount of Jewish ancestry
as possessed by Christoval Colon of Galicia, but that
blood gave us this kingdom."

"That is a claim of the iniquitous Jews."

"I never have heard it made by one; for two centuries they have hidden all they knew of the records, and the crown feared the anger of the pope if it was made clear. Even Spain had to think of what the world would say if it took a new world by the hand of one Jew, and at the same time drove his brothers into exile."

"And this has been the training you have had at the hands of Fray Fernando, and by the sanction of Fray Payo," said the priest coldly. "These records will go to Spain for his reading. We will see what the ship brings back. You will wait that coming in prison."

There was much wonder at such leniency and long waiting, though the fact was that the revival of the Lispano affair in connection with Don Fernando had aroused doubt as to the sound doctrine of other friends of the Lispanos. While the ship took letters of inquiry to Fray Payo in Spain, there would be many months in which to observe Tristan and the people who would seek to favor him. He was the first key they had found to secrets they suspected, and the Holy Brotherhood had no intent to wear out the key ere the door was found. The ecclesiastical mind had decided, to its humiliation, that Fray Fernando had lived a double life under their eyes, with his own son under his guidance. The fact that Tristan had not known it was, in a way, in his favor. Yet it all made a direful buzzing and all the books found under the tiles of Fray Fernando's cell were sent under seal to the church of San Francisco to await the final trial of Tristan.

In the excitement of those days, the arrest of Tristan in the palace garden was all but forgotten, or if remembered, no separate cause was assigned to it — the Holy Brotherhood took its victims wherever they were to be found. All smaller matters were swallowed up in the greater, and the going of Marco and Anita was but an episode to all but poor Luiza.

That good soul was in torture over all — the righteous act of Mateo, and the unrighteous words of Tristan as they were repeated to her by hearers, the child Anita out in the world of wilderness, and the honored Don Rodrigo at the door of death in her house.

He never rallied after that first examination. He was reprimanded for heretical silence on a matter belonging to the confessional, and it may be he saw in his mind the dispersion of the treasure he had been five exiled years garnering.

Be that as it may, he called a priest and an *alcalde*, and arranged his will, in which good Luiza was provided for, and the rest of his belongings divided between Marco and Tristan, the son of his friend. To me he left a good gift, and named me as executor, and then, as though in the dread of what he might yet have to face, he turned to the wall, and spoke no more.

And I, a lad not twenty, was alone in the big world of exiles with but one friend of the old days left alive near me, and the walls of a prison about him.

I took up my abode with Luiza after that, though it irked me to meet Mateo there. Yet he kept his distance, and it rested her heart to have one of the family to wait upon. Weeks went by like that — waiting what would chance Tristan, and waiting news from the north. The little we had from there was ill news, for Anita was unused to hard travel, and their first week on the trail

had given her illness, yet were they pushing on to join
the cavalcade.

"It is as well Tristan does not know," said Luiza,
"else bars would scarce hold him. He warned us and
we would not see."

As well as I could, I tried to comfort her; since Marco
had stolen the girl for all the world to know, he would
do what a Christian might, short of wedding her — for
there was Sancha back in Spain!

I had my own quandaries those days, but in the midst
of them was allowed the grace long asked for, that I
might provide the meals for Tristan in prison. So I
hid the letters and the glove, and went gladly forth to
visit.

As I expected, they searched me well, and I knew
they would set a watch lest I left, or carried away, a
message. But Tristan asked only of the death of Don
Rodrigo, and such matters of family. He had known
the old man would not recover, and was grateful that
he had lived to tell the truth, and had the courage to
tell it.

"And Marco? he got away?" he asked.

"Yes, he got away," I said, and professed to have
heard nothing more.

"It will not be so long a time now until a new ship
comes in," he observed.

"No," I said, "and so eager am I for news that I will
ride down the valley myself when the word comes."

He smiled on me at that, and understood. Despite the
guard, we had spoken our message.

Then the Brotherhood regretted that an able man
should be idle when there was work to do, and at a hint

from Fray Bernardino, Tristan was given sentence to perform certain labors calculated to enlighten his soul until the final sentence. Fray Bernardino was yet occupied with the chapel decorations and needed a helper. If Tristan was indeed a Christian, he had his chance to prove it with one not to be deceived, for it was a picture of the Virgin he was to paint, and it was his great chance.

There were many prophecies and prognostications over this. The more devout anticipated nothing less than a paralysis if he was allowed to attempt it. But Fray Bernardino had a good word to say of his craft, and of the money it would save if he succeeded. Even though he failed, no harm would be done beyond what prayers to Our Lady would cure again.

But that he did not fail, the picture is there to testify, and after the work was entered upon, Tristan went into it with all his soul. There is no doubt that he felt it was his last work for earth, as he was not lulled into hope by the special leniency shown him. However that was, the word went out that he had assumed the task and no eye but his must rest on the work until ended — then they could hang or burn him as they elected, but he would have done the one picture in his heart.

Doña Perfecta tried by all means to see it, but was told it was more than a penance put upon him — it was the work of a vow upon which none could intrude. So there was much wonder and expectation.

"How comes it that whether behind prison walls, or ranging free, there is no one like this priest's son to keep everyone at question?" demanded Doña Perfecta. "It has not been the custom to give prisoners the liberty of deciding who shall look in upon them, and his heretical argument makes it doubly strange."

"Have no fear," said her husband. "They suffer him many privileges that they may catch his heretical friends in the net ere the end comes. His art alone is no excuse for leniency. The Holy Brotherhood is not napping. They are busy on records left behind by Don Payo. No priest of any order since Bernardino de Sahagun has given such countenance to heretical knowledge of the false gods."

"And what was the end of De Sahagun?"

"He was discountenanced by his own order, and all obstacles placed in his way by the church. Not until he was eighty was he allowed to translate his papers on the pagan gods, and all the translation disappeared after his death."

"But Fray Payo, as archbishop, had more power than a mere priestly student."

"It remains to be seen how far that power can reach. All these mysteries of Fray Fernando, and the Lispanos, and the heretical books, came into Mexico some way while Fray Payo was at the head of affairs. Also it is shown that he was told the place of the death of Fray Fernando, yet kept silence. The Council of the Indies will hear all of this, and the curious encouragement granted to heretical scholars may even yet cause strange echoes for the ears of Fray Payo! It is not for nothing this free-tongued painter is granted rope to hang himself and perhaps others more exalted."

Doña Mercedes turned pale as she looked at me, and slipped her hand into that of Ernesto. Those two had been wedded the week after Marco's flight.

"You think, then, there is still danger that Tristan be put to the final test?" she asked.

"Say, rather, there is still hope for it," corrected Don Eduardo. "What else would you have for an apostate who hesitates not to say that Columbus and the Virgin, and the Son of the Virgin were one and all of Jewish blood?"

"It is of course an abomination, and to be deplored," she acknowledged. "It would have saved many lives if God the Father had chosen a virgin of another people."

"What are fleshly lives compared with souls?" asked Don Eduardo. "To me it seems your mind is wandering in strange and forbidden conjectures."

"It is in the air," said Ernesto. "People are talking of religions who never talked before. Tristan, with his open statements, has started it going, and the saints alone know what the end will be! But it is true, I think, the Brotherhood permits it for this time, and with a purpose! The end for Tristan will be the stake when they have netted his friends."

"And you are openly his friend even now," said Doña Mercedes to me. "Have you no fear?"

"I have indeed, for him," I agreed, "yet of his dangerous opinions I have no part. Don Rodrigo had love for Don Fernando though he married a maid of forbidden descent. It is said that Abarbanel was of the strain of David, and the Kahn is known to be of the caste of Aaron. Yet despite this friendship of Don Rodrigo for a suspect, he lived and died with evil towards no man. Why not I?"

"You may not die so happily, if you show approval of this heretic, Tristan," warned Don Eduardo.

"But I do not approve! I deplore and shrink from
the knowledge he has acquired. If I had influence I
would beg him to forget every written line but the *credo*,
and urge him to repeat it forever for the love of God!"
and I all but wept as I said it, knowing as I did that Tristan would rather be dead in the flesh than limited in
range of the mind.

But thus, in diverse ways, was I made to hear, over
and over, opinions and warnings, many for my own
sake, a few, I hoped, for his. I felt there were some who
sanctioned in him that which they never could imitate.
Forgotten ancestral blood within them clamored un-
voiced admiration of his daring. The very youth of
Tristan must have emphasized this, though I heard Fray
Felipe make statement that it was no youthful soul, but
some very old Jewish demon, who spoke through his
lips.

So, as Doña Perfecta stated, though hidden from sight
within prison walls, the spirit of him caused much controversy, and Doña Perfecta had more than a little
anxiety lest, if he be put to the torture, questions might
be asked as to the night of arrest, and the cause of his
presence there. All of his actions would be given
weight, and it was not to be supposed that he would sacrifice himself for Marco, or for her, a second time.

Names were not mentioned by Tristan during the
brief meetings when I took him food as permitted. In
a general way he asked of the outer world, yet had the
quiet content of a soul to whom the world is not neces-
sary.

"I am more free than before," he asserted when I
asked him of the weary days. "I am doing the same

sort of work, yet doing it better. My life is widened by knowing my origin, and my spirit unfastened its bonds when I openly took the burden of my race, and felt that others were not bearing my part of the load."

"But how can you, a Christian, feel the burden of a Jew?" I asked in dismay at his frankness.

"I do not feel it as to creed; it is scarcely understandable in its many sides. Yet it has nobleness, else it could not send forth both a Moses and a Jesus. Does the spirit of God descend upon a mean people?"

I could not answer, for I was oppressed by the sense of danger to him. He saw it, and smiled.

"Go you out, Juanito, without trouble or care for me," he said. "I am nearer happiness than you have ever seen me."

Which was another perplexing thing not to be understood at that time, for at that time I had neither glimpse nor thought of the picture to be done as a test and a penance.

Then came a day when the priests were let in to view it, and the viceroy and other dignitaries. Nuns of St. Dominic were there, and the ladies of the court, and all went in a soft rustle to their knees on the tiles before the chancel. I had but caught glimpse of the pictured summer sky — blue and white — under the shadowy dome, when Doña Perfecta, beside me, twisted her fan until I heard the sticks break.

"Santa Maria!" she whispered, "he has done it — he has painted the thing he grasped at in the sunbeam!"

"He has done the impossible thing," said Doña Mercedes, dropping to her knees. "It is a miracle sent as proof of a holy faith."

It may be that she was right. As she knelt I saw over her head, and from the painted sky I looked to the figure of the virgin in white, and then I sank beside her, and no one in the church stood in that presence. The nuns lifted up their voices and murmured the *Salve Regina* as a prayer offering for the beauty of it, and I, after that first look, knelt on the tiles with bent head, and the tears fell on my hands — tears for the hungry heart of Tristan.

I knew then what he meant when he said he was nearer happiness than ever before. After that picture I could never fail to understand Tristan. A man would have to live with a spirit of love, waking and sleeping through the years, to paint that consecration he had placed upon the altar.

He had painted her as she was, divine to him, and at her feet knelt his enemies and lifted their voices in adoration.

Though behind prison bars, he had won a victory beyond all dreams.

"It is a miracle — no apostate could win the power to paint like that."

"It is not as a painting, it is as if Our Blessed Lady had swept down from the sky to stand like that and look out upon us," said another. "I never will believe it a thing of paint unless my hands touch it."

"No hands should be permitted to touch it," said proud Fray Bernardino. "Did I not tell you a prize would be ours if you but let the lad do his will?"

"We will hold discourse of this," stated Fray Felipe; "there has been mystery about this work. Who is to prove the hand that did it?"

"I, who locked him in, and put no one with him," stated Fray Bernardino. "If he had aught of help, it came from Our Lady herself."

And thus was one of the legends begun.

Doña Perfecta stared, and stared. "He has caught his sunbeam and formed it into a woman," she said.

"But where," said Doña Mercedes, "is there a child-woman on the earth with that royal pride and gracious sweetness? The look in her eyes is a benediction."

"He has caught the sunbeam," repeated the other in a strange, grudging tone, "yet he has painted her as above the earth; her feet in the sandals barely touch the grass on that hill."

Thus the voices went around me, while I could not see for the tears in my eyes. As soon as might be I slipped away, and walked alone until the night came. That was the night I unfolded and read the letters. My boy's mind was so oppressed by the weight I had to carry that I had to know. And reading in them what I read in the picture, I thanked God that Sancha was safe in Spain.

CHAPTER X

THE COMING OF SANCHA

I SENT food and messages to Tristan but let days go by before I saw him again. On every side were voices speaking in awe and wonder of the painting in the chancel. There were many pious doubts concerning the work — either the accused man could not have painted it, or else he could not be a Jew and a heretic!

Doña Perfecta tried as she was able to strengthen the last idea — yet how could one accomplish much to contradict his own mad acceptance of Jewish ancestry?

" He shows pride in it, and not humbleness," stated her husband, " and in all ways is a dangerous man. Fray Felipe tells me that there are many pious people who firmly believe that he is linked with the devils of the pagans and inspired by them."

" Yet one thing given in evidence of his heresy is that he said the pagans had no devils, and were the better for having none." I ventured this with a certain trembling, for fear my privilege of sending his food should be taken away, yet it was occasion for Don Eduardo's reading me a lecture.

" How make converts but by scaring them with the devil? " he demanded. " How comes true form of re-

ligion but in the fear of the Evil One? This heretic
painter had best be reading the lives of the saints, rather
than the unedifying discourse of the pagan gods of the
sky. More will come of this, for his words of the high
priests here, and their clan name akin to the clan name
of ancient Jewry, are beyond all human or divine reason,
and these are the things by which he will be led to the
stake when the time comes."

"But it is not as if he had linked those pagan things
with Christian names," I said.

"Else his life would not be spared so long!" he
answered coldly. "He has declared that the Son of
God was a Jew, and after that, what evil thing would
he halt at?"

I could not say. Yet I went away knowing that
while the painting had given them an awe of him, it
had not lessened the bitterness of the pious — his art
was to them a certain indication of devilish possession.

I said some prayers of my own to the Saint of the
Impossible, and then went, after those days of pondering, to see Tristan.

"Have you been ailing?" was his first word at sight
of me, and I truthfully said yes, for my nights had been
without sleep and my days without security.

"The days of waiting are now grown irksome," he
confessed; "and my hands are idle, for my work is
done, and I have painted them a virgin."

"I know," I said. "I saw all the people kneel there."

"You did that?" and he was eager as a boy, "they
knelt to adore her? Ay, that is happiness, Juanito. If
you live to be old, and she does, tell her of it when I
am gone."

"No words could tell her," I said; "only the picture itself could do that, and the picture she never can see."

"That is so," he assented; "her paths of life will lead into happier places than this, and that is better. But they did kneel — they did see all the heavenly beauty of her?"

"How did you hold it in your mind all these years, and then glorify it like that?" I asked, and he smiled.

"Rather, how have I kept from painting it into each face I have had canvas for? You perceive I did resist that until they gave me a last task."

"Tristan, have you no thought of what the people say?"

"Why should I? I shall be dead and out of it before anyone comes who knows the face, and it may be that even now she is changed until only you and I, out of all the world, remember."

I could not say anything after that. His words, "I shall be dead and out of it," told me the Holy Brotherhood could have no surprises for him. He lived without hope while biding their time.

"I would wish to write one letter before the end comes," he said; "some day your eyes will look on her again."

I nodded my head and went away, for it was like hearing a man prepare for death, and I was only a boy. I asked Fray Bernardino to let him have paper and pen so long as he wrote no heretical record, for I knew Fray Bernardino was very happy over the picture, and disposed to think the inspiration of Tristan not an evil thing.

Gilberto Lanchitas met me at the palace with word

that a ship was in, and the carriers had been sighted on
the far slopes, so we rode out together to meet the mail.
I would rather have gone alone for my own reasons,
as Gilberto was constantly alert for all new enterprises.
Yet my anxiety was without cause, for there was no
letter.

I had planned every conceivable way to get and hide
it when it arrived, but for its non-arrival I had made
no provisions, and Gilberto laughed at my face when I
showed my disappointment.

"Is it a lover left behind?" he asked. "Your eager
riding and long face would indicate that."

Then he asked questions of the ship, and passengers,
and the journey. All arrived well but a noble nun of
St. Dominic, who had come with a band of sisters for
mission work. She was ill in Vera Cruz, and their
journey delayed, but the other travelers were coming
up the mountains soon as might be. I recalled the mention Sancha had made of the nuns, yet gave them little
thought. The lack of a letter was most in my mind. I
rode back, wondering, and went to Fray Bernardino.

"I had asked Tristan for help with a letter," I said,
"but a ship is in, and no letter has come for me. Will
you tell him?"

"I will tell him, but already the letter for you is written by him, and I am to give it to your hand. No evil is
in it, and there seems no fair reason why you should not
have it. A letter of love it might be, yet prayerfully
writ — as a farewell might be. It will make you a poet
to the lady, and anon is certain to bring you gracious
word."

The good monk looked at me, and smiled as if encouraging young love, and smiled more when my face burned red.

"Go with God, my son," he said in kindness, "it is the spring of the year with you."

I took the letter and went my way after slipping a gold piece into his warm hand. It was a comfort to know a heart like that was near Tristan, even though his power could not be great when it came to the things of life and death.

There was a note to me, and it said,

Don Juanito:
I would do much more for you than to write the letter which I send, but the things I may do are not many, and I dare not plan for the days of tomorrow. This hour I have is all I call mine, and in it I write. The future hours are yet with God. May they bring you blessings.   Tristan.

Then I opened the letter the monk had said would win me a gracious word from a lady. With Don Rodrigo dead and Marco gone, all the weight of the letters of the dice was mine to bear, and I had to know. The letter showed me that after the task of the picture was accomplished, Tristan expected nothing of future respite, for this was indeed the farewell.

White Virgo:
So long as the skies of earth are before my eyes, my mind sees you poised, serene and queenly between Hydra and Leo. It is thus I will think of you when the last hour comes.

The skies grow dark where I am, and I go, perhaps, on a far journey. Words of mine may not reach to you again for a long and weary while, but in the place you know, I will be waiting. You will never quite forget to look at the circling stars of night, and it may be that a wandering butterfly will help you remember. Hold close your dreams to your saint of the white bees, and lay a rose on her shrine for me, to whom she brought the joy impossible.

Give deep thought to a man before giving your trust, for your white life is so precious a thing that you are placed on an altar in a heart here in this far land. May all the light of the "houses of dawn" enshrine you, for this means the stars of the morning, and the young sun, and the white thoughts they bring to a soul.

More I may not say, and when this prayer comes to your hand, the writer may have found the long trail to the place at your feet — the place of rest to   Alphard.

I had been past all further wonder when I looked on her face smiling its glory on the world from the shadowy chancel, and the letters belonged to that dream life of hers, as she believed, through her Saint of the Impossible. The saint had decreed me the one soul left to help keep her dream as long as might be, and I folded and sealed the letter, and had it addressed and sent with the first carrier. Nothing gave me the feeling of safety and I never knew when I might be searched, or even placed where I could not start the letter on the way to her hand. Also I did not want the heartache of seeing again a hopeless man's farewell, and whatever the future might bring to Tristan, I knew I should never be able to see him as I saw other men. Whether heretic, or true son of the true faith, I should only see the painter of her wonderful face, the finder of the key to her wonderful dreams.

And then, having fought out my own battle with my boyish self, in spite of my own sorrows, and having made the letter safe, there was little to do but see him as I might, either within the prison or on the street

in the regular round of the penitents led to mass with
neck in halter, and the robe of shame. It was a sorrowful thing at best, yet he ever walked with head in
the air and eyes looking above and beyond the faces
of the street.

A week after the sending of the letter I saw him thus,
but his face was bitter and hard as he ranged his eyes
over the crowd until he saw me, then there was the
slight lifting of the chin, and the old look of command
in the eye. I knew nothing of what it boded, yet I
saw he was still human enough for anger, and that he
commanded me to come to him.

I went, early as might be, the next morning, and he
gazed at me in hard question and reproof.

"You have known it ever since that night," he said
bitterly. Then I knew he meant Marco and Anita.

"And I risked my life for a De Ordoño for that!"
and he laughed shortly. "Does he forget my promise?
I told him if he touched that child, I would trail him till
he died or I did. Does he hold my word so light a
thing?"

"But, Tristan, within these walls what can you do?
What but sorrow could the telling bring you? So I
kept silent."

"No added breach of their rules can add to the lesson they mean to make of me here when the time
comes," he said grimly. "Though I followed him
to death, they can only kill me once for all, and that
they will do in their own way some morning of holiday.
Juanito, if a change should come to me — and any
change means death whether soon or late — go you
back to Spain, and remember your blood kindred to

Don Payo if you have need of a friend. Take this to your heart and remember."

"Tristan," I said, and my heart was sick and shaking within me, "Tristan, have you heard, then, aught of your sentence?"

"Nay," he said, "it is only that I have sentenced myself for a task to be done if chance offers. Be safe, Juanito, go you back to Spain, and comfort as best you may the exalted maid whose name we do not speak."

I went back to Luiza, and told her Tristan knew, and was bitter, and said strange things I could not understand. And in trying to understand, I fretted myself into a fever of illness that night, and had two days of nursing and medicines ere I was on the street again, and then it was to see in the plaza and before the palace a gathering of people to give greeting to the reverent mother of the Dominican nuns who was to be the guest of the viceroy, together with others of her sisters. The viceregal carriage had gone with an escort to meet them at the borders of the city, and the superiors of other convents were already invited to the palace. Altogether there was an impressive group of ecclesiastics gathered there, and with Ernesto Galvez I stood at one side of the portal using my eyes as a boy will at any new pageant.

Don Tomas himself came there and bent the knee to religion as shown in the person of the mother superior, and led her graciously through the line of ladies to the seat of honor between himself and the archbishop. Following came the other sisters in their white robes of the pure in heart, and as one weary woman looked like another to me, I was turning away, feeling of no use, when from the carriage of the viceroy there came a high sweet call like that of a happy bird,

" Juanito! O Juanito!"

Eyes turned to me ere I could locate the voice, and then through the group she came running, with her hands outstretched and all her face alight.

" Juanito! I have come — I have crossed the seas to come! I am really here, Juanito!"

Gilberto — the lank cub — grinned at the dismay in my face, and that brought me to my wits.

I took her two hands, and kissed them and bowed in my best manner, and presented Don Eduardo.

" My cousin, the Doña Encarnacian, Marquesa de Llorente y Rivera," I said, and had my own revenge to see plumes sweep the tiles as she passed.

She looked all of sweet girlhood in the soft folds of the novice garb, yet she bent graciously as a young queen before the viceroy, and kissed with humility the ring of the archbishop.

There was more than the usual flutter over a pretty maid as the mother superior took her hand with a little smile of humor, and glanced at the viceroy.

" Here is a very worldly young mocking bird in the raiment of a modest wren," she said. " Our Doña Encarnacian would go adventuring, and had our protection to your court, Your Excellency."

" The court is honored. The apartments of Don Payo have had no occupant since his going, and are at disposal of his kinswoman."

While Doña Perfecta was introduced, I made bold to speak aside to Don Eduardo, asking that time for consultation should be allowed, for it might be that my

cousin would prefer not to be of the gay palace guests
when she heard of Don Rodrigo, and — of other things.
The convent might prove a more restful retreat.

Don Eduardo smiled as he watched her, all alive with
interest in new scenes and new people.

"Her excellencia does not give appearance of a seeker of rest," he observed. "She flashes color not to be
quelled by all the nun's robe."

Which was the truth. She was seated by the viceroy,
who warmed wonderfully to this sparkling masquerader.
Doña Perfecta joined them, and regarded Sancha curiously. Her gay freedom, which was yet not boldness,
made her difficult for the older woman to understand.

"Our men of Mexico will bless the reverend mother
for sheltering you on the journey, Marquesa," she said.
"Spanish brides are still so rare that our men speak
for wives soon as a girl child is christened."

"That is why I came!" confessed Sancha, smiling.

"Your pardon! You came because brides were
scarce?"

"Not that, quite," and Sancha blushed, and looked at
me — the only wretched devil-driven soul in all the gay
group — "I came because I was spoken for in childhood, and the man is here, Your Excellency."

"May I ask his name that I may add to your happiness by sending for him?" asked Don Tomas. With
an arch glance at me, she whispered Marco's name to
the viceroy.

His face changed, and he lowered his eyes as he
bowed.

"I regret I may not serve you on the instant as I
could wish," he said, "but Don Marco de Ordoño has

undertaken an expedition for the state into the deserts of the north. It is a journey of sixty days."

"I know it is far — his letter told me that — but sixty days more is not much when I have crossed the seas to follow."

"His letter?" I muttered, and got near enough to touch her arm, my wits all but gone in the sudden silence around her, "what letter?"

"One meeting me at Vera Cruz," she said eagerly. "Think of it, Juanito! I might have missed that letter if it had not been for the ship captain who knew I hoped for one. He brought it to me at the convent where we nursed Mother Maria Ynez. So I knew Marco was going — but I did not know where."

Then everyone began talking at once, and the viceroy kindly turned to speak to the Mother Ynez and left me to draw Sancha away to a window overlooking the plaza.

"Is it not wonderful?" she whispered, pressing my hand in excess of joy. "What difference can a little sixty days make after I am actually here? Tell all you know of him, Juanito, for I am not the girl you left in Spain — his letters have made all the world a different place."

"His letter has not, perhaps, told you the sad thing we have had to meet," I said, and then I told her of the death of Don Rodrigo, and that I alone was now in Mexico to do her will since Marco had gone — as the viceroy informed her — on an expedition for the state.

"Poor Don Rodrigo!" she murmured, "what a trial I was to him — and what a lecture I was prepared for! His soul to God — for he was a good and kind man."

Then after a bit of silence while my mind was in a whirl, she asked softly, " Tell me truly, Juanito — is it a journey of great danger on which he is sent."

" Who? " I asked stupidly.

" Marco. I feel sure it is so. His letter fills me with strange fears for him — every day was a week down there at Vera Cruz by the sea. I would have ridden alone to come, but the nuns were horrified, so I had to wait for them. But the letter of farewell for the far journey makes for me a heartache. He is very lonely — is he not, Juanito? "

" How can I know? " I asked, and she smiled and sighed.

"No, you cannot know, Juanito. No one can know but me, and for that reason is he more mine than we ever could have thought."

The reverend mother elected to remain at the palace while rooms were being arranged at convents, also she elected to keep Sancha with her. It was no pleasure for me to see her there, where Doña Perfecta held a suddenly discreet sway. Yet, since it was so decided, I could put forth no objection that she remained under the charge of Mother Maria Ynez, Countess de Monde-jar, for whom the palace became as a great reception hall for ecclesiastics of note. Mother Maria Ynez promised to be a person of importance in mission work and, as sister of a cardinal, was a social acquisition of value to any establishment.

The viceroy sent for me, and was in all things gracious. Mine was to be the pleasant task of page or guardian of the two noble visitors. My relationship to the Marquesa de Llorente y Rivera made me the most fitting and agreeable person to arrange their drives, and learn their wishes. Also I was to take up my old lodgings in the palace as in the days of Don Payo. To house in the cottage of a soldier of the guard was scarce in keeping with my importance.

When this had been concluded, he made excuse to send Don Eduardo from the audience, and smiled at me shrewdly.

"Now tell me of this brilliant and lovely cousin. It is true that the marriage is arranged?"

"So true that my wits are near gone at the shock of her coming at this most unhappy time!"

He had a bit of serene amusement at my dismay, and serene vanity enough to cope with it.

"Surely the courtiers of Mexico can serve to entertain her after a fashion until the wanderer can be brought back," he suggested.

"But who is to bring him?"

"There will be no difficulty in that. I can send a courier."

I knew he could — but would he? Lovely maids of degree were not so plentiful; Don Tomas had a record for gallantry, and a long waiting in the city might bring Sancha knowledge making her less eager for that one stray. So I voiced my doubt as to whether she would be content to wait; she was alive for an adventure, and had even spoken of going north to Sonora where a convent was to be established by Mother Maria Ynez — or by the money she donated to the task. Four nuns were to go, and already Sancha was studying maps and reckoning how short a way — on paper — the trail looked from Sonora to Sante Fe on the Rio Bravo.

"Let us hope she will be content with adventures in safer places," he said easily; "there are many novel things to be seen here in Mexico."

When I told Sancha this, she laughed. To her there was only one thing worth her while in all the world — and she meant to find it.

"By all means let the viceroy send courier," she said. "But why may I not cross the lands, and be of aid to the nuns, and meet Marco half way on his return? I am helping with the cost of this new convent. Why may I not, in courtesy, ride with them, and learn what other needs they may have?"

I saw that she was indeed a different maid from the one I had left in Spain. She was alert to every point in favor of the thing she meant to do; added to which, she had the good will of the mother superior. If the child wished to serve God by such labor, the nuns united in wishing that she make the journey with them rather than wait idly through the long months until the return of her betrothed.

What I could, I said, but she only took my face in her two hands, and laughed at me.

"Not only will I go when the train is ready, but you shall go with me as escort," she decided. "Think of it, Juanito, to ride through the forests together day after day, and see the wonders of it — the birds, the butterflies, the stars at night —"

"With the addition of snakes and other creeping things," I added, "and who knows what prowling savages to thieve each thing left unguarded."

"All the more will I need you, Juanito. We will ride north as two knights protecting the holy women on their mission, and you shall tell me all the wondrous things of him we are riding to find."

The wondrous things I most wished to tell of him grew silent on my lips as I saw her joy in the thought of him.

"You have spoke scarce two words of him since I came," she pouted, "yet you lived near him all these months, and heard him discourse. He has grown so very wonderfully wise, Juanito."

I said nothing to this — of what use was it when I saw that light in her eyes?

"Perhaps he does not talk to you as he writes me," she went on, a bit more shyly, as the little dimples deepened in her cheeks. "His letters to me are so wonderful — they drew my heart ahead of the ship all the journey."

She touched her bosom where I knew the letters lay. Though she had changed her garb of the nun's robe and wore silk of a sapphire blue, I knew that in all her magnificence her most precious jewels were the words written and hidden under her laces — the words decided by the toss of the dice!

I wanted to kneel at her feet and tell her she was cheated — that there was no honesty in anyone anywhere — and that the safer thing was to don again the nun's robe, and wear it forever.

"Little cousin," I said, "men are sometimes one thing on paper, and another thing in real life. If — If Marco should not prove what you think? Men are not saints, you know, and their rovings take them in strange places."

"I know," she said softly, "but he is very lonely in

the strange places; his heart tells that loneliness to my
heart, though no one else in all the world might think
it. Doña Mercedes says he is handsomer all the time,
and of course he is grand favorite — yet deep in his
heart he is the most lonely of men — and that is why
I am here."

"But he may be in a fury with me if I let you go into
the wilderness," I protested weakly, and she laughed
and caught my hand.

"Look at me, Juanito!" she said. "If you had been
writing your very heart out to me, and you suddenly
turned a corner and found me in your arms, could you
have anger with any soul on earth who helped me on
my way to you?"

"But I am not Marco," I said, and looked away rather
than at her as she commanded. It was quite true — no
man but must have been glad of her. Eyes turned her
way at every chance, and I saw more than one person
look at her in puzzled wonder, while I grew hot and
cold with fear because of the question in their minds.

Doña Mercedes voiced it when she said, "I have never
been in Seville, señorita, yet you made me feel that I
had seen you in a dream — somewhere. I thought it
was the robe of the novice which you wore — but it is
not. It is very puzzling — almost I place you, and then
you smile, or turn your head, and I lose you again."

I breathed more freely, for Sancha was smiling or
turning her head most of the time, and it was true that
only with her face in repose, and the eyes looking
straight out over the world, did she have likeness to
the Virgin of the Fawn in the chancel of San Carlos.

It was as Tristan had said — she had grown different.

The mouth was no longer wistful, but tremulous with the happiness of her heart. The face had more color, and only the eyes of velvet softness were the same — yet out of all the world, who but Tristan and I could be sure? The reflected light from the blue silk of the dress made even her eyes look different. So I praised the dress, and urged that she wear such color always.

"That may not be possible on the trail," she said, "for I shall wear, as I wore in coming, the dress of a novice. You know I made promise that I would wed or turn nun."

She laughed at the past promise, made in a temper, and then was led away by Ernesto Galvez to see some birds of wondrous hues brought up from the south.

"What if she knew what we could all tell her?" asked Doña Mercedes. "Are we friends that we do not?"

"It will all come right," said Don Eduardo. "The viceroy will send a courier. But a word would be wise in Don Marco's ear — when he finds his bride he would best wed as soon as may be, and take first ship for Spain. He is not high in favor these days except for courtesy to Doña Encarnacian."

"Think you he can wed, and take ship, and leave her none the wiser of his love days in Mexico?"

"Why not, if his friends are loyal?" asked Doña Perfecta, and at that moment Don Tomas halted outside the window, looking after Sancha in the garden below.

"Loyalty to Don Marco is a poor investment of either head or heart," said Doña Mercedes. "See what Don Tristan got for his loyalty — I shudder to think what would happen if he were free."

"It would make useless the journey of the Marquesa de Llorente y Rivera," observed Don Eduardo, "for she would have no gay gallant for the wedding day. Tristan would kill him like a dog. I hear he vowed it."

Doña Mercedes laughed. "Of murders I do not approve," she said lightly, "yet in my heart I feel as if it would be for the happiness of Doña Sancha if the viceroy should select Tristan as courier to the north."

"For her happiness," echoed Don Eduardo in horror, "when the girl is mad with love for him?"

"If he were sent to heaven she would keep on loving him — which is more than a sane woman could do who had to live with him," she retorted. "It is not Marco de Ordoño she loves — it is the man he pretends in his letters to be, and I maintain that a courier like Tristan would be the safe one to send. It would end all this tangle for a sweet and honest maid."

"What unchristian hate you have for him," said Doña Perfecta reprovingly.

"Yes — I think I have," confessed Doña Mercedes. "He is too pretty for a man — a sheltered, luxurious cat! But I will say a rosary in penance for my jealous dislike of his complexion;" and with a hard look at Doña Perfecta, she passed out the sala, and went to join Sancha and Ernesto in the garden.

"I am glad, my angel, that you inherit none of the waspish tongue of your relative," said Don Eduardo, and Doña Perfecta slipped her hand in his, and looked up in his face with the smile of an angel.

"Dear Mercedes, I am sure, will grow to have more charity," she said hopefully. "I will say a prayer for her."

Then they also passed out, and I followed after without turning my head. Yet I knew the viceroy still stood there by the window, and that he had heard the heartless suggestion as to the choice of a courier. Why had he not betrayed it, or as usual, joined the little group? Was some one member of it in ill favor at court? Since the coming of Sancha, he had been even more gracious than was his wont in regard to plans and pleasures for the ladies of the household. I walked away thinking of this, and of a remark of Gilberto that a new beauty at court took five years from the age of Don Tomas.

CHAPTER XI

THE PASSING OF THE PENITENTS

IN those two days of joy and dismay at her coming, I had seen naught of Tristan, and the wish of Sancha that I ride up into Sonora with her filled me with dread of what might chance while I was away. I dared not try to see him more often than was discreet, yet it was a comfort, so long as they let him live, that I might remain near enough for slight service.

On the third morning I strove to see him but was reminded by Fray Bernardino that it was the day of an execution of a witch, and all the accused were led to mass and to witness. That day, as I knew, no visitors were permitted. I returned to the palace little comforted at his respite, for I felt it a duty to tell him she was here — yet how could I? And I felt also the duty to keep her from the *quemadora* — many pious souls regularly witnessed the horrors there as a matter of discipline to their own souls.

But Sancha had made plans equally troublous. She was waiting for me in the garden, bent on being taken to San Carlos, where her letters had been addressed. I told her all I could to convince her that San Carlos was nothing remarkable, merely an old monastery, and an old chapel, and a century-old inn beside it, where the names of many notables were written on the plastered walls. But she had heard of the giant rose tree by the monastery, and that there was some picture of a late miracle there — all the nuns were talking of it, so, for pious reasons, it was a good place to go for prayer — Mother Maria Ynez was going.

Sick with dread, I walked beside her. The rose tree was in bloom by the monastery wall, and shed its petals over the stone benches and over the age-weathered table where the dice of the letters had been tossed. The inn across the little arcade was in holiday dress, and its patron saint, with the crown of feathers and dyed cotton, was placed in the niche outside the door, in honor of the visit of the reverend mother and her flock.

It was a morning with the smile of God on it in beauty, and the chatter of Sancha made music bittersweet to me — the odor of roses to this day brings it all back.

Fray Felipe walked with Mother Maria Ynez, and Don Eduardo on the other side, and Sancha and I behind all the visiting nuns, and their convent guides. Like a flock of doves in white robes they crossed the plaza, placid in their pious intent.

They entered the chapel, while I grew suddenly alive to the historic importance of the ancient inn where Don Rodrigo had lived, and been loved by the keeper, and had eaten his breakfasts under the rose tree, also I showed Sancha the names of famous soldiers and a viceroy or two whose rubricas made the old inn of San Carlos well known as the monastery itself.

"And he also came here — Marco?" she asked, for all her knowledge of Mexico began and ended with the thought of him.

" Yes, of course he came here, everyone does," I said;
" the cook and the wine are good."

" And perhaps sat here at this same table? " she said,
and slipped into the stone carven bench under the rose
tree.

" Yes he did," I agreed, and felt she should be told
that it was there, where her blue silks rustled, that he
had sat to toss the dice by which the other man was
given the way to her heart. I wanted to say it, but was
dumb before the radiance of her face.

" I am glad — glad that you brought me here," she
murmured, and sighed as she touched a drooping rose
over her head. " I feel closer to him here than in the
palace — closer to the thoughts in the letters he sent.
And he sat here — in this same place — perhaps read
here the letters I wrote! It is sweet of you, Juanito,
to bring me, for I feel close to him in this place."

Then Doña Mercedes appeared from the chapel door,
as if looking for laggards from prayer, and Sancha arose,
and smoothed her gown, and plucked white roses, as
she said, to remember the first place where she had
found him in Mexico.

I was dumb as a fish while I listened, and walked
beside her. At the chapel door I doffed my hat, but
kept beside her instead of following, and as we entered
the shadows of the portal, I slipped my hand into hers.

Without lifting my eyes from the tiles, I yet saw her
face turn to me in inquiry, convulsively my hand closed
on hers as I drew her to kneel beside me. I sank down
because my legs had all they could do to bear me, and
her silks rustled beside me, and then —

I heard the quick gasp, the choke in her throat, and

I coughed to hide it. But the cough could not hide also the fact that only one person in all the chapel was not kneeling in prayer, and it was Sancha.

The time seemed endless while she stood there, staring over the bent heads of the others. Then, almost by force, I drew her down beside me, where she half crouched, looking at me.

Heaven knows what of accusation was in her eyes — it might have been my own hand painted it, so hard was her gaze. She said no prayer there, only stared first at the picture, and then at me.

The nuns arose, and passed out into the sunshine, and the others followed, yet still she crouched there.

"Come," I said, "they will wonder, and you are saying no prayer."

"Why should I pray to an image of earth?" she asked, and rose to her feet. "Who did it, Juanito — who?"

"It is the miracle picture done by the hand of a man accused of heresy," I answered; "some say it was done by influence of demons — and others that a devout monk did the work. No one knows."

"They should know," she said coldly. "Has Mexico so many men who can paint like Murillo? That *vaporoso* feeling is his very own and — and — Juanito, if that is the miracle picture, how can I go out into the light facing all the people?"

She was trembling, and clung to me, half frightened as she faced that wondrous serene figure on the very top of the world.

"And Nanita, too!" she whispered, "I loved her so! Did I ever look like that? It is a saint who is also a child — I was never a saint, Juanito. Take me out and away from the others. I feel as if I am under some enchantment. I am frightened — take me away!"

I did so, walking with her out the side door and around again to the table under the rose tree.

"Is it enchantment?" she demanded. "What have I done that this should frighten me here? It is like raising the dead — for that girl is not I, yet once was. What have I done?"

She sat trembling, and tears were in her eyes.

"You have done nothing but let someone look on you some fair past day, and he did not forget — none of us forget, Sancha," I said.

"Juanito, do you know who it was?"

"No one saw the work or the worker — it is a mystery. The picture was painted behind locked doors. Only the officers of the Inquisition could tell what you want to know, and that, Sancha, is what we dare not strive to learn. It is better that we forget that the girl ever stood there as we once saw her — nothing is left of that memory but the Virgin of the Fawn."

"The picture is a glorified thing — it is more beautiful than any human maid could be — but even the sandals on the bare feet, Juanito — the sandals were of your making!"

"I know," I said, "but we must forget."

She sat a long time, her elbows on the table, and her face hidden by her hands.

"The Virgin," she said at last in a whisper — "Virgo!"

Then she slipped from her bodice the letters and read them one by one.

"Virgo," she repeated — "against the sky! Juanito — you do know — it is Marco!"

"Marco!" and at this last mad bestowal of love on him, I was near to losing my last trace of wit. "How could it be Marco? When did Marco ever learn to paint holy things?"

"O Juanito, he is wonderful, and you never have seen it!" she breathed softly. "When did he learn the wonderful things of his letters to me? The painting is no more wonderful to me than that! And here he tells me, 'I saw you once on the convent hill above the olive trees, standing clear against the sky with the white doves about you. You were Virgo to me — white and serene.' Juanito, that is what he painted! I did stand there with the fawn — and the doves did circle above us — and in his heart he glorified it all until that picture is on the altar, and his words are here for my heart! That is why there is mystery over the painting — he has done it in secret, and had the help of the priests to hide it. *That* is the work of a heretic? O cousin mine: only a true believer could have painted the soul of the Virgin into a little barefoot maid on the hill!"

Her eager words fell over each other in her great joy of discovery, and I, who could have laughed aloud, or cursed at the way all things worked together to exalt him — I could see only one gleam of safety in her thought.

"Since you think this, you must see that if he did the picture, he has striven to hide it in secrecy for reasons of his own. Ours is the task to help him keep the secret. The man who painted it did not dream that your eyes would ever look on it here in Mexico."

"That is true," she said, "it is his secret — but, O Juan! He has a genius greater than we could dream; all those silent years he has been painting secretly, and we never knew! Do you wonder that I followed him? No, I followed my heart that followed him! I did not know how he was great, yet he made me feel he was great." Then after a silence she added, "His last letter — the dear, sad, last letter — told me I was enshrined on an altar here — but how could I ever think how wonderfully?"

Tears were in her eyes, but when I made attempt to comfort her, she smiled.

"My weeping is for very joy, Juanito, yet it is also in humbleness. What am I, that he should place me so high in his heart?"

I dared not try to answer that, and she continued to discourse on the greatness of Marco until I all but lost control of my tongue, and arose to follow the nuns. She, however, slipped her hand into my arm.

"I can go in and pray now," she said, "I could not before — I was too frightened. But now we will pray together for his safety, and not again must you urge me to remain here in waiting. I must follow."

I knelt, but my prayers that day were far from clear. I did, however, thank my patron saint fervently for any excuse to prevent further question of the painting.

Sancha stood before it, her hands clasped over her breast where the letters lay. "O Love most wonderful," she whispered, "my Saint of the Impossible will find the way to you!"

Temptations came to me there — yet I held my tongue. My promise to Tristan overshadowed me — my promise to keep the secret until he himself should tell her. How wild and far away that chance seemed at that time, yet here she was before his work, worshiping the thought of it. And, scarce the flight of an arrow away, he waited beyond stone walls the sentence of death — waited the torture which all predicted would be needed to subdue his spirit ere it was sent to God.

"Come away," I said and took her hand. "You are right, Sancha; it may be that even the wilderness is a better place. No mysteries are there to overcome a soul. I will go with you when you go."

She sighed happily, and pressed my hand.

"It is the most wonderful day I have lived," she said. "His letters cleared my path to it. And some day — some happy day when we are together — we will build a shrine to Santa Rita, who has made the impossible come to be."

I went back with her, thinking hard as to how I could get away alone, and see Tristan in the morning. Sancha walked as on air and said little, her face illuminated by the revelation of the day.

There was much discourse among the nuns concerning the Virgin on the altar. Mother Maria Ynez spoke of the marvel of the picture, and compared it to certain work of Murillo, wondering much as to the training of the man who did it. From Don Eduardo she heard the opinion of many that it was the work of a pious monk whose identity was hidden.

I drew Sancha away lest the name of Tristan be mentioned — not yet had it chanced to fall on her ears. "The heretic" or "the apostate painter" had served Don Eduardo with the nuns.

Doña Mercedes slipped down beside me in the window of the sala, and her friendly eyes were keen.

"It is not so easy to make hourly a hero of Marco for the pleasure of a lady — is it, Don Juan?" she asked. "You look dead with the weariness of the task."

"Which is ingratitude in any man," I observed. "One should be willing to make a hero of the devil, if by that he could win so sweet a maid for company."

"You are too gallant for a cousin!" she said. "But I warn you, take a leaf out of Don Eduardo's book when your heretic friends are in question. Did you mark how little he knows now of that painter? not even the name! Who would think that so short a time is gone since Tristan had the open door here as had almost no other? And one would think that painting of Perfecta had been done ages ago and forgotten — so little are they inclined to mention his name in connection."

"They are very fickle — for he is no different as a man."

"It is the way with courts, and you are out of fashion," she retorted. "But truly, Don Juan, it would be better if you did go north, and let people here forget that you are ever at the call of Tristan."

"Who says it?"

"No one, in words. But take a leaf from Don Eduardo — he is preparing wisely for a storm if one breaks when a ship comes back from Spain. Go north in good company, since you can do him no good by a stay outside his prison walls."

"At least I can know he eats good food."

"He shall have the food — even when you are gone," she said kindly. "I do not speak in idleness when I urge you. The child is alone in Mexico, with her head full of false dreams of that pretty gallant. Who knows how she may meet him in the wilderness, and learn the truth?"

"That meeting is the thing I fear," I confessed, "and I am already of a mind to go — and hasten the going."

While we talked there, others entered the sala, and there was gaiety and soft laughter. Don Tomas was making a jest of Sancha's determination to wear a nun's robe on the journey, and he gave names of gentlemen who had suddenly grown devout and desired above all things to do guard service for the nuns into the northern wilderness.

Then, through the laughter and raillery, we in the window heard voices intoning a dolorous chant coming nearer and nearer along the street. Doña Mercedes looked at me and sighed.

"God find peace for their souls!" she said, and crossed herself, and then I knew it was the return to prison of the heretics who had been led to prayers and to witness an execution at the *quemadora*.

In the plaza below, people moved silently in groups to the place where the penitents would pass; some fell on their knees, and others took up the hymn as the flare of the candles of the "reconciled" came nearer, while the unreconciled carried green candles without light. That saddest music came up to us, and the gay jests were silenced by the shuffling of the many feet and the tramp of the guard.

"How terrible!" said Mother Maria Ynez, as she looked down upon them. "To this new land one could have hoped that no heretics would be allowed to take

The Recognition.

ship. The native pagans are in darkness until we come to them — and that is natural. But those unregenerate are against nature, and against God."

I could have wished to draw Sancha back from the doleful sight, but Doña Perfecta made place for her on the balcony, and together they looked down, in their shimmering silks and their glitter of jewels, upon the men and women who wore for their faith the robes of shame.

"God enlighten them!" said Sancha, and made the sign of the cross. In doing so she let fall a white rose as she leaned over the balcony. It fell, touching the bent shoulders of an old man, who saw it not, but it caused the penitent with unlit candle who followed him to lift his eyes to the window above.

Then there was a gasp as of fear from Doña Perfecta as she shrank back, for the candle of the penitent was let fall, and he stared, with a strange look in his eyes, directly up at her balcony.

It lasted but an instant, and his face, as he passed on, was not so clearly outlined as the others with candles lit. The guards closed up a space at the mishap, but the procession did not halt — and the twinkling lights went on down the plaza, and the sorrowful chant came back to us long after all the people of the street had risen from their knees, crossed themselves, and gone their way.

"How terrible were his eyes — he looked murder!" breathed Doña Perfecta nervously. "God send their ropes are strong to bind."

"Why should he do so?" asked Sancha, marveling at her terror, "who is he?"

"He is the son of a priest, and accused of heresy," I said before others could speak. "It is not a matter for the telling of maids."

The reverend mother nodded her approval to me; she plainly decided I was discreet and careful for my years. Sancha, at that hint, asked no more of the matter. She had scarcely seen the man who had startled Doña Perfecta with his stare. Except to add a prayer for them, Sancha thought little of those who had put themselves outside the grace of God. All her thoughts were for the wonderful lover for whom she had crossed the seas.

CHAPTER XII

THE LOVE TRAIL

THAT night was the night Tristan escaped to the hills!

There was to me a curious mystery about it for the reason that little outcry was made and there was little to be learned of it. Don Eduardo was plainly distressed, but the viceroy put it by as a slight matter.

"When the state or the Inquisition have need of him, he will not be hard to trace," he remarked. "Who knows that it is not another trap of the Holy Brotherhood to learn the friends who would shelter him?"

This was a natural thought. Yet if it were the true one, would he voice it in my presence, when, out of all the town, I was the one who had asked privilege of providing for his needs?

However placid the viceroy or the Brotherhood, it was far different with Doña Perfecta. The eyes of Tristan had frightened her as they glared up at the balcony; Tristan should either be pardoned and exiled that he have no animosity or revenges — else he should be guarded so close that none should get sight of him.

"That is a new thought — the thought of a pardon for him," said his excellency, the viceroy — "and you, Doña Perfecta, are the first to speak of it. One instant you are frightened of him — and the next you speak of pardon. Will you explain, Doña Perfecta?"

She saw she was trapped by her own fears, and said she dreaded what might chance if he crossed the trail of Marco and pretty Anita, and no one wanted a scandal now that the Marquesa de Llorente y Rivera was a guest at the palace. No one could guess what Tristan would attempt if free and desperate; his stare up at the balcony had been strange, and, she thought, threatening. It might be that even the highest could be in danger — and some plot against the viceroy —

But she blundered, and floundered, as the viceroy smiled at her.

"I am not doubling my guard," he said. "I can recall no grievance he has against me; yet if you know of aught —"

"I know his grievance against Marco de Ordoño and I fear a scandal for your guests," she said. "The reverend mother might not approve some of the deceptions we have all tried to make. If that heretic escapes your soldiery and finds De Ordoño far in some wilderness, it would be a simple matter, but if their meeting should be here under your windows Your Excellency would have difficult problems to face."

"Yes," he said.

Something in the way he said it made her turn sharply and look at him in silence, then her eyes narrowed in a strange smile.

"I see," she said — "I see! The game does grow."

Then she laughed shortly and walked to the window looking down into the court.

"The Marquesa de Llorente y Rivera goes with the

nuns and is very much in love, Your Excellency," she observed. " It is not worth risking too much in making plans for her, she is very capable of making her own plans — ask Don Juan here. Also, Tristan is a dangerous tool for any one to use — even to give so lovely a lady fair freedom from a ranging lover."

I did not understand this, but I could see that for some reason she was angry, and that the viceroy was half amused — and yet watchful.

" Then it is not for a reason personal that you advocate stronger walls of exile? "

" Personal? " and she seemed to take on an inch of height in her disdain — " if it was another than Your Excellency who asked that — "

" Let me show you something," he said, still smiling, and they walked into the other apartment where the portrait of Doña Perfecta hung. I could not hear what they said, but he pointed to the little figurine of the Mexican princess. I could see her puzzled amaze, then heard a sharp cry.

" No! He could not dare."

" Is there anything you can think of that he does not dare? " asked Don Tomas, as they walked back together. " Do you still ask pardon and exile for him? "

" No," she said very coldly. " I have asked nothing for him. I only asked you to be cautious for your own sake. Turn loose the dogs or the Indian trailers on his track and hunt him as you would hunt a brute in the jungle."

" The Indians would only trail him to warn him," said Don Tomas; " he has a certain friendship with the tribes, but every port will be watched, and there will

be only one trail open to him — we know what that
trail is, and if ever we want him, we can find him there."

" Then kill him there," she said bitterly; " never again
let him walk the streets, or look on me."

Their quarrel seemed half a jealous one on either
side, and a final adjustment through her sudden concen-
trated hate of Tristan. I did not understand it, but
I saw Doña Perfecta hold her head high in pride until
she passed from the range of Don Tomas, and later I
learned from Doña Mercedes that Perfecta had a strange
attack of rage by which she was made ill and was
locked in her room, weeping, and refusing to see any
one but Fray Bernardino, and she had sent for him.

For the first time I gave careful note to the portrait
of Doña Perfecta, and on the base of the little statue,
I spelled out the letters " Hija de Axiakatzin." The
daughter of Axiakatzin did not look a matter of importance, and the letters were so small that few eyes
would see it was not an Indian attempt at decoration
— yet I knew that no other thing but that statue had
caused the fit of sick rage.

I sought out Ernesto Galvez who had been long in
Mexico, and had ranged with Tristan.

" Who was Axiakatzin? " I asked.

" A king in Mexico."

" And who was his daughter? "

He smiled at that, for the daughters of kings are
many.

" But a daughter of his famous enough to have her
statue preserved to this day? " I persisted.

" I only heard of one — she was not famous — she
was infamous — the princess of a hundred lovers."

"That is the one — the princess for whom men died."

"They did indeed — and quickly," he said. "Her old favorites were secretly murdered to make way for new lovers. She was wife to a king, but she was put to death on the shrine of adulterers, and her family was disgraced. She was a very remarkable lady."

"Fortunately we have none like that today," I observed.

"None of them have the same power today — else — who knows?" he said, and laughed. "Why are you searching for word of her? Do you take up records of these pagan kings and gods where Tristan laid them down?"

"God forbid!" I prayed. "They are not of healthy flavor to my mind."

I could see plainly now what had happened. By some chance, the name of that Mexican king had come to the ears of Don Tomas, and his sharp eyes told him the rest. If he had ever, for a moment, felt a jealous mistrust of Tristan, it was cleared away by that statue, and he had used it now to check her remarks as to his interest in the latest favorite at the viceregal court — Sancha, Marquesa de Llorente y Rivera.

I saw that in wisdom the one thing for peace was to urge that northern journey soon as might be. The jealousy of a younger face might prove Doña Perfecta a maker of troubles for all of us.

I saw Fray Bernardino that day go into the sala where the portrait was hung and bolt the door, and in the morning I was not surprised to find red roses in the hand there, and no trace of the pagan statue left to cause comment.

"I like it better thus," said Doña Perfecta in my hearing. "Pagan and infidel things should not be put in the portrait of a true believer. Fray Felipe is also of a mind to have the fawn painted out of that Virgin of the altar."

"But the pretty fawn is not a pagan," I ventured.

"Animals have ere this been brought to trial by the church," she said coldly, "devils are known to possess them at times. Fray Felipe is making search to learn if such thing as a forest creature should be at the feet of Our Lady."

"The doves are over her head — they also are wild," I said.

"That is a different matter," she stated, "doves are permitted by the church."

I perceived that my opinions were not in high favor, and sought the reverend mother and Sancha to say that the arrangements for the pilgrimage north were well under way, and that the guard who had come with them from La Puebla de los Angeles was yet in the town and begged to continue as servants on the trail.

Mother Maria Ynez approved of this, for the reason that so many offers came from the town men that it was a task to make choice; but by holding the old guard it would be simple; also, Sister Maria Clemente, who was to be superior, already had confidence in the Pueblo men and they were not as strangers.

My own decision would have been different, for the men could know well the road to Mexico, yet were men of the lowlands, and might know little the life to the north.

But in this, and other matters, my opinion was not

asked. I was but the boy at court who chanced to be Sancha's cousin, and that most headstrong maid must have me ride beside her.

In plain truth I had to be content to ride behind her for the first few leagues, since His Excellency, Don Tomas, who chose to make a holiday of it, rode, as he often did, with his guard into the plantations of the valley, and this time Sister Maria Clemente and Sancha were taken in his own carriage while their horses were led by a guard. Mother Maria Ynez gave them her blessing, and Doña Perfecta smiled them her farewells, and asked many questions as to provisions for their comfort, while Doña Mercedes came forward with sweet blossoms for Sancha.

"That you may ride to peace, Excellencia!" she said kindly. But Sancha kissed her cheek, and smelled the fragrance of the blossoms, and laughed.

"I will find more than peace!" she said frankly, "for my heart is ahead of me on the road, and I ride to happiness."

Thus smiling, radiant-eyed, and sure of joy waiting for her at some turn in the love trail, she rode north, and the eyes of Mexico, either jealous or friendly, never looked upon her face again.

At the far boundary of a valley plantation, Don Tomas himself lifted her to the saddle with some remarks of gallantry, and assurances of service which Sancha acknowledged as lightly as a child. She rode into Mexico and out of it with no knowledge that the middle aged dignitary was caught in the snare of her smile, and that Doña Perfecta had her own content at the departure.

But to Sancha the adventure had not rightly begun until the viceroy's carriage had disappeared in the fringe of a palm avenue. Then she laughed, clapped her hands, and petted the horse that was to be her companion on the long trail.

I rode beside her into the new life, and we repeated tales of the crusaders, and dreamed that our pilgrimage was of equal importance, and in the pure high air of Mexico felt that we were above the world of mundane things.

For many days we rested at some plantation or hacienda or mission church on the way. Then, after a breakfast at early dawn, a call to prayer by Fray José Moreno, the loading of the beasts, we took the trail with good wishes of our hosts, who often accompanied us a full day on a journey, and more than one addition was made to our cavalcade by persons of degree who wished to journey to Guadalajara under our guard.

Thus the days were never dull for Sancha, who, in the freedom of the mountains and the forests, echoed the bird songs, and learned strange things from the new land where the atmosphere, pure and luminous, had its own charm, and each day was a golden promise taking her nearer to Marco.

At Guadalajara there was a week of rest and entertainment ere we went into the wilder lands of the north.

These were adventurous days to me, and I strove to read the brown faces of the Indians who brought out great baskets of corn for us from their little rancherias. They were courteous in many ways, but a sad people, and I wondered by what manner Tristan and Don Fernando had found the way to their dark minds.

Sancha at times gathered the little naked children
about her and to their delight gave them beads of glass,
and they would follow after her to the great distress of
Mother Maria Clemente, who could by no means come
by cloth to clothe them all, and lamented that the smaller
ones had seldom any cover other than the shade of their
vine covered *ramadas*, or at best a coat of mud when
near an arroyo.

But Sancha had joy in them in her own way, and declared that their brown skin was a thing of beauty, and
their nakedness not a thing to offend, as could easily be
with a people of white race. Thus our Indian guide who
heard this found way to have the freshest and ripest
melons brought to the maid who laughed.

Padre José had a good word to say for her to Mother
Clemente, for of such souls — so he said — came the
good workers in the Lord's vineyard. The primitive
mind responds always to the happy heart — and the
heart of Sancha was full of a joy not to be overshadowed by trials and mishaps of the journey.

For we had mishaps of many sorts, also word discour-
aging to Mother Maria Clemente in regard to that far
northland of pagans eager for divine grace. By reports
of a lay brother who was on the way south with messages to the Franciscan convent at Queretaro, they were
vastly more eager for new arms of the Castilian in order
to fight each other. The horses had been all stolen from
a mission north of the Haqui. No maize had been
planted in the low lands of the rivers, and word had
come south for stronger guard at the few presidios of
Sonora.

All this made no proper impression on the mind of

Sancha except anxiety for Marco. She asked all the reports of the cavalcade going into New Granada, and had joy to know that it was after their passing in safety that the tribal outbreak had come between Indians of the hunting grounds of the eastern highlands and the lowland people of the rancherias.

The grave black eyes of the Indios looked at us with inquiry as these tales were repeated in various forms through the weary weeks of the journey. Some of the packers understood Castilian, and in many of the towns were the descendants of red slaves captured at the north in earlier days. The deserts of their land and poisoned arrows and foul wells had taken rich toll for the captured slaves, and to my mind their eyes had the silent question as to whether we might not add to that toll claimed by the wide ranges.

At Culiacan came the final outfitting ere we left behind all the life of cities. Beyond that we could only hope to find Indian ranches, an occasional mission with its many *visitas*, and the rare presidio with its handful of men as guard over a land half the size of Portugal.

Sancha bought strings of beads many colored, in thought for the brown children and their pagan mothers, also bright ribbands and scarlet cloth, but as it fell out, she might as well have saved herself the costly troubles.

It is ill remembering occurrences and incidents of a long trail when each day carries us over a changing land. The Indian names of the wells, and the hills, the rivers, the arroyos, were such as no Christian soul could remember or repeat a day after passing over. The early mission fathers gave to nearly all of them a good saint's

name as they passed, but the next one who came did
the same thing according to his likings, and no two
maps yet made have much likeness to each other away
from the coast, but only by keeping inland could be
found the wells and pastures for the cattle. Of wild
life — our hunters sometimes sighted deer on the mesas,
and there were birds strange to us and of wondrous col-
oring. Natives were sometimes waiting on our trail
with quills of fine gold to exchange for anything we
might offer, but when asked from whence it came, they
evaded reply, or in one case, a man made statement that
it came to the earth by the hand of Elder Brother.
Mother Clemente was startled to discover that they
called their god by this familiar title — also by another
which I do not recall. To her pious mind each was to
be reprimanded, which proved difficult because of the
lack of a common speech.

But Sancha, riding beside me, smiled in kindness on
the poor pagan, and gave him some white beads.

"For the 'Mother Moon,'" she said, and the interpreter looked at her in a way curious, for he was a
Christian and the son of a Castilian father.

But for all that, he put it into the language of the
Indio, who breathed on her hand, and went away, and
at a bend of the trail far ahead he was waiting and with
him was his wife with honey of the hills in a painted
bowl. To Sancha it was offered, and she held such discourse with them as might be with gestures of the hand,
and smiles, and looks of the eye. Thus were the long
hot days broken by things pleasant to help us forget the
otherwise unfriendly land.

"You see how wonderful it would be on this journey

of adventure if Marco was here rather than ahead of us
— from him I learned that they pray to the Mother
Moon, and see you what a friend it has made for me!"

"Mother Maria Clemente is saying a prayer for you,"
I cautioned, "and surely the interpreter has his wonder-
ment. How should a pious lady of degree in Spain learn
of pagan gods in Mexico?"

But all the words of the letters were sacred to her
because of the lover who wrote them, and, to my inconvenience, she expected me to be wise because I had
lived in the radiance of his countenance. It was even
a worse thing when she called me in the night, or at
early dawn, to tell her things of the stars as they came
over the mountains of the east, and in my hearing she
more than once said good-night to King Polaris! We
watched together the stars in which she saw the Indian
serpent and eagle, and took note of other things of the
night and the wilds such as was no part of the natural
education of a maid of her family.

Thus, while every soul who goes into the pagan lands,
has his own troubles, I had more than my own. Mexico
City had seemed a good place to get away from, yet
there were hours when I would have had joy to change
the northern trail for any safe, sheltered abode there
even though it bristled with iron bars. The good nuns
had their recompense in thought of the souls they might
save for God, but I had only the devilish certainty that
I was helping take her nearer to Marco and her false
dreams.

At the fording of the Del Fuerte an accident brought
us ill luck in that Padre José had a fall by his horse
going into a sink hole. He was dragged out with some

bruises and a broken leg, and there was no other thing
to do than bind it with split wood, and make a litter on
which he was started back to the presidio in Sinaloa.
This took two men and two burros from our cavalcade,
and we could ill spare them.

We had reached the land of the Haquis who were
at war with their neighbors on the east, and a double
guard was kept each night. Thus the loss of Padre
José was important. The nuns had been aided by his
advice in all things, and the camp felt the lack of spiritual guidance until such time as the unfortunate priest
could reach a mission and send a substitute to follow
after.

We were aware that we were watched by Indios in
the wilderness, and from the mesas, but they showed
no ill will, and we were put to inconvenience by not
finding the families at the *temporales* or summer rancherias where their farms were. We had counted on
their local guidance as to water for the beasts, and more
than once went far either east or west of the trail for
lack of that aid upon which we had been assured all
travelers could depend.

All of one morning we had been journeying along a
dry arroyo bed because of tracks of horses and burros
there. With the hope that they were heading for water
and knew where to find it, we could think of no better
way than to follow after.

Desert willow was there, and palo fierro trees, and
at every turn our hopes were high that a well, or even
a camp, might be found. The hills on the east came
near, and in any land we had known there would be
wells somewhere in the cañons.

Thus I rode ahead alone while the scouts were spread out like a fan north and west in search of water as marked on a map of the trail. Sancha begged to go also, but for once I was ungallant enough to refuse, though the greatest joy I had on the long way was when we rode together ahead of the others, and she remembered poems or romances and repeated them for me — and called me at times the name of the hero, and made pretense that she was a captive Moorish maid whose soul I was to save by my own piety. This last jest was because of her joy in frightening me by spiritual converse with the pagans, of whom she asked no questions, but would offer a flower, or make them the sign of the cross, and the circle in the north sky, and looked with a child's reverence on their prayer things, until I was bewildered between her jests and her strange way of standing well with them. All my reason told me that a proper maid should have a godly fear of these as had the nuns — but not Sancha.

Yet I rode away from her through the white-green brush of the arroyo, troubled over delays and mishaps of the journey, and with ever near me the fear of danger for her in the wilderness, also a dread of that day when she must know the difference between a pictured lover of childhood, and the man whose thoughts held her heart as in a net.

Then, suddenly, my horse stopped short in fear in the willows, and I saw a small huddled figure of a woman on the ground with her back to me, and the sound of her weeping came to me while the cast of a lance away, a man bent over a dead Indio to place it in a shallow grave scraped in the sand.

He turned at sound of the horse, and stood erect, but I knew him at sight of the shoulders and the strong hand below the monk's sleeve — it was Tristan!

The thought of him had been so close to me through all the many leagues, that I should not have had affright to look on him. Yet so afraid was I that I fairly fell from the horse, and my first thought was of gratitude for the broken leg of good Padre José; which was a sin in itself. But Padre José would have known Tristan.

"You must go — you must go!" I heard myself mumble. "If anyone knows you they will take you back to death!"

"Not from here," he said, and the Indian woman came and stood beside us and her looks at me had no kindness in them. Tristan put his hand on my shoulder and looked at her.

"Quatzi" — he said — "friend of mine," then she nodded her head, and looked at the dead man, but turned quickly away again, tears of grief in her eyes.

I wondered not that she turned away, for the face of the man was no longer a face, a poisoned arrow had pierced the cheek and death had come only after all the bones were bare.

"She is of a north tribe — enslaved and knew not the remedy for poison of the south," said Tristan, "so I found him thus. Their rancheria is beyond the mesquite trees above."

"And water," he said, making a sign to the woman who took the horse and left us to bury her man. But ere the sand was over him, there was a sound of other feet, and two of our guard rode up with questions.

But they were men of Puebla, and saw in Tristan

only a lay brother performing a pious duty — his face meant nothing to them.

But the older man, Salvadore Serri, was given joy and courage even at sight of the robe, and plead with all respect that Tristan come with haste to comfort Mother Maria Clemente by word of these warring tribes, and tell us all how to avoid meeting them on the road to Kavorka.

"It is true then that women of religion are to risk their lives here as men do — and for what?" asked Tristan, but Serri scarcely heeded, so full of gladness was he that a man who knew the land had met them, and one who knew also the places of water.

From first to last I was tongue-tied; first with the surprise, and horror of the dead Indio by which I was made sick, then when Serri rode up. Tristan had no look or word for me. He took the horse offered and they rode away to camp while I could follow as might be when the pagan woman led back my horse.

But she would not speak to me, though I had seen she understood Castilian, she sat herself down again in the sand as if I had never ridden that way to disturb her.

I reached camp as Mother Clemente was speaking her pleasure, and thanks to God that a traveled man was with them on the trail. As no *cura* was now with us, she declared, it was a blessing from heaven that we had been without water and left the road to seek it as we did.

"But I am not in orders, Holy Mother," said Tristan, "I have only been an assistant with the Indios for men more exalted."

"Then be our assistant since no one else can have

greater need," she said in pleading, and I could see by his face that he was like to yield.

"I have a task set for New Granada, and go north as soon as may be," he said. "But that can be after I have seen you safe to your mission, though I am earnest to persuade that you go back on the trail and rest at Sinaloa while this tribal trouble rages. It is wider than you know. There will be no maize planted, and in the hungry months the Indios will dig roots and go to the hills for seeds of the trees. You and your holy ladies cannot live in that way, Excellencia. You can only make Christians of Indios if you have food to offer."

"Then the food will come if the work is to be blessed by Our Lady," declared Mother Clemente. "Were not the fathers of the church fed in the deserts by the grace of God? and is not our cause worthy? We will continue."

"You are a good soldier, Mother," said Tristan, "and while I do go with you, I give you earnest warning that this war of the tribes is not a little thing. If they come together where we are, your guard is not strong enough to turn them back. I have been tardy for my own task because I halted to work with them for peace — but the fight is on. I have already had Indio friends killed in this province and I buried one this day. Also you may not know that Indio war is a very terrible thing."

"We will continue," said Mother Clemente. "We feel more safe with you to guide us. The tent of Padre José will be yours, also there are garments his guard could not bear back with him, all these are for the service of God; I bid you make free of them. Don Juan de Rivera will conduct you to the place of storage. Juanito, my son, this is Señor Alcatraz whom the saints have sent to us."

I made my bow to the Señor Alcatraz, and grinned in my sleeve at that credit given to the saints, for to my mind the devil himself was taking a hand in both the beginning of it and the end of it.

I led him to the packs, and Salvadore gladly offered to find all the señor cura required, and bear it to him. So in courtesy I led our new guest to the shelter of a palo fierro tree where my horse was feeding on that gracious herbage of the Desert.

"I look in sore need of the reverend sister's gifts," he said, looking down at his frayed robe. "It is plain to see that I have traveled over no broad highway since leaving the fair city. I bargained with Indio friends for a deerskin garb — it was moving well in the making when this war swept them to death."

"Tristan — you trail him north to kill him?" I muttered, caring nothing for his garb, or his pagan tribes — but burning hot and cold with my fears. Though I spoke low, and no one was near, he put his hand out in warning.

"That is with God," he said, but smiled as he said it; and by the smile I perceived that he meant neither God, the Father, nor anything of earth to keep them apart. "She is there in Mexico" — he went on in a low, even, strange tone as though it was a thing he had said over and over many times in the solitude of desert days and nights. "In all her purity of a white soul she waits for him there — no, Juanito — do not speak!

You hid it from me until I saw her look down from the viceroy's balcony with that fair cat beside her. Between them, when he goes back, she will be trapped like a caged bird, and serve as a cloak for their intrigue. And north beside him journeys the ruined life of the maid who is become as his slave, and will be the mother of his child. This the Indios have told me who saw them pass. At one presidio he even tried to leave her because she was ill — to leave her there with an Indio woman and the soldiers of an otherwise womanless camp — to leave her there as the toy of which he was weary! This came to me because of the quarrel of two soldiers who were each eager to marry her and keep her in honesty, and thus, Juanito, will you see our little song bird Anita, if ever you see her again on earth! So, as I say, if there is justice at the throne of God, the Father, it is written there that I find him, and see him sent to hell."

He did not lift his voice, nor look at me, but as he said these words in that strange even way, he made me see all he spoke of — and see it with the deeps of misery held in his voice and not in the words he spoke. My throat ached, and I choked with weeping as I hid my face there and strove to speak — yet could not.

Then I heard him rise to meet Salvadore to whom he gave some directions regarding horses of his on pasture near the rancheria of the dead Indio. He said they had a friendly guard of the Pimas there, and that the woman they would find was also a friend. Then I heard my name mentioned, for Salvadore could plainly see I was weeping, also I was shaking with terror.

"The Señorito de Rivera was made ill by the sight of that dead Indio — which sight was indeed a terrible thing to view " — stated Señor Alcatraz. " Also he has a chill, and will have a fever if he is not given a quick remedy of herbs. Have water heated that I may prepare it. As to the robe — thanks, señor, I will don it gladly when time serves."

Salvadore Serri gave him two robes rolled together instead of one, and made haste to the cook, thanking the saints that at last we had a man at the head who knew the thing to be done, and how to do it, also vowing that my chill was from the last bad well, and was proof that the water there had not been boiled as had been the order of Mother Clemente.

And I, filled with a fury of resentment at thought of bitter tea of herbs, and at the easy and ungodly lies of Tristan, got to my feet and faced him standing there in his rags of covering, yet ruling already the camp.

At that instant it was that Sancha, seeing my horse browsing off the low branches of the tree, came over the sands calling to me, and in her arms were long stocks of that which she called star blossoms because they were as sunflowers yet not so big, and she carried also some creeping blooms of a wonderful blue and bade me to learn the name of it for her!

Not until she was near did she see that a stranger was with me, and was staring at her as eyes stare from the wooden saints of the Mexicans. She gave him no notice, for all her gaze was to me, who stood with tears on my cheeks, and muttered speech of anger in my mind.

"Juanito mine!" she breathed in a frightened way,

and came close, the yellow flowers of the sun falling at her feet, " Juanito, you have news of evil — is it so? Have you had word not good of — him? "

She half whispered the last word in her fright, and I strangled the curse in my throat.

" Señor Alcatraz tells me I have a chill — or a fever, and that is all," I growled roughly, " may one not have even an illness in peace? "

So strange was a cold word to her that she flushed red, and her head was held high as she passed over Tristan a slighting glance.

" Such chill, or fever, seems strange in its sudden coming," she stated, " and since you know not which it is, your new friend may help you discover."

She turned away, and walked slowly towards the tent of Mother Clemente, while we two stood looking at each other. But her good heart conquered her anger at me, and she called back.

" When your spirit is more friendly, Juanito, I will hear your word for pardon."

" So you — my friend — have cheated me also in this? " he said with frowning eyes. " There in Mexico you hid from me her coming, and here in the Desert —"

Then he was silent, for I laughed aloud with my tears yet wet on my cheek.

" Yes — she is here! " I declared, freeing myself of the horrors over which I had been all but strangled. " She comes north on a trail of love to follow the man of those letters — the wonderful lover who painted the face of her on an altar! His name is Marco; she is as sure of that in her heart that she is to wed with him, or die a nun in the habit she wears! Now you have it all

— the things of which I have cheated you. And you — you go north over the same trail to hunt him for death! Is it not enough to make mirth for the very devils who wait for him there in hell? "

And then I did in truth have a chill, or a fever, or a faint, and Tristan lifted me in his arms as he had done on a night long ago, and carried me from the hot sand to shelter. And in the end I had to drink of the detested tea at his bidding, and the only comfort I had was to hear Sancha argue against it, for the smell of it seemed to her an ungodly thing, and she had her fears it might be a poison.

But for all that, it was poured down me, and was the beginning of the rule of Señor Alcatraz in our camps.

CHAPTER XIII

THE NEW MASTER OF CAMP

SANCHA was in a strange way rebellious at his rule as was no other. Why should a man in rags who rose up from the earth in the Desert step thus to the lead of things? She pitied me much for my sudden attack of fever, and was a tender nurse on the trail. In a way she came more close to me, as if near to jealousy of the stranger to whom I talked when chance offered. It was the first time I had thought for any but her, and her eye was keen for the knowledge that often, though we did not speak of a matter, this Señor Alcatraz and I had mutual understandings.

"Who is he — this Señor cura who is no cura?" she demanded. "I have comfort that he is not in orders, for confess to him I would not. Do they train the priests for the deserts to ride like that?"

"Sanchita, you are hard to please," I said as reasonably as might be. "Each day you have made protest at the slowness, and the wasted time in morning start for the trail. We start now at starlight and the cool of dawn, because he arranges all things well."

"Also he has an unpriestly pride, and looks over the heads of people," she continued. "To see his high gaze

you would think we were not reasonable beings — or
that we did not possess souls."

I could have laughed at that, had my heart been gay
enough for laughter, for I knew there were few hours
of the night when he did not himself patrol the tent
where she slept, also I dared not put into words my
question as to reasonable beings, for none of the things
we were doing seemed to me reasonable, though it was
not in my power to change any of them.

After two days when affairs moved well, though the
heat was great, our new master of the camp made
changes by which our plan would be to travel at night
for the sake of the horses. The moon was growing
and the nights of the Desert were as a land of enchantment under the stars. With a week of night travel he
hoped to ride clear of the roving bands of Indios who
were seen more often now, and who watched us but
kept their distance. There was no longer the friendly
barter of the earlier days.

Mother Clemente and the nuns said their prayers and
were content with whatever plans were made so long
as their course held steadily towards Kavorka and the
crop of pagan souls to be saved. But Sancha laughed,
and asked if our new cura who rode so bravely was
afraid to ride in the light of the sun lest the poor pagans
see him?

Unnoticed by her, he was at the door of the tent when
she said it, and he stepped into the light and spoke.

"It is true, Excellencia, that I am afraid," he said
quietly — "never before have I had aught so precious
to guard. If it pleases you to think it is a coward's
plans I make — get your laughter out of it while you

may. But for your own sake I ask that you keep to the rules of the camp, for we need every man, and I can ill spare one for even a slight change."

"You have taken a man who was my special servant and added him to your guard," she said accusingly, and at that he smiled.

"I could wish that you had brought a cavalry troop as special servants, that I could take them as well," he said. "I should certainly take every man I could find."

"Is this a priestly custom in your Desert?" she asked turning her eyes haughtily towards him, yet dropping them at his steady gaze.

"The Desert is not mine, Excellencia, else I should have barred you out of it," he said, "also, as I have told the revered Mother, I am no priest. I wear the robe of one because at times it has been permitted to me — and at this time because this illustrious company found me in rags and showed itself generous. My one wish is that I may show service in return, and guard you safely to the place you seek."

"There he will be glad to see the last of us," she made comment as he bowed to her, and turned away. "You see, Juanito, it is as I told you; he looks over us or down upon us as if we were children playing a trifling game. Also he steals you too often from beside me, and our long talks are broken."

"But think of riding together under the stars," I made eager suggestion. "It is a most perfect thing he has made the plan of. Have you not rebelled each night of the moons that we had to sleep through the beauty of it? He has done the thing you wished to do — yet you have only disdain."

"Why should he know my wishes, and let them be done as if it was to humor a child — or forbids the doing as it pleases him? There is only one man in the world whom I want to know things as this man knows them. I am also jealous because you leave me to seek him out. He takes from me everything, and he would bar me from the land if he could — you heard him say it."

"Sancha dear, so would I," I confessed; "and I believe truly that if we ever get out alive from these endless ranges, it will be because of the man you do not like."

"He made you drink that stuff of the herbs, and I cannot conceive why you should take his part," she retorted. "I should hate him for that if I were you — also I asked him not to make you swallow it, and he did. Everything is different since he is here — and you no longer have any love for me."

At that, of course, my heart was all but broken, for I saw the anxiety of Tristan, and had heard the careful orders of which the women were to know nothing. He had made all plans for their safety, yet all preparations for their death if need be. It was a grim and dreary time over which we kept up pretense of light hearts, and I was accused of not loving her when I could have wept in very terror of the dangers, feared for her.

On our first night ride Tristan ranged his horse beside us in the warm moonlight, and bent his head to Sancha.

"May I speak with you, Excellencia?" he asked. It was the first time he had sought her, and I held my breath to listen.

"Is it to tell me again that I am not here by your will, Señor Cura?" she asked mockingly. "When you call me 'excellencia' you make me feel ancient as my own grandmother!"

"I could wish you safe with her," he said.

"My thanks to you — but she is dead!" she retorted, "and if I were with her someone on earth must needs say masses for my soul. If you were in orders I might ask you — but as it is —— "

"As it is we will all pray you need them not for long happy years," he said untouched by her humor or her words. "But prayers for life are needed as well as in death, and it is of that I would speak. I have here a thing of prayer very well known, and very sacred to these warring tribes; will you wear it until this danger land is crossed?"

He held out the rosary of Fray Fernando with the turquoise and shell beads in among the brown. She stared at it curiously, but did not touch it.

"I am well provided with a rosary," she said; "my own is of amethyst and gold. I think I prefer it to the brown beads, but my thanks to you."

"It is not as a rosary alone I offer it, but because the priests of many desert tribes have bestowed the beads threaded here. They make it a pledge of peace and friendship to the wearer."

"If pagan priests had aught to do with it, I should fear it bore enchantments," she persisted. "If you are brave enough to carry it, Juanito and I will ride in your shadow to win merit if it have any — but to wear it I should have fear."

"I could wish that Don Juan might prevail upon you," he said, and said no more; neither would she hearken to me, for she said, rightly, that I knew less of what might be pagan enchantments than did she, for the sacredness of certain prayer thoughts of theirs had been written to her very wonderfully before ever she journeyed from Seville.

Whereupon she began more amiably to hold converse with Tristan — asking of the ways of the Indio for finding roads in the darkness, and giving special notice when he pointed out the northern stars, and acknowledged to knowing a few of the Indian names, and their importance in the heretical religions they professed.

But he betrayed no special interest in these matters, and did little to quell her curiosity. Never, I knew, had she seen a man like him, and nothing in her well ordered life had ever made it possible for a man to arise out of nowhere, and without intent or desire, be given the ruling over respectable and pious souls. Her resentment was strange — as if she shrank from the power of him, and even tried to make little of it to me. And ever and ever in her mind she compared his knowledge with that of Marco, and found it very much of the earth cares — as to pastures and water wells and herbs of the field.

But not even the saints in heaven could hold their own in her mind if compared with Marco, yet she was a good Christian, and would have been in rage with me had I said that in her heart her lover of the letters was a new god enthroned.

The Pima friend of Tristan had gone back to the tribe and it appeared plain that the peace with these people had been marred by some young Castilians of the colonists who had passed north to New Granada. The Pima girls were hidden now if strangers came.

"Yet Don Juanito says there was a woman with you back there at the wells when you did us the favor to take charge of our camp and brew bitter tea," stated Sancha.

He turned to her with the rare smile by which his face was made a different one, and his eyes flashed their natural youth. It amused him that the herb tea remained an unforgivable cruelty to her mind. I knew even then it was not the bitter herbs she resented — it was the quiet dominance she had never before seen exerted except by ruler of church or state. It affronted her to feel such dominance in a stranger who came in rags out of the desert willows, and who confessed that even the rags were borrowed garb! Also, except in the matter of the beads he had shown no disposition to betray that in his mind she was exalted beyond the simple nuns who rode whispering prayers in the moonlight. This to Sancha de Llorente y Rivera, late favorita exalted at the viceregal court, was a change she could not readily bring herself to understand. She had raged to me that her sheep herders up in the Sierra Morena, where her people were masters of three towns in the ancient times, would not dare appear before her so nearly naked as had he in his ragged habit that first day. To remind her that she had admired naked skins in the brown Indios only gave her an impatience with me, though Tristan was burnt brown enough by the desert sun to satisfy anyone that he had a good dark serviceable coat. Few would recognize him for the man of the prison pallor who dared raise his eyes to the palace balcony.

Yet at that mention of the bitter tea, and of the

woman, his smile bridged over all her scornful words of pride.

"I thank your saint, whichever one it may be, that it fell not to my task to order herbs for your excellency," he said with a laugh in his eyes; "and as to the little woman of the rancheria — she has left her field of maize and calabashes to raiders, and travels back to the home in Tusayan for which her heart is sick."

"Could any heart be sick for desert life?" asked Sancha with slight belief, "and where is the home — a mud hovel by evil smelling waters?"

"So far from it that I could scarce convey in words the marvel of the difference," said Tristan. "It is scarce to be believed except by men who have looked upon the carven and painted temples of Palenque or Mitla, or the wonderful pagan palaces of Ho in Yukatan. Not that there are such carvings in the north, for there the people are as an island of civilization broke free from some mainland. Secluded thus they have developed more slowly — yet they are alive today and hold to their original gods, while the great body of their brothers who migrated to the hot lands built stupendously yet died as a nation leaving only carven records of their greatness."

"They must have been wicked and heretical as are the Jews, who also are dead as a nation," observed Sancha. "It is said they were once kings in their land."

"They yet remain kings in memory so long as the ancient Hebrew is read," said Tristan. "All the poetry of the Christian bible comes from them."

"Perhaps that is why our confessors forbid the reading of it," mused Sancha. "I had not thought of it before, for I knew not that infidels had the writing of it. Is it quite true?"

"They built a wonderful foundation of a wonderful edifice — and gave ages to the building," said Tristan; "then a new thought was grafted upon it — as a Norman tower built upon the frozen music of a Moorish temple, and the weight of the tower crushed its beauty of line, and the fragments are now scattered abroad in many lands."

"H — m!" murmured Sancha. "I never heard a thing like that before; but the church gives you to read things not allowed to women. You say you are not in priestly orders, yet they have let you gain knowledge of priestly things. Tell me more of the Indio woman."

At that I smiled in my silence, for the question of the woman had been curious to her; my own knowledge had not been enlightening.

"As a maid she was stolen by the Apache at a time when they fought her nation. They are the Hópitû — the People of Peace, and they live in great houses high on rock mesas. From the lower levels they are seen afar off like castles of enchantment against the desert skies. A thousand years they have stood there as islands of civilized people in the heart of a land where other tribes live in shelter of boughs, or under skins of beasts."

"What are they that they are civilized?" persisted Sancha. "If they are not Christian how are they people of reason? and if not that — how civilized? I cannot see them as you say."

"No — you could not," he agreed. "No one could see them by the eyes of another, and no woman who is white has ever seen them. They go not out to war, yet are not cowards. Their religion forbids anger or spirit of conquest, and they live to their religion. They wed with one wife, and she is ruler of the children, and the home. They grow maize and melons in their fields surrounding the high islands of stone where they live. Their weaving of garments is good and their making of burnt vessels of clay has merit in beauty scarcely to be given belief. They are gentle people, yet very strong people. They pray much, and give thank offerings each day to their gods of the sky. Never anywhere have I seen such peace as is theirs."

" And how came the woman so far in this land? "

" She was traded by the Apache to a Pima man whose son wanted her for wife. He was a kind man, and their home was a good resting place to me — and to other of the Castilians. Her life was content, yet when the poisoned arrow of the Seri struck him she knew naught of the art of healing such wound; her people have none such poison. Thus he died when I reached him too late, and I bade poor little Movi go north and weep for him among her own people and not in a stranger's land."

" Why should she weep at freedom when he had held her as slave? " demanded Sancha in high scorn — " it betokens a mean blood."

" Nay — love held her — and he gave her love," said Tristan. " Love serves freely, thus he was not as other men or masters to her. It may be that to woman such love makes man king even in a rancheria of small fields. It may be so."

" So it is," conceded Sancha after a silence. " I perceive now how it is. He was the greatest, mayhaps, she had ever had knowledge of, and I see how it would be if there is truly love; but how, holy father, do you know, when you are too young to confess women or maids?"

It was her first of gay mockery with him, rather than at him, and it told me that the good nuns with their endless devotions, and my poor art in providing new amusements, had wearied her more than I guessed since it drove her to seek distraction in fraternity with the man she disdained.

I already felt sadly enough my own lackings, and glad was I that she had at least called truce to her jealousy of him. But when I saw him looking at her in silence — looking at her with a gaze belonging to moonlit nights, but not to her desert love trail to another man, my heart jumped, and again I seemed to hear the cold voice of the viceroy when he said "What is there he has not dared?"

"You do not speak!" she said pettishly. "Juanito mine, how do priests in convents learn of pagan loves?"

"I have not had good luck to be a priest in a convent," I confessed, "and no one has taken pains to teach me loves — pagan or otherwise — for my own use."

At that she laughed, and said I was lacking in gallantry, for she had herself been instructing me always to slight avail.

"I said, 'for my own usage,'" I repeated; "to look at love through the eyes of another teaches only the hunger of love, and not any of its comforts — if it indeed confers comfort."

"Infidel!" she laughed, "have you doubts?"

"Have not you?" I returned. "We take this trail

for love's sake, and what comfort has it gained for any of us? The weary weeks, and bad water and now a forced trail in the night the sooner to get beyond scalping knives!"

"O — Juanito mine" — she breathed. "You are right, only a great love is worth it."

"Or a great hate," I said, looking at Tristan.

He turned his horse, and halted to speak to Mother Clemente, who was alarmed at a fire on a hill to the east. To her it looked a signal of danger. He assured her that it was from the west the danger was to be guarded against, and that two more days would see us safe beyond the Pima frontier.

"How is he so wise?" demanded Sancha, "or does he only make pretense to know? If he is not a priest, how does he know priestly things?"

"Oh, Sanchita," I said, "how do I know? He tells us he has traveled with mission priests, and studied to give them aid. You take any mongrel on trust who begs of you by the wayside, yet you give out only bitter thoughts to the one man who offers you the most holy possession of his."

"That is true," she agreed, "he did offer me the beads and it was a strange thing to do. Yes — I will believe with you that he means well, but he did not make answer when I asked how he knew about loves; he did not so much as speak to me again. I have conviction that the man owns a bad conscience. He only looks at me when he thinks I do not observe."

The night wore on, and the dawn came, but Tristan did not return to ride beside us. At times he was far ahead, and at other times he halted to review all, and

waited until the last of the rear guards came up. Sancha
grew silent, and slept at times briefly in her saddle,
drooping like a tired child, but rousing as her horse
made an uneven step on the wild trail.

The sun was high over the hills of the east when
we reached the next waterholes — having traveled
nearly double the distance possible under the hot sun.
Trees were there and grass in a near valley, a breakfast
was eaten, and shelters put up for the women where
they retired for the sleep they so sadly needed. I
fell into sudden slumber with my head pillowed on
my saddle, and half the guard slept near the horses,
with one of their number as sentinel, the others with
their heads under any shelter to be found near the camp.

It was late in the day when I was roused by voices
and smell of smoke, to find the cooks busy with the
evening meal, and saw Tristan coming into camp on
foot from the east, and without a word stretched himself under my bush and settled his head on my pillow
wearily.

"Tristan — you have ranged away on foot while the
camp rested. Why on foot?"

"To save a horse for the night — much depends on
their rest."

"And what on yours?" I demanded, excited and in
a bit of fear at sight of his tired face. "Where have
you wandered while we slept?"

"Three leagues east, and a bit north. I had to see
the old men of the clans."

"But — three leagues on foot, and return — no sleep
— and all this hell of heat!"

"Enough! A man of these tribes will make twenty

leagues on a handful of *pinole* to munch on the way. A wayfarer in their desert must do as well — or fade out of the land."

"The guard already brings in the horses," I warned him; "you have scarce an hour to rest."

"Then — if you love me — give me that hour, Juanito, and, boy, prevail that she wear the rosary."

In an instant he slumbered heavily. I, who toss and turn to nurse myself to sleep even on good feathers, stared at him in awe. To me it was scarce a thing of nature that a man should say "I will sleep," and on that instant go into a stupor. Yet that is what he did, and I, sorely troubled, still stood regarding him when Sancha came from the ladies' bower looking fresh as a rose in the cool breeze beginning to sift from the hills.

She came over to me, and then stood in her tracks looking down upon him in derision.

"I would that Mother Clemente would see him thus that her mind could be at rest," she said mockingly; "the good lady has fear that he never sleeps! Yet each lazy Indio and guard is up and alert save only he!"

"But — Sancha" — I protested, and took her hand to draw her away lest her voice wake him despite of all.

She shook me loose and pointed to him.

"O brave cavallero!" she said slightingly, "and see, how, even in his stupor, he clutches that rosary of the Indian gifts! He holds to the pagan enchantments to guard even his sleep — your brave cavallero!"

I drew her away, and tried to make clear that his sleep had been slight — yet, as I dared not alarm the women by telling the dangers he feared, my words were lame and careful, and she would not even listen.

"Is he worth so many words?" she asked in contempt. "Because he talks well of new things, and knows the water holes and red Indians, you and Mother Clemente speak of him as if he were an archangel sent by God, yet I see him thus when off his guard! Find other idols, Juanito."

She was very gay over this because she thought it teased me, and I perceived it was not a good time to follow his request, and mention again the beads. Because the Indians of the palm groves and the little adobes under the pepper trees had been to her as grave yet kindly children, she could not see that the savages of wild barrancas and brown hills were a different people, thus she attached no importance to the work of a master of camp beyond the fact that this one had a knack of making the packers move, and that we covered space in half the time as when Padre Jose had the word to give.

The supper was all but over before I dared let Salvadore arouse him. I knew he counted the hour of sleep of as much importance as food.

Carefully he looked over every horse in the herd when he wakened, and saw that every water bottle was filled ere he gave the word to break camp, and then with a quiet word to Mother Clemente he rode on ahead, and out of sight in the cañon.

Sancha looked after him with impatience in her eyes.

"It would be but civil to ask us to ride with him," she said; "it is not much pleasure to ride at the heels of another man's horse. You see how he has changed everything. You and I used always to ride at the head, and have races, and find surprises."

I tried to remind her that our races had been in a country where all the roads were plain — and where there had been no question of safety, but here for forty leagues was a reach of land of which the rule might change in a day, and all the trails be blocked.

"What could be done did that really happen?" she asked, incredulous, "our guard carry arms."

"They would only be a handful between two rival hordes of the sierra and llano," I said: "and I truly have not dared ask what might chance if we did ride into one of their battles, but the most likely thing would be to ride back to Sinaloa and pray for a better year to build missions."

"Ride back!" and she turned startled looks on me — "ride back I would not. To ride over these hundreds of leagues to meet him — only to turn and ride back to Sinaloa? No, I would not. Rather would I ride the other leagues north to New Granada."

"That could never be. The other ladies are already much worn with the travel, and even the guard did not engage to fight the savages. No, they would turn back, and be held justified."

"You commend all the things for which I have no liking," she complained, "and it never used to be so with you. I think it is the fault of that man."

Thus she at least gave him credit for strength, since she felt the influence of him in all things.

The ride thus in the evening was as through hundreds of wonder pictures, for the changing lights of the low sun threw strange colors back to the sierras — yellows and reds, with deep purples where the shadows were. On the llanos to the west high fog would drift in from the sea of Cortez, and cast bars of shadow over the yellow land. There was no darkness, only a dim half light between the going of the sun and the rising of the moon, and the tall sahuaros stood out like gray phantoms against far silver hills.

"Yes, it has beauty," agreed Sancha, "but it is a beauty like no other living thing. Each rise of a hill one looks to see some castle of enchantment in some oasis, and there is only an arroya or a tinajia, and we are gladdened if there is water for the beasts. Also when the sun goes down there is a hush about it all. Our guard do not sing in the night here as did they in the palm forests of the south; it is not the weariness of the trail alone, it is the spirit — the land has no spirit of joy."

"True, it does not seem to us joyous, yet it is good to watch the stars come out, and give thanks each time of waking that we are yet guarded safe."

"Safe! safe!" she repeated. "Now again you repeat that man. I grow so tired of his strict ruling that I can almost feel myself riding in spite of him far ahead, for the adventure of it."

"For all our safety do not dare that until he gives us the word," I pleaded, and would have said more, but she laughed at me.

"Dare?" she said, "and — wait his word? Have you then forgot that we De Llorente y Rivera let not even the priests think for us? Why then a priest's robe?"

To quell her rebel spirit, I talked of Marco, and the fact that he was now safe in the turquoise land of

New Granada, and she fell a wondering if there were white butterflies there, and the things of flower and field loved by him, and then she was back, discoursing of his wondrous letters, and his genius, and the bigness of his mind that he sought no credits for the pious work of the picture in the chancel!

So, no matter which of the two men we talked of, I had my own troubles. But in my heart I had no thought but that when she learned the truth of Marco, she would decide for a nun's robe, and the journey into the wilderness for planting of a mission was a most satisfying novitiate for any mortal maid of proud temper.

She laughed with me over the wisdom of primitive things she had gained in the Desert — of making fires, of cooking maize, and of mending things with leather thongs or thread of yucca. For a jest she had mended with yucca thread that day her robe torn on thorns of the pale fierro tree, and she confessed she had patched the pocket in which she kept the letters of love always close to her.

"I pray each night and morning to my wonderful Saint of the Impossible that at some turn in the trail I find him close beside me," she said, "and there are times, Juanito, when I close my eyes and dream that the horse beside me may be his — almost I reach out my hand to touch him — so real is the sense of his nearness. Does that seem strange to you?"

It did not, and I told her so, for she had lived with the thought of him all the long journey until the thought was part of her, but I warned her no other would understand, for no other could know.

"He will understand," she said, and her eyes were all aglow in the moonlight as she looked at me. "O Juanito! he is the wonder man of all the world, and it is as though his heart was beating here in my breast. I waken in the night and feel that he is close even though I have not been dreaming of him — it is very strange, that! Think you, Juanito, that it is because he has ridden his horse over these wilderness trails ahead of me? Now — this instant — it is as if around the mesa we will find him waiting."

She laughed, and lifted her hand, and her horse broke into the easy lope of the range while I followed with what haste I could, yet urging her not to go beyond sight of the cavalcade.

And around the foot of the mesa was Tristan, his horse across the trail — black shadow against the night silvers by which the desert was all a gray garden under the moon. She pulled her horse up short.

"Santa Maria and Santa Rita!" she whispered as if in fear. "That is how it is at each turn! I wish for the one man in all the world, and ever, for my sins, the one sent is the one who makes me have fear, or I know not what! Juanito, does it not seem a thing of reason to you that the pagan beads of that rosary are of evil enchantings?"

I made the sign of the cross for fear it might be. My own doubts and troubles were many.

Yet his presence there was a simple matter, for he but stood across the trail and talked with an Indio who spoke briefly and softly in the shadows, and then faded away again among the low shrubs and strange shapen cactus.

Tristan turned to us, and I could see he was troubled.

"We must take great care, yet cover ground this night," he said. "The Pima sentinels are watching from the hills and see the Haquis come in large bodies from the west."

"Yet they travel on foot while we have horses," I observed.

"That is true," he said, "but footmen can run ahead of horses on this trail, and we need to take each short cut until the great body of Pimas and Papagoes are reached."

Sancha talked to her horse, and petted him, and could not credit that a footman could outdistance him, also she had confidence in our guard brought from the south.

Tristan looked at her, noting her pettish humor, and rode in silence near us, and after awhile finding no one to argue with, she too fell silent with weariness as the night wore on, and Tristan took the reata and led her horse, so that often she slept.

CHAPTER XIV

RIDING THE TRAIL ALONE

THE dawn broke with coral pink beyond the blue walls of the sierras, and Sancha aroused to the beauties of blossoms of pale lemon scattered among the shrubs and cactus of the trail. We were in a pass where the walls narrowed, and the space between was level as a floor. The way was plain before us, and she looked at me and laughed.

"You were not gallant," she said accusingly. "I thought you were leading my horse, but when I wakened, it was that man. I will show him I can ride the trail alone, also that I am tired of never getting away from his eyes — so — *adios!*"

She lifted the bridle, and used the whip only one stroke, but the horse had felt it seldom, and leaped forward.

"Sancha!" I called, but she lifted her hand high in salute, and rode her mount to the utmost. There was nothing to do but follow, which I did. Tristan was somewhere at the rear end of the line of travelers, and no guard followed us. They thought it but a bit of childish play, and the road was good.

I thought little of the road, only of keeping her in sight. Once I did miss her in the jungle of low growth where another cañon branched, but it was only for a moment, and I rode my utmost to reach and hold her by force if need be until Tristan should come and place her in the very middle of the cavalcade instead of at either end.

The first bend took us out of sight of all of them, and the second into a beautiful cañon where the sun was gilding the view on the west, and the sunflowers reached to our saddles.

"Sancha! Sancha!" I called, and the walls echoed back my cry, for my horse labored wearily after — both animals could only be aroused for a spurt, but her weight was the less, and I could only keep in sight her robe, or high flung hand.

Her laughter came back to me mockingly, and then one scream made the cañon walls echo strangely. My heart seemed to be in my throat as I rode forward fearing to see her horse fallen, and with my mind filled with visions of broken bones — weary leagues from a surgeon.

But it was not a fallen horse I found at the bend of the cañon, but a girl with a very white face sitting her horse in still horror while around her circled a sea of red brown faces.

My first thought was to ride forward to her rescue, but my second was to call back for help to Tristan — first and last, to Tristan!

The thought was scarce formed, or my bridle touched, till I saw how useless it was. From a side cañon, the Indians swarmed, and above the edges of the cliffs they peered, and there was no calling back.

I looked in their faces, and without word, I rode forward and halted my horse beside Sancha.

"Listen," she said.

I did, and heard back of us the echoes of firearms. The guards were using arquebuses against an enemy in the rear.

Even while we listened, the groups of Indios divided. At the word of a man who stood at Sancha's bridle, the mass of them raced back the way we had come, and, with another brief word, a score of the devils circled us, and our horses were led through a narrow break in the cliff.

I looked back; four men stood sentry at the narrow pass, and behind our horses walked others with lances leveled, and the points of them were the sharp cutting knives of smoked volcanic glass.

"Thus have you shown him how you can ride the trails alone," I said, furious with her as I heard the far distant reports, and the savage yells.

She only looked at me, and I felt like a coward. The Indios watched us with smiling faces in which there was little of threat — they were rather as exultant children who had made an unexpected point in a game.

There were no words to us — only the dark bodies trotting ahead and back of me, and Sancha at times out of my sight in the winding cañon.

Then we reached a wider place between walls where water trickled at foot of a cliff, and a tree of size spread wide arms.

Some women were there, and a fire of mesquite poles sent up meager blue smoke, while a boy turned a rabbit on a spit, and a girl heated stones to cook some mess in a basket.

All let go their tasks to stare as we were driven in like cattle before the lances. Sancha won most of their notice for no white women in nun's robe had come their trail. Somewhat in awe they looked on her until her captor pulled her roughly from the saddle, and with some words in their devilish jargon, thrust her towards the women.

I strove as I might to reach her, for I had still my knife — and the orders of Tristan were plain if the end came for the women, and this seemed the end.

But a stroke from one of the brutes left me senseless, and when I came back into knowledge the blood was holding sand caked against my cheek, and Sancha was roped to the tree. Two women had stripped from her the robe, and a boy had her shoes. Girt as she was with the reatas from our horses, she was a figure of pitiful appeal. My tears blinded me, and I felt for my knife — but it was gone!

The women were having dispute for the robe and the stronger wrenched it free from the grasp of the other. As they did so, there fell on the sand beside me the rosary of Sancha, and something else. One woman with a squeal of laughter saw the jeweled strand and let go the robe. I had lifted the rosary and gave it up, reluctant, to her eager clutch, and in their wrangle, and in the new treasure trove, neither of them saw the flat packet over which I laid my arm. Then I rose and went over by the water to slake my thirst and wash the sand out of the cut, and though I was watched, no one halted me.

I had wonder as to why I was not deprived of garments and liberty as well as Sancha, but I soon discovered that the horses were being given water for the trail, and while the leading Indian took Sancha's horse for himself, I was tied on mine, and the men spoke together with many nods in my direction, and back to the trail we had come.

It seemed clear I was to be taken with them while Sancha was to be held in camp with the women and boys. The tall fellow gave some scowling directions indicating that the girl tied to the tree was his property, and then we were headed back between the cliffs, and never once had I been let get within touch of Sancha.

"They have not harmed me," was all the word I had of her, "but your head —— "

The Indio riding her horse heard, and smiled with evil, half closed eyes, and then to my surprise, he spoke Castilian.

"No time for women, time tomorrows," he said. "Now you people learn how Pimaria like when you take their maidens."

As I had taken none, or had will to, his taunt had no sting for me beyond the horror of the thought of Sancha. I was certain that his scowling instruction to the women was to guard her for his return — and Sancha, perhaps, like myself, without a knife!

All that ride between the cliffs I saw not the arrow-bush, or the mesquite or the long shadows, but Sancha, bare armed and bare of foot, bound to the tree trunk within cañon walls, and the evil-faced native smiled as he saw me striving at every chance to loosen my bonds.

"No good," he said. "Take you to make talk plenty good — many horses maybe for one girl Castilian."

Thus I saw his plan to make a deal for stock, and hold Sancha for ransom, and the other man smiled when he said horses — that much they knew of the white man's language.

"You are not Pima?" I said as I looked from his face to theirs, and they ceased to smile, and stared.

"What is your medicine to see?" he asked. "It is true. I am Apache once — when little. Know you also my father's or my clan?"

I perceived that my careless guess had given him suspicion that I had power of divining. I remembered the lore of Tristan, and used it.

"Do these people with whom you live mention the names of the dead?" I asked in reproof. "To tell your clan, and the name of your father might bring evil on the trail."

"That is true," he said. "You have the knowing. You can go south for the horses; a man of medicine we let go in peace."

To go in peace, and alone, was the last thing for which I craved. My prayers were silent ones as we went on over the brown sand, and fervently I remembered Sancha's Saint of the Impossible. If ever the seeming impossible must happen, and happen quickly, this was the time. I thought ruefully of the holy beads offered by Tristan and disdained so lately — would they have proven more potent than the jewels of gold and amethyst?

As we emerged into wider space between the walls I perceived the thing I had not when I raced by eager to keep her in sight. We had turned into one lane of rock while another had been the main trail where a battle had been fought. The trampled sand and a dead mule told me little of the outcome of it, but the red men scattered north and south, and climbed cliffs like so many squirrels, the while my renegade Apache looked and smiled evilly.

"All what was caught, we caught," he said with satisfaction. " The Haqui are driven back with the thunder arrows of the white men — and look you here — they carried with them their dead."

Then, by pretense of knowing more than I in reason could, I learned that north of us there had been fights with the Haquis the day before, and that two companies of Pimas had been waiting in the gulch and on the heights to trap a southern group of their enemies who were on the war trail. The thing, as it chanced, had turned in a different way. Sancha and I had ridden from the true road into one company, and our friends had met the fierce Haquis, and each had retreated — in what order none could say.

No doubt Tristan thought us captured by the Haquis, and my mind was certain on one point, the retreat of the expedition meant — perhaps not great defeat or injury, but the willingness at last of Mother Clemente to accept advice of Tristan, return to Sinaloa, and wait a more peaceful year for the planting of a sisterhood among the heathen.

Men from above the cliffs came down, and told of the Castilians turning back on the trail, after their men, headed by their priest, had fought the Haquis and made the cañon walls echo fearfully with the thunder of their arms.

"Have the Haquis followed the trail by the south?"

asked the Apache, and by gesture and tone, and nods of the head, I learned they had not. The clash with the white people had been accident, and the enemy of the Pima were not eager to fight against thunder, lightning, and lead hail.

The Apache scowled and looked at me, and then they sat in the sand and talked. His plan for me was changed — if I was sent to ride after the Castilians now, it would not be horses they would get in exchange for the white maid, but more of the same gun fire; also I could tell how small was their own company, and there would be time to call on help from other Pima clans.

I could see that the sullen Apache was alone in his scheme for a herd. They quarreled among themselves, and one man pointed to Sancha's horse. Already the Apache had one while the Pima men walked. It was easy to follow their argument. Through it I learned that the Apache was called Kasia, and when no settlement could be made an older man said some words ending with "Matiwa," whereupon all nodded and said "Matiwa" except Kasia, who looked sulky that he was voted down.

Again I was tied on my horse, but driven north instead of the way we had come. Later I learned from the sulky Kasia that Matiwa was an older chief and a Piman; also that there was to be council to decide if I was to be sent back to ask horses in ransom for Sancha. Evidently his adopted brothers were not so eager for trouble with Castilians once the excitement of the adventure was over.

But ere the night fell we learned it was not over, for up from a barranca swarmed nude brown bodies following their spent arrows, and my captors fought back, but a running fight, for they were outnumbered, and out of the scramble the horse of Sancha leaped riderless, for Kasia lay with an arrow piercing his eye, and a lance thrust in his throat.

Another Indio leaped on the horse and led mine out of arrow range, and as I had no mind to change captors now that the Apache was gone, I rode right willingly. To my surprise the enemy did not follow; evidently the two horses and a Castilian rider caused them suspicion that the Pimans had strong allies.

There was no sign of grief over the death of Kasia; he had been a strong man but not a favorite and of no blood kindred. His going left me even more alone, for only one youth had few words of Castilian which he used with little meaning.

The dusk of night came on as we reached a place of water, and a little apart from it was a small shrine place of stones, circled crudely by the dried skeleton ribs of the sahauro. It was still light enough to discover willow wands to which bird feathers and seed pods were tied with the fiber of yucca — some pious pagan had made thanks or prayer there for the dribble of water in the pool.

Stiff and sore though I was from the rope and the saddle, I was alive to that flat packet rescued by me in the cañon camp, and having little doubt but that my garments would be divided as were Sancha's, I had cast about for some way of hiding or destruction for the letters ere the fragments of them be used for charms in medicine bags. To attempt burning might fail, and the shrine place was the only likely haven.

While *pinole* and a bit of dried deer were doled out to us, and the horses were held at graze, I broke four twigs of mesquite evenly, stripping the bark, and from my shirt tore bits of linen until four newly garnished prayer plumes were finished.

With solemnity I did the work — putting aside the parched maize until the prayer was made, and then as if not noting the awe-struck, curious watching of all, I arose and walked slowly to the little hedge of the shrine. With gesticulations and bowings, I stood by it, then knelt with my back to the men. One by one I raised the twig with its shred of linen, and lifted a stone that it might be planted firm. Under the largest of the stones went the packet, and it was a true prayer I planted there though the way of it was pagan.

I felt their eyes on me, and returned to my seat silently, and gathered up my few grains of maize without looking at any of them. They were as solemnly silent as myself, yet I could feel that they were not disapproving. I had learned from Tristan that the religion of every man is sacred to these people so long as there is no attempt to impose it upon them; for their gods are jealous and peculiar.

It was plain that the planting of prayer sticks with fragments of my garment did impress the minds of all of them, and I blessed the days with Tristan and the learning of the things I never thought to need.

My captors were plainly not happy that they had to carry to an older chief the burden of the act of Kasia — yet they had decided it thus with the dead man, and it may be that some superstition of their dark minds compelled them to abide by it.

I was let sleep in comfort, but two were ever standing sentinel, and before dawn when I lifted my head to observe location of the horses, one of the men stepped forward to show me it was of no use to plan escape.

Breakfastless we took the trail when gray came into the east, and we made our way over the strange land with an energy in proof that neither food nor water was for us until we reached the end. A line of palo fierro trees showed where a river ran in the season of rain, and to the east rose a gray hill one would not forget after once having seen it — not that it had a height so great — but it was of a character peculiar.

A village of wattled huts was there, with *ramadas*, and woven baskets as granaries. The children ran after us staring at my face and my bonds, but no insult was offered, as I learned later was done with Indian captives in war. My captors were yet in doubt as to my standing.

Matiwa, the ancient of the village to which I was taken, ordered them to unfasten my hands and give me food. A woman, who looked strangely familiar, ran past me with words and gestures to Matiwa. She was let enter his dwelling with my captors while I was led elsewhere, and no word came to me of the council that day.

There was much inspection of the horses, and my heart sank next morning when the youth of the few Castilian words mounted mine, and led away the other.

"Come — womans," he said with a grin, "come womans, all good;" and then, with a great dash to display his riding, he plunged south again into the desert of hills.

Weary though I was, it was a day of restlessness for me; every bone ached from being bound in the saddle, yet the spirit in me was quickened by endless conjectures concerning Sancha and the pious cavalcade of Mother Clemente, and Tristan. Of Tristan I could only wonder how far he would go south to see them safe ere he turned to seek us, and if chance should lead him wrongly on the trail of the Haquis?

I tried to read in the faces of the villagers their disposition toward me, and with little success. They were not evil in look as had been Kasia, but my presence was a trouble, and the old chief Matiwa gave me no smiles. He did, however, let me range free with a guard ever beside me, and my garments were not divided as had been Sancha's.

The strange hill noticed when afar had allurement when in its shadow, for stupendous though it was, it looked as the work of human hands in the long terraces of stone, line above line, rising to the top where vultures nested; and up there was the outline of strange walls or upright columns, and between them the sky was seen in slits of light.

I paced back and forth, gazing up at them as they seemed to march in line as I moved. It was all most curious, for across some of the upright pillars could be seen a coping or canopy.

I tried by word or gesture to ask my guide, but he only kissed a feather and blew it upwards, and smiled, and then an Indian woman grinding mesquite beans in a stone bowl spoke haltingly.

"Señor, it is House of Light — very ancient — same old as the stars — ancient House of Light."

She was the dark little woman who looked familiar. Her hair was cut curiously unlike the others, and was not comely, but to my mind she was a very gift of God after the sound of strange languages; yet her familiar look was a puzzle.

"Where? maid of my language," I said, and sat beside her in eagerness; but she moved her bowl a little distance, and I learned a lesson.

"The House of Light, that means House of the Dawn? Is it not so, sister?"

"That is true, the ancient House of Dawns. It is true also, if you are friend to Ivava, I am as sister."

Then I knew! It was the weeping woman by the grave in the willows of the south.

"But what is Ivava?" I asked, and at that she smiled.

"Ivava is brother: 'friend' you were named by Ivava. So I am telling this ruler Matiwa. That makes you held in this place, and in safety."

"And you?"

"Movi — me, I grind grain on the trail to my own people."

Joy and sorrow have I known since that day below the strange worship place of the ancient years, but out from them stand the moments there when I felt the friendship of Tristan cast as a mantle of protection around me even in this far village of red heathens.

Yet my heart was sick that it had not been in the Indian camp of the cañon Movi ground her grains. Her good word might have served, and Sancha's garments and Sancha's letters remained her own.

I thought much of the letters, for since they were

hidden away it seemed wisely done — as if her patron saint had shown the way to take from her the emblem of a false idol.

I asked the woman Movi where the horses had been taken — and what was meant by the " womans coming " of the rider.

" That I no can help," she said gently. " The wife of Hotaku, son of Matiwa, was taken in strength by Castilian men. She come home, she told, and she has gone to Those Above! Now to pay must the white woman come to Matiwa for his son, Hotaku. Thus it is to be."

I set myself to explain. I made pleadings to her that she take me to the chief and speak for me. All that was possible I said, and all was of no use.

" You I could speak for — Ivava is as son in the heart of Matiwa, so you are fed and you are held sacred. The woman I do not know, but Castilian people owe a wife to the clan of Motiwa. They think their gods have sent this woman for the wife — it has been spoken."

I walked the plain below the great hill of the temple and thought until my heart was sick with thoughts. I looked in the wattled dwellings with horror at the picture that might be. I knew in my soul she would find a way to send her spirit to God ere the son of the red chief claim her — and this rude village of the cactus land would thus see the end of the love trail.

In misery I fled from even my one friend and made my way apart from the voices — the chatter of women and children, and all the sight of horrors to which they doomed her — our Sancha! My guard followed where I walked, bow and lance as his armament. When I reached the great stone terraces of the lone mountain, he halted me, but in wildness to get above the human things, I pointed upward, and after a moment of steady regard, he nodded his head gravely. There was no doubt that he remembered that I did respect to their shrine near the pool, and without doubt he thought I again craved place for special prayer.

As we climbed from terrace to terrace, and out on the bastions of stone where the vultures rested, I could have thought it a fortification but for singular weaknesses. Once upon the strange work, each terrace the height of a tall man, there was a temptation to go on and on, for at last I was facing one of the great primitive records of the ancient people. The mere climbing of this one made me understand why Tristan had ranged far in the seeking of these things of old which were mighty.

And on the summit was truly the remains of a temple very ancient — small wonder that the people of the wattled huts, and the brush shelters, deemed that House of the Dawn of an age with the stars. All the stone had been square and huge, and the lines of pillars held, I knew, some strange record or calculation. Was it the dawn of the various ages of the peoples by whom the land had been possessed, or the dawn of the living sun itself? I was only a boy, but to my mind great wings of mysteries of some Past seemed to hover over the place like a brooding bird. It was a very strange feeling which came to me — as if I must stretch my hands high in salute to Those Above!

It frightened me as a witchcraft would, and I made the sign, and whispered a prayer. The Indio was watching me, and at the sign of the cross he smiled, and led me to the center of the lines of stone, and there he pointed to a strange thing for a pagan place — it was the four arms of a cross in stones, one fitted close in square blocks, and now worn by the storms of centuries to rounded edges. East and west, north and south the arms reached, and where they joined there was a bowl-like depression blackened by burnings of gums or incense.

I would have given much to question the man, but could only point to the east and appear to understand. He pointed to the north, and the sky, and smiled as if he would ask if I understood that also — which of course I did not, except for the pagan records made by Tristan of the great significance to Indians of the stars of the north.

It was easy to understand how vast this work, and the thought it held, must seem to the smaller village people of smaller lives. To me it was a cathedral of the sky, and about our feet lay the broken slabs with which it had been walled. Only a few of the upright pillars had the coping left to show where and how they had been placed; these were the fragments giving so strange a line along the sky as seen from below.

I gazed down from the height, and to my mind came remembrance that a House of the Dawn was also a house of refuge, and wild hopes came that by some plan, as yet formless, sanctuary might be found there for Sancha, and if Movi could somewhere reach Tristan —!

I went down from that place with a light of comfort in my heart; at least a hope had come and wild plans were made by me in the days to follow, each move of the people being noted by me. To the old chief, Matiwa, I made attempt to be little less than a lackey, so eager was I to show affection and be claimed, like Tristan, as friend or son. My righteous endeavors, however, did not meet with the success I could have wished. He did smile upon me at times, but there was a grimness to it, and without Movi the village below the great altar would have been a friendless place.

Not that she showed her friendliness in words after that first day; there seemed a decorum to be observed by a stranger woman who ground meal to earn her way on the trail, and the records left by some ranging Castilians did not place our superior race above reproach.

But by reverence to their holy things — when I could divine them — I was at least deemed harmless to range abroad as might a straying puppy, yet ever followed after by my amiable guide. Thus, each day I was allowed to ascend to the place of ancient prayer and gaze southward, the way Movi said she would come. I never met any of the heathen on the summit, though I did note the coming down of youths at sunrise, and occasionally even the boy children in the care of Matiwa, thus I knew they kept alive some cult on the height even though they did nothing to protect the crumbling ruins.

"Why not?" I asked Movi. "Is it not the honored work of their fathers?"

"Who knows?" returned the little brown woman. "When a well is dug four times the measure of a man in this place, those who dig bring up cups and broken bowls of most ancient days. The land is an old land, but these village people have record of their coming from the great water of the sunset, and who knows the record of the buried ancient people — or the high altar builders? "

After the first visit, I but climbed the terraced height to gaze southward where Sancha was already riding toward me. I thought of her journeying unaware past the shrine where the letters were hidden, and I cursed the fatal trail on which those mad letters had led her. It was one mistake in which Tristan had been a boy at heart, and a foolish one.

The fourth day the joy was mine, for away in the distance two moving dots were discerned coming slowly through the tall columns of the giant cactus. The pagan shrine was truly as a place of light after darkness at that sight, and the tears were in my eye as I leaped down terrace after terrace, to greet her as she came.

But my guard was alert as I. His warning call summoned his fellows who circled me as in a trap! My freedom was gone, and I was hedged in a hut with bonds about me, and could only peer out as she passed to the house of Matiwa — a weary drooping figure in grass cloth mattings, and bare arms burnt in the sun.

Again Movi was called upon, and the older people of the clan of Matiwa were sent for. It was plainly a thing for council, and Sancha was given place in the *ramada* of his house where all might look upon her — poor proud little marquesa whose wealth had dwindled to her smock and torn shoes! It was evident that other wearers had used the shoes, slitting them for comfort, and as failures they had been given back to her.

She looked at none of them, her gaze was over their heads — wide eyed, listening! I felt she was hoping and was not daunted; for weary though she was, her head tilted in arrogance. I could smile at that, even while my tears fell, for her Saint of the Impossible had surely held her unbroken of spirit.

I could hear the words of Movi, who asked her the questions ordered, and told her she was chosen by the chief, and would be married into their clans. Sancha stared at her and shook her head.

"Tell your chief I am already chosen — and already promised to a man who would sweep to death every village of your people if hands touch me."

Movi spoke a word of warning.

"If I tell them you belong to a man, that will please them best, for it was a young wife taken from the son of the chief by the Castilian men."

"Tell them my man will come like a wide fire and leave only ashes here."

Movi repeated this threat, and Matiwa smiled grimly as he looked on her.

"But once can we all die," he said. "The white strangers take our maids and our wives until now we tell them we will only trade. So it is. This time we trade. When Hotaku, my son, comes from battle to claim his new woman, I send the white boy to Mexico. He can take the word to Christian men. It will teach them the thing they some day must learn. Always they have taken, now we take!"

Word for word Movi spoke the words to Sancha, and her face became white. She was to be used by the pagans to teach the wandering Castilians a lesson their own religion should teach them. But in all her horror, she caught at the one threat.

" The white boy? And where is there a white boy? " she asked as if in unbelief, but I knew her heart was trembling.

" I am here, Sancha! here in bonds," I called to her. " Be brave, for love of God until he comes — Tristan! "

She called to me gladly though I was out of her sight, and at sound of the name " Tristan," Movi spoke lowly to the chief, and they had quiet talk. Then question was again put to Sancha.

" Know you him — the Castilian — Tristan? "

" Say yes! Say yes, Sancha," I begged, but she looked at them coldly.

" Who is he — Tristan? " she asked, " and how should I know him? If it is the man who has taken their woman, why should I lie for him? "

" Sancha! it is a man they hold in honor, a man whom, for some reason, they honor more in these wilds than the viceroy. Sancha, it is only a name — have wisdom and say yes for safety."

But Movi answered me.

" Not thus must Ivava be used," she said. " The maid does not know him, and does not lie, and that is best."

" Ask the chief to set me free to speak," I pleaded, and after some words with my guard and companion, it was done. Sancha rose to her feet and held out her hands, but men stepped between when I would have clasped her.

" You do not understand," I said to Movi, " she is of my house. If freedom is given me because of Ivava, I claim freedom also for her because she is of my own blood."

Matiwa smiled when I spoke, and turned to Movi.

"Ask the white woman if this is the man to whom she belongs, he who would sweep us into the sleep of death."

Poor Sancha tried to be loyal, but knew I was all too much of a boy to threaten tribes with.

"I do belong to him as to a brother," she confessed, "but he is not the man I meant."

I could have groaned at that, for what difference would a brother mean to those stolid red devils bent on their own revenges?

"Then," said Matiwa, "must she rest content and wait Hotaku, my son, and if the other man comes for his woman, he had best come before that time."

A sentinel from the terraces sent a call, and at once there was excitement and scurrying of feet. The name of Hotaku was spoken. I looked at Sancha, but Indian names meant nothing to her. I looked at the Indians who had knives, and measured distances, and thought of how I could get a blade and use it for my hands were no longer bound and all minds were on the coming of the son of Matiwa.

Then I heard another name, and Movi looked at me and nodded her head and smiled. I was dazed with the suddenness of all things after the still days of waiting. The sense of what she meant did not come to me until I saw a horse and a wounded Indian sagging in a saddle. The horse was that of Tristan, and my heart sank, while my eyes went again to a knife in an Indian girdle.

Not until the horse was halted did I see that Tristan, who looked like the dead, walked beside and held the Indio in the saddle.

Sancha gave one look — one choking cry, and dropped her head on her breast — her hair covering her face, and her tattered and slashed shoes were drawn under the manta of grass matting.

"Water — for God's love!" muttered Tristan, but Movi already had it in a gourd. He drank it with closed eyes, and dropped where he stood. The others carried Hotaku into the house of Matiwa, and Movi helped me bathe the face of Tristan, and the hands, and she brought broth of a rabbit, and a little at a time he swallowed it, and finally looked at us with bloodshot, yet seeing, eyes.

"Juanito," he said at last. "I have come. Where is she?"

No one answered, and she who covered herself with her hair seemed to sink more low on the trodden earth under the *ramada*.

"Alive, and — unharmed," was all I dared say. "Rest you now till we learn how this has come about — you are starving!"

"For water — water," he assented. "Searching, I found my friend wounded, we made the start home for help in the search, and, you see! He was mad with fever and striving for a hidden spring he knew. I fought him, took his arms, and made him ride. He is dying, I think, but he sees his father, and he is my friend."

Matiwa came out, and took his hand, his face was sad, and Movi spoke for him.

"Ivava," he said, "come, speak to Hotaku as you know. He calls for his wife. Tell him there is a new wife, white and young. Make him hear. You have kept life in him, now give him strength."

Tristan stared at him, and arose, staggering, striving against weakness.

"A new wife, white and young!" he repeated.

Matiwa pointed to me, and Movi again spoke.

"This boy would claim her, but the maid is for my son, tell him — you — he listens for your voice."

"The maid — the white maid — is for your son, Matiwa?" said Tristan very quietly — "and what am I?"

"You are Ivava — you are also son, and you are brother," said the old man, "and you bring back to his mother our youngest born."

"And what may I ask of your clan?"

"All things we may grant to a friend."

"Then take me to the maid whom my younger brother has asked of you. Of her have I come in search. Of your clan I ask only the maid."

"She is yours?" And the eyes of Matiwa were narrow and keen.

"She is mine," said Tristan and looked at him squarely. "Your son, who is going to God, was to help in search for her — she is mine."

"Yet she calls not out to you in gladness," said the old man with grimness, "and your own eyes do not know her though she sits at your feet."

Tristan stared at him and at me, but I dared not speak though I saw the wary eyes of Matiwa who thought it all white trickery. Then Tristan looked on the crouched figure hidden under black hair and the manta of grass cloth, and his cry was as if his heart had been struck.

He moved toward her with outreaching hands, then halted — aware of Matiwa's suspicion, and turned to his horse. There, tied to the saddle, was rolled a blanket, and the extra robe given him by Salvadore Serri that first day.

Quickly he unfastened it, and I could see the great beads of water on his brow. He was weak from starvation, and desperate, and the sight of her thus turned him chalk white.

He shook the robe loose from the rawhide straps.

"Arise, Doña de Llorente y Rivera," he said, and his voice was shaking, though his words were cold, and she arose and stood, her eyes on the ground, and he cast about her the robe, and took the brown rosary, with its scattered turquoise and shell beads, and put it around her neck.

"She is mine to claim before the clans, Matiwa," he said. "By the beads of your friend Fernan, you see that she is sacred."

"I see it, and my heart is troubled that she was shamed by our people, but it is a time of war. No man shall claim her but you, and my son will be glad."

"He will be glad," assented Tristan, and then to Movi he said, "little sister, take my lady where she will have rest and comfort. My eyes are glad to look upon you here."

And Movi touched the hand of Sancha who turned and followed her. Not once had she lifted her head or looked at him.

"Watch over her, Juanito," he said haltingly, "let her not feel shame."

And then he sank as if to pray, but from his knees fell prone upon the ground. His last strength had been given, but he had come in time.

CHAPTER XV

THE FINDING OF ANITA

SANCHA wept when alone, and was curiously silent, asking few questions. Of that I was glad enough, for in his delirium of the night I heard strange things — memories of old days in Spain, secret things of forbidden books, and names I dared not whisper even though all those desert leagues from the Holy Brotherhood — a word here and there of his escape in the night time — Fray Bernardino, and an open gate — a saddled horse — his own saddle!

All this, and then the search for trail of the Haquis — and white Virgo! The mumblings of thirst, and the records of stars jumbled together. I listened to it through the night hours while herb brews were made and poured down him; also dried blossoms were burnt as incense, of which I half strangled. Yet the pagan cures did have power, for the fever abated, and in early morning he slept.

But the son of Matiwa went to his gods in the night, and I strove to find excuse to lead Sancha apart from the village ere the ceremonies of death add horror to her mind.

I found her fresh bathed, her hair smoothed by a broom of grasses, and clothed from throat to feet in the consecrated robe; but while there was sanctity in her garb, there was little hint of it in her expression.

"Tell this woman she lies," she said, pointing to poor Movi, who was much impressed by all the happenings.

"Come away, Sancha, that we may talk alone," I begged; "there are great reasons. You have lately escaped one danger, are you eager for more?"

She did not answer, but followed me out across the level until we were in the shadow of the hill. I noted that Movi looked after us strangely. She thought I was stealing the property of Tristan while he slept!

"Now tell me where no one hears," I suggested, but her mood had changed.

"She is but a foolish savage," she confessed, "and I should not heed her words, but she thought the giving of this cloak was a marriage gift! Does your friend sleep?"

"Sancha — Sancha!" I said, and looked at her. She stared back at me with haughtiness for an instant, and then her tears fell, and she turned away, fairly running until she reached the terraced hill.

"Go you back and leave me," she said weeping. "You mean that he is my friend most, and that I — O Juanito, how is the debt to be paid? What can one do for a man like that?"

"Is it that you fear to own the greatness of the debt?" I asked, but she shook her head.

"I do not know what I fear — it is like a witchcraft, for Juanito, I tell you truly, I knew he was coming!"

"You knew — !" I felt myself go cold at that.

"Night and day *I knew*. I seemed to hear the sound

of his horse even in my dreams. I thought of you, also I wished with all my heart and prayers for Marco; yet it was neither of you, but always the steps of that man I heard. And when he staggered in from the trail, I was not even surprised. It was as if I had been waiting a thousand years until he found me there — half naked and ashamed."

I said nothing, but sat down, my head in my hands, while she paced back and forth restless, in the fresh dawn of her new day of freedom.

"It is very strange," she said, "and this extra robe — it is as if he too had been waiting this time."

Some men came down the terraces and passed us. I could see their minds were of their prayer, and made no salute, she turned to look.

"What do they?" she asked, and I pointed upwards.

"They go for prayer in the ancient place of refuge," I said. "It is their high House of the Dawn."

She gave a low cry and stared at me.

"Are all things coming at once?" she asked; "the things of witchcraft, and the shrines of which his letters spoke? O Juanito, my heart was in the letters — and his — and they are gone and have changed all things — the letters — the letters!"

I strove to comfort her with the thought of her safety and her freedom, but she shook her head.

"All is changed, Juanito. This girl in the monk's robe is not the Sancha who rode with you under the palms out of Mexico. The letters were as the touch of his hand — they led me on! They are gone, and it is as if the end of a trail had been reached. It is most strange!"

Then, after a little she said, pointing upward, "I want to go there, I want to find such House of the Dawn as the letters told me of."

But I urged that she wait another time. I strove to keep near enough to Tristan for service if need be.

"What is it that woman calls him — Señor Alcatraz?" she asked, and I told her Ivava meant "brother" in Movi's language, and it was all they called him.

"And Tristan — who is that?"

"I have heard that a man of that name journeyed these parts with a priest for whom they had much love. It may be they confuse the names," I answered. And already her thoughts were afar, and she was easily satisfied, which was well for me.

"Is there anything I might do for him — your Ivava?" she asked, and I thought that when he wakened he might need to be assured by her own words of her safety.

So, after the dead body of the Indio had been carried out, I led her to the rude shelter, and Tristan opened his eyes to find her there, trembling and staring at his thin cheeks.

"I owe you much — Señor — I scarce know how to speak of it," she said; "words are not much — but if I may serve you —"

He smiled at that wanly enough.

"There is no need of words, Excellencia, I regret I have no fitting seat to offer — or —"

"Cease, I beg you! My own pride has brought shame to me — and has brought you to this!"

"It is a weakness, no more," he answered her; "we lost the way of the water — and the days without food

— yet the lack of water was worst. But you are safe and perhaps you will not again disdain the beads I begged you wear? "

" Never," she said, " never."

The next day he was up from the couch, and eating the food or broths Movi was ever intent upon. Sancha was courteous, but ill at ease in his presence; a strange and new thing for her. She would wander away restlessly towards the terraces, or gather strange desert blooms to learn their names and uses.

Thus he noted the wretched slashed footgear under her robe, and sent Movi for rawhide, at which Movi laughed aloud even while she complied, and her smiles were ever apparent as she watched him cut the leather with his knife and fashion small boots of deer skin with rawhide soles, and all sewn with the glistening sinew of the deer.

To me Movi laughed.

" It is true," she said. " His lady makes me silent when I say he is her man — but you see! Each man of our people makes the boot for his own woman; no other man must do — and you see."

He gave them to me when finished that I might get them to her, and then he proceeded to mend his worn raiment, and take note that the horses were getting rest and food for the trail.

No word had been said of it, for I waited his strength ere bringing forward new questions, but a trader from the north — a Pima man — came in with turquoise and blankets, and told of trouble with the Apaches, and of the Castilian colonists who had gone to Santa Fé, and of a white woman they had left for dead with the

Pimas, but who was still alive. The Pima medicine had
more of virtue than the white magic of the Castilians.

"Anita!" said Tristan, and the Piman thought that
was like her name.

"In another day we will go," said Tristan turning
to me. "Another day of rest and water for the horses
and we can take the trail — my poor little Anita!"

I did not know that Sancha had walked close and
halted in the shadow when she heard an Indian talking
with us, but when I went to look at the horses I met
her there, and her look was strange.

"Where do you go?" she asked, and I pointed where
the horses grazed.

"Where is the trail you go?" she persisted — "the
trail for his Anita?"

"I think he goes north," I said.

"I do not!" she decided. "To Kavorka we started,
and there I will go!"

"Sancha!" I begged, but she walked away.

"I learn now why he was sleepless on the trail —
and why we were made ride in the night — it was for
a woman!" she said.

"It was indeed, Sancha," I answered, "he went
sleepless to guard a woman who disdained the sacrifice."

She halted at that as though to question me, but I
gave her no chance. Later I told Tristan Sancha had
set her mind on Kavorka.

"With the Haquis thick between?" he said. "I
could find no guard strong enough for that trail these
days. She goes with us."

"But — she has set her mind," I ventured doubt-

fully, whereat he laughed with a grimness in which there
was yet sorrow.

"And her mind has, until now, been the rule for all
who came near her," he conceded, "therefore will her
dislike of me be even greater that I am the first to
change that. She goes with us, and I go north."

"To find Anita?"

"Ay: and to find the man who cast her off among
savages!" and he looked a savage himself as he said
it though his voice did not reach beyond the *ramada*.

"But — Sancha?" and my soul was full of fear between the two tempers of fire.

"Tell her it is no more distance north where there
are white people and priests than it is back to Sinaloa;
also, the southern trail is fenced now by fighting savages, and in the north I am as with my own people, and
my people will guard my friends."

"And I am to be the one to tell her?" I grumbled
with no liking for the task.

"Why not? Will she not see him — Marco —
the sooner?"

That seemed a good reason, though his bitter smile
was not comforting, and in truth I found myself for-
getting in those days that Marco was in the world.
I could even understand Sancha's word that she hoped
for him, prayed for him, yet ever heard the voice or step
of the other man in her dreams.

So I took to her the boots, and helped her with them
while Movi smiled at us.

"Now she Hopi womans," she said, "good Hopi
boots."

Sancha asked no questions, but put them on with

our help, and Movi showed her the fastenings at the
knee.

"Good boot for trail — much strong — good mans,"
approved Movi with her gentle smile, "good trail boot,
me too — I go."

Sancha gave little heed to her comment, or its meanings, and I preferred to tell her when alone that we
were all to go north.

But when I did, she stared at me in disapproval and
walked away. Her disappointment in me was plain.

"But Sancha!" I argued, "what else is there to do?
He goes north, and this kind Hopi woman goes north.
What is there for you or for me alone in this village?
Also their fighting men are away fighting. If their
enemy is conqueror, who is to say what tribe may cover
the land? Six months may pass before Castilians go
the south trail; and even so, this village is not on the
trail."

"He will come — Marco. He will find me," she
asserted defiantly. "You know he will come."

"It may happen," I agreed, "and he will find you
tied naked under some other tree, or dead in some other
cañon."

She pointed to the ruins on the summit.

"I am going there," she said. "In the letters he told
me a House of Dawn was a house of refuge. This is
the first House of Dawn on my path — and the angels
know my night has been dark!"

"You must save your strength for the trail," I called
after her, but she set off across the little plain.

"You are with him, and against my wishes," she retorted. "Everyone is with him, and I am forgotten."

I could make little of that, for daytime and nighttime our thoughts were for her good, yet I could do nought but go back and tell him.

"And she has gone — and alone?" he asked.

"Gone she has — to find a place of refuge from us," I grinned. "This comes of your teachings. Her heart is set on finding a sanctuary in which to wait for the man who wrote the letters!"

He arose, and took a stout stave for walking.

"It is the better place," he agreed. "I will go up."

I walked beside him, for I feared his weakness, and we stood and looked as she climbed terrace after terrace where the young vultures tried their wings.

"She is a child in humors, but she has braveness," he said — "look at the black wings above her, and she does not once falter."

I thought it a strange hour to praise her bravery when it was causing him a climb for which he was none too fit.

"That height is not a trifle," I warned him, "it is near a thousand spans, and your strength is not returned."

"The climb is good to test it," he returned — "and it may be we all need the high places of prayer in these days. Strange things come to pass in lives. I never thought to stand beside her at any House of the Dawn."

Beyond that we did not speak, for I could not well follow his thought. What could he hope to gain in any prayer place, when she fled there in angry mood?

And there we found her at the very edge of the flat rock of the height, and between us was the ruin of slabs and broken pillar.

Over her head she had drawn the cowl of the robe when among the great birds. They were settling themselves in their roosts because of the low sinking sun.

I halted there by the pillars, but he crossed the summit, and his step was so light on the stone floor that she did not know until he stood beside her.

"May your prayers in the place of dawn bring to your heart happiness, Excellencia," he said, and so startled was she that she made a step away, and would have slipped at the edge but that his hand caught her.

"Your pardon for me!" he said, as she stood steady, and he drew his hand away. But she stared at him as if more afraid of him than of the depths below.

"Are you in league with Indian enchanters?" she asked. "How knew you that I made prayers? and have you hidden wings that you come to this place without sound?"

"It is a place for prayer, and I know your spirit though you strive to hide it from me, Excellencia. I may not bring you the answer to the prayer, but it seems a good place to speak with you, for in the village it is not so easy."

"That is true," she agreed; "down there I can only see you as you entered — staggering, and myself as I was — but how know you that it is hard to talk to you before the people? You have helped me, but you make me fear you — the thought of you — more than the Indians can do, and that leaves me bewildered. Who are you, Ivava Alcatraz?"

He did not reply to that at once, and I, beside the pillar, held my breath and heard my heart thump — would he tell her?

"At least you have called me by the Indio word for brother, and that is much when two people share a trail, and it is also gracious of you, Excellencia. But my name should be written Kahn Alcatraz — for Kahn was the name of my mother."

"It is a strange name," she mused. "Kahn! Is it — Indio?"

"No, even though Indians have the word, and the meaning of the word, while it is lost in the older world."

"There," she said suddenly, "it is the things like that which seem enchantment. You are not old, yet you know the things of old, and you walk into a tribe and change their rules, until it seems they too fear you. Is it wonder I deem it strange?"

"If affairs seem strange to unpleasantness on the trail, ask and I will change what I can," he said.

"Then you will turn back with me?" and there was gladness in her voice, "to Kavorka if not to Sinaloa, you have come to tell me this?"

"I have come to tell you, Excellencia, that we start north at dawn, and that the next white faces you may see will be at Santa Fé in New Granada."

"But I told Juanito — "

"Yes, you did, but this is a trail Juanito cannot make plans for. You gave no reason, Excellencia, and — "

"How dared I give the true reason? and why now do you call me 'excellencia' in that tone?" she demanded. "Is it in mockery?"

"Mockery — of you?" he said, but she was blazing in quick anger, and the tone of his voice meant nothing.

"You have shamed me more than the garb of grass,"

she persisted. "You came to my rescue, but made me a laughing stock. You tell these savages that I belong to you, and now you would drag me north on your trail because of some woman you were seeking when you crossed our path. Well, I will not go! This I did not tell Juanito, else there would be a day of reckoning for you, and — "

"Would you try, even in your anger, to save me that day of reckoning?" he asked.

"I must remember you did me service: that I must remember, even though you did tell them you owned me, as if I, a Llorente y Rivera, were but a chattel."

At that I stumbled forward, and found my tongue.

"Sancha, Sancha!" I said, "if he is exiled from your friendship for that, I too must go, for I did likewise!"

They both stared at me as if I was the Father of Lies.

"Ay, did I! but with no effect, you, Sancha, know that is true. Did I anger you when I told them you were mine, of my family? Should I show anger that he called me his brother — and saved me? And you — your life he has given back, and from your head to the tip of your toe he has clothed you, and — "

"No!" she broke in sharply, "you — yourself — "

"I, myself!" I mocked. "What could I do here but by his grace? Sancha, you foster a pride that is against all reason. This is not your life of ceremony in palaces, it is the Brotherhood of the Desert where men and women strive for life together, or loyal death together; are you above that brotherhood?"

"Boy!" he said, and put his hand on my arm looking at me curiously. I do not know what I appeared to them, but her face flushed red and went white again as she stared at me, and I was shaking as I flung aside his hand.

"I am no longer a boy — she will make old men of both of us on one summer's journey," I persisted. "Even now she does not measure aright your sacrifices, and *you* will never speak!"

"There is nothing to say," he stated looking at me with a sternness as if in fear I would lose my wits utterly, and blunder further.

"There *is* something to say!" she retorted. "Am I a fool that I do not know it, and feel it? The very air is full of the unspoken; it weighs me down — it makes me afraid. It may be Juanito is right that it makes me also unjust. But it is not pride, Juanito, it is the fear of some unknown thing. Even my dreams make me fear! I come up here above the earth to the House of the Dawn — yet the dawn I do not find."

"It is in your heart you must find the dawn, else a false dawn may bring its deceptions, Excellencia," he said, and I wondered at the steadiness of his voice, for his eyes were devouring the proud loveliness of her face.

"If it is so, it will be for the reason that neither you nor Juanito give me confidences. You make plans as if for a child; you keep secrets, and your thoughts are all for some one else — some woman on that north trail."

"If you see her, Excellencia, you perhaps will not have wonder at that," he said gently, "and some day you will forgive Juanito and me any harmless secrets we may have."

"I do not think I will see her. I do not think I will

go," she said pettishly. "Why should I travel deeper
into a desert where there is no comfort?"

"Have you forgotten so quickly the man you crossed
the sea to find?" I asked with brutal curtness, at least
I was rougher than I meant to be, for she turned away,
and her hands went to her face and she wept despair-
ingly. I strove to make excuse, to comfort her, but
she waved me away.

"Go, both of you!" she said. "You are only men,
and you are without heart, and go north I will not; why
should I?"

"Because you are mine to save, and I can only
save you by claiming you, and taking you with me,"
he said steadily. "Never fancy it is a journey of
pleasure I am planning for any of us."

At that she ceased weeping, and turned to me.

"Since it is made so plain that it is no pleasure to
take me, I may at least be excused from gratitude,"
she remarked coldly. "I am only carried as extra
baggage for which there is no safe warehouse!"

He made no reply, but his eyes held all of sadness
as he watched her walk back to the worn trail. Silent
he stood there against the darkling sky, for the blue
haze was covering the mesas of the east. In his still-
ness he looked akin to a detached pillar of the ancient
altar. A ray of the afterglow illumined all with a
strange golden green light for an instant, and Sancha
caught my hand.

"He looks as if he had stood there from the beginning of the world," she whispered, "and waiting — waiting for what? He is like no other man on earth." Then
after a little she continued. "My first hour at a shrine

of the dawn is not what I prayed for, but that man; —
Juanito, he makes all things fit his own plans, even
prayers!"

Between the two of them, I was past asking questions of her meaning, and I got her safely down the
terraces as the dusk came, but the stars were out before
he followed.

My sleep was over light because of my doubts of her
going in willingness, yet she came out of the hut at the
first call of the white dawn, and looked like a most
lovely martyr sacrificed to our selfishness.

We had our three rested horses, and a burro brought
from the hills for Movi, who plainly said she would
prefer to walk. Sancha listened to the argument which
ended in the obedience of the Indian girl, and then
in proud silence she mounted her own animal, and said
her farewells to the old chief and those who had shown
good intent.

"It is a new thing for one of our family to leave
a poor village no richer for a visit, Juanito," she said
with a sort of self pity. "We seem to have fallen into
mean estate in the new land."

Beyond that she favored me with few words, as if to
punish me for what she deemed adherence to his cause.
She showed her disapproval of us both by riding beside
Movi, and that little person was vastly flattered, discoursing, on request, concerning her own wonderful
home of the northern desert, and her eagerness to return
to the ancient land of Tusayan.

We were well supplied with all the outfittings of an
Indian camp — ground meal, parched maize, and dried
deer meat — and with an archer's bow for myself and

the arquebus of Tristan, we were fairly provided for defense. For the first day we followed the river to the north and east and reached a peaceful village where we rested for the night, and an Indio guide kept us company for two days longer, trotting beside the horse of Tristan as if the leagues were but a holiday run over the desert, where, to my untaught eyes, there was no sign of a road. At need we made long days to find the best water places, and passed from the desert bloom and giant cactus into valleys where the palo fierro and aliso trees were things of beauty, and the desert willow gave its yellow bloom.

At the *temporales* — the summer ranches by the fields and water holes — the friendly Indians showed us courtesies in their own way; offerings of mescal roots and sahauro wine were brought, also fresh killed antelope, and brown beans cooked in vessels of burned clay. All these became things of enjoyment to Sancha until she seemed ashamed of idle hands, and had much amusement in being taught the ways of primitive women, until at one place of rest she strove to form a vessel of clay, and was sweet tempered again, and laughed with me when I showed her its crooked side.

There were hours when she became gay over trifles, and wreathed flowers and vines to wear as shade from the sun, and then there were long moments when she watched Tristan in converse with Indian friends, as if in silent query as to the secret of his influence, and to me she called him " Your Señor Ivava."

Once he heard this, and smiled.

" It is honor, Excellencia, to be given as brother even to your kinsman," he said.

"Without kindred to the others of the family!" she retorted, mockingly. "Juanito, you alone are adopted. You can expect an Indian naming and baptizing when we find leisure — and find water enough! Movi tells me the baptism of her people is a headwashing in a bowl of foam. Have you shared that pagan rite, Señor Don Kahn Alcatraz?"

"It was my good fortune," he assented, "else Movi here could not call me brother."

Thus with quiet courtesy he met either her mockery or her silence, but she regarded him curiously when he said that.

"And you did not fear it as a pagan enchanting by which your soul would be dangered?" she asked.

"If ever chance should take you to that people of peace — whose very religion is against angry thoughts in the heart, you would know their simple ceremony of baptism could work no ill," he made answer.

"Would the officers of the Holy Brotherhood agree with you in that?" she asked.

"I shall not return on the trail to make inquiry," he answered. "None of the officers have ever seen the peaceful lives of the Hopi people."

"Yet, as a good Christian, you must know there can be but one baptism," she persisted; and at this speech of religions and the Holy Office there came back to me the dread for him, and I begged them to consider more cheerful things than religion, since we were such weary leagues from even a chapel.

"Talk not of chapels either, Juanito," she said. "I would I had waited back there by the chapel with my dreams."

She walked away from us, and sat alone under a mesquite until the saddles were on, and when I went for her there were tears in her eyes, and she pointed to a white butterfly drifting over low creeping desert blooms.

"He called me that in the letters — and I have lost the letters," she said. "He painted that dream picture of me in the chapel, and I have wandered into the deserts away from the chapel. Juanito, that is not all, that place of the House of the Dawn had witchcraft — I know it! I have never been the same in my dreams since that time, and — yes, I was weeping because of it! for never once have I thought of Marco until that butterfly comes and will not go away. I am frightened at myself to whom I am a stranger, and my thoughts are of new and different things. What but a witchcraft could make that, Juanito?"

"Come, he is waiting," I said, and at that she laughed.

"Come, he is waiting!" she mocked. "All things in the Desert begin and end with him! You also only echo what he thinks. We are dragged along on this trail to some woman whom he seeks, but never makes discourse of. There is some wrong thing covered in all this, Juanito. Why should a white woman remain with others than her own kind?"

I did not answer, and she caught my hand.

"Is it that — he loves her?" she asked watching the still face of Tristan.

"I think it is so — or has been so," I answered truly, "for at the last camp he had word that she is on the way to death, and as you see, he is a troubled man."

"I see," she said softly, "death must be a sad thing where there is love, and love itself is sad enough."

I could not see how love could teach her sadness since only the shadow love had come to her — the mere dream of a maid, and not the knowledge of truth. Also I rode beside her with a strangely divided mind at thought of love and the lessons of love; for while, as a Christian, I must pray for the life of poor Anita, I found myself wishing that if the end was near, it might come before we reached her abiding place at the north village, Tuquison.

But this was not to be. Indians with horses came out to meet us on the trail, for their heralds had seen us afar, and after spoken words of friendliness for our care, Tristan accepted a fresh horse and rode on alone quickly.

Without word to either of us he went, and Sancha, gazing after him, had a white face of dismay. It was the first time he had ever ignored her presence, or left without courtesy to her, and I tried to explain, but she shook her head.

"You are good, Juanito, you think it is my pride that is hurt, the pride of a Llorente y Rivera. How it all dwindles and fades here in the great wilderness. What is our rank worth here? Would the viceroy himself have power like this stranger whose word saves us, and whose hand clothes me? Juanito, when a debt is heavy as this it weighs, it weighs! And, cousin mine, he flings us all this without thought, and rides to find the other — the woman who makes him sad."

It was the first time she had ever betrayed so much, but I could see that despite her resentment, and moods of mockery, she did not underrate his importance as guardian in the wild places. She meant to be just, yet the woman in her resented what she dared not disdain.

And into that village we rode as in state, for beside us were his Indio friends with smiles and kind welcome, and on Sancha in the monk's robe they looked with wondering eyes, also one of the older men touched a turquoise pendant on the rosary she wore, and pointed to himself that we might know the jewel was his gift, and that it was pledge of friendliness.

A dwelling was given us at the edge of the village, and there water was brought, and food, but we saw nothing of Tristan. Sancha asked no question, but wandered, restless, about the village, or stood looking north where the heat waves rippled upward, and the candelabra of the giant cactus made dark lines against the blue. When she returned, Movi had disappeared — sent for by Ivava, said the wife of the village chief.

Sancha looked at me half accusingly.

"You should have kept her until I came," she said. "I — I have been thinking about that — and if the woman is white — "

"Sancha! Sancha!" I said, perceiving her struggle, and knowing her pride. "The Brotherhood of the Desert asks neither rank nor color when sickness comes, or death comes."

"But it was Movi he asked, and not me," she persisted.

"Have you not thought that he also may have his pride?" I asked.

She pondered this a moment, troubled, and pale under all the tan of the sun.

"I have failed in all things," she said at last. "I resented that woman because he explained nothing, yet it was no fault of hers. You shall take me to her."

I scarce knew how to do so for Tristan had given me neither word nor hint of his wishes. It was as if he left for Fate to finish that which Fate had so strangely begun.

With the wife of the chief as guide, we went out past the gardens or little fields to a wattled hut and *ramada;* beyond were the pools where women filled their woven and waxed water vases. As we approached, Movi came to meet us, and her face was very grave.

"Ivava goes for other water because she asks it," she said. "Yes, it is far. He is knowing there is no use — yet she asks. Sometimes the mind is gone away, and she called for many things — but none of the things can he bring but the water."

Even as she spoke, Tristan appeared beyond the dwelling with a water vase of the desert, and in the shadow of the *ramada* we saw him kneel, and lift up to drink the woman lying there.

We had not seen her before — so still she lay that it looked like a mere heap of deer skins and a striped blanket of Indio weave. Her face was very white and her eyes had the strange glisten which comes before the end. I had seen it with Don Rodrigo, and thus I knew.

"Drink, Anita, dear little one," said Tristan in a voice of tenderness Sancha had never heard. She caught my hand, and I could feel her tremble.

"It is good," whispered Anita, haltingly, "you have come far — they call you here, Ivava — Ivava, and that

The Finding of Anita.

is dear to them! You will not do him wrong? You will not?"

"Comfort you, and sleep content, Anita mine," he said lowly, for even as she spoke, her eyes closed, but as he drew away his hand, she muttered, "Do not go. Do not leave me, belovéd. I will grow strong — a little rest, and I can ride beside you — a little rest, belovéd."

"She sleeps, Movi," said Tristan as he arose from beside her, "guard her again until I come."

He turned away without even sight of Sancha and me standing close beside the wattled hut. I would have spoken, but her hand held me with a grip for silence, and her eyes were fixed on the girl there, and a ring on her hand. It held an emerald, and was the one painted into that portrait so admired by Sancha as a child.

"The ring of Marco!" she whispered. "See you, Juanito, it is the ring of Marco she wears! They have killed Marco — these savages *he* calls friends! it is the ring of Marco!"

It was, but I tried to lie out of it with some pretext of a copy made of it — or such reasonable thought — but it was a useless effort, for Anita opened her eyes full on Sancha at the name of Marco.

"Is — he come back — Marco?" and her thin voice was sharp with eagerness. "Was it you — said his name? Tell him — for God's love tell him to come quickly. But how is it? and who are you? and why —"

Her voice trailed out in weakness, and I moved back out of her range as Sancha went forward swiftly.

"I am Marquesa de Llorente y Rivera," she said. "Who are you to wear that ring?"

"How — wonderful you are — as they said," murmured poor Anita, "yet — he never gave love to you — never — never! With me beside him he rode north, and left Tristan to write you the letters — Tristan, so dear — so good! But Excellencia — he never loved you — never — never — never!" Then her eyes closed, and she lay whispering — "Marco — Marco."

The face of Sancha was staring white.

"Who is she to say these things?" she demanded, and put her hand on the shoulder of Anita as if to shake her into senses again, but I stopped her.

"A poor soul who will soon be no more on earth, Sancha," I said, "also she has loved much, and been left behind, is not that enough?"

"No," she said, and flung off my hand. "No — it is not true — not true of Marco — not — " then she stopped and looked at me.

"The letters!" she whispered, "did you hear? How did this creature by the wayside know of letters to me? And Tristan! who is Tristan?"

"Sancha dear — come away!" I begged of her. "You might as well ask who is Juan, or Pedro, or Pablo. Her mind is going, she uses names she does not know."

"She does know," she insisted coldly. "I heard that name also in the village by the hill of the dawn — yes, I did! Not know? she knows too much of me and mine to die not telling. Juanito, if you love me, take yourself out of this matter. Awake — girl — arouse and tell me! Who wrote the letters?"

Poor Anita, shocked into life again, lifted her head and strove.

"Excellencia, he adored you always — I think — always! Marco did not know that — no — he did not know."

"Tell me — of the letters!"

"It was a jest — Excellencia. They tossed dice to decide which man should write the letters to you, for Marco had love for none but me, not Doña Perfecta — not you — for me only — Marco! Marco!"

She sank back with his name on her lips, and Sancha knelt, trembling, looking down in the blue white face.

"It is a lie!" she said. "It is all a lie!"

But even as she spoke she fell limp, and when Movi brought Tristan, he found me between a dead girl, and one who looked like death.

CHAPTER XVI

IN THE PAINTED DESERT

IT WAS the third time I had seen death on the long trail — the husband of Movi, the warrior Hotaku, and now the poor little maid who had been all alight with the sparkle of love when last I had seen her. What I could, I did, to help Tristan, but his wish was that I wait upon Sancha, and leave to him, and to Movi, the last care of little Anita.

To Sancha I gave no sign that my eyes had ever before looked upon the poor waif of love left by the wayside, but when told the grave was ready, she arose and took my hand.

" Come, Juanito," she said, " she is to us a mystery of the Desert. Yet you say there is brotherhood here among men, why not also sisterhood? I think that she was false, but that is between her own soul and God."

So she stood beside me, and looked in the placid face of the dead girl, and her voice joined with that of Tristan in the prayer for the dead, while the Indians, sad faced, yet curious, ranged at either side and listened.

I felt as if in some strange dream as I watched the white man and the maid at either side of that grave, and heard their blended tones in prayer. It was the unbelieveable thing which had happened — it made the way clear for Marco and happiness, if only chance could wipe the memory of the girl's words from the mind of Sancha. But to me that grave seemed as the close of a chapter in those lives. It was the two living people who filled my thoughts, and not the poor child on the bed of dry grasses in the shallow trench.

The hands of Anita were folded over her breast and the ring was there. Sancha looked at it, and at me.

"That is well," she said, "for surely it meant much to her. If it is duplicate, it is hers, and if it is the true ring of Marco de Ordoño, then he also is hers if alive, and none of mine. But that I do not believe."

Tristan heard her, but said nothing and motioned me to take her away as the crude hoes of the Indios scraped the earth on top of the cover of dry grasses.

"He loved her so that he followed her far," said Sancha, "yet he weeps not at her going. The love of men is a curious thing."

"Yet if she loved not him, would a wise man mourn?" I asked.

"She was fond, that we could overhear, and so was he," she replied, and so strongly was she sure of his love for the dead girl that it seemed a safe belief to encourage her in. I was willing she should think all things but the truth.

With some of his Indio friends, he ate the evening meal, and came not to us until the sun had gone. The Desert was sinking to rest in the blanket of misty blue greens, and the mountains to the north were against the sky in faint amethyst. Sancha had stood, as if fascinated by the beauty of it while it changed through the many tints of pink and purple, and then blended with the dusky plain.

Tristan coming slowly towards us, noted her gaze and turned to look.

"Forests and running streams are beyond there," he remarked. "For a little journey we will see no desert."

"But — from here we go back!" she said. "I was looking into the north as a land we will not cross."

"Cross it I must," he replied, "and in safety must leave you with Governor Otermin of New Granada."

"The Governor of New Granada is a stranger to me," she said, "and I feel no call to visit his province, my wish is to free myself from this endless trail, and go back to Sinaloa."

For a moment they faced each other in mute battle of wills, then he smiled slightly.

"Excellencia, when you chose to ignore my rules of march, and rode your horse out of reach of the guard, you closed behind you the only gate to Sinaloa this year. In October you may have chance with the *conducta* of traders to go south from Sante Fé to El Paso, and thence to Mexico, but first we must guard you safely to Sante Fé. We are at the edge of the Apache lands where only large cavalcades feel safe — yet we must find a way past them. Here you could not remain, the water alone would kill you."

She looked at him with mutinous, unbelieving eyes.

"You have thought this out for my safety that it may fit your own will," she said coldly. "I heard her — the girl who died — beg you off from some plan — some vengeance perhaps, and it lies on that north trail, she begged you to do him no wrong."

"But you heard no promise," he reminded her, "and it will not be wrong I do, but right."

"Because she followed his trail, how was he to help that?" she demanded, "and because she died on the way ere he was found, you would follow for vengeance, Kahn Alcatraz?"

He only looked at her, letting her think what she would.

"If she gave him love instead of you, how can vengeance alter that?" she persisted. "Love goes where it will, it is not to be bound. Who appoints you judge? As a Christian you will do the thing she, in dying, asked of you — and you will go back?"

"No, Excellencia," he said with a little sigh as he looked southward where prison or the stake waited him, "no, it is not so written. I shall not go back."

"And I must go north beside you whether I wish it or no?" she asked frowning.

"So it seems," he said quietly, "there is no other way. None of us wish it, Excellencia — but the way through the land of the Haquis is closed these days — there is no other way."

"Do you know that the man you go north to reckon with is the man to whom I am betrothed?" she asked, and he bowed as though receiving a gracious confidence.

"I would it were another," he said, "but the Fates often arrange affairs without consulting us."

"To be loyal I announce that I will only ride north beside you to warn him against your intent," she said, and again he bent his head.

"That is as must be, and we will lose no time on the way."

"Never fear that I shall be laggard," she retorted, "my — love — will keep pace with your evil intent.

I rejoice you are so frank even in injustice to him, and I shall ride north beside you to — to learn some truths," she ended, lamely enough.

" God send you learn all truth of comfort to you in this world, Excellencia," he said quietly, " and that I may be your guide on the way."

" I do not know how I may accept guidance or courtesies from one who bears him ill," she debated. " I know nothing of your family, or even if you are nearly enough to his rank for fighting."

" God, the Father, will enlighten us on that when the time comes," he said, " but of the man you trust, and the little maid in the grave, we will not speak, and on your trail to truths the rank of a desert guide will not be an important thing. We start at dawn."

He bowed to her and walked away, and she turned to me with appealing outreached hands.

" Juanito, what other thing could the saints send for my trial of the spirit? " she asked. " How or why should I do else but hate him? Who is he to set himself a task against an Ordoño? "

" Sancha, when we accept food and shelter by his courtesy, it ill beseems us to question whence he came," I said, " for without him we would both be dead in this far wilderness. Hate is the last thing we should give him."

" I do not agree," she answered, " his gifts weigh too heavily. I tell myself over and over the different ways I should give him dislike."

" Is it so hard a thing to do that you must school yourself to the task? " I asked lightly enough, but she did not take it lightly.

"You admire him too greatly to be just, and you are no help to me," she accused. "We should both remember it is an Ordoño he is set against. Have you no loyalty?"

"Loyalty? Sancha, we may both have our loyalty tested on this journey of yours to learn certain truths." This was as far as I dared go, for she stopped me with a cry of protest.

"Juanito! You don't believe it! That girl was ill to madness, and — yes — it is true perhaps that she loved him, and that strange things were in her mind at the last, but Juanito, do you not see he could not be to blame regarding her? Why, it proves itself: she was alone — would he — noble as he is — have left her alone if there had been any bond? Never, never in the world! I do not know who the girl was — or how she learned " — then she halted, and I knew she was back again at thought of the letters.

"Go you to sleep, Juanito," she said, " and — be loyal as you can until the truth is learned."

She did not make clear to what or whom I was to be loyal, so I gave it my own reading and went to sleep as she bade me, well content.

She was at least started on the path to the truth, and if the break came when she met Marco, it could not be the shock it might have been but for Anita and her lightning flash of disclosure as to the letters. What a fool he had been, Marco, to flatter a little peasant's vanity by telling her how much she excelled the ladies of rank who waited for him! Yet that was the Marco I knew, and the Marco Sancha had never heard record of.

A day further in the journey we learned that the peaceful Indians of the rancherias had been raided by their hereditary enemy, the Apache, and a heavy smoke to the north and east showed us that one of them had fired the grasses to halt pursuit; that way we could not go with horses to be fed.

"It must be the trail past Sivanoki — the Casa Grande," decided Tristan, "and you, Movi, will be the sooner home."

I was not ill pleased at the word that we go through the land of strange contrasts of which I had heard much on the trail. Movi had told willingly of the mystic rites of the Navajo who made prayers in deep cañons, and made wonderful singings of ancient songs to their gods. These tales of wild chants of the night, and the strange dwellings of the Divine Ones who once lived on earth, filled my soul with desires for which my confessor would have set me a stiff penance, and the enchantment of it to this day remains in my mind as do the tales of the Arabians or the romances of the Crusades.

There, however, at the gate of the province of the red and jealous warriors, we outfitted in a different way than when we took departure from Culiacan and Sinaloa. Shields of bull's-hide carried we, every one, with lances and knives, and bows and arrows also for the women. Movi could send an arrow like a man, and in the village where we were captive Sancha more than once had entered into the game of archery with the young savages; not that she shot well, but her arm was strong and her eye steady, and all she needed was practice.

And well pleased she seemed with the new weapons, for, as she explained to me, she would not feel so much the need of being cared for like a child.

Strange enough they looked, those two in the garb of monks, yet armed with painted shield and good strong bows. Movi made pleasure for us by reading the pagan symbols on the shields we carried. Mine had the lightning, Tristan's had lines of falling rain and a sacred plant of their priests, while that of Sancha was the most important — it had the Father Sun and the Mother Moon, and the morning star.

"But it is not a star, it is a cross," said Sancha.

"Morning star," insisted Movi. "Morning Star is the son of the Mother Moon. He is in the sky when she goes away, and he calls the Father Sun to come and smile on the earth for people. He is ever between them, and is their child."

"There," said Tristan, "Excellencia, on that one circle of bull's-hide, you have set forth, without words, the foundation of all religions of man, and their kindred with the sky."

Sancha made the sign to ward off evil, and looked away from him.

"Have we not enough of trials on the way without invitation to heretical thoughts?" she asked, but he only smiled at her, and refused to be reproved.

"If you heard it in a poem such as comrade Juanito is given to recite for your pleasure, you would deem it a pretty thought," he ventured. "The pagans of Mexico were only won to faith in the Virgin and her Son because it fitted with their ancient belief of Mother Moon and the Star which brings in the Day. Also

the star is the child of the great god, the Father Sun;
in no other way can these dark people be made understand a king in the heavens. The king of whom the
Christians tell is beyond their sight, but the primitive
sky gods they see daily or nightly."

"Still, they should not use the cross of Christians,"
she insisted.

"Why not, when they used it as a symbol of light
before Christianity had emerged from the mists of
the past? On your shield it stands for the bright son
who is born of the god and goddess of the sky. Who
knows but that some such primitive symbol was not
foundation for the legend of the cross which you regard
differently?"

"Juanito, you must not give ear to such heretical
surmising," she declared, turning her attention to me.
"As you came into this wilderness for my sake, your
soul is my care, and it is my opinion that Movi, as
well, needs some godly teaching."

"Mayhaps, if you were inclined to priestly instruction,
I also might present myself as pupil," said Tristan, and
at that she smiled, though she would not look at him.

"Juanito, tell your friend that the simple faith I
own would seem too slight a thing for notice among
his vast collections," she said.

"Juanito, tell your cousin that if simplicity is the
thing desired, the symbols on the bull's-hide, and their
visible gods of the sky, far outrank us. No matter how
we disguise the same creed with words, or weight it
down by priestly ceremony, they have the better of us,"
said he.

So, as between two fires, I escaped from them both

to discourse with Movi, who smiled her pleasant smile on all of us alike, and when she heard those two near to quarrel, she would look at the shoes of Sancha, and then at me, and laugh. To her mind there was certain magic in the boots of white deerskin, and to quarrel with the man after wearing the boots made by him seemed to her a useless thing.

For a day after our minds had been given enlightenment regarding the symbols on the shields, Sancha had no word for Tristan, and gave her undivided attention to Movi, and strove to bring her into the ways of church, lest evil or death might meet us on the trail and find her unprepared.

Movi listened with interest to all the beauties of the heaven in the sky for true believers, and then told her cheerfully that the Underworld of the Hopi gods was the place of her preference, for there the melons were always ripe, and the peaches never failed, and the Father Sun spent the nights there, and all were glad of heart.

The dismay of Sancha made Tristan smile.

"She is very honest, Excellencia, she has not learned — as perhaps her grandchildren may — to pretend infidelity to her pagan faith. Their honesty is the strength of their clans; it is a perilous thing to strive to weaken that, even for a new religion."

"But on my own soul will the blame lie if I strive not," said Sancha, sore perplexed, and he smiled again.

"You too are honest," he said. "You want credit for a convert, and do not know you will only make her unhappy with the old, and incapable of understanding the new. I need to have little Movi happy on the trail, for on the friendship of her clan may depend much of your own safeguarding, so be content with the garb of a missionary, and let go the preaching, or, as I ventured to suggest, turn your discourse to me."

"I would if I had hope, for — you trouble me much," she said soberly; and her tone was so changed that I could believe, like Movi, in the magic of the footgear made by him.

We reached the great house called Sivanoki, and it looked a palace in form after the wattled huts of the Pima people. Movi ran about it eagerly, looking for stray beads of the ancients, and told us it had been built by southern clans of her own people, but that dwellings on the open plain were no longer safe for reason that the roving tribes had grown too strong. Other things of the strange ruin she told us — legends and traditions heard in the winter nights around the fires of her people — and the massive walls, and its four stories, surely gave reason to think it built when the clans were indeed strong and sovereigns in a wide land. All about it were crumbled walls and sand-filled ditches where the water had once been led from the river, and the sight of the vast ruined place of Indio pueblos impressed Sancha as words could not.

"Why, they were indeed people civilized and of industry," she said in amaze. "The thickness of the walls will measure the height of Movi, and that ruined tower — was it for sentinal or priest?"

"I shall use it for the view, to learn if other travelers are in sight," said Tristan, "and if you, as priestess —"

He glanced at her robe, and smiled.

" I also will go up if the way is safe," she said. " I wish I might know it also was one of the high places of light."

I was content to stay below, and content also if her curiosity took her alone with him as guard, for dear though she was to me, her moods of discontent and disdain of him made troublous work for me in camp or on trail.

With a fallen beam he made a ladder up which she could walk with help of a reata held by him, and as there was no roving enemy in sight they took time to investigate the old tower, while Movi and I were content to pick garnets out of an ant hill when her search for beads proved useless.

And the Indian woman looked at me and laughed when the voices were heard returning to earth, for Sancha was in a pleasant mood, and was voicing thanks.

" For without you I should never have found it," she said, " and for a certainty the bell proves it a place of ceremony, and the height of it makes clear it was their substitute for a mountain in greetings to the dawn, or study of stars."

" You learn fast," he said, " and I have joy that it was your hand found their music thing of prayer. Many have gone through the rooms and never found it."

She carried a little copper bell in which a pebble tinkled, and it had been hidden in the dust of what appeared a break or hole in the wall. Movi looked at it gravely, and said it was a sacred thing, and that the place in the wall had been built for it when the house was built — it was still the custom.

" That is the second time I have stood in a House of

the Dawn," remarked Sancha, showing the bell to me,
"and this time the little bell is as music in the heart,
for I come down happily."

"Their prayer places perhaps keep a holiness of
spirit despite the pagan blindness," I agreed; "and if
you can find understanding of it, you will add much of
happiness to your own heart on the trail."

"I think that is true, Juanito, for in each House of
the Dawn I have learned a new thing."

Tristan turned and looked at her, then walked away
where the horses were. I could not think what she
had learned on the mountain except the thing giving
her anger at him, but the trophy of the bell had quelled,
for the time, her mutiny, and I was the last to wish it
reawakened.

Few signs of danger had crossed our path, and the
spirit of holiday trails did at times come between those
two, for, though all their world looked tragic, they were
young in life and heart, and the beauties of the days and
nights were many. All the wild things of bloom were
at their best, and the horses were faring better than
we could have hoped. The water was not good until
we entered higher lands where the pines grew, but we
had few dry camps, and we often traveled by the stars
of morning to earn rest through the hours of greatest
heat.

It was in these times of dawn and dusk that we heard
from Movi, and sometimes from Tristan, the Indian
legends of the stars at the edges of day and night. It
was the one theme of which Sancha never tired, even
though she made many words of objection to the pagan
readings of them. And for comparison Tristan would

bring in Greek or Arabian meanings until she confessed that the Indian had its own charm when inter-
preted by the faithful Movi.

Thus journeying, and thus entertained, we crossed
the wide lands in safety until we reached the great
Desert of Wonderful Color, where a sunrise glow made
all the earth of rose, and a sunset would give a sky of
green and purple and pink amethyst. Nothing like
that had come to us in the south, and the glory of color
was like magic to Sancha. She spoke of jewels, recalling all those she had ever seen, and comparing them
with the colors in the sky. In the strange place where
our trail led us past forest trees leveled, and turned to
stone, she looked at Tristan with wide eyes of question.
Many unbelievable things had she seen, but the petrified forest seemed a thing of enchantment.

The heat was intense. Many times on the trail the
heads of the horses had to be covered from the storms
of sand. Many times in crossing the higher ranges we
were all but chilled into sickness and fever by the tor-
rents of cold rain. Many nights of exhaustion the
Indian woman changed guard with us when danger
came near. Yet we had fared safely withal, and reached
the pass of the petrified forest in good condition, and
the eyes of Movi glowed with gladness as she recog-
nized the wonderful landmarks.

"Homolovi is near — then all good," she said to
Tristan, and he nodded and looked the horses over
approvingly and then regarded Sancha and me much
as a general who had brought an army through a hard
campaign.

And hard and long it had been, though no pen could

make record to tell the difficulties lived through. That I have not the courage to even attempt. After a certain period of exhaustion, or thirst, or daily threatened dangers have been lived through, no one day stands out clearly from the rest. We knew the names of neither the streams we forded nor the hills we crossed, and there was little to distinguish one day's journey from another. Of all the trail from the river of the Gila where the ancient ruin was, to the north where the Painted Desert blazed its glories of color, and its fantastic forms of mound or mesa, there was nothing to record except the fact that the common dangers drew us very close to each other. I think of that little brown Movi today as of a loyal, ever cheery, sister, and we emerged from that long trail with all the smaller vanities and prejudices burned out of us. Tristan had not changed, for to his unselfishness there was only one duty — service to us all, but Sancha had grown more meek even as she grew more self-reliant. Instead of argument or resentment at new things and pagan ideas, she grew thoughtful of them until at times she fairly divined the Indian meanings before they could be explained to her. Thus almost without our being aware of change in her, Sancha was one in the Brotherhood of the Desert at last. To Tristan she gave the respect due a commanding officer, and in those later days there was no reference to his unholy quest and her loyal intent to defeat it. She talked to him little, but watched him when he spoke to others, and as to the best thing to be done on trail or in camp she had ceased to assert an opinion. It was as if the very wilderness had tamed Sancha!

Thus we came to the village of Homolovi one evening of red sunset when the new moon and the evening star gleamed in silver out of the blaze of the afterglow. Tristan halted, and let me pass him while he turned to Sancha.

"At last I have brought you to the first village of the people of peace," he said, "and we may thank God in our different ways that it has been in safety."

"The debt is great," she confessed.

"Yet not enough to buy forgiveness?" he asked.

"Forgiveness is only bought by repentance," she returned, "and I have had no word of that."

"True, neither have you," he said.

Then the herald from a tower of the village wall called loudly to the people, and out on the terraces swarmed men and women, and some of them ran out gladly to greet us when a woman of their own race was seen to be in our company.

So great was their glad amazement at safe return of her that they made it like a home coming for all. Their best of provision was put before us, and around Sancha, the first white woman they had seen, the women and children gathered in wondering admiration. They said "*Lolomi!*" to her, and of her, and by that word expressed all the good and beautiful thoughts they gave her.

But a more substantial testimony of their good will was given when one of their priests led in four fresh horses from the range to exchange for our own animals. The burro ridden by Movi was especially desired by them, and to gain it they were willing to either trade or lend us their best for the trail.

A runner had been sent the seventy miles north to

tell clans of Walpi of the return of Movi to her people, and for that space we were to go under friendly escort for the reason that it was the season of their solemn serpent ceremony to the God of Sun and Growing Things. At that time the people from the far rancherias gather at Walpi as the faithful gather at Rome, or fare forth to Jerusalem.

It may have been the sense of protection we felt in company of the friendly guard who ran beside our horses, or it may have been the smiling joy of Movi by which our days were lightened, but nothing on the long trail had wakened in our hearts the happiness of new life in a new and enchanted world, such as came in the Painted Desert.

"But it is not a desert, it is a garden so vast and so beautiful that the angels surely gave help in the planning of it," insisted Sancha. "There are as many blossoms as stars in the sky, and every shrub carries some blessing or fragrance."

As we journeyed north it had been a growing wonder for her to observe the full sweep of stars around Polaris, but in the great desert of the peaceful people, there was time to observe and delight in them. On the bank of a river we had to wait until a sudden flood subsided, and that night she learned new Indian names for many stars while Tristan sat silent, smiling at her efforts to pronounce the difficult words.

Suddenly she turned to him.

"You know so many things of the Desert," she said, "it may be you could tell me which lamp in the sky is the light of Virgo."

It was the first mention she had made to remind us

that the letters were a living memory, and Tristan
stared thoughtfully at the skies a moment ere he pointed
to Spica glittering in the south.

" And — Alphard? " she added, but at that question
he shook his head, and smiled.

" The great serpent trails across the sky to clear the
way for Virgo," he said; " already the star which is his
heart is out of sight over the edge of the world — the
rest of him is under her feet, hidden in the blue veil."

" Is that what you think? " she asked, " or did you
find it in a book of poets' writing? "

" My days, as you see, Excellencia, give me small
space for the reading of poets even if I could come by
them," he said.

She sat in silence a while and then said, " You are
a strange man, and know strange things. I would that
your heart was clear before God of all revenges."

" Few of us but have some human fault," he said.
" Only the angels in heaven can boast perfection."

" You are not — not politic, or you would include
ladies," she said; but I, remembering her moods and
tempers, laughed, and so did she, so that the spirit of
jest and comradeship was between us all as never before.
She went to sleep that night after telling me that all
her fear of the northern deserts was gone, and all her
dread of the red tribes. These people had a laughing
joy of life by which content was won.

Then as I agreed with her, and spread a blanket for
her where Tristan had plucked a bed of sage, she added:

" You are dear and good, Juanito, and I talk to you
as to my conscience, but do you also find this life in
the open a thing to live for? and do you remember once

when we were very little, and I wept to follow the strolling Zingara who came out of France?"

I remembered, for I had to bribe her with all my small belongings to be good, and not win me reprimand as a careless guardian.

"Yes, so it was," she said and laughed, and looked up at the stars, "and after all, I am strolling over half the world, as I wished, and sleep under the open sky, and find it good. Juanito, do you regret Mexico?"

I thought of the ceaseless intrigues, and endless cruelties, and then looked over the quiet and peace of the desert night.

"I have no answer, Sancha. This is to be ever remembered; but that life more befitted your name and state."

"So it did," she agreed, "but why should the life of a maid be hedged about by weighty dignities of state? This sky teaches more than I ever learned in school, Juanito, and — if only the letters were with me ——"

After a little silence, she remembered again my presence, and bade me go and find sleep, and half in mockery reminded me that I was to give no heed to words of hers when the stars swung low as they did over the Painted Desert, for they wove enchantment, and made music disquieting to simple minded maids!

But if the desert stars touched her with witchery, it was only preparation for the day when we descended a mesa trail, and passed fields of growing corn, to see a gray mesa beyond growing into something more than a mesa. So suddenly did the change come to us that Sancha checked her horse with a little cry of wonder and put out her hand.

It fell on the arm of Tristan, who was watching for
the moment she would realize it was an eagle's nest of
a dwelling-place rising out of the level, and terraced,
roof above roof, against the sky.

"It is a part of the desert enchantment," she said,
"for how could savages build like that?"

"As I told you, Excellencia, these people are not of
savage tribes; I have hoped that you might know it
some day. They are the people of a great mystery; surrounded on all sides by warlike enemies, they yet hold
their fortresses and their independence."

"And they are — your adopted people?" she asked.

"Rather they have been courteous, and I am grateful," he answered. "More grateful now than I ever
dreamed I might be."

"Because of me?" she asked, and he nodded his
head.

"Their island of rock above the sand dunes would be
a haven of refuge, if refuge be needed."

"Have we not journeyed through all the lands where
enemies might wait for us?" she questioned, but to my
surprise he had no ready reply. He was staring
upward, where at the edge of the cliff a dark robed figure stood beside the watching, half-nude figures of the
boys and young men.

It was amazing to me to see our companions from
Homolovi run up those heights like squirrels with no
sign of weariness from the desert trail. The training
of their boys from earliest youth is to fit them for
speed. No horse can keep pace with them on a long
journey.

But we who rode left the steep path to them while

we wound between the sand dunes, and up the rock trail where the harvests of the fields were carried. So gradual was the rise, with the rock wall on one side, and the sand dunes and clusters of peach trees below, that we did not know the height we had reached until suddenly we emerged from the shadow of walls, and I caught my breath in amaze as we stood in one of the wonder paths of the world.

There is no pen can give to another the wonder of that place of the meeting of the trails at the rock shrine of Walpi in Tusayan. There are times when a sun setting will wrap it in flame, and a dawn will lift it into a mysterious world apart from all one could dream. As the red sun set in the west there were strange reflected rays shooting upward from the horizon in the east, and between them we stood on a high trail, where, on either side, the cliffs dropped away, leaving great reaches of the Desert below, in changing colors and shadows so full of beauty that tears were in the eyes of Sancha, and her hands clasped over her breast at the wonder and beauty of it all.

" It is a very benediction," she whispered. " Juanito, it is as if we stood on a throne of God, the Father. Yet is it the earth, and the haven of a strange people," then she turned to Tristan.

" This justifies you in much, señor," she said. " To starve or freeze, or to burn on desert trail, is slight enough payment for this you have brought us to. It is the very gateway of a Place of the Dawn. Are the others but lesser copies? "

He looked at her, quickly smiling.

" How soon you learn when you let your thought

have freedom," he said. " Yes, all the artificial hills of sanctuary are in memory of a greater one. The high places of prayer are not alone in sacred books."

A line of men were coming down with ceremonial greeting and welcome, and Movi slipped from her horse and ran eagerly to meet them, for her brother and father were with them, and they wept in gladness at her return.

Then they crowded about Tristan, with every sign of fondness and gratitude, and when he spoke of Sancha, and pointed to the beads of the man they had honored, the father of Movi breathed on her hand, and led the horse of Sancha proudly up the trail to the terraced dwellings, while we all followed.

At the top of the trail waited the man in the robe; it was a priest from a near-by settlement, Oriabe, and his name was Padre Juan de Vallada. At first he had thought it two brother priests who had arrived, and his amaze was great when he learned of the dangers we had passed in the country of the Haquis, and the strange reason for a lady of De Llorente y Rivera wearing the robe of a priestly order.

He had been for a year in the province of Tusayan, with another priest to share the work, and all the news of the world was dear to him. Letters came from Santa Fé and from a priest at Acoma. The youths of barbaric clans were ever eager to serve as couriers between the tribes, and thus the priests kept in touch with brethren; so also the young men learned the world. Padre de Vallada was at Walpi to frown on the iniquity of their serpent worship, for which ,his brown charges were eager in the August moon. He was a garrulous man, eager to hear words of good Spanish again, and we learned much as we crossed the stone floor of that high cliff, and observed the fortress-like arrangement of all things. In that place a few men could hold at bay a thousand.

Because these were the days when the pagan priests fasted in the sanctuary, none of us could see the leading men of the snake order. Movi could not see even her own grandfather for the reason that no priest in communion with the gods may look upon a woman. It seemed that Tristan might enter the sanctuary because he had been taken into the order, but he could discuss no worldly matter there.

Padre de Vallada looked at him curiously when the message of invitation came from the priests of the snakes.

" Do you wear the sanctified robe of church into dens of iniquity where the symbol of all evil is worshiped? " he asked.

" Nay, holy father," answered Tristan. " You have been ill-informed. It is not the symbol of evil to them, rather of immortality, since it comes new out of its old cover each year. But in my visit to the _kiva_ I shall wear no robe."

" You have no fear? "

" I have gone in once before, and it may be I have made this day's journey on a lucky day," said Tristan. " Their minds will tell them I have crossed all lands to keep the fast here where they made me a brother."

" At Santa Fé each priest is ordered to serve at mass before each harmless pagan ceremony, but that the hideous ceremony of the snakes be especially forbidden," stated Padre de Vallada pointedly, " and it seems a curious matter that a Christian should join in their horrors."

" They have made me brother, and opened the way for me two summers gone," returned Tristan. " All was done with the knowledge and blessing of Fray Fernando. In that way he learned they do no evil; it was the best way in which to learn. Also it has won blessings for me with southern tribes, for it is the most famous order of all these nations."

" Yet opposed to the church? " insisted the priest, but Tristan told him it was opposed to no order of any religion; all their thought was centered on prayers for strength to the Spirit of the Growing Things.

Sancha listened in silence to their words, yet it was plain to see her distress at any argument with the priest, for the sight of him had been a great comfort to her own mind, though I liked little enough the suspicious regard he gave to all of us.

In a house of Movi's clan, a room was given to Sancha —a room of white walls, and white floor, a roll of blankets, and great vase of water. Movi and one of her small sisters slept by the door, and my chosen place was on the terraced roof beside her portal. Weary though we were, all were too excited for sleep. The return of Movi, stolen, and given up for lost, was a wonderful thing to her people, and to be brought back by Ivava out of the land of an enemy was of vast importance. He had proven himself truly a brother to the clans of Walpi, and on the word of Movi they accepted Sancha as a person greatly exalted, since Ivava looked first of all to her comfort.

After a supper of green corn and the flesh of deer, Tristan, who was now called Ivava, left us on the terrace in the purple twilight.

"I would that Fray de Lombarde had made the return from Awatobi," mused Padre de Vallada looking after him. "This to me is a strange thing. I have seen no white men to whom their sanctuaries are open, and it has a strange look. What Fray Fernando did he mean?"

"One very holy, and no longer alive," I told him, and in gossip of other matters he seemed to forget Tristan. He told me conversions were slow, and he thought it a serious matter that only half-breeds should be punished for apostasy, since it was the old men, of pure Indio blood, who were most rigid in evil practices, and little could be done for converts, even by the Inquisition, until the old men had died. One most troublous warrior-priest named Popé had been a thorn in the flesh of the godly these several years, and had evil power over many pueblos to the east.

From that he told of the Indians in the turquoise mines, and their troublesome dislike of work underground, for which reason the unruly converts were enslaved to that task; so, while Sancha was listening with open ears, my thoughts drifted far, and my mind was not so easy as I could wish over that matter of the sanctuary and the snakes — and our one friend down there in brotherly converse!

And then I was brought sharply back to Sancha, who said, "But that was even more strange than to fare safely through the Desert. Two white maids in an open boat saved by Indians — do you hear, Juanito?"

I had not, and I asked what questions I might. Fray de Lombarde had heard it in Santa Fé, and the word came from the great river Miche Sepi to the east where the French were; a half-French trader told of two sisters lost on the sea in the south, and guarded safely by Indians to a hunting camp of the French. The sight of the maids fitted in with some legend of white-water spirits of that coast tribe, so they were given food and raiment, and they arrived at the French and Indian camp, decked in all feather fineries, but near to death for the proper food of white people.

No, Padre de Vallada knew nothing except there had been others, and all died but the two sisters; perhaps a ship had gone down, he did not know. But the sisters were started north along the great river to the French possessions where they would be welcome to the colonists, for white maids were rare in the wilderness. Padre de Vallada only told of this matter in evidence of the power of Indian superstition, for the maids were fair and were regarded as twin gods or goddesses of the water, and thus were saved.

I had joy to hear this, for well I knew that the death of the Lispano family was a heavy cloud to Tristan, and if the daughters had thus escaped, perhaps the others might, and the sacrifice of Don Fernando had not been all in vain. There was in my mind no doubt left of their identity when he spoke of their fairness, and again I could see that far-away, stone-paved street of Mexico, and the proud riding of Marco with the young girl tied with his reata, and the sweet bell voice of Doña Perfecta who spoke her wonder that a Jewess should be so fair!

And well content with the news of the evening, I bade the priest good night, and rolled myself in my blanket to sleep on the terrace.

The moon was gone, and the still night was a-glitter with stars, when I wakened and heard the voice of Tristan.

" The trail is not ended, Excellencia," he said, " and it is the time for rest and sleep."

" It is a night for wonder at the very beauty of earth," she answered. " I have been watching the stars and the land below ever since the priest went away. He looked after you as if in no good mood, Señor Ivava. Is it true there is no evil in these pagan chapels? "

" No evil is meant there, that is all I can tell, Excellencia," he made answer; " but the order is secret even from their own people, and the church frowns on secrecies. Almost a hundred years of white priesthood here has won no snake priest as convert for confession."

" But you — is there no danger for you? I could not sleep — the thought of all those serpents! "

" Vex not your mind, we have now crossed the deserts of danger. You have reached the priests of your own people, and even though I halt by the way you can find many guides to Santa Fé, Excellencia."

" Do not call me that — it spoils the night," she said.

" Then must I keep silence when you speak to me? " he asked, and at that she spoke impatiently.

" You are so proud, Señor Ivava — also you are hard. I was a child when I began this journey, and I followed the dream of a child. That life slipped from me in the Desert and I am different. I was seated here in this place of wonder thinking of that. Yes, you are

hard. You use words to exalt me, as if in mockery of
the unclad beggar you found on the way. Also my debt
is so heavy I cannot sleep."

. There was silence after that, and I heard him walk
across the roof and back.

"I may perhaps then call you Doña Sancha without
offense?" he said. "But you are a great lady in your
own land, while I am only a landless brother of desert
tribes. Your kinsmen could think I presumed if I forget
that difference because of the chance disaster to you on
the trail."

"My kinsmen!" she retorted, "the one nearest me in
blood, Juan, asleep there, is devoted to every thought of
you. Nothing you could do or say would seem but right
to him. He tells me often enough you are above us
both, and for this, perhaps, I was jealous. I was ever
first with him until you crossed our path and made
unwelcome rules."

"First you always will be, Doña Sancha," he answered
gently, "but Juan can scarce speak for your illustrious
kinsmen of Spain, and, when he has double his years,
he also may not look back on our desert trail through
rosy glasses. The days of this summer are now but a
boy's romance with him. He calls Movi of the Desert
'sister,' and he is enchanted with the changes of the
wilderness which is yet a garden."

"Are we not all?" she asked. "If it were not so,
would I be sleepless here on this terrace lest the serpents do harm to you? You are enemy to the man
I will not name to you; an unjust thought in your heart
is against him, and I ought not to have care what
chanced you down there in the serpent den with your

red brothers! Yet here am I, awake under the stars, and the peace of the life, and the people here give me strange thoughts. I wonder why peoples and nations should strive for power in the world, for gold, for the fame of a day? Here there is no strife of that kind — and no anger. Is it indeed true these people assert that wrath causes a poison in the blood to drive away the spirits of good? It is a strange thought, yet the curious thing is that no thought, even the wildest, seems strange here! The stars come so close they lift the spirit and make our little plans of life out in the world seem small. All men are equal together here, and the women aid in the governing and claim the children, and sit in council of the clans. That would be a strange thought in another place, for our people are ruled by kings or queens, and are always in strife. But here they have peace without a ruler, and nothing seems strange or wrong — not even this, señor," and I knew she smiled — "that I sit on a house roof in the night time without a duenna, and talk alone with a man who tells me he is only a landless brother of desert poeple."

"You are kind of heart, Doña Sancha," he said, "but it is no jest that I am as I say. Whatever of ill you, in the future, may be brought to think, none shall add that I made pretense of more than I am."

"How could you?" she asked with impatient force; "are you not stronger here than the very priests of Holy Church?"

"That is an ill power to covet in any land," he said. "Do you not know it alone might shut me out from doors opening wide to you?"

"You are his enemy, therefore you are mine," she

answered, " yet you have been salvation to me in the wilderness. No Llorente y Rivera could be ignoble enough to forget a favor because of hatred, Kahn Alcatraz, and the doors where I go will be open to you when you speak."

" I shall not hold you to that, or ever remind you of the words, but I will never forget them," he said. " Tomorrow you will remember it was the enchantment of desert stars by which you were made gracious. Good sleep to you, Doña Sancha."

Then he went down over the terraced roofs, and she stood looking after him, and I went asleep again with the picture of her, wrapped in the blue light of the stars, high on the upper terrace against the sky.

CHAPTER XVII

AMONG THE SERPENT PEOPLE

I DO not think either of them had the sleep they needed that night, for when I wakened, she was below me on the eastward edge of the mesa, where a cool wind of the early morning carried to her the odor of wide lands of sage brush. Already she had gone for prayer to the house used as a chapel by Padre de Vallada, and then, leaving him with his scattered flock, more curious than devout, she had found her way through an arcade past a strange, natural stone monument in the plaza, and out to the rim of the great rock. Below in the Desert patches of mist yet lay in the shadow of far blue mesas.

I also went down the ladder for prayer, and before I was out again, Tristan had joined her. The evening before she had given him the copper bell as gift to the head of Movi's clan. To her it seemed a trifling thing to give in gratitude for the clean dwelling, and courteous greetings, yet it meant much to the men in the snake kiva. It was as a voice from their ancestors of the ancient days, and their hearts told them that the gods had sent the bell at this time, and in this way, as a sign that the woman who brought it must be sacred to the clan as Ivava was sacred.

I joined them as he was telling her this, at which

she was gay. It seemed to her a great jest that the crude copper bell as a gift would lift her into importance with a strong tribe.

But Tristan did not laugh over it, and asked her not to treat it lightly.

"Also — if they bring you today a garb such as their maidens wear, I beg that you accept it," he said earnestly. "It will be meant in great kindness, and — there may be need of their kindnesses."

"Shall I also see her with her hair in whorls of the squash blossom?" I asked, and had joy at the picture. After all her disdain of him, and his pagan friends, it would be a thing for laughter to see her in proper ceremonial garb of a desert tribe.

"With all my heart I hope I see you both in the dress of these clans if the thing is to happen which I fear may happen here," he said. "I may not leave until after the ceremony of the serpents — and that is at set of sun today, also I may not again have chance to speak with you both, but we must take the trail at the earliest hour tomorrow. Get what rest you can — betray no need of haste — leave that to me! But I do ask that you accept every kindly offer or gift, for it is a strange time we have come to this place, and they wish you well."

Sancha spoke of Padre de Vallada, and ventured to think he would scarce approve even the gift of the bell, if he learned they thought it a sign from their ancient gods, but Tristan was suddenly careful.

"It is better that you tell nothing to Padre de Vallada of that, or any other thing these people would use as a bond of friendship," he said. "I may not say more, and this only here where no one listens. Things have

changed since I was in this place before, and Padre
Vallada is not welcome for their days of prayer. They
do not tell me this, I only read it in many actions. You,
Juanito, keep close as may be to Movi or Doña Sancha
when I am out of sight; you bestowed no sacred bell.

"That is sadly true," I agreed — "I could not even
conjure a likeness to a pagan divinity as did stray maids
in the boat on the south coast."

I looked at him as I said it, and he frowned at me,
puzzled and incredulous.

"When was this?" he asked.

"Not so long ago as time flies in the Desert," said
Sancha, "Padre de Vallada told it to show how easily
the superstitions of the red people were influenced. I
wished he could have told us more of the sisters than
that they were fair, and were taken north at their desire
to some French camp of explorers."

"Also they were taken in safety up the great river
to lakes of the north where French settlements are
made," I added. "It is a great journey by water, but
it would lead them to safety, and that is good to know."

"It is, in truth, good to know," he said, and drew a
great breath as he turned away his head. "We will
give thanks to God, who found the way for them."

He walked back to the plaza without looking at us
again. I knew it was that Sancha might not see the
tears in his eyes, but she did not understand.

"It is curious," she remarked, "that in the affairs of
white people his interests are so small."

"That you should say it, Sancha!" I mocked, and
pushed the sleeve up from her round arm. "Despite the
desert tan, you yet show enough of white to be given

audience in civilized courts, yet I see no lack of his interest in you."

She twitched the sleeve loose from me, and flushed rose red under all the tan, yet she smiled where a month before she would have withered me with her disdain.

"Well, the saving of two women through a superstition of the tribes is to me a marvel," she persisted, "yet he asked but when it chanced, and then hastened away to his friends of the serpents — does that show interest?"

"He made clear that affairs new and of import were on his mind," I urged.

"Yes, and treats us as children who are not trusted with affairs of men!" she made retort. "But we care little, do we, Juanito? He can go to his serpent sanctuaries, and leave us to go adventuring."

"We will first go adventuring to break our fast," I suggested. "I think we are late as it is, for Movi was busy with the fire as I came down."

We walked back, watching from the mesa the men far down in the fields of maize and melon vines — they looked like mice for size — and we learned that the dawn always found the workers there, and when the sun stood above, they were back at their homes, resting in a change of work such as fashioning arrows, beads of stone, or weaving robes of rabbit skin for winter. The village was a beehive where each worker did his share. No one seemed idle, and no one hurried unless it be in the ceremonial races with each other, or with the sun.

So quiet were they all in their waking, and going, that we did not know the young men, and even small boys, had gone at dawn to plant prayer plumes at a spring far to the west, and from there made a race with the sun to reach the mesa as it came out of the east.

From the terraced roof we saw the last of them come up the steeps where the mothers watched in pride the first run of the younger ones, and received them, breathless and exhausted, in their arms.

Very gay they were in eagle plumes and paintings of white on their brown skin, and all the brightness of turquoise beads and red shell from the far sea. The old runners disappeared at once in one of their *kivas*, or sanctuaries, but the little fellows paraded all the day with a pride in their nude importance.

Movi had our breakfast waiting, and was almost as much of interest to the women of the clans as was Sancha. Visitors were gathering for the snake ceremony from the towns on other mesas, and already were climbing ladder and terraced roof to see the only Hopi woman who had journeyed so far and come again back to her people.

Her relatives were bringing large reed platters heaped with the colored feast bread, red and yellow and blue, that she might give food to all in gratitude, and in memory of the long time when food had been given her by strange tribes.

Thus, without making question, we saw much of tribal things curious and often pleasing, and to Sancha one of the most interesting was a strange and continuous song in a woman's voice drifting out from one of the many houses. It sounded like a high chant of supreme content.

Movi laughed when Sancha asked of it.

"Some day you sing that song — maybe so," she

said. "That song is the grinding song for wedding meal — I let you see."

She led us over roofs and down a ladder to a room where a woman was coiling the whorls for the head dress of a little maid, and a woven blanket screened a corner where the song was.

Great meal jars stood in a row against the wall, and in an alcove were ears of corn in even layers piled like fagots from floor to ceiling.

The floor was freshly whitened, and Movi had pleasure in our approval of the orderly arrangement of all things, for the people were of her clan, and she drew back the screening blanket with a teasing laugh at the girl behind it. The girl was on her knees at a grinding stone, and the fresh meal was piled beside her in a shallow plaque. Only an instant the curtain was held back and then let fall in mock fear, as if the shy black eyes of the maid held a threat.

"It is so," she said sagely. "When the work is to do first, and the meal to grind, and prayer songs to sing, it tells the woman if she wants the man — for long days is the meal grinding."

"That is not so bad," I agreed, "it does away with any decision of haste. Thus a bride serves an apprenticeship, and it is a good thought."

"That is as may be," retorted Sancha, "but what is the task for the man?"

"He works fields for her father, or gives robes, or some way he is friend."

"That is not so bad," mocked Sancha — "it does away with all the drones. When I wed, the man must also serve apprenticeship!"

Of all this we made jests, and were about to go up the ladder, when the Hopi woman whose house it was, touched the arm of Sancha, and held out to her a long woven girdle — narrow and of yellow and black. Their sheep were few, brought from the far eastern pueblos where the Castilians were, and I knew the girdle was precious.

" We cannot buy — we are but poor strangers among you," I said to Movi, but the woman smiled and looked only at Sancha, saying something in a low, pleasant tone.

" She says it is not to trade — it is the first time you are in her house, and she, Lenmana, makes you the gift. Also, because you are friend, she makes the wash for your hair in this house —— "

" Is it — the custom? " asked Sancha, doubtful, yet with interest. " True enough the washing is needed. Think you I had best ask the padre? "

" He would say no, and perhaps lose you the friendship Ivava bade us foster," I reminded her. " He asked nothing of us but that we help him in some way by acceptance of all kindness. That seems an easy enough task, and if you are made choice of for first favorite, why not be gracious? "

She consented, after insisting that my own locks needed care as much as hers, and our hostess courteously showed pleasure that I would accept a head bath — a curious custom, but a most grateful one after the long weeks of desert travel.

Thus, in turn, our hair was lathered and rinsed and lathered again, to the joy of the household, for each one put his or her hand to the task though ever so lightly, and the woman was smiling, and over the head of Sancha said " Poli-kota " and the children also said it shyly, and ran out again into the sunshine. Over my head there was not so much ceremony, but some laughter, and when it was all ended, we sat on the terraced roof in the sun to dry it, and to watch the visitors streaming in from south and east. There were even a few traders of the Navajo who came with browned deer skins, and lumps of turquoise. They had their wives and horses, and were great rangers, also they were tall, shapely men.

Padre de Vallada found us thus among the curious pagans, with the hair of Sancha drifting about her in a dark cloud, and my own inclined to extra bushiness not so becoming.

" Have you had heretical baptism? " he asked, and looked us over suspiciously, but the fright of Sancha at the thought reassured him.

" Still, they do it that way," he stated. " A bowl of suds in the house of any of their magicians, and no sanctity about it; also they change gifts and it is done."

But he approved the use of the yucca root they used for washing suds — it was good for all things, but especially for the hair. He used it when a good chance came. Then he became interested in some of the newcomers, hailed a convert occasionally, and pointed out those of the aggressive pagan element; they were usually the old men. Some of them did not even look up at us on the terrace — but most of the younger element was openly curious.

And I saw Sancha drawing the girdle under her robe lest Padre de Vallada note that it was not there by

chance. That was her first definite move to shield her
exchange of courtesies with pagan friends — this from
our Sancha, who, in the spring of the year, had taken
the trail to found a convent, and wipe out all pagan
thought by proper conventual prayer!

But when I teased her about it, she would not laugh.

"How was I to know the desert tribes have two
prayers to every one of ours, and that the smallest
children glory in them?" she asked. "My own thought
is that our priests should learn the old here, before
striving to engraft the new. They do worship some of
the same things under different names, but it takes time
to learn the names. Their plan of life is not bad at all.
Mother Clemente never heard true things of these
northern people; they are gentle people and kind."

"Yet when persecuted they did battle with the fierce
Apache," I reminded her. "You need not think because
they love you that they are angels; we all do that, yet
our feet are on the earth.

She smiled, but gave my open avowal of devotion no
further attention. With the approach to safety, the
spell of the Desert had fallen over her, and she saw all
things through a golden haze of illusion. All priests'
tales of the unregenerate red man in need of civilizing
had been denied by her own days among them. Even
when a prisoner, she had been treated better than if
captured by wild Saxon tribes, or even chiefs in war of
other Europe lands. These things she knew, and was
just enough to acknowledge after her first rebellion had
burned itself out. But now, strangely enough, with no
one to give word or influence, she suddenly glorified the
common things of life about her until she no longer

lived in the real but in a seeming world, full of a beautiful strangeness in which mysteries touched her on every side. Always the sky and the stars had been above her and plain to her sight, but now she walked sleepless to watch their beauty, and felt cheated if weariness caused her to lose a single glimpse of the gorgeous dawns.

I was more bewildered by her in those days than ever before. Her tempers I could understand, and her sweetness; her stubborn loyalty to the ideal lover of her childhood, enhanced as it was by devotion of letter and pictured face — all that was the natural impulse of a nature meant for love; but the still dreaming in dusks and dawns when she slipped away from voices to pace either the sands or the terraces alone, and her sudden great gentleness with all things heretofore disdained, and her quick will to turn critic of even herself and the thoughts of the clergy — that was a big and serious thing. Also it was a dangerous thing where we were going. Since the Holy Office in Santa Fé was strong enough, as had been proven for years, to displace any governor not to their liking, what chance was there for even a maid of degree who came out of the Desert with good words for the pagan lives so abhorrent to all proper devotees?

Thoughts like these had been my company more than once, but were given point there in the terraced town where the clash of pagan and priest had suddenly become vital to me in the dark looks of the old men, and the natural intolerance of Padre de Vallada. He confessed that the old men would have to die off before any but a few women and children would accept the

faith in truth, though many came cheerfully, even gaily,
to baptism, as it was one of their own ceremonies, and
they gave no more weight to a sprinkle of holy water
than to toss upward a pinch of prayer meal, or puff of
smoke, as they did when speech was made of their devilish gods.

Padre de Vallada asked for Señor Alcatraz, and not
finding him, called a Walpi youth to interpret for him
to the few Navajos. He had hoped he could gain converts among them if once they were led in by friendly
Hopi. I listened while they told whence they came,
which place was great Tséye — the rift in the earth
from which their gods had surely emerged. The Walpi
interpreter listened politely to this, and later told us that
in the ancient days it was his own people who had lived
sheltered in the deep cañon walls, but the clans had
come — a few, and then many — out into the sunshine,
until now they all lived like the eagles, very high above
the lands — higher in the air than they had once built
deep in the bosom of the earth; also he added that the
graves of the ancient fathers of the Hópitû were in
Tséye to prove his words, while the Navajo were people
of a yesterday.

Padre de Vallada properly rebuked him for unseemly
pride of ancient ancestry, since the pagans of course
were all brothers alike, and none of more importance
than his fellows. But Sancha smiled on the pretensions
of the interpreter, and reminded the padre that it was
by such pride of ancestry that every ruling family of
Castile held claim on eminence. By their accounts, the
Hopi were older than many proud lines of Hispania, and
for her part she was hopeful the journey might take us

to that oft-mentioned wonder cradle of the clans —
mysterious Tséye.

The Navajo watched while she spoke, as did also the
other Indio people, for their women speak gravely and
seldom before strangers, and do not smile on all as did
Sancha. They looked on her robe and rosary, and asked
if she was of high medicine orders, also they said that
when she journeyed to the east they would be as guide
for her through their lands.

The older men in the Hopi circle exchanged quiet
glances when this was said, but Sancha and the padre
were in some friendly discussion and did not note it. I,
because of the words of Tristan, was alert and making
note of all things, and wished him with us to prompt us
for reply to this offer. I had to content myself by smiling on one and all most amicably, and let it go at that.

As the day wore on, all of Walpi assumed its gala
dress. Children ran about garbed in a little paint, the
warm sunshine, and strings of beads, while the maidens
appeared on the terraces in sober native weavings, with
red or green girdles, and their hair in the wheel-like
dressing over either ear. There was a subdued sense of
importance everywhere. Each good housewife had
foods prepared, for visitors or relatives. The Navajo
women in their dress of skins, peered with a child's
interest into bowls and cooking pots, for they were
as folk of the wilderness on visits to a central city. All
these things filled the day for Sancha and me, though
each of us thought often of the friend who was somewhere underground in that place of the serpent den. A
great sheaf of green boughs was erected in the center
of the plaza and appeared of special interest, for the

visitors and Walpians gradually moved in that direction, chatting, and placing themselves comfortably along the edges of the roofs, and perching on ladders, until from the stone floor of the mesa to the sky line above there was a sea of Indian faces looking down.

"But for the difference in color and dress, one might think it a fight at home with a bull," said Sancha. "Is it not so?"

I could not agree that a gathering of pagan barbarians in an infidel ceremony could have likeness to representatives of the finest families of Castile gathered for royal sport. My imagination had its limits. Sancha's had none.

"Well," she said finally, after I had expressed my thought of it, "if it is danger makes the sport, I should say that these pagans at their prayers handling serpents show more brave blood than all our ancestors sitting in rows to watch a trained man and old horses tease a bull to death."

We almost made a quarrel over that, but Movi interfered with her slow smile and gentle voice.

"Soon the Antelope priests will come from the *kiva*, and after that the priests of the snake will come," she said. "The clan of my father is of that people, and because of the gift of the bell they ask a new promise of you — will you come?"

Sancha was all alert with interest, yet feared to leave the plaza lest the ceremony of the day be lost, but I reminded her it was a time to return all kindnesses.

"Yes — we will go, but why wait so late, Movi?" she said. "This is the time when all are waiting and watching in the plaza."

"That is so," agreed Movi — "and that is the time when no one sees us."

"Juanito must also come?"

"Yes — that is best, come," said Movi.

She fairly ran to an opening in a little plaza to the west, where a ladder came up out of the ground, and a woman stood watching. I thought it Lenmana, the woman who had been our hostess in the house where the girl ground wedding meal, but the dress was different, and I could not be sure; she wore a white shawl, and very white boots.

There was some hesitation about allowing me to follow Sancha, but I had been told to keep near, and the haste to get her away from the crowd was curious to me.

"Take no trouble for me, Juanito," called Sancha from the cavern place. "I think it is a well intentioned thing — and you will laugh. Sit you there on the ladder until they are through with me — the time will not be long."

After Movi had finished as interpreter in the *kiva*, she came up, and sat by me on the ladder, smiling.

"I am not told why it is," she confessed, "but the clan of my father wish to do a kindness, and he thinks it is good she puts off the robe of a priest here this day. There are men from Oriabe here, and they are in anger — that is all I know. Your priests have angered them, and a maid in a priest's robe is to them crooked magic. At this time all are making prayers for power that is strong. My people want Poli-kota safe, as Ivava is safe — so it is they give to her a Hopi dress, as Lenmana gave to her a Hopi name."

Then I knew what they meant by saying the curious word over Sancha's foam white head. It was a Hopi name, and so ugly it would cure her of fancy for Hopi custom. I chuckled over the thought, while Movi patiently explained that Oriabe men had many jealous days concerning Walpi clans, and it seemed as if the priests of the Castilians put them in confusion with each other. Also she said she had never seen a ceremonial day of any of the brotherhoods when so many of the old men looked darkly on each other. What it boded she did not know.

My interest in their various factions was slight, and, whatever their discord might be, we would take the trail at dawn and see no more of it — or that was my comforting thought.

So satisfied was I with it, that I listened more to the laughter of Sancha in the woman's *kiva* than to the quiet tones of Movi beside me on the ladder. Whatever was going forward down there in the underground room, it was not a thing of trouble, for Sancha was as gay as a child in accepting their friendship offering.

But, when she called up that I must close my eyes until she stood beside me, I had little preparation for that which I saw when I looked upon her. It was not alone the dress and girdle, but the hair dressing of the maids of Tusayan, which is, in my mind, the real test to a comely face.

I knew not whether to laugh or disapprove, for in mockery of me she stood smiling shyly, with the manta of white about her, and the wheels of her dark hair coiled over her ears.

She looked it all too well, and so I told her; no one

who had ever seen her in the palace of the viceroy
would know her now for the Marquesa de Llorente y
Rivera.

"I make you my compliments, Poli-kota," I said
with my best bow. "I find comfort that you retain at
least the rosary of civilization!" In my heart I dreaded
having the padre see her.

"Poli-kota! what a thing to call me," and she
laughed as she whirled on her toes and then made
mocking courtesy. But the small sister of Movi called
to us from the terrace, and Sancha caught my hand
and made me run with her.

"Am I not fine?" she asked. "It is a garb of good
service for the trail, but I will need a tirewoman for
the hair dressing, so difficult it is, Juanito. They tell
me there is a wide well on the mesa beyond the shrine
where the trails meet; you must take me there before
the light goes — I want it for a mirror."

We had reached the plaza, and found again our place
on the terrace by the strange column of stone. There
was a quiet "Ah!" went round the swarthy circle, and
some said "Lolomi!" and there were smiles given us.

But we had scarcely been settled, when, as if far off,
we heard muffled voices and rattles, and up from a kiva
came a fearsome group who circled the plaza, and then
did a shuffle sort of dance before the green boughs. I
turned to Movi, who said it was the Antelope priests,
but more than that I could not learn, for a louder and a
different note sounded and every head turned to watch,
and Sancha took my hand.

"Listen, Juanito! even the Indios show their awe of
this which is coming. I would he were beside us!"

She did not say who, but there was no need, for her wish was my own. The painting of the Antelope priests made them aught but comely, yet their appearance was fairly mild compared with the Snake priests who swept into the plaza with a ruthless force dangerous to anything in their path.

They circled the plaza, they sounded before the altar of green boughs their message to the spirit priests of the shadow world, and then the thing they did is a thing not to be believed, but my own eyes saw it, and the shudder of Sancha and the muttered execration of Padre de Vallada told me I was not in a devil's dream.

For out of that altar of green boughs they drew handfuls of serpents big and little, they circled the plaza with them coiled around neck, shoulder and arms. Their shuffling dance, which was of a strangeness in itself, was done with serpents darting here and there between their feet, and all the while there was a monotonous droning, like a wordless chant to which they circled — the Snake priests with their coiling serpents, and the Antelope attendants, who stroked with eagle feathers the loathsome reptiles. At the last they were all tossed in a great pile and sprinkled with prayer meal, and then gathered in bare hands and borne to the four ways to carry messages to the gods that the faith of the people was great, and the devotion of the Snake priests was strong!

"It is diabolical sorcery flung in the face of the church!" declared Padre de Vallada. "What further evidence is needed that devils out of hell still walk the earth?"

"Yet harmless to all," said the voice of Tristan back

of us. "Did not Jesus, the Teacher, say all faithful to God, the Father, could thus deal with serpents and scorpions? These people do this thing in natural faith, and for that are they condemned, yet in all their ceremonies we hear of no one injured."

"Is not the spirit of man injured if not the body?" demanded the padre, who was livid with horror. "I have heard of these abominations, but now my own eyes have looked upon them, and I shall tell these pagans ——"

"Tell them nothing today, Your Reverence," said Tristan lowly, "their temper is not good for a sermon after what they have gone through. It has meant eight days and nights in the *kiva*, and fasting since set of sun yesterday. They are exalted for any sacrifice, and it is a time for wise silences."

"They send you out of their den of evil with advice to a priest of the church?" accused Padre de Vallada, but Tristan shook his head, and kept his voice carefully lowered because of Indians near who were silent and intent.

"No one has told me, no one has sent me, but there are converts here today, men from Oriabe, and they are not well received in this place. That may seem to you a simple matter, but nothing these people do is without meaning."

"Even that?" said the priest, pointing to Sancha, who stood with face turned away, suddenly conscious of her hair, half shamed before Tristan though it had only been a jest with me. "Are we to choose their customs to suit their vanities? It is a new way!"

Then Tristan saw her and smiled.

"It is so good a way, Padre de Vallada, that I could wish the clans would offer the same garb to every Christian in Tusayan this day," he said with so much force that the priest frowned back, sore perplexed.

"Why this day, and why Christians?" he asked.

"I do not know. I am not told. You and your comrade priest should know each word here, and the cause of it. I came yesterday, I go tomorrow. I give thanks that they welcome my friends, but I am glad to go quickly."

I led Sancha away lest she have fear at the words. On the long trail the dauntless spirit of her had been a rare comfort, and I had no mind to have it spoiled by Indio factions and their troubles, now that we were at the far gate of the land.

As it was, she feared Padre de Vallada disapproved of her, and that was bad indeed, but not so serious as would be his anger at Tristan that pagan sanctuaries were open to him when closed against the priests of holy church.

I thought as much myself, but cared little to dwell upon it, and reminded her of the well on the mesa to be used as a mirror. The sun was sinking, and it was the time when maids and matrons filled the water jars for the morning.

Willingly she consented, for it was her last chance of seeing herself as a Hopi maid; also, she was eager enough to walk where we could speak freely of the unbelievable thing we had seen.

"Were they killed — the serpents?" she asked, and glanced warily about the trail when I told her they had been carried to the four points of the compass and

let go to bear witness to native gods that the faith of
the Hopi priests was strong.

"I would that he might tell us what other wonders
he saw underground," she ventured, "but it is scarce
to be hoped, since all is secret even from their brothers.
It is strange."

As we passed the great shrine, an Indio followed us
by another and narrower way, and halted at the western
edge of the mesa watching us.

"He also sat near on the terrace," she said, "and I
think he is of the family of Movi — each place I go, I see
him near."

Movi heard us, and smiled.

"It is my brother, Wisti," she said, "also he speak
Castilian and Pueblo for the padres, and now he goes
the trail with you to Santa Fé. It is his work to see
you all with your own people."

The man must have heard her, but made no move
towards us. Later I learned that his indifference had
a reason. He was to guard and report all things, yet
run no risk of being thought over friendly lest another
be put in his place. The Oriabe visitors had decided
that a white woman in the Painted Desert meant a colony settlement as at Santa Cruz and Santa Fé, and that
was the least desirable of things, so it was the task of
friendly Walpi clans to bear the task of proof. He
watched, listened, and reported.

Above the shrine, ancient steps were cut in the point
of the cliff, and up there we followed the maids with
the water vessels. It was their hour of laughter and
careless jests with each other. Some visiting youths
were crossing the trail there, and despite an older

woman who served as duenna, there were looks exchanged, and gay railleries as the maids teased each other, and ran up the incline, pausing at the edge to glance down at the men on the west trail below.

It was a wonderful place up there on the mesa of the well. A cool air followed the sun, and the moon showed silver white above the far blue cliffs. There was the scent of sage in the air; and some other shrub, nearer and sweetly penetrating. Sancha asked of it, and was shown small roses of yellow and its low growing green on the trail. Further ahead it had more height and strength. Sancha was gay as the most carefree maid of them all; in great good humor with herself when once away from the chiding eyes of watchful Padre de Vallada. She even ran races with them, and was left behind, whereupon the visitors ran back to her with smiles and comforting words. Then they led her to the pool that she might kneel there on the stone and bend over to view herself in the curious hair dressing reserved for maidens.

They were like children in their humor with her, and I stood apart, a guard who was needed as little as silent Wisti, who remained at the head of the stairway. I watched him with a friendly desire to fraternize if he was to be a companion of the trail, but the fact that he spoke Spanish, yet had not betrayed it to Sancha or me, withheld me.

Noting that the Indian maids were more free when I was not near, I found myself a seat and idly watched a man who ran to the east, past the cornfields. I strove to keep him in sight, but he faded into the shadowy places where cañons were, and over all drifted the turquoise and soft gray of the sky, and the evening star like a glimmer of gold in the west.

The place had a beauty so strange that nothing but the quaint garb of the Hopi people seemed right for it. My own worn apparel would have spoiled any picture, and I was as well satisfied not to use the mirror of the pool. But while watching the others, the thought came that even the peaceful tribes of the south dressed and looked like savages, but these people of many mysteries had a great correctness in their dress regulations. The little children ran naked, and the men in the races almost so, yet when they did put on garments, it was after a rigid manner; and no woman, old or young, was without the enveloping manta, by which, in modesty, the lines of the form were concealed.

I heard one of the maids laugh and say "Poli-kota," while others flicked water from the pool on Sancha, at which there were little shrieks, as she, with a clay dipper, gave back as good as they sent. Thus without a common language, and only the spirit of youth as medium, they got along very gaily.

I had never before seen Sancha with groups of young people except when backed by all the convention of Castilian forms. Always I had seen her with people of mature years, and the nuns, and the ecclesiastical flavor of life where there was little of freedom.

I was thinking of this, and noting how rosy her cheek, and how sweet her laughter, when a step sounded back of me, and Tristan was there.

He was breathing quickly as if from running, and I asked the cause of haste.

"None, now that I see you both in safety," he confessed — "but I was not told where she had gone, and if by chance it had been on the lower trails —— "

"What then?" I asked, and he smiled.

"Nothing, since you are not there," he said. "But the Oriabe men go home that way, and they are in some way jealous that we are here. It may be a matter of religion, for there is a special feeling against the wearers of robes."

"Yet you wear one," I said.

"The Walpi men understand that, but the Oriabe men are of different mind," he said. "I only anger Padre de Vallada when I try to make him see, but there is a strong feeling against his brother priest because white children are born now in Tusayan. The heads of the clans have held council on the matter, and there is a brewing of troubles to come. I was even warned that it is better we all turn south again from here, and not try to cross to the Rio Bravo. But since that is not to be, the Walpi men will send a strong friend who knows the speech of other tribes."

"You mean Wisti?"

"You learn fast," he said, "and so does your lady cousin; there is no thing more wise that she could do than to wear the dress today — and use that coiling of the hair."

All the vessels were filled, and the women had started back along the trail, when Sancha saw him, and laughed.

"Have you come with a sermon from the padre on my vanity of spirit?" she asked. "Since it is only once in my life, I come to look at myself."

"It is worth your trouble," he answered, "but keep to your priest's robe for the cloak you may need in cold rains. You must not remain away from the village until the dusk comes. I am as the shepherd, whose duty it is to guard you back."

"Sleepless shepherd!" she said. "When do you rest? And is it the serpents you have fear of here after dusk? I shall see them in my dreams for many a night."

"Nay, Excellencia, keep them not in your mind as things altogether of horror. They have a double tongue and carry messages to the gods, also they have ears, and are thought to hear when evil is said of them. An Indio does not say evil of any of the things of nature — not even a hurricane — because God is in all."

"We may learn from them in that," she said. "What shall I do to make my peace, or my thanks, that they did not eat me? Movi, what do you to make thanks?"

"We place prayer plumes for gifts or thanks, and we make shrines for that."

"Then will I," declared Sancha, "in memory, and when I am gone, you will come to it sometimes and think of the days when we were wanderers in the wide Desert."

"That will I, Isiwa," said Movi, "and *isiwa* is sister."

There was a natural elevation in the rock floor, and on it Sancha placed small stones as a child builds a home. Movi helped by bringing others.

"But ai me! I have neither prayer meal nor incense," lamented Sancha; "and, after all, it will only be a pile of stone on the mesa floor."

"Could you lack incense when you have this?" and Tristan broke sprays of the sweet smelling shrub on

which were yellow, roselike bloom of much sweetness.
As he offered it, Sancha uttered a little cry, for a white
butterfly fluttered from its resting place, and hovered
over the blossoms, unafraid.

Movi clapped her hands in delight.

"It is good! It is truly most good!" she said. "This
day you get the name, 'White Butterfly,' and at the
star time the white one comes to your memory shrine.
It is a sign from Those Above, and it is good to you."

Tristan laid the flowering branch on the little heap
of stone, for Sancha did not take it, she was staring
at the white thing on the odorous offering, and her
eyes were wide, and the laughter was gone from her
face.

Tristan was silent as she. I was half afraid at the
way the thing had chanced.

"What is this, Movi?" I asked, "what is it you say
of the butterfly name? We have not been told."

"Today — Poli-kota — 'Butterfly white,' that is the
name. It is now the Hopi name for the sister of you.
Have you angry thoughts that you are now sad?"

"Not sad," said Tristan, "only it is a new thought
and it had not come to us before. The name is a beautiful name, and it is fitting it should be made very sacred.
Surely, Excellencia, you will accept the little rose of the
hernava when lacking other incense?"

"O God of my life!" said Sancha, and it was as if
she spoke through shut teeth lest she scream, "it is in
truth a sign, it is in truth! It is fitting that I should
build a memory shrine — I who have forgotten! We
were to build a shrine, the two of us, and the butterfly
has come to me in the Desert to show me how far I

am now from that thought! It has come to tell me that."

"Nay, Excellencia, it did not come. I brought it," said Tristan. "It was asleep in its quiet resting place, so the fault is mine."

"Do not call me 'excellencia,' and it is not a fault," she made answer. "It is my own saint has sent me a sign, and it is you who have made the shrine with me, Kahn Alcatraz!"

"If it makes you sad, I stand ready for any penance, Butterfly Maiden," he said.

"I should be sad, yet I am only sore bewildered," she confessed. "Out of all the things of the Desert, why should that name be the choice for me? And of all the growing things, why should you bring the one on which the butterfly slept? O, you think me deranged! You cannot know what the white butterfly has meant in my dreams; you never dream, because you so seldom sleep!"

The afterglow was flaring its rose tints where the blues and grays had been, and as she sank on her knees beside the little memory shrine the reflected light gave her the unreal glamour of the mysterious. Movi touched my hand.

"At shrines one must not weep," she said, and Sancha heard her.

"I do not weep, I only remember," she said, "and this place of the shrine is not now a place lightly thought of. It is made here to my Saint of the Impossible, for the impossible has come in the deserts where I have been protected by her care. It is right I should leave a memory of that on the trail, and what place so

fit? The mesa itself is as a great throne or altar place.
You are right; the incense is on every side, and strange
it is that such fragrance should be rooted in the crevice
of the great rock."

"The fragrance lasts through the years," said Tristan. "Will you take a branch? It may survive the
journey."

She took that which he offered, but after a moment
laid it on the little shrine of stone, and lifted a bit of
that on which the butterfly had rested.

"This will go with me," she said. "And now come
away quickly. I want to go while its wings yet make
beauty on the yellow bloom."

We walked in silence along the mesa and saw the
shadows changing and deepening while the moon gave
silvery light on the gray sage.

At the head of the stone steps she stood last, and he
beside her.

"It is strange," she said, "how dreams are dreamed,
and vows are made, and we drift far, but a vow made
must be kept even in places strange as this — the saints
who guard us bring it to be."

"That is often true," he said.

"I am glad it was here," she added as she looked back
over the exalted and lonely height. "Never shall I see
it again — but it will not be forgotten."

Our silent guard stood by the ancient shrine of the
pass as we went up the trail, and looking back, I could
see him follow in the twilight. He did not speak even
to Movi, his sister.

CHAPTER XVIII

THE CAÑON OF THE DIVINE ONES

WHEN the herald star of morning shone over the mesa of the east, we descended to the plain, and shadowy forms sped beside us. It was a silent group, strangely silent.

Movi had wept at our going, and in the house of her father, Hongovi, there had been no sleep. Her brother told Padre de Vallada the route we would go, and he gave us perfunctory blessing, taking his own trail to Oriabe.

We had scarce left the foot of the mesa when I noted we were going north instead of east. Tristan observed it, and spoke to Wisti.

"It is so," he said. "It is better you go where no enemy waits on the trail."

"We make no enemies, for we are friends with all," insisted Tristan.

"So says my father in council, and so it is I who journey by your side for your happiness," said Wisti briefly, and he bade us not spare our horses the first day — for the first day was a trial.

His father ran beside our horses, and when we reached high places would ever pause to look back over the trail. We were riding away from the strange mesas, and into a land of rolling hills and trees; flower

carpeted plains and arroyos between. At a curious red
cliff where there were cavelike openings suggesting
windows we halted, and found there some of the
Navajos who had left Walpi before sunset. Wisti
showed gladness at sight of them, as did the older men.

"Now it is over," said Wisti. "Men of Oriabe will
not follow into this land if your trail is with Navajo."

And that was the first I suspected that our comrades
were along to guard us from some of their own tribe!

"It is so," insisted our guide. "They went away
from Walpi, but not to home. They wait for you in
the cañon of Motsovi, for they were jealous of the
horses. Their thought was that our tribe should have
these horses and not the Rio Bravo men."

I wondered how much Tristan suspected, but he was
ahead with Sancha, exchanging greeting with the
Navajo. We made a halt at the nearest place of water,
and all ate together, and when it was over, Hongovi,
the father of Movi, smoked, and then spoke.

"When the tornado comes, and levels all standing
things, it gives the warning of thunder and shakes
the earth. I am your friend, and the Dawn and the
Day hear me. Go you back to the south and live. That
is the little, far-off trembling of the air for you as warning. I am your friend."

"I also am friend," said Tristan, "but to the south
I may not go. If the trail is closed to the east, then I
will find my way back to your clan where my friend
is."

"That is good," was the answer. "But my son goes
with you. It is his work. If there is life for you, he
will help you to it. But if death finds you where I say

not to go, then not again may I, your father, smoke with you on earth."

"That may be so," assented Tristan, "for after the ride to Santa Fé my trail is covered by a cloud, and I have no light by which to see."

Sancha looked at him strangely, with something like fear in her face. It was the first time she had thought of him as going out of our lives, and my own heart shook. I had striven with myself against thought of that which I knew must come.

"There are high places of refuge where the Dawn may bring you Light," said the old Indio, "for this, my son goes with you on the trail. But these — the friends you love — send in haste back to their homes that they may live, and remember me — Hongovi."

"That I will surely strive to do," promised Tristan, and then smiled and glanced at us. "But these, Hongovi, are very exalted people in their own land; I but serve them on the way, yet have no rule for them at the end of the trails."

"Make rules, if they are dear to you. I have spoken," said the chief, and then he, with his comrades, bade us farewell and turned back, and we journeyed on with Wisti and the Navajo. We had to wait at a village of theirs by a river while the men sought out a safe crossing, for the quicksand made it a place of danger for horses.

So the night was spent there where the curious hogans, or huts, were built of brushwood and clay, and had a mean appearance after the high place of Walpi above the sands.

But the people were tall and finely made, and were

kindly disposed to us. Sancha noted that their infants
were wrapped in the fine inner bark of the hernava
shrub, which was soft as moss and sweetly odorous.
The fragrance of that shrub stays with me strangely
like mingled cedar and rose, and while I saw it many
times on the trail, I only think of it as I saw it first,
— where it served as incense for the shrine on that
mesa mysteriously beautiful.

Sancha wore her Indian dress, but her hair was
braided and a wreath of leaves served as shield from
the sun. Wisti talked to us freely now that duty or
ceremony did not seal his lips, and noting the interest
of Sancha in the women and little children, he came to
tell us that there was to be a marriage of the daughter
of one of their men of importance; for that reason had
the relatives hastened back from Walpi, and there
would be a feast.

The little bride — for she was very young — looked
with shy smiles at Sancha, evidently honored that
strangers from afar were guests. There was a fire,
and a special vessel of food, and there was neither
priest nor other official — only the man and the maid,
the robe and the dish, and their relatives around them
in a circle. Over the shoulders of the maid the man
placed the robe, and seated himself in silence beside
her.

I endeavored to make some jest as to the lack of
ceremony, but Sancha rebuked me.

"After all, what matter?" she asked. "Can you not
see that they are fond? Could the words of a bishop
make them more so?"

What I began to say in comment I did not say, for

Tristan had entered silently and stood by the door, and at her words I saw him for the first time off guard, and gazing at her with half at least of his heart in his eyes.

Sancha, looking up, saw him, and what she read there made her own face change. In like fashion had he clothed her in the southern desert! A long instant their eyes met in strange steadiness, but while his face looked gray in the light of the hogan fire, hers flamed red and turned aside.

That shadowy hogan, with its circle of dark pagans, was a strange place for a revelation of soul. I scarcely breathed, and all our little world stood still, only the eyes of those two spoke.

Then the Indian lover took from the side of the dish some of the food, and offered the dish to the bride. Her hand took food carefully from the same side, and together they ate, and later drank from the same cup in the presence of their respective clans, and the ceremony ended.

"If the simple form has your approval, you scarce could improve on that," I ventured, in attempt to lift the strange chill fallen on all three of us; but Sancha stated coldly that it was time for sleep, and walked past me out into the night. There was nothing for me but to follow, and Tristan was left to make a more ceremonious withdrawal. We found the bed for Sancha already prepared, of high piled sage branches with her monk's robe over it, and she dropped down there and covered her face with one of the sleeves.

"All my life I should keep this robe to humble my pride, and remind me of my nakedness," she said —

" also to remind me of other things! Sleep near me, Juanito, but waste no words on me this night, for the day has been over long."

The night seemed but an hour of darkness, when the hand of Tristan was on my shoulder and we woke to eat grilled deer meat, and maize that was parched. All were ready for the trail when he waked us.

We forded the river ere the gray dawn had merged into the yellow dawn of the desert, and the four Navajo men of Walpi went with us, well armed with knives, arrows, and steel lances. Already the coming of Spanish men had improved the war implements of the natives.

These men we could not speak with except by the help of Wisti, though I had more than a little interest in them. Often they sang as they rode — strange songs in which sounded all the calls of the wilderness, and Movi had told us things of their magic which kept me as keen in desire as had the tales of the ceremony of snakes.

Tristan only smiled with his usual patience when I would have asked of their great healing by prayer and songs, but would not allow me to question.

" Through some especial courtesy they go with us for our safety, but it is a mystery to me, and the journey requires caution. I dare not take risks as to question of their religion. But at least I can promise you one strange trail in their land which inspires to much, and it may aid you to understand a little of the people, for their legends are often of it."

More than that he did not say, and when we entered a cañon where water ran, and the wood doves fluttered ahead of us from the stream, we were glad for the sake of all, yet gave it not much thought until of a sudden, huge walls shut us in, and before us was a great spear of a rock like the monument of a giant. This was where two ways divided, and as we went onward the spell of mystery and beauty lowered every voice, for we were in the true cañon of the Divine Ones as believed by these people, and no soul could journey into the heart of the land there and view the habitations of the ancients — stone walled under roofs of great rock ledges — and fail to feel the spirit of awe breathing there. The age of it, and the bigness of it, made us feel very little and even weak, for the men who had built the eagle nests of homes under eaves of gray rock had been strong men and their building had beauty. The outer walls were white, and the inner walls of many colors — pink of the rose, blue of the turquoise, yellow of the sun, all these in many tints were there — and strange designs of decoration.

Before one of these Sancha stood with curious regard. It was the imprint of a woman's hand dipped in white earth paint, and impressed on the smooth brown stone.

"It is the hand of a lady, that," she decided; "see the beauty of the fingers, slender as if used only for fine embroiderings; yet it would seem as if she had been a worker in clay."

"Perhaps not so," ventured Tristan. "This was a *kiva* wall, a sanctuary. Here are the seats for council, and there the altar place. All the designs are prayer symbols, and the mark of the hand may be for a vow made."

"And long ago?"

"It may be centuries. This is the place so ancient it is called the home of the gods."

"Centuries! and the mark of one woman's hand stands record as if it had been made yesterday!"

"The hand of a woman, though slender, may weigh heavily, Excellencia," he said, and she looked at him reproachfully.

"I told you it did not please me to be thus called," she replied, "but this hand interests me. Then the women of these enchanted lands made vows as today?"

"And broke them, as today — it may be so," he said. "Their hearts are as our own, except that our life has given us more cravings and arts than they knew."

"Do we need more?" she asked wistfully. "I never knew how little ceremony life and happiness needed until we found this magical land. I wish I might leave impress of my own hand here in record of that."

"Truly?" I said, for he only looked at her as if in wonder if his ears had told him aright. She did not know how much her words had expressed.

"Truly, Juanito. These places bewitch me, so I think. I want to be of them because I feel the spirit of them is of beauty. Have we not passed many good and profitable places for dwelling? And some of to-day's people live in them. But the places of the ancients, whether walled by their own hands, or by nature, are the places of most wonder and beauty in their world. Do you not see it everywhere?"

I had, but not to spell it out like that.

"Their ancient prayers are the same," said Tristan.

"If they came from Persia and were in a book, you would learn them and repeat them as poems."

"Know you any?" asked Sancha.

He glanced below where the Navajo men were resting, and the horses were feeding on the grass thick and high at edge of the stream. Wisti was also there.

"I know one invocation to a sky god of theirs, but this is not a time to repeat it in the hearing of any of them. Our priests have made them distrust all our interest in their religion."

"Say it for me while Juanito stands guard," she begged, and he did so. It was very long, and I never heard it all again, but I recall the opening words for the reason that Sancha afterwards chanted them as we rode, and said they made her think of words from the Bible read by a padre at the convent.

"Repeat it not to a padre unless you are ready for a penance," said Tristan — "for this prayer is very pagan, and is joyous in its faith."

O You!
Who dwell
In the House of the Dawn,
In the House of the Evening Twilight,
Where the Dark Mist curtains the doorway
The path to which is the Rainbow!

Sancha stood looking at him in curious wonder as he began the prayer as Fray Fernando had made translation of it, and when he ended with the joyous

Impervious to pain, I walk!
Feeling light within, I walk!
With beauty before me, I walk.

> With beauty above me, I walk.
> Happily may the roads all
> Find the way of peace,
> And the end of the ways in beauty!

Her hands were folded over her breast and her eyes closed as if to shut out all but the meaning or feeling of the words. When his voice was silent, she opened her eyes, and put out her hand to him, and it was the first time.

> "O You who dwell
> In the House of the Dawn!"

she said, and tried to laugh, but her voice had a tremble in it. "I have heard their prayers are beautiful, but I never knew how they were beautiful until now! Were you one time an Indian, Kahn Alcatraz? And are you now born on earth again to teach us beauty?"

He looked at her hand. It lay in his by her own wish, and he turned towards the wall and spread her hand there as had been placed that other hand of the woman of the ancient days.

But over Sancha's he placed his own.

"This of record in the house of many prayers," he said. "You are a generous comrade, Doña Sancha, but if the beauty were not in your own heart you would not perceive it in my poor chanting of their prayer to heal ills."

"And it does heal?"

"It does heal — my own eyes have seen that. Thus the prayer always ends happily, and with blessings for every one."

"The things of wonder I am learning!" she mused. "I wish I might leave the mark of my hand there."

He picked up a piece of soft stone, and broke it to a point to which his knife added.

"So slight a wish is easily met. I would that all others of yours were likewise."

Thus I left them there while he used the soft spear of stone as a pen, and made for her the outlines of her hand. The last I heard of their speech they questioned writing her name within the outlines, but decided against it, and he gave her an Indian symbol instead which only she would know, and marked it there. I found her marking the same symbol in the sands when we stopped to camp.

"But has it a meaning?" I asked, for to me it looked not so much.

"It has meanings — and many," she answered with a pride in her new knowledge. "It is the star shining over Walpi when I made the shrine to my Saint of the Impossible."

"That star was Venus, and it has a record of its own aside from Indian symbols," I told her, but she gave me little heed, and went on smoothing the sand and marking it, only to smooth it again for another trial.

From the cañon of the Divine Ones we emerged with some difficulties of trail into a land of piñon and shrubs and nodding blossoms, then through the grateful shade of pine forests where antelope nibbled tender grass in the sheltered places. Birds of many kinds were seen, and I was told that the blue bird and the eagle were each prized highly for the feathers used in symbols of prayer — one for its strength, and the other because it carries the color of the sky depths and of deep waters.

After the forests, the Navajo men were more cautious on the trail, for we passed through lands where the Apaches ranged, and our party was small to withstand any important band.

One nameless river we followed eastward towards its source, and netted fish in its many pools. To our taste they furnished desirable feasts after the steady meat foods, dried or fresh, of our desert living, but not an Indio but Wisti would eat them. The Navajo men had some religious prejudice against the eating of fishes — a myth of theirs gives some clans brotherhood with water creatures. So they satisfied themselves with meat, and the wild batata growing in that land and baked in the ashes of the night fires. We also ate it with the fish, and there were many wild berries in cañons where water was. Thus we fared well, and on more variety than in the lands of the Pimaria. Also the animals we rode were the better of running water and rich grasses.

In all this journey, Tristan had sought in vain to learn from Wisti the reason of the warning of Hongovi. But Wisti confessed that he himself did not know; also that his heart was troubled about it, for it was no little thing. He was sure of that by the orders given him, but the orders he dare not tell. And finally, on his own account, he begged that Tristan act on the bidding of Hongovi, and linger not at all in either Sante Fé, or north of the great lava beds.

"Is it for me alone there is a danger?" asked Tris-

tan with the thought of the long route he had come
north to avoid traders, and the shorter route of the
east by which messenger of either the Holy Office or
the State might have borne word in advance.

But it was plain that Wisti knew naught of special
trouble for Tristan; he stated that none of the younger
men knew: it was a thing in the hearts of the old men,
and it might be that one of them had a vision. Wisti
thought that must be so, and visions are very sacred
things.

Then came the day when a thing of importance was
met on the trail, a spring where there were tracks of
sheep — many sheep, and one lone burro — plainly we
had reached the edge of a Spanish range where some
lone herder moved up and down the land with his
flock.

The Navajo looked with sharp eyes over all the
ground, and affirmed this, then said they would go
back to their clans, for we would now be safe with
our own people.

Wisti urged them to continue to the villages of the
Jemez and there was considerable argument concerning the matter. It seemed that the Jemez and Navajo
had twice fought together to overthrow the white men
and failed, and after that they drew apart and the
Jemez men were suspected of stealing Navajo girls
and selling them as slaves to the Spanish.

Sancha was affronted, yet curious as to the purchase
of Indian maids by the Christians, and was very certain the padres had no knowledge of the traffic. But
Wisti told her that when a young Spaniard married,
it was a custom to present at least one slave girl to

his bride, and if the Spaniard could not steal one, he had to buy her. It was a common matter in the settlements, and young men who wished to marry sometimes banded together and went on a hunt for women as gifts to their promised brides.

It was at the breakfast time these things were talked of, and the Navajo said they would go beside us one more day. Tristan did no persuading, but was content to have them. He felt safe now as to Sancha, for in Jemez he was known, and as we rode along together he told me he had painted for them some of the god beings they had described to Don Fernando. They deemed painting great magic, and had shown him special friendship. For this reason he felt that, if need be, he could secure us a safe guard in case he should part from our trail ere reaching Santa Fé. I did not welcome that prospect, so made no mention of it to Sancha. She had grown very quiet after the sheep trail, and the evidence that at last, after living through the impossible things, she was again on the border land of her own people.

And when the shadows began to lengthen that day we saw on a far hillside the moving mass of wool bearers spread like a creeping blanket over the green, and a shepherd dog gave warning to the herder that strangers were abroad.

The herder was a Jemez Indio in camp by a spring, and part of a freshly killed sheep hung to a tree limb. The man looked at us, startled and uneasy, and asked Wisti if the Navajo men were after women. Even when told no, he continued to give us careful regard not free from suspicion.

But he was generous of both meat and water, and cuts were broiling on the coals before the saddles were off, and after he had been assured that Sancha had come the incredible trail, and that we were her guard, he opened his mouth, and told the thing of his fear.

He was all alone, and had his sheep to guard, and on no account, and for nothing, could he leave them, and he did not want that the Navajo men should hold him to blame, but the facts were as follows:

The sheep had been killed at this place because other company had been with him. He would not give names, but it was three Castilian men, and they had come from the south and had captured two girls. The girls were Navajo, and he thought they would camp early, for they had traveled fast and their horses were wet. At first sight he thought we were on their trail. His own tribe had been blamed often for the stealing of Navajo women when it was indeed the white men who took them, and he thought this was not a time for neighbor tribes to be enemies to each other because of acts of the white men.

Wisti watched him with sharp eyes like black beads when he said this.

" This is a true thing," he said — " also my father who is Hangovi of Walpi tells me this is the time when the tribes should be friends and brothers."

" Your father is wise," said the shepherd, " for it is the time."

And the two men who were of different tribes, and unknown to each other, exchanged looks of import, and said no more.

The Navajo men talked apart with each other, and

then decided. The horses were tired, but those of the white men were in no better condition according to the shepherd. Their plan was to ride down the thieves, kill the men and take the women.

"But if the women can be bargained for without battle, would that not be the better way?" asked Tristan.

They agreed it would be the safer way, for the Spanish had firing pieces — yet they doubted any bargain. Navajo girls were much desired. Also to bargain would give time for the raiders to plan escape.

"If we are friends let me do a brother's part in this," said Tristan. "I will demand the girls as your right. If they are not given, my own arms will be for your service — this because you have been faithful in spirit to poor wayfarers who can make no other return."

"The Divine Ones have at times come to earth as poor wayfarers," was the reply they made, "and men who have helped them fell heir to blessings. We will do as you say. You are our friend."

Sancha was troubled over it all, for the wise and lawful and Christian thing was of course to carry the tale to Santa Fé where the church or the governor would decide for justice, and the women would be sent home safely to their clans.

"With whom would they be sent?" asked Tristan, but of course she could not say.

"The only safe guides are these men with us," he said, "even if they were sent from the town, which is not a thing to hope for — they would be sold or traded to pueblos on the trail, and would never see their own people again."

"But — with you to speak for them?"

"I, as I told you, am but a brother of the Desert, a poor wayfarer, and my word of little import with dignitaries," he made reply. "We like little enough to plan for troubles while you are of our care, but if speech fail, then the women must be taken by force of arms. We are enough."

Meat was cooked while we ate, and was then wrapped in leaves and lashed well to our saddles that we need not halt for food on the way. The shepherd told us the best trail, and the springs, and passes of the hills, and we rode on in the long shadows of the late day.

"I know now how it was when you took the trail to rescue me," said Sancha riding beside Tristan. But he looked at her with the wonderful smile in his eyes.

"No, Doña Sancha, you do not know," he said, and she did not argue, but rode on beside him into the rose and gold and azure lights of the highland sky.

The rose and gold was cloaked in the blue mists of twilight, and the stars came out, and still we rode on. Wisti was far ahead on the trail leaving signs for us to follow, halting at times until we came near, and using every caution that we not ride close on the quarry, and startle them ere their camp was made.

And at the last, when the night was late, and all well wearied, Wisti stood in our path, and pointed far down where a glimmer of light shone.

"They have reached the camp of a Jemez hunter who goes for the sacred eagles," he stated. "He has a cage with the young eaglets, and the fire is his fire, there the three men have stopped, and the girls are there."

"Then it means one more native man to help against the raiders," I ventured, but Tristan was not so sure.

"Slavery is sanctioned in high places if it is properly cloaked and named," he said. "It is called bringing in converts for the glory of God, and the pueblos have it drilled into them as a just affair. Thus there is no telling where the eagle catcher may stand in a dispute."

We left our horses and crept forward. Sancha still wore the Indian garb, but Tristan unstrapped her robe and gave it to me to carry. The way was steep and movement slow, with every caution used against the starting of rolling stone down the cañon wall. And it was Tristan who led Sancha by the hand through the dark of the Indian trail.

The glint of fire was on a plateau where the forest hid it as we reached the level, but Wisti never wavered in direction, and led us between the pines until we reached a thick scrub where young growth made a jungle. We could hear voices there, yet see no one.

There were no words among us. Tristan on the way had used all needed speech. Now he put the robe about Sancha and put her hand in mine, and we all moved forward quietly until we could hear the words, good Spanish words from well-content rangers — and the first name spoken clearly was that of Marco de Ordoño!

Sancha gripped my hand, and I know Tristan laid his hand on her shoulder for silence.

"Let Governor Otermin give him lieutenant's rank for his pretty face and his name!" said one man. "All that favor would fail to get him in on a hunt again with me! He took the girl who by right belonged to Roberto here, and for that reason we have to make another, and a more distant raid, before Roberto's favorita will go to the priest with him."

"O, Dolores would go with me," said Roberto with a certain pride, "but who wants his wife to have not even one woman to start the home with? But I owe Ordoño for that trick. The girl had beauty."

"For that reason was Ordoño's claim made," said the first speaker, and laughed. "He has a trained eye of his own. They tell that the girl he left in the Pima land was also a beauty — and white."

"True, but no one has dared tell the Don Antonio of it. White women are all too scarce, and even Otermin might have frowned on that."

"He did not frown on him when he bore back the Navajo girl I should have had," grumbled Roberto, "also De Ordoño had no need of serving woman, as there was no marriage day set for him."

"I thought the girl was Jemez — that pretty Marta," said the third man, "she is slender as a red lily, and worth more money than a mere drudge."

"She had a Navajo mother. It is the mixed blood gives the better grace," stated Roberto. "These two we have here will give good service to the house, and no fine gentleman of rank will come our way to covet them."

There was laughter at this, so we could guess the captives were not too well favored. They had ended their supper, and began to speak of who should stand first guard of the night, when Tristan said very quietly.

" Señors ! "

There was a movement, and then a voice.

" Who speaks? "

" A Castilian," answered Tristan, and walked through the tassels of the young pine until he stood beyond its close knit, though narrow, barrier.

" Life of my soul! " said the one called Roberto, " you suggest the devil rather than a padre bobbing up from the earth in this hell of a cañon. Whence come you? "

" From Hopi land."

" It is a strange way of meeting," said the other voice, " and strangers in New Granada are mysterious to all. Will you favor us with your name, Señor priest? "

" My name is Kahn Alcatraz, and my business you will not approve, though I come in all honesty to save your lives, and it may be, your souls."

The hand of Sancha gripped mine in breathless tension, for it was a weird time there in the thick pines where the odor enveloped us as a veil, and we stood, hearing words, yet having sight of no one; only the firelight flared on branches of trees high above.

There was silence for a space after his words, and then a man laughed.

" Surely, padre, always are you after souls and lives, but it is a curious place to seek them. We are all safe Christians here, unless it be this catcher of eaglets, yet he has been civil enough."

" It is the trappers of other eaglets with whom I came to deal," said Tristan. " The tribesmen of these maids are here to guard them back to their clans."

"By all the saints!"

"Señor," said Tristan. "I have evidence, Juan!"

At that I let go of Sancha, and went through the jungle into the light.

"This, Señors, is Senor Don Juan Rivera, and is nephew to the Reverend Fray Payo, late Viceroy of Mexico, and of power in both church and state. The reports of the capture of women for barter have not been made special record of in this province, but after today it may be done, if Don Juan here has a mind for it. This is our side, the Spanish side. But the Indio side of the question is a different matter. Unless you go home at once, and leave these girls and the horses on which you brought them here, you will never go to Santa Fé alive."

"You threaten us?"

"No, I only tell you. I will call my interpreter and he can bring two of the Navajo warriors to show you that men are here for these women. Wisti!"

Afterwards Sancha confessed she sank to the ground in terror at the going of Wisti. She had never known how close he seemed to us until he spoke to the Navajo, and they followed me into the circle of light.

And a grim trio it was who faced those wonder struck raiders, the Navajo men seemed to loom more tall, and Wisti stepped forward lightly as a cat, and smiling. There was something curious in that smile. The Hopi have disdain of anger for any reason whatever, as it is evidence of lack of control, but to myself I thought I would rather face an angry man than the smiling devil he betrayed himself.

"I bring only two, Señor. If the women are given

back, I bring no more than two. They have no Castilian words. I speak for them."

At sight of the Navajo, the eagle catcher, a man not old, but with gray in his hair, stood up beside his eagle cage, and spoke a few quick words; one of the Navajo nodded his head, and the eagle catcher, with his lance and axe, and bow, stepped across the little circle of light and stood beside them, and the two crouching Navajo women turned from one to the other with smiles.

"You see, Señors," said Tristan, "thus it will be on the trail. Each Indio will stand with these men, and I can not say the word to save you after you move out of the light of this fire. Also it will not be long I can save you even here. Look in the faces of these men and see."

He could well say that, for they were like bronze animals, still and poised to spring, four of them. Roberto tried bravado.

"I see, but they have none but savage arms, while we Castilians — with you and Señor Rivera to aid — "

"Yes," agreed Tristan, "but Señor Rivera and I have another task. We may not aid you."

"What is your task that you would not aid a Christian against savage murderers?"

There was a moment of pause, as Tristan looked at me, and it was I who spoke.

"We are a part of the body guard of a lady of rank, Señors, the Marquesa de Llorente y Rivera and niece of the former archbishop and viceroy of Mexico. I think, Señors, you will agree it is the right time to give up the captives, and not risk the word her Excellency may carry to Governor Antonio Otermin of New Granada."

The men stared at us, and then looked foolishly at each other.

"If it is a game, it is a good one," said one of the men, "but it will take more than a priest's robe, and some titles to make us believe that, and no offense to you either! Since there are six of you in sight, to our three, and the devil only knows how many more around us!—it is wisdom to let the women go. But for myself, I have a fancy to see this exalted lady who comes through these hills of the wilderness. It would be worth the price of two red women—if true!"

I looked at Tristan for some sign of wisdom, but ere either of us spoke, I heard the quick stepping of Sancha, heedless now of the noise she made. The three incredulous stared at that wall of green as if demons were using it as a nest of iniquity for their undoing, and when I saw them lift their hats and sweep the ground, I knew without turning my head, that she emerged into the light.

"My cousin, Don Juan, and Señor Alcatraz are in the right of this, Señors," she said very bravely. "I claim these women, and if you have complaint, I beg that you make it to Governor Otermin of Santa Fé. For the advice given you by Señor Alcatraz, I will take responsibility. There has been no desire to threaten —only it is fair to show you the thing to happen if you refuse. We are only three white persons among our Indian friends. To control them might prove a task beyond us."

"Excellencia," said Roberto promptly, "you need

give no command twice, and if you care to add to your white guard, I am at your service."

"My thanks, but I have no orders. Señor Kahn Alcatraz gives all commands, and it well that you remember you would have died somewhere between these cañon walls tomorrow, but for his word tonight."

"Little danger we will forget," stated Roberto ruefully. "It seems the devil himself is against my wedding day! Come, Ysidro, what must be, must! The cards fall not our way, instead of winning girls, we lose horses. Small use in striving to wed and lead a virtuous life."

Even Sancha smiled at his idea of virtue, though she was neither glad nor gay at the bloodless victory. It seemed a matter of fate that Roberto should have lost the first girl through Marco, and the next one by Sancha. And we knew that the idle comment on him made by his comrades had sunk deep.

But she made no sign, and stood there, a serene picture in the firelight, while the captives were unbound, and the horses were separated for their use. I had become so used to Sancha in the robe, or the Indian dress, that my sense was dull as to how she must appear to others, but the regard of the men was so open, and so amazed that one could but note it. They made no comment, but her words of authority scarce fitted her Indian garb.

The Navajo men talked with the women, who smiled and were very gay in their own manner, but the eagle catcher stood apart listening to all — saying nothing. His gaze followed Tristan and Sancha in a curious, watchful way.

I asked Wisti what it was that made the bond with the Navajo, and was told the eagle catcher had a Navajo wife, also that he could understand Castilian a little, and that the name given him by the priest was Manuel.

There was no time lost in starting the raiders on the trail. Tristan told them it was better not to trust the temper of the Indians — it would be a surety for safety to seek other sleeping place. So they took themselves off, with Wisti and one Navajo to see that they made no halt on that side of the range, and Manuel, the catcher of eagles for prayer plumes to his gods, stood guard while we dropped quickly asleep from utter weariness.

When I wakened there was a cheery bustle about the camp. The Navajo women had brought water from the cañon deeps, also berries in baskets of bark; meat we had, and there was fair show for an appetizing breakfast, but I was the only white person in sight to partake of it.

The sun was at the edge of the eastern world, and there was flecked gold and rose over the far black line of the pine forest. Wisti still slept, and beside him the Navajo who had, with him, trailed the women-hunters well on their way.

He wakened as I spoke, and asked a Navajo where the master of the camp had gone, and the lady who was their friend.

It was then I noted that Manuel also was out of sight. He had stood the guard alone and called no one until the dawn, at which time the lady had wakened, and had spoken with him.

The Navajo said the morning star was still in sight

at that time, and that their speech had been earnest, and he thought, was of ancient prayer places in the hills, for Manuel had pointed upward and used words of ancient things.   Then the man who was master awoke, and together the three had gone qiuckly into the forest as the great star began to fade in the dawn. That was all he knew, but Manuel was much their friend, for the daughter of Manuel had been stolen by woman-hunters of some tribe, and he was in search wherever he found himself.   Both Wisti and the Navajo had been questioned by him.

While we talked, and all happily lent a hand at the simple breakfast, we heard them coming through the pines, and Sancha appeared, wreathed like a goddess of dawn with pink roses, found, dewy and fragrant, near the trail.

"And, oh Juanito!" she breathed as in ecstasy, "to think I have been shown the wonder place of all our many wonders, yet may not tell it to you!   It is a vow, an Indian vow, see my hand!" and she held out her palm.   It was white as with powdered lime upon it.   "Only to save a life dare we take that trail again, for it is, above all, sacred.   It is a true House of the Dawn, Juanito, and we made the vow of secrets as the sun came out of the dawn to watch!   The sacred eagles nest there above a wonderful sanctuary, and we are given these as sign that we have the right of the eagles."

She showed me an eagle feather marked on one side by the stripping of its fringe in four places.   There was a certain individual token in the marking.   I noted that Tristan also carried one, but not in special display.

"Is there any other gift or honor left to bestow upon you by these desert folk whom you enchant?" I grumbled. "How am I to be a proper guardian for your Excellency if you steal out to secret meeting places while I get my sleep?"

She only laughed, and patted my cheek, and promised she would put me under her wing when she fled to that sanctuary of the dawn place for refuge.

Then she ate her share of breakfast heartily, and confided to me that the secret adventure was a joy to her because of the eagles. That first wonderful place of the terraces in the south gave its own memories of a greatness, yet the wings of the vultures there oppressed her. The place of the shrine at Walpi lifted the soul because it was an unbelievable nature place. But the temple where the roses grew was the work of ancient man, and truly great, and the most sacred bird of strength held guard over it that it be kept inviolate.

"When we have left the desert life far behind, I may tell you of it, Juanito," she promised, "but not between these ranges. The honor was shown me, I truly believe, because of these beads I wear, and Manuel seems to know of some virtues of your friend, Kahn Alcatraz; thus the two of us were asked to leave record there on the temple wall. But he is more modest than I — he does not boast, nor flaunt his whitened hand."

Tristan heard her raillery, and his eyes were never long from her direction, yet he was very silent, and I thought, had a look most anxious.

But he was brief in all arrangements for the dividing of the trails, and the Navajo women gladly climbed on the backs of the horses, and regarded Sancha as more than mortal that she had come, white from out the Desert, and helped to give them freedom. One offered her a narrow obsidian knife, and the other a pendant of turquoise.

"It is good that you take them," said Wisti. "It is the proving that you have come out of the Desert with friends in three tribes of people. If days come when you need friends, it is good to have a sign to send. These gifts are as the eagle feather, and — it is a pledge."

Then he touched the turquoise in the rosary she wore.

"This also," he said. "Each man who has given a bead knows — or his clan knows. See how it has made easy your way!"

The Navajo men asked Wisti to make clear to "the chief" their names and their clans, and if again he crossed their lands, he must send word to them.

Then they made their farewells, and went back up the trail through the forest, while we went down and outward on the great plateau of a land that is like no other.

The catcher of eagles went before us, and was of much help. He was a man of few words, and would walk hour after hour beside Wisti and no speech between them, for that is the Indio way. And Tristan grew almost as silent and watched their faces, strangely alert. He left Sancha to my care, and gave much time to the men.

When I asked if he had doubt or fear of the new man, he shook his head.

" I have had no doubt of any since we left the Oriabe men behind in Hopi land," he said; " not even of the three Spaniards whose names we do not know. But strange things are on this trail. I came over the land once with a man they thought next to God, yet these things did not happen. Do you not see that each tribe is giving a pledge, or sign, or symbol, by which we may call on friends in need? There was nothing like this before. It is not doubt — far from it! It is their jealous care of us by which I am made anxious."

" Think you it could be word from Mexico — your escape, reward or — "

" No, it is no thing of church or state. It is an Indio matter, and so great a thing that it touches three tribes wide apart from each other. The white men know nothing of it; all is peace in the province, else men would not be abroad to trap women and plan weddings; such pastimes belong to peaceful days. I have met nothing with so much of mystery in it, for I truly believe that Wisti does not know — yet his father in Walpi does know! Also I think Manuel of the eagles knows, and he tells me he is going with you to Santa Fé."

" Why say it in that way? Do you not go also? "

" Juanito, comrade," he said with gentleness. " Do you not know there must be a parting of the trails? This is not to be said before your cousin, but I can help her to nothing in New Granada. There she will find people of her rank to make all smooth for her. You alone must stand as her guardian, and Kahn Alcatraz will be only a name of a desert guide for whom no one is accountable." Then, when he saw the pro-

test in my face, he added, " Think back, Juanito, remember what you have seen of Inquisition work in
Mexico, and know it is stronger here. My stay in
Santa Fé will be only long enough to find one man,
and after that it is not to be hoped we will meet again.
I am, even now, a dangerous person for her to know,
she will learn this in time; but neither of us can tell
her. I came to you out of one desert, and I will dis-
appear in another wilderness; beyond that you must
know nothing of me. Never you remember hidden
things, Juanito."

" But where — in all this land —" I began in wonder, but he stopped me.

" Compared with what we have crossed, it is but
a summer's day travel east to the great river Miche Sepi
leading north to the colonies of France," he said. " If
need be, I could live hidden with these tribes where
neither priest nor soldier could ever find me. But where
those women in a boat could go, I surely could go, and
there are yet great lands to discover."

" You say nothing these late days of Marco," I ventured, " and I wonder — "

" It wastes time," he said. " Nothing has changed
as to him. She will grieve for her pride a little while,
and then wed with some governor or viceroy, and remember the desert days as a long dream. Be very, very
patient with her, Juanito."

I knew I should surely need patience and courage,
and several other helpful attributes if he dropped out
of our lives and left me alone to her questions, and my
heart grew faint within me on that part of the trail.

Then we reached Jemez, and spent the night in the

house of Manuel. His Navajo wife had a few words of Spanish, and showed every kindness to Sancha.

Tristan left us to rest, and disappeared somewhere with Manuel in one of their sanctuaries; no doubt the one where he had so easily secured rank or place by painting their gods as they had dreamed them. It left Sancha and me free to roam, but she confessed herself oppressed by the regard of these people — they gave no such sunny welcome as had the people of Walpi. There was a somber note in the life, and Sancha wished for a priest who could tell us of these people who gave us food, but no smiles. Padre Morador of the mission, was absent, visiting some men brought home crippled from the turquoise mine where twenty men had been crushed to death by the caving of walls.

Wisti learned this and told us very gravely, adding, as he pointed to the turquoise of Sancha "I am telling them you wear it from Navajo, and Pima, and Hopi, not from men made slaves by the Castilian god."

This death of the enslaved miners made explanation of the dark looks given to white strangers, but Manuel's wife was kind, and noting the worn foot-gear of Sancha, she brought out maiden boots, almost new, and asked Wisti to offer them.

Wisti looked at them, and then at her own feet. For whom had they been made?

"Manuel — he make — for Marta," said the wife, then Sancha came in, and gave thanks when the boots were offered, looking at her own oft mended ones ruefully.

"But I think I must keep these always," she said — "they are my record of the Desert."

And no one but I seemed to note the name of the girl for whom they had been made, and I wondered not so much then that Manuel meant to journey with us the rest of the way. Those hunters of women had given hint to the trail of the lost daughter for whom he asked of each tribe he met. And he had sat silent beside them at the camp fire in the pines while they told of her slender build, her Navajo mother, her name, and her owner; silent had he sat with no pretense of knowing Spanish — that was the Indio!

CHAPTER XIX

THE END OF THE TRAIL

FROM Jemez I remember less of the way than any other, for that land is a land of bleached cañons and forgotten cities. Rifts in blackened rock showed where fires yet burned deep in the earth, and in other places ancient lava cut the leather of shoes and the feet of horses. After we left the high forests, and the Jemez valley, each turn in the trail towards the river showed deeper scars of monstrous cleavage — it was the rock ribs of a world bleached white in the sun.

Sancha murmured prayers in some of the danger places, and bade me do likewise.

"For it is a place where terrible forces have left record," she said, "and where things of terror might happen."

My mind was full enough of shadows for the future, since I could not count on Tristan after the passing of the Rio Bravo del Norte. I knew that when all dangers were over for us, he would go out of our lives, and I rode with him ever in sight, though at times tears blurred my vision, for he had been salvation to us, and I was only a boy.

We passed a village ere the river was reached, but Tristan advised against camping there. Several of the

349

Indians killed in the turquoise mine had been taken from that place as slaves, and the looks of the natives were not friendly to white people.

"If you have a river to cross in the Desert, always cross before making camp," advised Tristan, "lest a storm, or cloudburst near headwaters, may lift the stream high in the night."

No one gainsaid him, for we had grown a silent group. I, because of my own fears, and Wisti and Manuel because of some words exchanged with the people of the village, but they would not tell what they were.

"It is the tragic death of all those men in the mine of the slaves," decided Tristan. "These tribal men have done great works, as is shown by their ancient building, and canals, yet they never have worked as slaves until now, and to die in that slavery is a serious thing, and the white conquerors should know it is a dangerous thing."

"What could happen?" asked Sancha, and I noted that Wisti and Manuel listened while one made a fire and the other prepared rabbits for cooking.

"Much could happen if the tribes knew their strength and were not so constantly fighting little wars between themselves," he said. "No white conquerors have conquered either in Mexico, or here, but by the help of Indians. Moctezuma was conquered as much by Tlascalans as by Castilians. These tribes have greater power than they know, and it is the good fortune of the white people that they do not know."

What else he said, or Sancha said, I did not hear, for my mind was held by the two Indian men. Neither spoke, neither made gesture or ceased their work, but over the little blaze of the new fire Wisti looked at Manuel, and Manuel met him with strange question in his eyes. It was a curious look, and it told nothing; each questioned, and each was on guard even with the other. I recalled afterwards that I had a chill because of that look, and got to my feet to walk it off.

When I came back, Sancha and Tristan sat above the river and tossed pebbles like children, and he made a balsa of willow twigs, and launched it with a white primrose as freight.

"There is your ship of life," he said, "all a white blossom on a muddy stream, Excellencia."

"Make one for yourself, and I will forgive you the 'excellencia,'" she said, and laughed.

"Will you so?" he asked, and wrapped the twigs and tossed them. "Will you indeed forgive, O Desert Comrade most Wonderful?"

She put out her hand to him, but leaned over the edge of the bank.

"O look! look!" she said. "They drifted wide, and mine halted and swirled in the eddy, and now the current bears them together until no eye can tell which it is carries the cargo of the desert bloom. Can you?"

"I do not want to," he said, and looked at her, and she gave one quick look at his face, and bent again over the bank.

"I know," and she spoke lowly. "If they drift apart each would seem in danger of wreckage, and it fits the peace of the twilight better that we see the two go together like that, lit by the white flame of the white blossom. See! they have passed the place where the ripples are, and no drop of the yellow spray has touched the white."

" That is how it will be — O White Butterfly Lady."

" Why do you call me that? " she asked, and he stood up and looked at her. His arms were folded, and to me there was a certain finality in his manner.

" Perhaps because of the shrine on the desert mesa, and the white-winged thing there. I think I have always wanted to call you your Indian name, and this is the last night."

" What! " and I could feel her terror.

" I have made your bed of the fragrant things under the stars for the last time on this trail, Marquesa de Llorente y Rivera," he said grimly enough. " When the twilight comes on the morrow, your trail of the Desert will be ended. You will be safe among people of your quality, and there will be silken covers for you, instead of desert stars."

" And you? " she asked.

" I shall always have the stars, and there may be summer days when white butterflies cross the trail."

" And you will be content with that? "

" That will mean freedom to range, and I have been content with less, White Butterfly Lady."

" You are a mystery to me always, Kahn Alcatraz," she said. " In all these days you ride beside us as a creature of power — yet the power always wears its mask even to me. I do not approve of that. Good night, Kahn Alcatraz."

" God be with you, Lady of White Butterflies! "

I stood in my tracks, making no sound, and they turned their different ways without getting sight of me, and that was the last night camp on our unforgettable trail.

But in the morning I was startled by a cry from Sancha in the dawn. Close beside her pillow of sage brush, lay a handful of the white primrose of the Desert, and beyond that no sign left of Tristan — it was his farewell! He had lain down to his rest as had the others, and no one knew when hè had risen and taken the trail.

In vain I assured her I did not know, and had distress enough of my own without borrowing from her. If the man was weary of our company, I did not feel to blame. I assured her I had ever given him friendly courtesy, and knew no cause of his going without farewell to me.

She only stared at that, and gave me cold disdain for the first mile or two on the way, then she turned to me after moody silence.

"But he forgave me my early discourtesy," she protested, and thus I knew where her thoughts had been. "He did forgive it all in a comradely way, and I had intent to have all honor shown to him before the governor; for God knows, Juanito, he has been as a very Saint of the Impossible on earth for us."

"But that saint was a woman," I reminded her.

"Ay, so they taught me," she answered, "but in the New World there are bewildering new things to be learned."

That of course was, and is, a fact, and I kept my tongue between my teeth for I knew she had more of the unexpected still to meet, and she would need a litany of saints, or a heavenly faith, to see her through.

And to meet it we journeyed over a trail of lava in
the hills, but when we went into the lower lands, we
could view great pastures and comfortable herds of
cattle, which brought the proof that we were at last
coming near the governor's seat of the most northern
Spanish province. There I turned to her, and made my
endeavor to cloak his presence in the land.

"Sancha dear," I said humbly enough. "He has
other cause than we know for his comings and goings in
this land. It is as well to say little of a white
comrade on the trail. If he is enemy to friend of ours,
that comradeship might be hard to explain. We are
young, Sancha mine, and we will have to live the rest
of our lives on the plans we make in this town of
Santa Fé at the end of the trail. Let him go as he will,
and mention him only as Ivava, if you mention him at
all; it is a good name."

"It is a good name, for it means brother," she agreed,
"and you are not trusting me, Juanito. But if either
of you think I will not see him again, it a foolish
thought. He had love for that woman, but I have
my own reckoning day as well as he in this land, and
when it is over I shall see him again. The thought
that he is utterly gone is foolish — he is only out of
our sight. But I will call him Ivava to please you,
Juanito."

So it was decided, and when we halted at a pueblo
where good water was, we heard clatter of horses, and
a troop of the governor's guard rode up and saluted,
and the chief officer, Captain Roque de Lara, gave us
welcome. His word was that a padre of Mexico — Fray
Domingo — had given the word to Governor Otermin

of our coming, and of our rank. The mystery of this was made somewhat clear by the added fact that Fray Domingo had met some hunters who crossed our trail.

"But we were told there was a white man with you, and I see none," he said.

Whereupon with as careless a manner as might be, I stated that the man was but a ranger who had served as guard, and when we were at the edge of safety, he had gone his own way.

Sancha looked her disapproval of my slight opinion of him, yet she said no word, and permitted herself to be mounted on a fresh horse, and gave joy to Captain de Lara by riding beside him into the town of the Holy Faith of Saint Francis.

There was excitement enough, and to spare, over our arrival from the wide wilderness of the pagans. So many were the questions, and the strange faces, that it is a blur in my mind to this day.

His Excellency, Don Antonio Otermin, and his wife, Doña Zelinda, looked to the comfort of Sancha who was housed in the Governor's Palace; a long adobe building, of insignificance to our eyes after the wonders in the ancient homes of the Desert.

But there was clean linen, and Christian welcome, and De Lara was my friend to lend me needful garments in which to make proper appearance at the governor's table. Manuel had asked with civility to be my servant on our arrival, and as Sancha and I might well employ one between us, I asked courtesy of De Lara for him until we two bankrupts had time to discover what would chance us next.

Neither of us asked for Marco, and nothing was

seen of him, but my friend, the captain, laughed and made a remark concerning him, and concerning the chance that Marco would slip into town the back way, and come with no tooting of horn from San Yldefonso.

When I asked the meaning of that, he told me Marco had gone north a day's journey on some business of Governor Otermin, and had taken his pretty family along lest she be stolen by some one else in his absence! — also that her excellency, the marquesa, might not relish so pretty a serving maid as had been secured for her.

And by that I saw of course that no secrecy could be made of the betrothal. The vanity of Marco made known all his conquests.

"But it is by fateful and unexpected adventure that Doña Sancha has reached this frontier land," I explained. "Her destination was a convent instead of the Governor's Palace."

De Lara and his comrades were tireless in their question of the wide trail and the tribes of the west. A padre from Mexico had arrived, weeks before, with tales of the Apache war on the Pima, and the difficulties of the eastern trail; we had done well to keep to the west.

I pricked up my ears as to the padre, and the latest word from Mexico, but my new friend knew only that his name was Padre Domingo Orellano and that he had some business of import for the Holy Office, and was a man made of whalebone by the look of him, and the endurance. In the Apache land he had traveled two days without daring to approach a water hole — and was confidently hoping for martyrdom.

I met the man, and bowed before him in the house of the governor, and felt his cold gray eyes measure me, and weigh me.

He asked where our guide had left us; also his name. I replied that it was Ivava, and he had only remained with us for courtesy and our safety; after the latter was assured, he had gone about his own business which had to do with Indians.

"Ah!" he said, "ah-h! Indians?"

I made my face a blank against the gaze like a gimlet in its searching, and his smile was not to my liking. I had a chill of fear at thought of this man hoping for martyrdom for the Faith — and on the trail of Tristan!

Then Sancha came in with Doña Zelinda and a Doña Ynez Tafoya who had shared the adventures of her young husband in the colony. I was glad of heart to see Sancha safe again under a roof, and garbed in a gown of white linen, and a rebosa of lace over her shoulders.

Every eye was turned her way — and she was well worth it. As a personage, and the niece of Fray Payo, the well beloved, all homage and courtesy was her due, but it was something more which caused each man's eye to lighten at sight of her. Favorite though the Sancha of the viceregal court had been, she was but a hint of the royal beauty the Sancha of the Desert had become. She had been a pale bud of promise, and in the dusty garb of the long journey I had grown used to the change in her by degrees, but the garb of dignity, and the burnished tresses, made her suddenly a revelation; she radiated beauty graciously as a flower its perfume.

The women were her adoring admirers as well as the men: for to them she was as the spirit of a romance such as women's hearts feed upon. Welcome diet it was in that adobe town of the frontier, for there was little of change there but to change the guard, and protect the settlements as might be from Apache, Navajo, or roving Comanche.

Her eyes went quickly over every face in the sala. Then she looked at me in question, but I kept my attention steadily for Doña Ynez, who was exceedingly gracious. She told me her husband, Don Lorenzo, was expected back from Santa Cruz a day later, and she would pray that he come by San Yldefonso and bring Señor Lieutenant de Ordoño quickly to so fair a sweetheart. All the town, with its hundred and twenty soldiers, would celebrate the wedding day.

"Wonderful proud one!" murmured Doña Ynez, and looked half pitifully at Sancha; "it is as well there is a day for preparing, for there must be no thorns on her roses."

She was a lovely lady, who had come north with the colonists; and there was a comfort to me in having one new friend who knew of Anita, and would help cloak, if need be, all truths from Sancha.

But it was thin ice we all stood on that night of the first supper at the table of the governor, for Padre Domingo was ever as a watchful puma coming back on the trail; and suddenly, after Sancha had told of the disaster to the hopes of Mother Clemente, and the capture of us by the Sonoran tribe, the padre suddenly asked:

"Did you, by any chance, hear of the heretic, Tristan Rueda, on that trail?"

Sancha looked at him curiously, half smiling, yet wrinkling her brows.

"How strange to hear that name away here," she said. "A heretic, good father? Truly?"

"You have not seen him on the trail?" he asked again, and she laughed and shook her head.

"I never have seen him since I was but a child in Seville, and he angered me so that I was long in forgiving. I never have seen him in this land, but no one told me he was a lost soul. I am sad at heart of that thought, for Don Rodrigo loved him."

"And Fray Payo and — many others, Doña Sancha," said Doña Ynez. "He was high in favor with Don Tomas, and had painted the most lovely picture of Doña Perfecta de Dasmarinas. It was enough to cause love for her but to look at it, so beautiful it was — like a golden poppy of a woman."

"Why — yes, I saw the portrait, but no one told me it was by the hand of that Rueda," said Sancha, perplexed, and looking at me. "If he knew enough to paint so well, small wonder that he angered me long ago by slighting a portrait I thought entirely the work of inspiration. I was but a silly one at that time."

"Ay, he knows enough — with Satan for his master!" agreed Padre Domingo. "Angels for the chapel of San Carlos he did, and there is grave doubt now concerning them — it is thought they will be painted over by a true believer."

"But they were quite things of wonder in beauty!" said the amazed Doña Ynez. "I went there for prayers on my wedding morning, and closing my eyes, I can still see them."

"Things of beauty, yes," agreed Padre Domingo grimly, "things of wonder to make poor souls forget the sins and souls, and remember only the fleshly beauty of color and likeness to life. Spirit is what he was told to paint, and he did instead graceful wenches wreathed in cloud. That is the time he should have been curbed, and never let do that Virgin of the Fawn, which is a pagan false goddess, and not the holy Santa Maria at all."

"The — Virgin of — the Fawn!" repeated Sancha with stiff lips, and paling face.

"Why — we never heard of that Virgin," said Doña Zelinda.

"Nor did any one else in Christian faith ever before," stated Padre Domingo. "The painter was a heretic Jew on trial for the faith, and was given the task in prison to paint an altarpiece of holiness, if Santa Maria, the Virgin, gave him leave. Well, an altarpiece was painted, and his friends say that the Holy Mother helped him. But there is another side of the story; we have painters in holy orders who are modest, and — all too lenient. Also after the painting was done, the apostate painter escaped from prison. He started north, but has touched no point on El Paso trail. Thus my question to you; He escaped prison before your excellency took leave of Mexico."

"Juanito, did you know?" asked Sancha.

"I did hear, but who knows the business of the Holy Office? Because a man is no longer seen does not mean he has escaped."

"But, as to the picture?" she persisted, and the good food was forgotten on her plate, and her voice shook despite its coldness.

"Of the picture there were rumors, as the reverend father rightly says," I replied virtuously. "No one saw the painting of that picture. No one but Fray Bernardino truly knows. The decoration of the chapel, and the altar, was in the hands of Fray Bernardino."

"That is the true word, and the sorrowful one," said Padre Domingo, "for Bernardino has ever had a soft place in his heart for that adventurer apostate. The evidence points one way; the painting was credited to the Jewish heretic that true believers might vote him innocent."

"No heretic could do that picture," stated Sancha. "I saw it. No, no! the painter of that was not heretic."

"So I say," decided Padre Domingo. "He may have given help, for he has the devil's cleverness — or the Jews'! He has been upheld by men who should be disciplined for it, and all will come out when we find him again."

"But we knew Tristan Rueda, and he was honest Christian, or so it seemed," said Doña Ynez. "Fray Payo gave him countenance in all things, and he could have mounted high if he had cared for worldly possession rather than profitless learning. How could he so quickly turn Jew?"

"A Jew he was born, or of Jewish ancestry, so the curse is in the blood," said the padre.

"This is all very strange to me," said Sancha. "I never knew the man, but he stood high in the thought of Uncle Rodrigo."

"Your excellency has not been told then that it
was the death-bed confession of Don Rodrigo de Ordoño
by which the Jew's ancestry was made known?" demanded Padre Domingo with a keen look at her, but
she shook her head, white, and bewildered.

"All these things are heard by me for the first time,
and they give me a soul sickness instead of joy at the
end of the trail," she confessed. "If it is true that the
word of Don Rodrigo sentenced that man, then Don
Rodrigo died in torment, for he loved him well. I pray
your excellency —"

She turned with pleading eyes to Governor Otermin,
and he smiled upon her, and lifted his goblet of wine.

"You are overtired to be entertained by tales of
heretics and the laws, Excellencia," he said, "but ere
Doña Zelinda and Doña Ynez claim you for the night,
I would empty a cup to the most distinguished lady
who has ever braved our northern wilderness. We drink
to your high courage, to the honor of your house, and
to the noble example you have set to ladies of rank. I
may hope to double my army on this example, for men
will ever come in plenty where maidens venture forth.
To your happiness, Marquesa de Llorente y Rivera!"

Sancha smiled with stiff lips, as all stood in her honor,
and lifted goblets high, and then made a little lane
through which she was led by her host. My last sight
was of two reproachful eyes, gazing at me above the
head of the governor as he bent low over her hand.

Then the door closed, and the men sat again at the
table and voiced their admiration. I alone sat silent,
I, and the gray padre watching me, and, after a little,
he spoke.

"Is it not strange, Señor Rivera, that the thing of greatest scandal of the Mexican winter has never reached the ears of your cousin, Doña la Marquesa, until tonight?"

The governor turned a quick frowning face on the padre.

"That scandal drove away our most lovely guest, father," he remarked. "Is it your intent to send the rest of us to bad dreams?"

"Nay, rather to get trail of an arch enemy to Mother Church," he said softly, crossing himself. "These children from the Desert might have traveled in perilous company, Excellency, and none to warn them."

Their exchange of words gave me time to gather my wits.

"Your Excellency," I ventured. "The reverend father has reason on his side, for Tristan Rueda was a favorite of two viceroys, and much in the speech of men. His brush made one portrait of a lady of rank in the palace —so he was a Somebody. But fashions change at court as elsewhere, and when the Marquesa de Llorente arrived, his was a forbidden name there. I am witness that Doña Perfecta, for sake of policy, had a priest to alter points in that portrait of hers, and, as the Marquesa lived in the viceroy's honored circle, and knew no other, how should she hear of this outlawed man? He was never known to her by sight even in her childhood, and for this reason I gave her no confidence in the matter, lest it bring her grief for Don Rodrigo's painful duty, as you are witness now."

"True," said Governor Otermin, "I have heard it was that honored old soldier who made the betrothal, and won such a treasure for Marco de Ordoño. By the Faith, she is too rare a creature for a lieutenant; a viceregal palace would be better shelter for such a face!"

"It is whispered, your excellency, that she could have even that, and without striving," stated Padre Domingo impressively; "this young gallant should know somewhat of that."

"I know only her words — that she would wed as arranged, or re-enter the conventual life. All her years were lived thus until now."

"What a waste of beauty!" said Roque de Lara. "His excellency is right, as always; such proud loveliness would grace a palace. How think you Lieutenant Marco may measure up to it? She looked like Sheba's queen to me, though in an Indian dress, and a man's cloak."

"I started a runner at once with a message to him," said the governor — "the most gracious thing I could do for one so proud that she makes no mention of him when his voice is not here to speak welcome."

"More than pride, that," said the gray padre. "More than pride! It holds its own mystery; which does not fit with her path half-way round the world."

His tone was quiet and thoughtful, but his eyes never left my face, and the curious smile of his thin lips had too much satisfaction in them for my content. There are nights even now when I dream of those crafty eyes watching — watching from under the gray overhanging brows. I had little chills and flashes of fever at his gaze, and I cross myself now when I think of all it meant.

There were questions asked me of the western pueblos, and their appearance of content, but I was well near to being tongue tied, and could only tell that they were friendly, and the guides they sent proved loyal. Cochiti village showed some sullen faces, but we did not halt there. The governor listened closely.

"You see, gentlemen, the trouble is not in the west, and is not general. It is the northern groups for whom the guard must never be lax. That crime lately at San Juan is the most troubling thing, for it was Popé himself who strangled the Indian governor there, and Popé has heretofore been politic with all the clans, striving with constancy to incite them to return to the pagan faith. Padre, cannot the Holy Office help us in this matter? This red apostate claims to talk with spirits, and excites the poor natives to distraction. If you have leave to trail one renegade painter for execution, why not a rebellious leader who is against church and state?"

"The execution of that rebellious Indio, your excellency, should have been carried out before he gathered his bewitched and fanatic guards about him. He moves about in state with more courtiers than the soldiers in your garrison. He will be dealt with when the time comes, but the trail of this renegade Jew is a different matter. His knowledge of other secret Spanish heretics may be great. It is not for death he is precious, but to be put to the question as a most learned apostate. His friends in high places did win him respite, and he has been let run the length of his chain, but it is only to be drawn back as witness for the Faith."

His words were to the Governor, but his eyes were on me with that mocking, endless stare, as if to read all the thoughts I had ever dared cultivate. Boy as I was, emerging from the months of desert silences, it was a nerve racking time I put in there, with the consciousness of that death's head gloating over me.

I welcomed the first move of the captain to go, for I had not the courage to take myself away, much though I craved to.

As the other men bade good night, and went out, De Lara halted to speak to Governor Otermin of some private matter, and I stood near the door, afraid, in truth, to go out alone lest I should run wildly in useless search for Tristan, and shout to him my warning. Someway I knew he had either evaded the town, or was well hidden, but who was there to tell him the breed of tiger on the trail?

The knowledge of Padre Domingo was very wide, and I was clear as a piece of crystal to him, for he continued to smile as I fumbled nervously with the cuff of my borrowed garment, and strove to look comfortably placed.

"The length of his chain," said the padre softly. "Don Juan Rivera, you perhaps do not know that Padre de Vallada in the Desert, has the swiftest couriers of New Granada at his call. Do you know now just how long is the chain for Tristan Rueda Alcatraz?"

So he had known all the time!

I could only look at him, struck dazed with all it meant. He had played with us as a cat with mice. He had given me a chance to damn myself in the eyes of the Holy Office by withholding testimony. Thus, no matter how long a chain was given me, they could also draw me back for service if a day came when I was desired.   And their strength on the frontier was above the power of state!

More than that one crafty question he did not speak. It was as if he meant to kill me by inches of torment, yet I was so slight and helpless he could afford to let me walk free, knowing the limit absolutely of my range — he held the other end of the chain!

No one heard him but me.   He did not mean to make a scandal in the governor's circle of guests, but I had my warning.

Someway I got outside, ahead of Roque de Lara.   I was voiceless with dread, and began to understand why there had been so little comment on the disappearance of our guide.

Had I known then that Tristan, supperless, lay roped and tied in the adobe cuartel not a bowshot away, the fine supper at the table of the governor would have choked me.

CHAPTER XX

ON SANTA FÉ HILL IN NEW GRANADA

M Y NIGHT under a roof was one of sleepless dread, in terror at thought of facing Sancha, and in even greater terror of what the keen gray padre meant to do with us all.

At dawn Wisti was waiting me at the door, huddled up in a blanket, and his words did not bring comfort. He asked that I get for use the dress in which the White Butterfly Maid had ridden away from Walpi. It had been presented to her for wearing. In the patio of the house of the governor he had seen her in a garb of fine white, but the tribes only knew of her by the Hopi dress, and the gray cloak, and if she was indeed my sister of the heart, I must at once get ready the garments. Also his word to me was that it would be well to take the trail without delay for Mexico; the tribes in New Granada were not content, and it was an ill place to come for holiday.

But he did not tell all this so plainly as I say it. Except for his tremulous anxiety of the dress, no other statement of his was clear. When I strove to learn the thing he hinted, I could get from him only the fact that he was a simple man of the wilderness, and a stranger in the Christian town of Santa Fé. He also made statement that Manuel would take good care of the garments for me, and Manuel was a friend and server.

Thereupon I undertook, as early as might be, to come by the desired articles by the hand of sleek Rosita, a half-breed serving maid of Doña Ynez, for Wisti advised that it be secured without question or alarm to Doña Sancha.

So, after breakfast, the affair moved well enough, and the garments were slipped to me out of a barred window, and Manuel disappeared with them as Doña Ynez herself came from the patio in time to ask if I was already finding myself brown sweethearts among her maids!

Over this we jested, and I vowed I was only there to ask of her health, and to learn how my cousin had rested at the end of all her adventures, and at that the kind eyes of her looked sad.

"She is without doubt mad with love for him— is it not so?" she asked. "I think she slept little, and twice she sat at the window looking out in the night, and listening to each sound as if waiting some sound of his step."

"That listening is a habit of the Desert; I did likewise," I confessed. "But it may be that she is indeed deep in love, and that she has her own anxieties. She does not speak of them."

"That is true; did ever you see a girl so cold and proud? Don Antonio insists she should be a vicereine at the least, even the padre spoke of it with warning of too much pride in youth. But the Llorentes and the Riveras have their own excuse for pride, and always they have been an honor to church and state."

I had scarcely acknowledged properly this fine compliment, when Sancha appeared in the patio, fastening yellow roses in the bodice of her white gown. She had no pleasant looks for me, but a cold decision in her voice.

"Juanito, O wise one," she said mockingly. "You know so many ways of this world, know you also the trail to San Yldefonso? They tell me it is only the ride of a day, and San Yldefonso seems the bottom of the well where Truth lies for me. I have asked for our horses, and have the mood to ride that way."

"Santa Madre!" whispered Doña Ynez, "never in the world must she do so. Another girl rides with him — a slave girl of his!"

"I know," I said, and stole another look at Sancha. Her face was a mask, but her eyes were aflame — she looked as if she also knew!

"If you ride forth to the north take me as guide," said Doña Ynez with sudden thought to help. "I was once at Santa Cruz, and know some of the trails, also my husband is there."

Captain de Lara advised against this plan, and offered instead to take us pleasuring to an extinct volcano not far away, and by nightfall, without doubt, the Lieutenant de Ordoño and Don Lorenzo would have reached town, also there were various trails to the north, and we would surely miss them in the wilderness.

Sancha listened, and smiled at us.

"I do not think I care for dead volcanos," she said; "there are too many living things of interest to me. I may save a life by riding north, and my cousin here knows the meaning of that."

Doña Ynez stared at her and crossed herself.

"If such be true," she begged, "come first, for the love of God, and tell the governor or the padre. Padre Domingo has safer messengers than you could be — or any of us."

"That is true," said Captain de Lara. "The Holy Office can pay its messengers more than the state, and controls the best. I heard this morning a new thing — a Roberto Sanchez trapped some renegade on the range for Padre Domingo yesterday, and how, think you? Roberto is a lad from the far south and uses well the reata; swish, it circles a man's shoulders, and drags him from a horse. An Indio carted the man in, roped and tied, under a load of corn. He is now in the cuartel back of the church waiting the pleasure of the priests. One man with a greased rope — and the job is done for the church, and no one in the town the wiser. But for the state we would have been sent in company, and every street boy know our errand, and the result. It is true, Excellencia, that if you desire haste, the padre has the greater power."

My own interest was suddenly lost in the desire of Sancha. That cuartel back of the church held all my thought. That was the prison for the Inquisition: not a strong place, except by guard and rope, or chain. The story of the captain had its own suggestion: Roberto, who was a handy lad with a reata, and thought he had an honest grudge of his own to pay! Padre Domingo, by whom the people of Santa Fé learned our coming! I dared not question, yet I was sick with fear. If the long arm of the Inquisition had indeed touched him again, it must have been in the dusk of dawn when he rode away to free our skirts of all stigma through comradeship for him.

Small wonder if Padre Domingo could smile contentedly over the game he had come a thousand miles to win! and well I knew that but for the encumbrance of Sancha and me, Tristan could have ridden, unheralded, safely into New Granada, and safely out again.

Filled with dread of that which I dared not voice, I walked apart where the roses grew, and watched the wall of the cuartel. It was not high, and looked a mere walled square back of the church. It might have been a monastery garden for all one could see of it, but I had been told that the prison adjoined the monastery there, and was back of the church. It was the place of restraint for all detained by the Holy Office, and the place of punishing for novices.

It was again the very mockings of fate if he should be chained within hearing of her voice, and she the honored guest of the governor. I remembered the thing she had said to him on the terrace roof that night at Walpi — that doors must ever open for him where she was!

So oppressed was I, that I lost track of the words of others there; only Sancha had her mind decided upon San Yldefonso, without any messenger, whether churchly or military.

Doña Zelinda joined them, and plainly agreed with Sancha. The governor's lady had a heart for romance, and Sancha fitted all her dreams of adventurous love. She ransacked her chests for garb worthy her wear, and in her mind's eye she already saw every chance for the most sumptuous wedding yet seen in Santa Fé:

all this though no one had heard the bride elect mention Marco by name. But that, they all agreed, was maiden shyness, and more than maiden pride. In later days Doña Zelinda confessed to me that Sancha was overpowering to her in three different ways — as a simple convent maid of high degree, in the glowing beauty of her which fitted well a love romance, and in the still pride of all the Llorentes and Riveras by which it was plain she would rule wherever her lines of life were cast.

"Don Juan is not gallant this fair morning," said Sancha loud enough for me to hear. "He walks apart and mopes to show us he is weary of riding beside a mere cousin. Doña Zelinda, I beg that you find for him a lady worthy his fancy, while I go begging for a cavallero!"

"A fine jest," I grumbled, "with all the presidio at your nod. But I have ridden with you on headstrong rides of folly ere this, and once more is a trifle."

The others laughed, but she put her hand on my arm very meekly.

"So you did, Juanito mine," she said, "and in weariness have you paid for the other times; but — this is the last one — and it will not be long."

With a proud or angry Sancha a man might argue, but Sancha with meekness in her eye was a power none might resist, and I swept the ground with De Lara's holiday hat, and bent knee before her, playing courtier. She patted my hair much as if I had been a faithful watch dog.

Manuel came with the horses, and at sight of him I had a new fear. I had no good reason to guard Marco from any justice, yet I had no fancy for having Manuel meet his pretty daughter on the highway in the midst of all the troublous coil.

He looked searchingly at Sancha, and at the rosary, and yellow roses.

" The feather of the eagle — where? " he asked, and Sancha slipped it from the bosom of her gown.

" It was a pledge," she said. " I remember, and I keep it."

" It will be good that you do not forget ever in this land," he said guardedly. " It weighs little, but the spirit of it is big. Also the day may dawn when you need that spirit."

" Manuel," she half whispered that the others should not hear, " Manuel — there were two feathers; you said they were mates, but we have lost the mate. Manuel — can you help with the finding? "

" That is true, Manuel," I added, eager enough to give him other task than to go with us. Then I drew him apart while Roque de Lara helped Sancha and Doña Ynez to saddle.

I told him all I dared, leaving him to think that if it were indeed our friend who had been roped and thrown in prison, that the man who did the roping was the woman-hunter whose slave we had set free, and that the capture was in vengeance.

I had touched the right thought, for the eyes of Manuel blazed, and his smile was wicked.

" I will learn," he said. " Converts of our clan are here with the padres. The eagle feather will win their heart if he shows it. I will learn."

Well satisfied, I rode out to join Sancha and Doña

Ynez. De Lara could not leave. Don Antonio offered to send fitting escort, but Sancha wanted only Wisti as her guard.

"This must be only a family party, Juanito," she said. "Wisti has been of us these many days, and Doña Ynez already is a comrade."

To me Doña Ynez privately expressed the hope that if we met Marco and Don Lorenzo on the way, that it would be her husband the girl rode with, and not Sancha's betrothed. Also she gave as her opinion that Sancha had heard some foolish gossip of the matter, else why this sudden notion to ride north?

As we rode, I noted little work was being done, and groups of Indio men were coming in from many ways. They looked on us with curious interest, and some of the older exchanged words with Wisti. Once, when speaking, he pointed to Sancha and spoke her Hopi name, and an old man came over, and very gravely looked at the rosary, and the feather she wore, with its curious marking. Then he unfastened a blue bead of turquoise, slipped it on a thread of sinew, and offered it with a gesture indicating that she wear it on her wrist.

She did so, thanking him and smiling her most gracious, but the man did not smile, and he stood in the road looking after us.

"That man is Ruler — what you call Cacique of a pueblo," said Wisti. "Forget not his kind heart thought, Excellencia, for you he will not forget."

"Have you had such easy conquests all your long road?" asked Doña Ynez wonderingly. "You do not have even a surprise that an ancient comes out of the

wilderness to offer you a jewel. They do nothing like
that for me."

" On the long trail we learned to value each kindness,
and each one seems a link in a chain of service. It is
by no virtue of my own that I am heir to these," said
Sancha humbly.

We had reached the top of a long hill where it was
worth the time to halt and watch the shadows of the
clouds drift over the pastures and fields of corn. North
was the forest range of the Sangre de Christo, and
back of us the walls of Santa Fé shown yellow, glim-
mering in the August sun.

" It looks a picture of endless peace," said Sancha,
and halted her horse, " yet my mind is troubled at the
strange looks in the eyes of all Indians who pass. Why
should that strange and stern old man have chosen
me to receive his gift of a blue bead? "

It was at that moment of her perplexed looking back
at the adobe walls, and the straggling Indio travelers,
that Doña Ynez did a quick and clever thing. She was
ahead on the trail, and with a gesture to me for secrecy,
she slipped from her saddle, and ran forward without
sound. At the same moment I heard the beat of the
feet of horses. Sancha was speaking to Wisti and
heard none of it.

But when she turned, she saw the empty saddle,
stared at me in startled question, but never voiced it,
for from the trail beyond she heard the voice of Doña
Ynez and laughter, and then the tones of a man, and
guessed the truth.

Women are wonderful things! My own blood was
jumping, and I fairly shook with the unexpectedness

of it all, but Sancha sat her horse like a queen at a review, her face a cold mask, her eyes glowing and steady. She did not even urge her horse one step nearer, but held him in his place on the very summit of the hill.

Then, up from the trail of the scrub oak, walked Doña Ynez with the arm of her husband about her. He led his horse, and back of them rode a young Indian girl of beauty and wistful eyes.

The saints alone knew how the wife of Don Lorenzo had so quickly commanded her husband in one breathless sentence, but command him she did.

"This is my husband, Señor Tafoya," she said, smiling and elated at her triumph. "I heard his voice and slipped down to give him the great surprise. And see how thoughtful he has been to bring me a maid who is pretty as a painted saint!"

I agreed that the maid was good to gaze upon, and knew I had heard of her beauty in the Jemez mountains. She looked puzzled and even frightened, glancing from one to the other of us, and turning her horse in the road.

But I rested my hand on the bridle, while Don Lorenzo bent over the hand of Sancha, and spoke his wonder at meeting a lady of Old Spain on a hill in New Granada.

He had not seen the messenger sent north, neither had Don Marco. He had cut short his stay in Santa Cruz for the reason that there were strange, treasonable matters going forward in the north, and he felt his duty was to bring warning to Governor Otermin at once; more of a guard was needed at Santa Cruz.

Lieutenant de Ordoño felt the same regarding San Yldefonso; both were riding with all haste to make report.

Sancha had uttered no word, had only clasped hands
with Don Lorenzo, and smiled her gracious greeting,
and the smile of Sancha had a satisfying message of
its own. But through that still smile of hers, and the
explaining words of the puzzled man, I could see that
her every sense was centered on listening — listening!

I could tell the very instant she detected the sound
of hoof beats above the nervous chatter of Doña Ynez,
for her shoulders squared, and the smile did not vanish,
but it did change. By the suppressed excitement of
Doña Ynez she knew there was something concealed
from her.

As I learned later — many terrible days later, when
the Tafoyas and I camped together for the winter at
San Lorenzo — Doña Ynez had rushed through the
thicket to meet them, and bade Marco de Ordoño halt
in his tracks long enough to recall all his sins for confession, while she claimed the Indio maid and saved him
his honor.

More than that there was no moment to speak, for
her husband had got out of the saddle, and she drew
him away, leading the horse of pretty Marta. Marco
did halt for the reason that Doña Ynez appeared ter-
ribly in earnest, but his list of sins was brief according
to his reckoning, for his halt was only so long as one
might count a hundred on his fingers, and then the
forced chatter of Doña Ynez halted on her lips, and she
made much to do about getting in the saddle again,
for she heard his horse coming.

Sancha saw him first, as she was highest, and he

came upwards, his hat in his hand, and his face lifted
as if seeing visions of heaven instead of a slender maid
who sat her horse well, and watched his coming with a
look mocking and strange.

No one spoke because of that look, and Doña Ynez
drew a sobbing breath, half of fear. Truly it was a
strange welcome for so handsome a gallant. Me he
did not see because of the bulk of Don Lorenzo's
blankets back of the saddle.

Thus it was Sancha who was first to speak — Sancha
of the deep, sweet voice, and the strange smile.

"The way has been long, Don Alphard, long as your
trail across the sky," she said.

He bowed to the horn of his saddle, and gazed at
her in open admiration, and wonder, and did not know
her!

"Excellencia," he began with adulation in his tones
and his eyes. Doña Ynez strove to speak, but Sancha
lifted her hand in quick warning.

"Wisti," she said. "The gentleman does not remember my name. Will you tell him the name I have?
the name given me in the house of Lenmana ere we
came east across the Desert?"

"It is Poli-kota, and the thought of it is the 'white
butterfly,' Señor," stated Wisti as he was bid. "So
the Excellencia is to us, and to our clans, the White
Butterfly Lady."

"A name of exceeding beauty, Excellencia," said the
bewildered gallant. "I — I appreciate the honor of
being told. But you mention that I do not remember
— I, if ever I had known — "

He halted, and let his eyes speak for him. They had

been eyes well trained in service to ladies fair, but the smile of Sancha was not encouraging.

"Then the name is not a name of meaning for you, Don Alphard?" she asked.

"Only that the beauty of it is well placed," he said glibly enough. "But — may I correct you, Excellencia? The name you give me is one I have not heard, it has a sound of the Moor or the Arab."

"So it has," she conceded, "and yours is — ?"

"A sound Christian name, and at your service," he said with another bow, "Marcos de Ordoño."

He looked so handsome in his eagerness, and his admiring wonder, that it was an effort to stand speechless there and let him condemn himself out of his own mouth. But if it was the end of her love trail, why not let her decide it her own way? So I thought and held my tongue. Doña Ynez and Don Lorenzo strove to conceal their smiles at what they deemed but a little Comedy of Love begun long ago in Spain and played out on the Santa Fé hill of the north frontier.

Sancha saw it all, but Marco saw only her.

"Ride more close, Señor de Ordoño, since that is the name you have preference for," she said. "I would see your hand."

"I think you mock me, Excellencia," he said, as he drew his horse touching shoulder with hers, "and I do not know the game you play — but if it is for your pleasure, I will be either cavallero or clown," and he held out his hand.

"You wear no ring, Señor," she said. "If you are the man I brought message for, he wore a ring. Doña Perfecta spoke of its color."

"Doña Perfecta?" he said eagerly. "Yes, she did know me to wear a ring —"

"A ruby — was it not?" she asked mockingly smiling, and he smiled back, straight into her eyes.

"It was not a ruby, Excellencia. If you have a message from Doña Perfecta, it was to a man of an emerald ring; but why seek to confuse me by the strange Arab name?"

"Can you show me the ring, señor?" she asked. "How may I give the message unless the proof be sure?"

"Nay, I can describe it as she saw it," he said entering into her mood, "but the ring itself I cannot show; it was lost in the Desert."

"So?" she said with lifted brows. "Well, there was also a glove — a maiden's glove of white, with a fringe of silver. Was the glove lost to the same slender hand, Marco de Ordoño?"

Her voice was like steel. Doña Ynez and her husband ceased smiling, and Marco flamed red as he drew back.

"I know not the glove, nor ever saw it," he said, "nor do I understand —"

Sancha put up her hand.

"I do believe you, Señor de Ordoño!" she said, and drew a deep breath, turning her face to the sky. "Mother of God! How glad I am to believe!" Then in a very different way she added, "Who wrote the letters, Marco?"

"Excellencia?" and he stared at her incredulous, yet fearful, and I got out from behind the horse and stood beside Sancha.

"Are you entranced, Marco?" I asked. "Have you no wit left to tell you the truth?"

Then he saw, and went deadly white.

"That damned Tristan!" he said. "God send the priests burn him at the stake!"

"Tristan! always Tristan!" she said with a sob in her throat. "God send that I find him first!" then she looked at me, and laughed.

"Tell him, Juanito, where he can find his ring," she said; "and you tell him also that it might be as well to send that comely slave of his back to her hills. I heard gossip about the matter under my window last night. You have tried to trick me — all of you! Come; — Wisti, it is good for me this day that I have red brothers of the Desert."

"Yes — it is good for you," agreed Wisti quietly; and she wheeled her horse, and touched him with the spur. It was the best animal of Don Antonio, and little used to urging. He fairly skimmed the ground over the sloping range to Sante Fé, with the Indian as close to her as his horse could keep him.

There is little to tell of that ride back for the rest of us. Doña Ynez openly wept at the wreck of all her pretty plans for the lovers. Don Lorenzo asked if the beautiful Doña Sancha was not a mad woman, and Marco rode sullenly beside us, cursing his luck, and cursing Tristan Rueda whom he was glad to know was a damned Jew who would be garroted or burned some fine morning. And when he got tired of plans for Tristan, he flung an extra curse at me, and even at the poor Indian girl who strove timidly to express sorrow that some shadow had fallen over him.

For myself, I rode along in the unhappy group feeling that one curse more or less could not make difference to me after her bitter words. Marco had been given his deserts, but I could see no justice in her choice of that Indio brother.

CHAPTER XXI

THE INSURRECTION OF 1680

THAT was the day of panic for all to remember, for the news Don Lorenzo brought of the northern pueblos was no news to the Holy Office, or to Governor Antonio Otermin when we rode into Santa Fé.

Two Indians from Tesuque had crept away from that pueblo under cover of the scrub brush, and in fear of their lives, and the word they brought made clear all the strange things of the clans from Tusayan to Santa Fé.

For the word was out secretly over all the land, and in two more risings of the sun, every clan and tribe was joined in conspiracy to rise against the Castilian priests. In every pueblo they would wipe from the frontier all trace of the white man's god, under whom they and their children were made as slaves!

So secret was the plot that only the older men knew all. The informers begged that if they could not be protected, they be killed quickly by the men of Don Antonio, and not be given up as captives. Popé, the leader of the revolution, had strangled Nicholas Bua, the husband of his daughter, and the governor of San Juan de los Caballeros, because his loyalty to the cause of the insurrectos was even suspected.

Governor Otermin was given, according to this in-

384

formation, only two days in which to take all his people, and his loyal Indians, and remove to the south, for it was too late for the saving of Santa Cruz, or any white people outside of Santa Fé, and no hope for them unless the warning was taken quickly. When I heard that I remembered the word of Hongovi in farewell — the little far-off trembling of the wind before the tornado — and against his urging we had ridden into the tornado path!

The priests doubted the extent of conspiracy, and Padre Domingo had the informers cast into the cuartel for whipping unless they told all names concerned. They would, or could, tell no names except of course that of Popé, the magician whom all knew had a fine record as a breeder of troubles. Then there was Jaca of far Taos, and Francisco of San Yldefonso, but of Tesuque, or of Santa Fé, they would give no names.

"Five years ago when Fray Andres Duran, of San Yldefonso, was bewitched by the shamans of the Tegua nation, you all know the only way to find justice for that holy man," stated Padre Domingo. "The records tell that forty-three Indians were whipped and enslaved, and four were publicly hanged as a warning to all the clans, and it served. When Popé, that red enemy of Christ, marched here with his seventy followers to ransom the forty-seven conspirators, he and every rebel of them all should have been put to death by the state or the Holy Office. There has been too much leniency with these infidels. That was the time to nip all threatened insurrections in the bud."

Governor Otermin listened, but as fast as his pen could write orders he was sending calls to the south for all scattered troops. The lieutenant-governor was at Ysleta with extra men, and his adjutant, Pedro Leiva, was at Alamillo with forty others.

"All this is as you say, padre," he agreed, "but in that day Governor Juan Frecencio did his best, according to his light, when he called special tribunal to investigate. He was, as I am, Padre, but one officer with a handful of soliders to guard this province against thousands of the wild tribes. We have begged for colonists here, and now that we have them, we must risk all things for their protection."

"You forget, Don Antonio, that this word of insurrection means a religious war and not a political one. It is final battle for their false gods against the True Faith. You will have much more than your handful of soldiers, Excellency; you will have back of you the Holy Office, and all its converts."

"But who will guarantee the converts in the face of swarms of pagans who number thousands?" asked Governor Otermin.

"Are not the two Tesuque informers, converts?" returned Fray Francisco, the superior of the monastery, with a desire to smooth over the little difficulty. "They show zeal for the cause in the face of estrangement from their people."

"Ay," agreed the governor. "But they refuse to give names of conspirators here within our walls, and zeal without knowledge may lead us into traps of danger."

"Don Antonio," said the superior with quiet meaning, "the report of the two men was made first to their confessor. This makes it our affair to see that they do speak. Padre Domingo will see to this. They have been thrown into the prison with a purpose; every man within the wall will report their words or take the whip in the plaza, for all to witness."

"Not the men who are prisoned there for other and trifling faults," protested Don Antonio.

"A spy has been chained with them to make them talk," said Padre Domingo easily; "never fear but that we will get at the right of it with no loss of time."

"Padre Domingo," ventured Don Antonio, perplexed and troubled, "though you are appointed Inquisitor here by the Reverend Father, you are new to this north land. You have not lived here with the records of these people as have I. May I show you what has been done in one generation, and the difficulties made by the Brotherhood for the governors of this province? In 1640 there was special religious exercise in the whipping, imprisonment, and hanging of forty natives because they refused to be converts to our faith. That ecclesiastical action brought on a revolt to be quelled by the soldiers of the presidio here. The Jemez people were also driven to rebel for like reasons, and never laid down their arms until twenty-nine of the leaders were punished by General Arguello through death and slavery. In 1650 the natives realized that the kindly help their fathers had given the Castilians as friends, was exacted from the children as slaves, and the infraction of religious rules which they did not comprehend, sent many a man for life to the mines. There was then another rebellion, but again a convert betrayed the leaders, and Governor Concho had the task of hanging nine, and selling the others into slavery. In 1675 the feeling against the superior of San Yldefonso became too bitter to quell, and the governor, Don Juan, had the unpleasant task of enslaving many of the leading men, and hanging others. These are but a few of the records, but they are enough to show two things, señor: first, that the strong leaders of the tribes oppose conversions, because it has always been a convert who betrayed his own people in an uprising against ecclesiastical authority; second, that the civil officers of this province are continually occupied in the quelling of religious troubles, leaving neither men or money for the efficient development of colonial enterprise. By these figures, Your Reverence will plainly see that neither deaths, or slavery, or use of the whip, has ever done aught but check them in a temporary way. It is a lesson of years, Padre Domingo, and if these men who have turned traitors to their tribe, in order to serve us, are whipped today in the public plaza, I dare not even say I could guard the man who used the whip! I would do less than my duty if I laid not this matter before you in all clearness. You, Padre, have come from Mexico where there is a standing army to protect the church. I am hundreds of leagues from an army, and have only one hundred and twenty men against twenty thousand natives!"

"You protect yourself well, Governor Otermin," said Padre Domingo, who had listened with half closed, watchful eyes. "But you forget that while the local government of state is, and must be, temporal, the rule of Holy Church remains eternal! Bernardo de Mandizaval forgot that in the fifties, and was removed from the governor's seat by the power of the Holy Office.

Governor Peñalosa repeated that forgetfulness, and instead of the palace of a governor here, he was given the cell of a prison in Mexico. Don Antonio, these are things to remember when the Holy Office has plans to learn the enemies of the True Faith in this land!"

"On your head be it!" said Governor Otermin. "This is not the time for a house to divide against itself. What I can, I will do, but the word of these men of Tesuque was very plain. We have two days before the outbreak is planned. If we make a public example of them in order to learn more, we only hasten the evil hour. We need every hour of grace, Your Reverence."

All this had come too quickly to bring enlightenment, or clear comprehension to my mind. I was stunned by sight and hearing of these leaders of men as they calmly faced the thing we must prepare for. Don Lorenzo and Marco were detained because of their reports, and questioned as to their suspicions of pueblo principals, while I was unnoticed at the edge of the group.

Curiously enough, my thoughts were of Sancha in the Indio dress rather than the argument of the men. I saw them with my eyes, but in a strange double way I saw her with my mind, and every little act of the trail from Walpi flashed before me — the Indian gifts of childish things, which yet became important things, ran between the gray padre and me as beads on a string. Hopi and Navajo and Jemez — she wore their pledge — and the stern old Tehua of the morning had added his blue bead to the others! All this at first had been because of Tristan, and the rosary of Don Fernan, and now, I could but think it was for her own sake.

My head was in a whirl with it. I forgot her disdain of us all on the hill, and when the superior and
Padre Domingo left the governor to the planning of
guards, I slipped out, and made my way to the sala.

Doña Zelinda was there, and in tears; not for dread
of self, but for Don Antonio, and his probable fate if
he opposed the officers of the Inquisition. Her own
memory was alive to the discipline former governors
had suffered at their hands.

"It is days like this in which we remember how far
we are from Mexico!" she lamented; but Doña Ynez,
who had wept at what she thought a quarrel of lovers
on the hill, now sat with wide, dry eyes, and pale face.

"I do not think anyone has ever seen a day like
this," she said. "Lorenzo tells me that on one excuse
or another, the Indios swarm the hills. It is too early
for the hunt, yet in the north there are bands of them
with hunting spears."

I asked for Sancha, but was told she had not come
in. Our Indio, Manuel, had been waiting for her with
some message, and at once she had ridden to the monastery with Wisti to see the prior there.

"But that is Fray Francisco, and he has been with
Governor Otermin in consultation," I said. "This is
no day for careless riding in a new town. Wisti is a
treasure in a desert, but scarce a proper guide for Santa
Fé. I must find her, and make her listen, though she
hate me for it."

"The saints guard her!" said Doña Ynez. "I had
forgotten her temper out there. Her anger was natural when she found the maid was his — and the poor
maid was not to blame either. He turned her to me

as lightly as you would cast an old cloak — yet the girl is worth a good price."

"I lack even a *marivada*, and so does my cousin," I said, "but we know the father of that girl, and he has done us kindness. Will you sell, at your own price, and await long the paying?"

"What day is this to trade for slaves?" she asked. "We will do well to save ourselves, and every extra Indio is a danger. Take the girl, Don Juan, and get her quickly as may be out of our sight. She weeps with fright in the kitchen."

I scarce knew what was in my mind to do, but as I went out in the sunshine of the street, Manuel stood, watchful, and erect, in the narrow strip of shade. His eyes were to the street of the monastery and I knew he waited the sight of Sancha even before he spoke.

"The mate of the feather is tied with ropes and is behind prison bars," he said. "The padre has done it, and not the governor. A man of my clan is convert, and tells me."

"Does he tell you of your daughter?" I asked, and he regarded me gravely.

"He does, and she is in San Yldefonso," he said. "I have not seen her, yet I have found her at last."

"Come," I said, and led him back through the patio to where, under the *ramada* of a giant grape vine, the poor, disdained young slave, wept because forsaken among strange faces.

He turned to me with a wonderful look on his face as he had sight of her bent head. In another instant she was in his arms, and the people who think the Indio disdains love, should have seen them there!

"She is the gift to you of Doña Sancha," I said.
"There is no one to stand in her trail home."

"And the man?" he asked.

"Doña Sancha was to be wife to the man, but now
she will never be his wife," I answered.

"That is so," he said gravely. "No one shall be his
wife."

Not until afterwards did I give thought to his speech
— and then it gave me many thoughts.

"I would say that you send her quickly to safety,"
I suggested. "This looks a busy day even without
women or girls to care for."

He looked at me very steadily, and nodded his head
in assent, and he went with her out the back way, while
I started again to look for Sancha.

In the plaza I saw the man Roberto with one of his
comrades, and he lifted his hand and laughed at me.

"Will he again play dog in the manger with the
maid of another man?" he jeered. "A fine 'padre'
you take the trail with, Señor! He fooled you well
with his high words and his monk's robe, for he was a
renegade heretic in borrowed plumes."

"It was you who lay in wait and roped him?" I
asked.

"None other, and he is safe bound now with the
other apostates they are bringing out for whipping."

"You did this at the word of Padre Domingo?" I
asked.

"Why not? He is made Inquisitor General here to
deal with the red heretics, and that is an office higher
than governor, and higher than superior of the monastery. When he speaks, we all jump."

"So it seems," I said, pondering in my mind if any power might secure Tristan respite there on the frontier. That mention of the whipping made me sick. Few men, Indio or white, would retain secrets of danger under the lash of the Inquisition. Padre Domingo meant to show the clans that no partiality would be shown. A white skin was no safeguard when the fight for Holy Faith was in question.

I felt all this rather than thought it, and as the guard suddenly swung into the plaza ahead of the priests, I knew what it meant. They were bringing out all the prisoners the better to flog the poor Tesuque men into telling more perhaps than they could humanly know. If ever I could win a word of help from the governor, this was the time.

But the bell of the monastery was ringing a doleful note by which the people were warned of executions, or special disciplining of prisoners, and the houses were soon emptied, and the little lanes and the plaza filled with wondering, questioning people. Yet among them all, I could get no sight of Governor Otermin. Don Lorenzo I saw, and De Lara, each fully armed, and very grave of face, as was every soldier who knew the truth.

"Find him — for the love of God! find the governor for me!" I asked each frantically. "There is a man of blood, of rank, of dignity, roped there among those bewildered cattle! Get an order for a shot, and quick death for him if it must be — the death a soldier should have — but no touch of a lash to fall on him!"

Roque de Lara caught and held me, and Marco de Ordoño stood near and laughed.

"I owe you a shot for your damned treason to me, Juan Rivera," he said, "and I wish it were a whip promised to your own back."

"Marco!" I begged, "for the honor of your own house, stand by the honor of your house, stand by the friendships of the house! He was loyal to you — loyal all your life. Your fathers were faithful, and this is your one chance, Marco, your last chance!"

I only remember he pushed me back against De Lara, and said I was a crazy fool, and that he knew nothing of my meaning. Then, in the midst of his words, he gave a shout of exulting, and laughed.

He had seen Tristan, whose hands were roped, and whose head was bandaged with blood-stained linen. The concealing banda prevented me from seeing his face until he was very close, but the laugh of Marco told me that hate had found him first.

"Hi! the Judaizing heretic!" he called above the tolling of the bell, "and *that* is the friend of rank and blood and dignity for whom he asks a soldier's courtesy!"

"Yes, it is!" I shouted back; "of blood more nearly royal than our own, Marco! The blood of men who were high priests of God before Christ was born! He asks nothing, and we owe him much. Find the governor; this is our day for payment!"

The yellow face of Padre Domingo pushed my way through the crowd.

"Is this so?" he asked. "Open confession is good for the soul, Don Juan. For what do you owe the heretic in bonds there?"

"For life, and a safe journey here," I answered

boldly. " He could have saved himself in comfort, yet strove to shelter us."

" Ah? " he said with a cold smile, " and what is the debt of Señor de Ordoño? "

" That is for him to say," and I turned to Marco imploring.

" Alcatraz, turn your face and look on these men," commanded Padre Domingo. " You have heard their words. What is the debt they owe to you? "

The eyes of Tristan rested one instant on mine, a wonderful look, and passed me by to look on Marco.

" The boy owes me not anything, Señor Padre," he said clearly, " and the man owes me for the life of my foster sister whom he stole, and left to die with Indians of Sonora."

There was a strange hush as he spoke, and Don Lorenzo glanced meaningly at De Lara. All of them knew of poor little Anita.

But back of me I heard a cry from Sancha.

" O Ivava! Kahn Alcatraz! your *sister?* "

She had ridden up, pushing her horse slowly through the mass of people to the portal of the palace, and I had not seen her coming. Wisti was close behind, and there was a strange meeting of Indian glances when she called " Ivava."

But Marco scowled in fury.

" What is this heretic to you, Doña Sancha, Marquesa de Llorente? " he demanded. " Does a lady of Spain claim knowledge of outlaws in the street? "

" What is he to me? " she repeated clearly. " He saved me from Indio slavery! he has gone hungry that I might be fed! he clothed me when I went naked!

All I have to put in the balance would weigh but little towards my debt to him! Padre Domingo, will you do me the favor to find for me the governor, and the father superior of the monastery? I must speak of this matter to them, and go surety for Señor Alcatraz. A mistake has been made that he should walk in bonds like this. I beg you have him loosed."

"What is this?" asked Governor Otermin from the portal. "What mistake is this?"

"It is witchcraft, no less!" stated Marco. "This lady is to be my wife, our betrothal is of many years, and here, suddenly, she claims she owes this heretic Jew her friendship above all others! It was known that he half bewitched Don Payo ere he sailed away, and this is not the first woman on whom he has worked enchantment! In Mexico he was in league with devils until they fear to use for the altars even the pictures he painted. That is a truth that our reverend father here knows more of than I."

"It is quite true, Excellency," said Padre Domingo. "He is a man dangerous to the Holy Office because of his heresies. When his bonds are loosed the stars will shine at midday, or you, proud maid of Llorente y Rivera will step down to walk barefoot beside him!"

"But the stars do shine at midday!" cried Sancha, with a half triumphant, half-tearful note in her voice. "I saw it so in a deep cañon on the way, and — quick Wisti, untie my shoe!"

"O great soul, and loyal comrade!" breathed Tristan. "Juanito, let her not touch the dust!"

Marco caught the head of her horse to turn it.

"Let her not shame herself here in the eyes of your

slaves, Don Antonio!" he called. "I tell you it is a witchcraft. As the lady who is to be my wife, I claim the right to protect her from her own madness, and I ask the church to aid against this apostate!"

"Apostate! is it so?" said Sancha looking down at Tristan. "O faithful apostate! Take your hand from my bridle, Marco de Ordoño, and choose better your words. Neither betrothal or marriage will ever be between you and me. Since I must say it before all these people, I say it!"

"Ay!" he snarled, catching her wrist, "why not confess the rest — that this accursed Tristan has you bound in some spell of the damned letters until you would lower yourself to the dust with him?"

"Tristan? The *letters?*" she said, and stared, white-faced from one to the other. "Tell me, tell me! This is Kahn Alcatraz — this is —"

"Kahn — yes, the name of a Jew!" said Marco, "and Alcatraz, yes, the name of Fray Fernando Alcatraz, his priestly father! But before that, he was Tristan, the shepherd of our herds! The boy you hated, but the man sent you letters of witch charms until you crossed the seas to him. I see that now — see all too plainly! Is there no pride left in you? Are you held in bonds to this outcast? He is convicted by church, and outlawed by state. Do you still choose to walk barefoot beside him?"

"To the end of the world!" she said, and more quick than I could see, she slipped the Navajo knife of obsidian from her belt, and sunk it into the hand of Marco holding her wrist.

There was a scream of pain from him, and then an-

other, but she neither heard or saw what happened
when Marco crumpled to the ground with another
Indio knife between his shoulders. Manuel left it there,
and like a flash was beside her as she slipped to the
ground, and cut the bonds of Tristan.

"O Glory of God!" Tristan cried as her arms circled
his shoulders. "White Virgo come to earth for me!"

But above the surging tumult, the terrible voice of
Padre Domingo sounded in my ears as echo of the terrible bell.

"Seize that shameless woman for the trial of Holy
Faith!" he thundered. "No rank of earth can save
her here in New Granada! She shall indeed walk beside
him in the dust — walk excommunicated, and in chains
— to the *flaming stake!*"

So sudden was all the rest that no one could tell who
gave signal for battle; yet Manuel did make curious
call as Marco fell there in his tracks before the portal,
and at sound of that call it seemed the very earth
swarmed Indians. They dropped from the flat roofs
by the score, while the Padre shouted, and like a red
wave of war, they launched themselves between Manuel and the guard. I saw Tristan with Sancha in his
arms crowded farther and farther away by the mob of
fanatic Indians who had been placid servers a moment
before, and were now reckless warriors.

The guard was swept back against the wall of the
governor's palace, and then we knew indeed that the
Tesuque men had brought the truth. The pent-up rage
of fifty years was loosed by that knife stroke of Manuel,
and the most terrible insurrection of all the colonies
was precipitated by a private hate.

CHAPTER XXII

UNDER BLESSINGS OF PAGAN GODS

ONE dear memory comes out of that surging hell in the plaza of Santa Fé. Sancha remembered me, even in the arms of Tristan, and her voice came high and clear where we beat off the wild devils from the portal of the palace.

"Juanito! Juanito mine! adios!"

"Adios! O Sanchita!" I called, and leaned, panting, and battered, against the wall. Padre Domingo staggered back, and fell, bleeding like an ox, from a swift blade in the side.

"You too!" he said with lifted hand of condemnation. "Her name is blotted out from Christian souls forever! Bear you the word to Mexico — *excommunication!*"

Then, with his hand dipped in his own blood, he drew the sacred sign on the stone paving, and strove to lay himself on it, but fell there, dead ere Fray Francisco could reach him. Thus Padre Domingo indeed found the martyrdom they say he coveted.

Once only after that had I glimpse of my lost comrades. Manuel had striven to lead them out of the mob of the street by way of the church of San Miguel, but the sacristy door was barred, and there was delay long enough for word to reach us that the church was seized as a fortress by the infidels. Extra troops had joined the prison guard, and the red swarm launching itself in disorder to free the convicted men, found itself giving way under the solid front of the governor's soldiery. Back and back, they went with face to the foe, covering with lance and knife the trail of Tristan and others of the cuartel. I reached the door as the relief soldiery entered. Indians were using a broken altar as a battering ram to break through the sacristy door, and there, on the altar place in the dim church, stood Tristan with an Indian spear in his grasp, and his arm around her. One niche at the side held a statute of the Holy Mother, where three candles burned, and the light from it touched the white dress of Sancha, and the white banda on the head of Tristan. Only a gleam of her white dress showed, for he had wrapped about her a gray robe. A moment later I saw how that had chanced, for I stumbled over a lay brother stripped and dead on the stone floor.

Then the door at the back gave way, and the Indians rushed into the light, while the walls echoed the explosion from the firing pieces.

" Save the man and woman alive! " called Fray Francisco. " The blood of God's anointed is on his head, and the woman makes her choice of perdition with him! Save them alive! "

But they should have known that if those two were saved alive, it must be in freedom. I saw them go out the door, and in all the smoke and turmoil and dead and wounded about them, her face was lifted to his — exalted as if to welcome even death beside him!

Manuel was also there, thus I saw that from the first

The Excommunicated Lovers.

signal for death in the plaza he had never wavered from the trust he had given himself.

After that there were ten days of hell with the tribes swarming from the hills after the killing of all priests of the pueblos. They came, flushed with victory, from north and south, to aid against the capital, where we fortified as best we could, making short dashes out with small success. The plaza ran red with blood of the prisoners taken, which served us little. On every side we were surrounded. A thousand people to protect, counting women and children, and less than two hundred fighting men to do it with. Three thousand barbarians sang their songs, danced their victory dances on the hills, and cut us off from the water. We killed more than they, but of what use was it, when the various tribes stood ready to send other bands to the siege as needed? We could not know it until long after, but eighteen priests were slaughtered in New Granada in that week, and every Castilian farmer and his family.

On the tenth day after the Tesuque men risked lives to warn the people of Santa Fé to go south, and go at once, there was a very sorry cavalcade of us who took that trail — ten days too late! The barbarians sat on the hills, and watched us go in peace after all the horrors. All they asked was the Indian land for the Indio.

But they sent warriors to follow us, thirty leagues on the way, that we gain no courage from reinforcements to turn back on the trail.

A dreary march was ours, with not enough horses for even the sick and wounded, and dreary the winter for us in the huts we built for shelter south at San Lorenzo.

A year later, I went north again with General Mendoza, only to be turned back by the warring infidels. Governor Otermin, as he had anticipated, was removed from office, and Governor Ramirez appointed, but he would risk no men in the north lands. In eighty-eight I again entered the forbidden land with General Cruzate, a considerable army, and seventy priests for mission work, yet we were turned back at Zia after many skirmishes, and ceremonial councils with many chiefs.

One chief came who was gorgeous in cloth of scarlet and otter skins. All Spanish names and customs and religion had been wiped from the land, thus I dared not call him Manuel, who had been trapper of eagles in the Jemez hills. I have changed, as all men do if the years are hard; and while he looked at me much, I had no sign that he had ever looked on me before, and he betrayed no knowledge of Spanish speech.

But I remembered the twin feathers and their markings, and idly, during the council, I took from a hawk's wing fan the broad brown feather, and, little by little, without turning a glance his way, I trimmed it in four spaces divided curiously on the quill.

I twirled it idly, while the general, and the priests, and chiefs, held weighty converse, and I left it on the seat when the council was ended. As idly as I, he lifted it as he passed, and went out without word or look to me.

It was two nights later when that which the guard said was incredible, occurred. A boy, who carried a message for me, was challenged by the sentry and my name was written plainly on a strip of fine parchment,

such as was used for church records. He spoke no
Spanish, but when we were alone, took from under his
blanket a roll of the same, well fastened in a painted
case. There was no address (it was like their care for
me!) and it read:

At the House of the Dawn.

Brother Mine:
I truly live here in the ancient place of sanctuary not otherwise to be named. Each time you have come to the forbidden
land we have known it. Come not again, lest all our love should
not save you. We are outcasts and happy. Have you memory
of a marriage night in the magic Navajo land? Such simple
marriage was ours with Indio witnesses, and it has grown
more sacred with each of the years. To only you could I say
it — and not to you again. Has the Holy Office weakened in
power that the excommunicated dare be sought in friendship?
This you must answer to yourself, and bear in mind that a task
is yours for which you need smiles of church and state. The
honor of the family is yours to preserve — and it is a family of
old names, and great pride.
For the nameless one who stepped out (I cannot say down,
brother mine!) you must have no sorrow, and no doubt. We
have all the world to wander in, yet we remain happily in this
land of enchantings. Here we build our own shrines and make
our sacrifices. The stars of the Desert are above, and we have
more books than you ever read, for the padres were often
learned men, and their written knowledge remains in this forbidden land for us.
Our days are not idle; the work he did of old, he does here,
and every star, with its guardian god, is made record of in the
two tongues. Their herbs of medicine, their words of the laws,
all these, with the legends of ancestry, and even records of
earth-born gods, he has written as work of joy.
I tell you this that you know we lack no thing of content in
our high place of the dawn prayers. And if men of Spain should
some day re-conquer — there will be other trails for us, and the

world is wide. Here the intrigues of church and courts are far away. I wear boots made by his hand, and a pet fawn is by me as I write. It looks like your pretty gift across the seas; for that it is dear — and for the other reason, not to be named.

Of him I can no more write than could I of God the Father. But my Saint of the Impossible caused the unbelievable thing to be, and for that a shrine is built to her here on the hills of New Granada — it faces the east, and Old Spain. We write your name there for happiness!

You seek us, beloved one — to save us, or serve us. Go back and take up your burden of the world. I have confession to make. I have seen you once, and been very close, and made no sign. I heard his name spoken, and the tale of his evil deeds. Thus also, I learned that my own name is blotted out from Christian speech. A young soldier sang by the camp fire, the song of " Doña Perdida " as he said they sing it in Mexico. Never let it hurt your heart, dear brother-comrade. My soul was not lost in the Desert — it was there I found it!

This is sent for your own soul's content.

Then, instead of a name, there was a butterfly drawn with folded wings, and under it was the sign he taught her to make in the cañon of the Divine Ones.

And on the other side of the parchment were his words

Comrade of ours:

You, who live by your rank and order, dare not approve, yet the content of her heart is my justification. The blessing of neither pope or priest could make more white the loyal soul of her.

For myself, I am learning (as no man could learn in another place) the strivings of primitive priests from the time the Spirit of God moved on the face of the waters until the records were made, thought by thought, which we are taught is the word of the living God. Here, today, these red priests strive, in like ways of fastings and prayers, and sacrifice, to learn the Power back of all earth power, and go up daily to search for their gods on the heights.

There is work here for a pen through a long lifetime. We strive to do our little share, ere we find deeper wilderness, or wider range.

To you, until the end, the blessings of the Divine Ones, and all the stars of light above the trails you tread.

Tristan.

I read the blessing of his, over and over, and was reminded of the prayer chant in the sacred cañon of the Ancient Gods:

> Impervious to pain, I walk!
> With beauty before me, I walk!
> With beauty above me, I walk!
> Happily may the roads all
> Find the way of peace,
> And the ways all end in beauty!

So I have that last message of theirs for my comfort, and the other letters hidden in the stone shrine of Sonora were brought back by me on the last trail from the north. I know well she did grieve their loss, but it is beyond my power to have them go to her.

Meanwhile I am learning many things of the French and English and Dutch lands of this new world. There is a great north, and a wide east, where they may find safety when the time comes.

With Doña Mercedes I talk of these chances at times, and of what might happen if some day I should get word to meet them on the other side of the world! Doña Mercedes is a woman of heart, who remembers our youth, and knew the heaviness of my task when I bore the dying command of Padre Domingo to the bishop of Mexico, and heard the excommunication from the altar. For awhile I had my own troubles with the Brotherhood, but Fray Payo reached a strong hand across the seas to help. Since all the men of importance, from the archbishop and viceroy down, had held Tristan, at some time, more or less in favor, I was finally cleared of evil intent for accepting freedom at his hands; also my blood relationship to the excommunicated maid of beauty was at last condoned as no fault of mine.

But though she is called " Doña Perdida," and they sing today love songs of their mutual enchantings and of his wickedness, I close my eyes, and remember only her joyous voice intoning in the desert nights,

> O you!
> Who dwell
> In the House of the Dawn!
> In the House of Evening Twilight
> The Path to which is the Rainbow—

And I know in truth that he led her into a Dawn beyond the shadows where we grope.

In memory I go again over the many wonder places of the long trail, and live again, with my comrades, the life of desert ranges and cañon deeps, but the picture clearest in my mind is of those two in borrowed robes at the edge of a cliff in Tusayan.

Boy as I was, I was vaguely touched there by the force he strove against, and the enchantment our Sancha dared not confess. Voiceless they were, yet bound — so great a love it was — by bonds defying even fears of hell. Though the padres do deny them sanctification, deep in my heart — and I cross myself as I write it — there lingers ever the message sent to me out of the Desert, "The blessing of neither pope nor priest could make more white the loyal soul of her."

The End